PRAISE FOR JERUSHA AGEN

"Jerusha Agen once again delivers top-level suspense and thrilling action. *Covert Danger* kept me looking over my shoulder and flipping pages. Fast-paced suspense at its best."

DIANN MILLS, BESTSELLING AUTHOR OF
CONCRETE EVIDENCE

"Hang on! This action-packed story doesn't let up until the good guys win!"

NATALIE WALTERS, AWARD-WINNING AUTHOR OF
LIGHTS OUT AND THE *HARBORED SECRETS SERIES*
ON *COVERT DANGER*

Hidden Danger kept me reading and on the edge of my seat from page one through the end. Jerusha Agen writes a gripping suspense filled with danger, romance, and K-9s complete with a strong faith thread.

SHAREE STOVER, BESTSELLING AUTHOR OF
FRAMING THE MARSHALL

LETHAL DANGER

BOOKS BY JERUSHA AGEN

GUARDIANS UNLEASHED SERIES

Midnight Clear (prequel novella)

Rising Danger (prequel)

Hidden Danger

Covert Danger

Unseen Danger

Lethal Danger

Terminal Danger

SISTERS REDEEMED SERIES

If You Dance with Me

If You Light My Way

If You Rescue Me

LETHAL DANGER

GUARDIANS UNLEASHED  BOOK FOUR

JERUSHA AGEN

SDG Words, LLC

ACKNOWLEDGMENTS

Getting *Lethal Danger* from conception to published book was almost as harrowing and nail-biting as the story is for the characters. I'm so thankful that God provided me with the right people at the right time to bring *Lethal Danger* to the printed page.

Thank you to Kylie Grant for helping me ensure the CSI elements were realistic and correct. You are a connection God provided at just the right time!

Thanks to my fabulous beta readers and proofreaders, Angelique Daley, Natalya Lakhno, and Jeanne Crea. Your first impressions and sharp eyes are such a help and encouragement!

To Mom—we did it! Thank you for being my co-brainstormer, biggest fan, and faithful partner in work and life. I'm so thankful God gave me you to cling to in the dark and rejoice with in the light. I couldn't do this without you.

To Allie and Leah, the dearest friends I've ever had.
God knew I needed you for such a time as this.

Soli Deo Gloria

Fear not, for I have redeemed you;
I have called you by name, you are mine.

Isaiah 43:1b

ONE

Excitement and anticipation buzzed through Jazz Lamont's veins, taking her back to when she was eight years old, and she believed dreams could come true.

Jazz couldn't help it. The first day of the Tri-City Fair was always full of hope, the promise of fun times and reliving memories, and—she inhaled deeply—the mouthwatering aroma of fried foods.

So what if she was an adult, part of the fair's security detail this year, instead of a kid hanging with her best friend for the greatest time of their lives? She was still determined to enjoy the fair as much as she always had.

"Help! Stop him!"

Jazz jerked toward the woman's shouts as Flash growled.

She let the Belgian Malinois tug on the leash to hurry them toward the source of the yells. Jazz stretched her neck to see above the moving people on the midway. Good thing it was early in the morning and not very crowded yet.

"Stop him!" A middle-aged woman flailed her arms as she pushed through people like she was trying to follow someone.

Jazz darted her gaze ahead of the woman.

Fast movement caught her eye. Someone running.

A slim male darted through the crowd, something in his hand.

Purse snatcher.

Jazz took off, Flash easily kicking into gear beside her.

"Out of the way!" She barked the order as she tried to run around the people congesting the paved path. No use. She'd never catch him this way.

She dropped Flash's leash. "Flash, *halt schnell.*"

The Malinois took off like a bullet, darting through pedestrians and vanishing from sight.

Jazz picked up her pace as much as she could, navigating the crowd as she strained to see Flash. Didn't really matter if she had eyes on him. He'd get the job done.

She pushed past a group of visitors, reaching a clear space she could sprint through. Until a group of teens slowed her down.

Then she spotted him.

Flash stood on top of his fallen target, paws on the purse snatcher's back as the guy sprawled on the blacktop.

Jazz slowed her pace and grinned at the magnificent dog, standing so tall and proud on his quarry.

A small cluster of bystanders gathered to stare. And record everything on video with their phones.

Good thing she hadn't had Flash bite the guy, or there'd no doubt be some objections.

"Good boy, Flash." Jazz tossed him a treat as she stopped beside the perp. "*Pass auf.*"

Flash gulped his treat and dashed off the perp's back to get into guard position as she'd commanded. He swung back to face the thief, feet planted as he stared, ready for any wrong move.

"You can get up now." Jazz looked down at the brown-haired guy who twisted his head toward her. "But I wouldn't try to run. I might have to tell my K-9 to use more force next time."

The perp, probably about eighteen, slowly planted his hands on the pavement and pushed himself up. He swiped a long patch of brown hair out of his eyes. Eyes that widened as he stared at Flash.

"Hands behind your back."

"What for?"

"Don't think that purse belongs to you." Jazz shot a pointed glance at the beige purse the thief had left lying on the ground.

She activated her coms earpiece. "Base, this is PT3. I've caught a purse snatcher in Sector Two, near Judy's Sweets and Treats. Respond an officer to this location."

The three police officers on loan to the fair during daytime hours meant she shouldn't have to wait long for one to show up.

"Officer 1 to Base." Jazz recognized the voice of Officer Davis Leeland. The guy had already had a busy morning. "Will respond. ETA two minutes."

The perp shoved his hair back off his sweaty forehead again and moved his gaze away from Flash, scanning the surroundings. Not good.

"Don't even think it, pal. My K-9 can run circles around you." Jazz stepped closer to the perp and gripped his slim arm. "Did I mention he's a tracker, too?" She could zip tie the thief's wrists, but she'd rather let a cop with cuffs do the honors. Better to keep the bystanders from getting rankled in defense of the criminal.

"You caught him." The breathless statement drew Jazz's gaze to the heavyset woman who approached, her chest heaving beneath the low neckline of her tank top.

"Yes, ma'am. Take it easy." Jazz held up a hand toward the victim to discourage her from acting on the anger that flashed in the eyes behind her glasses. "It's a hot day." And the woman looked like she could drop from heatstroke at any moment.

"I want him arrested." She pointed a finger at the teen past Jazz's shoulder.

"Yes, ma'am. He will be." Jazz glanced at the bag on the ground. "Is that your purse?"

"It most certainly is." The woman huffed as she stomped over to her discarded purse and started picking up the contents that had spilled onto the blacktop.

"Is anything missing?"

The victim's face was bright red as she stood and marched toward Jazz with the recovered property. "Well, my wallet's still there, but everything's filthy now, thanks to this criminal." She moved close to the kid, lifting a fisted hand.

Jazz shifted to block the woman with her body. "I need you to back up, please."

"Why should I?" The victim's sweaty face pressed close to Jazz's shoulder. "He thinks he can rob innocent people without any consequences."

"Ma'am, please step over here." Officer Leeland appeared behind the woman in his police uniform, shooting Jazz a commiserating glance.

The irate woman swung toward him. "The police. Good. I want to file a complaint or whatever I need to do so this thief is arrested."

"Yes, ma'am. I'll get your statement after I secure the suspect. If you'll head for the main entrance to the grounds, you'll see the Public Safety Center. Go inside and have a seat until I get there." The fifty-something cop guided her with a hand close to her shoulder, not touching her as she walked with him six feet away. He said something to her that Jazz couldn't hear, and the woman left, hopefully agreeing to do as he'd directed.

Leeland headed back to Jazz. "Lamont, right?"

She nodded.

"Good work." He stepped behind the suspect and cuffed his wrists.

"My K-9 gets the credit for this one. Chased him down when the crowd blocked my way."

Leeland cast Flash a glance, the K-9 still in his ready stance, intensity shining in his eyes. "Duly noted."

"Flash, *in ordnung*." Jazz put her hand on the Malinois' smooth head as he relaxed his stance with her release command. She stooped to pick up his leash and watched the stocky officer lead the perp away.

"Well, back to patrol, bud." She turned to continue the patrol pattern that had been interrupted by the theft. "Nothing like a little excitement to start the day, huh, boy?" She glanced down at the K-9.

His mouth was open unusually wide, and his tongue extended out farther than normal. "On second thought, maybe a water break is in order." Flash had gotten used to intense heat during their tour in Afghanistan, but the cooler climate of Minnesota was probably undoing that. And the dog had just sprinted in the sun in humid, eighty-degree weather.

She headed for umbrella-shaded tables near the Zilly's fried cookie dough stand, reaching for the strap of her slim backpack where she kept his water thermos.

She glanced down at Flash. "Maybe I'll grab—"

A scream rent the air.

She spun toward the sound.

Just in time to see a Ferris wheel passenger cabin freefall.

"Coming through!" Hawthorne Emerson barreled through the crowd to reach the Ferris wheel.

Screams and shouts fell from the cabins of the giant wheel like an echo of the cabin that had crashed to the earth two seconds before. Had anyone been inside?

Please, God, let no one be badly injured. Somehow.

He hadn't noticed a long line for the wheel when he'd passed by ten minutes ago. Maybe it was early enough in the morning that some cabins were empty.

He broke through the bystanders gathering along the fence that bracketed the waiting line for the ride. Thanks to his security guard clearance, he didn't have to weave through the maze to reach the wheel.

He unlatched the gated shortcut and dashed through, sprinting for the downed cabin.

The enclosed capsule lay on the pavement beneath the ride, not quite as cylindrical as it had been a moment ago. The lower half had smashed into the blacktop, bits of glass and metal pieces spread around the carcass like confetti.

Were any human bodies inside it?

He reached the door, now aimed toward heaven, and peered through the cracked window.

Couldn't see anyone.

He yanked on the door.

The safety latch must still be in place. He flipped the latch and swung the door open.

"Is there anybody in there?" An anxious voice behind him drew Hawthorne's gaze.

A young man, probably early twenties, watched from a few feet away. His name badge and terrified expression identified him as the ride operator.

Hawthorne stuck his head into the cabin to verify what he hoped was true.

It was empty.

"Thank you, Lord." He breathed the prayer as he backed out and swung toward the operator. He pressed the button on his coms. "This is S4, I'm at scene. No casualties or injuries. The cabin was empty." He glanced at the ride operator as one of the security dispatchers acknowledged his transmission.

The young guy stared at the crushed cabin without moving.

"Go back to the controls. We have to get the remaining people off."

The operator's gaze slowly drifted toward Hawthorne. "Okay."

Movement by the secured access gate caught Hawthorne's eye.

A tall woman with a leashed K-9 walked toward him at a quick clip. She seemed to scan him as she approached. Probably checking to make sure he should be there, similar to what he was doing with her.

She wore a gun holstered on her hip and a black T-shirt that had the word, *Security*, printed on the front. Her dog's vest was labeled *PK-9 Security*. He'd met a team from the Phoenix K-9 Security and Detection Agency when he'd come on duty that morning. A shorter lady with a German shepherd. He assumed the back of this agent's T-shirt would also read, *Phoenix K-9*.

"Any victims?" The woman stopped a few feet away, her attention skipping past Hawthorne toward the fallen cabin.

"None. It was empty."

She gave him another long look, then nodded and glanced up at the Ferris wheel. "Let's get these people down before another one drops."

"You want me to do it?" The operator's voice nearly squeaked as he stared at the new arrival.

Hawthorne considered pointing out the kid was the only one there at the moment who knew how to operate the ride, but the K-9 agent beat him to responding.

"That would be best, yes." Was that a twitch at the corners of the woman's mouth? Amusement?

"But slowly." Hawthorne added the direction as he followed the operator to the controls. With how nervous the kid seemed, he might spin the wheel fast enough to produce more casualties.

"Yeah. These people have been scared enough for one day." The woman stepped to the other side of the operator and gave Hawthorne a quirked smile that definitely communicated humor.

A woman who was cool and calm in the face of disaster. Didn't encounter that every day.

As if to prove her point, raised voices cut through the air above them. The passengers were probably more than a little frightened and eager to get off.

Hawthorne glanced at the operator's nametag. "Go ahead

and bring them down, Kenny. A little slower than you usually would at the end of the ride."

The kid nodded, moistening his lips with his tongue as he put the ride in gear.

Hawthorne glanced at the attractive woman as the cabins started to lower.

She watched the action with a confident gaze, her thick red ponytail tilting with her head. Slim and fit with curves in the right places, she was taller than most women. Probably about five nine in her flat sneakers. On her left thigh, the side he could see now, a black leather sheath rested against her jeans. Was she packing a knife?

The ride stopped, drawing Hawthorne's attention to the middle-aged couple and young girl Kenny let out.

They clung to each other as they hurried from the cabin as if they couldn't get away from the ride fast enough.

A muffled yell came from above.

Hawthorne peered up into the bright sunlight. Hard to tell which cabin.

More shouts. Sounded like a male voice. Getting louder. Panicked.

The ride started to move again.

"Hold it, Kenny." The redhead echoed the thought Hawthorne had been about to voice.

The operator paused the wheel.

A smacking sound broke the air. The door of a cabin near the top of the wheel flung open.

"Help! Get us down!" A head stuck out the opening along with the man's hysterical shout.

A woman shrieked.

The man's leg protruded from the cabin. Then his whole body.

Was the guy crazy?

"No!" A woman yelled from inside the cabin.

"He's trying to climb down." The redhead's voice lifted with disbelief.

Hawthorne couldn't tear his gaze away from the man above. "Kenny, do not move the wheel, whatever you do."

The young guy didn't answer, so Hawthorne threw him a glance.

Kenny stared up at the panicking passenger with his mouth hanging open. At least his hand wasn't anywhere near the controls.

Hawthorne jerked his attention back to the man above.

He seemed to be trying to navigate directly down to the next cabin along the rim. There weren't many handholds there. He'd have a better shot climbing onto the spokes that were doubled on this Ferris wheel with X-shaped support beams between them.

"Fool's going to get himself killed." A new female voice pulled Hawthorne's attention to the petite Phoenix K-9 agent he'd met earlier and her German shepherd on leash.

The redhead gave the new arrival a quick glance. "Yeah, not—"

A scream cut her short and yanked Hawthorne's gaze back up the wheel.

The man lost his grip. And fell.

Hawthorne's breath stopped.

The guy landed hard on the support beams between the spokes below.

"Base, this is PT3." The redhead spoke into coms, her tone steady. "A passenger tried to climb down the Ferris wheel and fell. He's still on the wheel. Appears to be unconscious. Call a rescue squad."

Hawthorne stared at the man. He hadn't moved. The Phoenix K-9 agent was probably right. And it could be a good thing if he was out. At least he wouldn't panic and do something additionally foolish.

But he could wake up at any moment. And fall to his death, if he wasn't already terminally injured.

They couldn't wait for the rescue squad.

"I'm going up."

"What?" Both women said the word at virtually the same time. They stared at Hawthorne but didn't actually look like they thought he was crazy. More like they doubted his ability to do it.

"Can you free-climb?" The redhead's expression was intense, her eyebrows lowered.

The rational question took him by surprise. He'd expected her to protest or try to stop him.

"I do it all the time." Normally on rocks or climbing walls, but a Ferris wheel shouldn't be much more challenging. He hoped.

"You know that's fifteen stories up?" The agent with the shepherd appeared to be assessing him with her dark eyes.

He chuckled. "Yeah, I've heard."

"I'll call for some rope so we can lower him down."

He gave the redhead a nod. "Good idea." He turned and walked past the controls toward the base of the wheel, eyeing the best place to begin the climb. At least he'd worn his broken-in tennis shoes today. Should be fairly flexible with a bit of grip.

He scanned the massive base of the wheel. Not the best handholds there. He glanced back toward the cabin that had just been vacated in the loading dock. That should be easier.

He went to the enclosed pod and clambered up to stand on top of it. No sweat.

From the roof of the cabin, he reached for the X-shaped beams that crisscrossed between the vertical spokes. Gripping the middle of the X, he found footholds where the beams connected with the spokes.

He pulled himself up, switching out his handhold to put his foot in the middle of the X as he climbed. He continued the same pattern, sweat moistening his forehead with the effort. The holds were pretty good.

He looked up beyond the next beams. Might as well keep climbing vertically until he reached the center of the wheel.

The passenger had fallen onto the support beams and spokes that were locked horizontally at the moment. So long as Kenny didn't bump any controls.

Hawthorne grimaced at the thought as he pushed on. By the time he reached the center of the wheel, sweat dampened his skin under his blue security uniform T-shirt.

Thanks to the interconnecting spokes and beams at the center, it wasn't hard to climb from there out onto the horizontal spokes.

He stayed in the prone position, essentially crawling as he carefully gripped the crisscrossed beams between the spokes with his hands and wedged his feet in the corners to be sure he didn't slip through. The parallel spokes were much farther apart up here than they'd appeared from the ground. Too widely placed for him to grip them instead.

He looked up from his holds as he neared the fallen passenger.

The man didn't move. Was he alive?

Hawthorne picked up his speed to close the distance between them.

"Sir?" Hawthorne braced his knee against the beams, ignoring the discomfort of the metal digging into his bone as he let go with one hand to reach for the unmoving passenger.

He pressed his fingers to the guy's clammy neck, feeling for a pulse.

Soft beats thumped against his fingers.

Thank the Lord.

Hawthorne leaned forward to get a better look at the man's head where it had slammed against the spoke.

Blood oozed onto the steel from an apparent wound. Not good. Was it still actively bleeding?

Hawthorne mentally cycled through the First Aid course he'd received years ago in basic training.

He should apply pressure, but with a clean cloth. Given how sweaty his clothes were by this point, a torn scrap from either his shirt or pants wouldn't suffice. Maybe he should wait for the rescue squad to try it.

Hawthorne glanced down below.

Wow. Way below. Glad he hadn't looked down earlier. And he was especially glad heights didn't bother him.

Wait a second…

Something moved, but not on the ground. On the Ferris wheel.

A person in a black T-shirt climbed up the spokes and beams exactly as he had done. Was that the redhead?

Sure enough, a dark ponytail swung as she shifted her body toward a spoke.

A strange feeling stirred in his chest as he watched her. She moved quickly—faster than he had climbed, actually. Her movements were fluid and strong. No hesitation or caution. Only athleticism and skill, not missing a hold in her almost rhythmic climb.

She disappeared under the cluster of connecting beams at the center. But only for a moment.

Then her head appeared above the horizontal spokes where he waited with the injured man.

She sprang onto the beams and crawled toward him nearly as fast as the monkeys he used to watch at the zoo where he had volunteered. Coiled rope hung from her shoulder and angled across her shirt.

"How is he?" She didn't even sound out of breath as she came up beside Hawthorne, close to the passenger's head.

Hawthorne turned toward the injured man. Probably should've been watching him instead of the remarkable woman who'd just free-climbed halfway up a 156-foot Ferris wheel without breaking a sweat.

He rechecked the man's pulse. "Pulse is steady but weakening a little."

The redhead crawled closer and pushed up to sitting, balancing on the middle of the crossbeams' X with her feet braced on the two beams where they angled away. She aimed big eyes at him. "The rescue squad is on the way. ETA ten minutes. But one of the onsite nurses is waiting below. If we can get him down, she can start treating him."

The woman was fascinating. With only a few feet between them, there was no missing she was even more beautiful than he'd first thought. And she wasn't slathered in makeup like so many women her age who wanted to be attractive.

Her smooth, creamy skin was sun-kissed to perfection, and the rays glinted off her shiny red hair. Her full lips didn't need more than the gloss he guessed she wore. But her eyes were her most stunning feature. A brilliant emerald green that made him rethink his statement that he'd never seen a green as intense as the color of the fields in Ireland.

The woman had beauty, brains, courage, and toted a gun and knife he was sure she knew how to use. It couldn't get any better than that.

"I'll get on his left side here. You can go on his right, and I'll pass the rope under him to you." Her directions brought him out of his observations to see she was hefting the coiled rope off her shoulder and over her head.

Occupational hazard to get lost in observations and imagination. But he couldn't help it this time. He'd been searching for weeks for the right idea for his next book series. And now, she was staring him in the face.

"What's your name?"

"Excuse me?" She shot him a glance with raised eyebrows as she unwound one end of the rope.

"Sorry." He scrambled for an excuse for the oddly timed question. An excuse that would also get her to answer. "I just want to know what name to yell if I'm about to fall."

His joke earned a charming laugh that sounded like she was hitting the notes of a musical scale.

She bent over the passenger to slide the rope under his back. "Jazz Lamont."

Jazz. Even her name was perfect. Though she'd probably never agree to let him use that in print, too. But either way, he'd just met the heroine of his next bestselling thriller novels.

A groan screeched his excitement to a halt.

The injured man's hand moved as he moaned.

He was waking up.

TWO

"Hurry. Lift him." Jazz paused with the rope by the victim as the security guard took her cue and raised the passenger's shoulders a few inches above the beams. Jazz quickly fed the rope under the man's torso.

The security guard grabbed the other end as he lowered the victim.

"Wha—" The injured man's head flailed side to side, his eyes widening.

"Sir, we need you to stay calm." Jazz kept her voice steady while the security guard tied the rope around the victim's chest.

The passenger let out a sound between a yelp and a groan. "My leg. It hurts!"

She glanced down at the left leg she'd noticed was at an odd angle when she'd approached. Probably broken.

She put her hand on the man's chest, hoping to keep him in place. "I know you're in pain. My name is Jazz, and this," she glanced at the distractingly cute guard, "is a security guard." She swung her gaze back to the panicked look on the victim's face. "We're here to help you and get you down."

"Down? I'm still on this—" Expletives spilled from the man's lips as he twisted his head and shoulders to see below.

"Ahh!" The yell exploded from him as he recoiled and tried to plant his elbows behind him on the beams.

"Sir. Please hold still." The security guard paired his gentle command with two hands planted on the passenger's shoulders. "We will help you down as soon as we stabilize your leg and other injuries."

Which would require a splint, bandages, stokes basket, and other equipment they didn't have. The rescue squad would bring those items up when they arrived. But would the guy sit still that long?

"I can't stay up here." Fear tightened the passenger's voice. "I'm getting down. Now." He tried to twist from the guard's hold.

The guard clamped down, muscles in his tanned arms cording as he pushed the man's shoulders with enough force to make him lie down again. "It'd be better for you to lie still, sir. You have a head injury, and your leg may be broken."

"I don't care!" The passenger thrashed, straining to see below as he shrieked. "Gotta get off! Help!"

The guard leaned his body into the passenger's torso, struggling to keep him from falling. The guard's eyes flicked up to Jazz. A startling electric blue. No, maybe more of a teal color. Though this was hardly the time to be admiring the guy's eyes.

She rallied her focus enough to realize the message those eyes were communicating. They had to get the man off the Ferris wheel now. Before he fell off. And maybe took one of them with him.

"Okay. I understand, sir." She tried a sympathetic tone to reach the passenger through his panic. "We'll get you down right now."

The man kept twisting and struggling.

"Sir." Jazz shifted closer. A risk, given the man's arms flailing out from his body. "Sir." She reached over the guard's shoulder to touch the passenger's frightened, twitching face. She placed her palm gently on his cheek.

He stopped. His widened brown eyes shifted to her face,

holding steady as surprise pushed out some of the terror.

She smiled. "What's your name?"

"Wienke. Bob."

"Nice to meet you, Bob. I'm Jazz." She figured he hadn't heard a word she'd said earlier. "Would you like to see your wife and family now?" Just a guess, but maybe the woman who'd screamed when he had jumped was his wife.

Bob nodded under her hand.

"Good. I'm sure she wants to see you. I'm going to help you get off the ride right now so you can see your wife, okay?"

A flicker of fear reignited in his eyes.

"My friend here is going to help me, and it'll be over in seconds." Or at least it would hopefully feel that fast to Bob.

His gaze jumped to the security guard who still held his shoulders.

"Trust me, Bob. You're perfectly safe."

Bob returned his attention to Jazz.

"Ready to see your wife?"

He gave a small nod.

Jazz pulled her hand away from his face. "Great." She glanced at the guard. "Tie him off?"

Something she couldn't read flickered in his teal eyes before he released Bob and grabbed the coiled rope she handed him.

Bob watched as the guard rapidly knotted the rope around one of the thick spokes.

Jazz stayed where she was, close enough to grab Bob if panic took over again. Or he looked down.

Which he suddenly did.

"Bob, look at me." She grabbed his shoulder, but the intervention was too late.

His gaze darted around, eyes wide as his breathing quickened, and he sat up again. "Get me down. I can't—" A strangled sound cut off his exclamation as he lurched past her, reaching for the spoke.

His hands slipped.

"Bob!" She reached for him as he fell with a scream.

Her hands caught rope. She winced as it seared her palms, but she clamped as hard as she could, trying to halt the heavy man's plummet.

The rope stalled in her hands with a jerk, stopped from behind.

She heard the guard's grunt before she felt that he stood behind her, probably a couple feet back. "Nice save." She glanced over her shoulder.

He gave her a stiff nod. "Happy to help. Let's let him down slower the rest of the way, huh?"

She grinned as she turned forward again. "Good idea." Bracing her feet carefully on the support beams, she kept her grip on the rope and peered below. "Looks like over fifty feet to go yet."

"Roger. One foot at a time." He started to feed her more rope, which she passed on to Bob below.

They created a smooth rhythm, working well as a team to make the rest of Bob's ride a smooth one.

People gathered under him as he neared the ground. Jazz couldn't be sure who they all were from that distance, but there was no missing Raksa, Sofia's German shepherd, and Flash.

"Slower." Jazz gripped the rope tighter as the people reached for Bob. Though she'd been able to tell the entire time that the guard didn't really need her help. Good thing, since her palms felt like they were on fire from that initial burning.

She watched as people laid Bob on the ground and removed the rope from his chest. "Okay. He's down."

She released the rope, turning toward the security guard who'd helped her save Bob's life. "Thanks for the assist."

The tall man let the loose end of rope drop to the cross-beams below them as he watched her. "Likewise." Splotches of sweat darkened his pale blue shirt, making it cling to his lean, muscled torso.

Wow. Broad shoulders, trim waist, and sculpted muscles

on every inch of him as far as she could see. Topped with a face that could grace a magazine cover any day if they wanted to sell thousands of copies. And he was taller than her. Probably six foot two or more.

Now that she got a good look at him, she wasn't sure she wanted to stop looking. But the heat of a blush crawling up to her face told her she'd better.

Especially since he was watching her watch him. His head tilted slightly to one side as his teal eyes seemed to study her.

Probably wondering why she was staring at him. Or maybe he knew.

The thought sent a fresh burst of flame to her cheeks. She turned away, and her foot nearly slipped off the beam. *Duh. Try to remember you're on a Ferris wheel and not on the ground, would you?*

"Race you down?" The security guard's voice was closer behind her than it should be.

She twisted her head around to see him just a couple feet away, holding the rope out toward her.

A twinkle sparkled in his eyes above a mischievously angled mouth.

A surge of heat that had nothing to do with the summer temps lit up her insides. Was he flirting with her?

Two could definitely play that game.

She took the offered rope. "At a time like this?"

His mouth flattened as the spark left his eyes. "You're right." He moved his hands to his hips. "Sorry."

Jazz turned away to hide her smirk as she stepped onto the spoke at the far edge, bringing the rope between her legs and up over one shoulder. She spun toward him, clasping the rope above her body with one hand and gripping it past her back with the other. She sent him a grin. "Last one down has to buy dinner."

She only stayed long enough to catch a glimpse of his surprised smile—one that would've curled her toes if she wasn't busy rappelling eighty feet to the ground.

THREE

The security guard's laugh followed Jazz's descent for the first several feet, sparking a surge of butterfly tingles that almost made her forget the pain in her palms.

He waited until she was on solid ground before he added his own weight to the rope.

She stood at the bottom and watched him rappel the first few feet.

"Nice rescue." Sofia's amused tone came from behind Jazz.

"Thanks." Jazz turned to face the raven-haired stunner.

"A little showy, but I approve." She glanced down at Raksa and Flash as the dogs vied for the best position to smell Jazz's jeans as if she'd been to another planet and back.

Jazz reached to pet Flash, but he buried his nose in her hands instead.

Sof chuckled. "I guess you have Flash's approval, too. Though he wasn't too happy with you leaving him behind."

"Aww." Jazz stroked the Malinois' smooth head as she took the leash from Sof. "Next time, I'll take you along. Okay, bud?"

"That'll be an even better show." The twinkle in Sof's dark eyes signaled she was teasing.

But was there some truth in the joke? Did she think Jazz

shouldn't have climbed the Ferris wheel to help? Maybe the Phoenix K-9 Security and Detection Agency didn't get into rescues of this kind. Though they did standard search and rescue all the time. She wasn't sure when she'd learn all of Phoenix Gray's unwritten rules.

"Jazz. There you are."

Recognition came fast on the heels of the woman's voice. Only Aunt Joan could make it sound like Jazz was tardy or had been goofing off when she'd been saving a person's life.

Jazz turned to see her aunt walking her way in a navy blue pantsuit that must be stifling in this weather. But it was expensive, elegant, and professional. All the things Aunt Joan prized, and Jazz could never achieve.

"Have you seen the damage?" Aunt Joan's makeup and hair were still perfect, even in this humidity, but lines crossed her forehead. A rare sight for her foundation-slathered skin and always-controlled demeanor.

"Briefly."

"Come with me." Aunt Joan led the way at a brisk pace toward the damaged car lying on the ground.

Jazz scanned the area as she followed.

Two EMTs rushed toward Bob where the man lay on what looked like a blanket.

Sofia and Raksa went to join a line of other security guards at a perimeter they'd established outside the fence.

A larger crowd than Jazz would've expected gathered there, given how many entertaining activities they could be enjoying at the fair instead. But some people apparently thought injuries and disaster were always the best entertainment.

Jazz slowed as Aunt Joan stopped near the fallen car.

Butch Klika gave Jazz a gruff nod as she approached. But everything the head of security did was gruff. Even the way he wiped the sweat off his forehead with his large hand was gruff.

"Well?" Aunt Joan looked at him, then glanced toward the

two police officers crouched by strewn parts from the damaged cabin.

He tilted his broad head toward the officers who must have come from an offsite department. "They have a theory."

Aunt Joan took three steps to stand over the officers. "Hello, officers. I'm Joan Cracklen, General Manager of the Tri-City Fair." Her tone cooled to the patient and pleasant one she used for public relations. "Have you found anything?"

The men stood and faced her, their expressions calm but serious. The taller of the two men gestured to the shorter guy. "Officer Burns. And I'm Sergeant Wentworth."

Aunt Joan nodded. "A pleasure, though not under these circumstances, perhaps. Have you been able to determine why the car fell?" Her features relaxed as if she wasn't worried at all. But Jazz spotted the barely perceptible vertical depressions on either side of her mouth. They only showed when she was tense or upset.

The sergeant pointed down at small bits of something on the blacktop. "These rivets have come apart. They're nearly rusted through."

"Hmm." Aunt Joan kept her face as unreadable as she could.

"If you'll come this way, I'd like to show you something." The sergeant picked up a long piece of flattened metal and headed toward the crushed car.

Aunt Joan shot Jazz a look before she followed. A look that said Jazz was supposed to come, too. Though why her aunt wanted her there was beyond Jazz. She usually had the opposite desire where Jazz was concerned—to get rid of her as soon as possible.

Jazz kept a couple feet between them, preserving what Aunt Joan called the polite personal space window, as they stopped at the rear of the car.

"See here?" The sergeant bent to place the metal piece against the indented section of the cabin that seemed to be fitted for that part. He pointed at holes that aligned with other holes drilled in the metal piece. "Looks like the rivets were there."

"I see." Another careful answer from Aunt Joan. She needed to be cautious. Couldn't leave the door open for accusations or liability.

"So the rusted rivets broke off and allowed the cabin to fall." A man's voice drew Jazz's gaze over her shoulder.

The security guard.

Her pulse hopped at the sight of the tall, very swoony guy. How long had he been nearby?

Flash apparently didn't consider him a threat, since he hadn't given any warning.

Aunt Joan looked at the handsome guard but didn't appear impressed.

The sergeant nodded. "Looks that way."

"Thank you, Sergeant." Aunt Joan stepped closer to the policeman to shake his hand. "We'll have an inspector come immediately to conduct our own accident investigation, as well. Accidents with fair rides are sadly common, though we've had very few at the Tri-City Fair during our long history." She sounded like she was warming up for the press conference she'd have to hold soon. "If you'll excuse me, I need to contact the inspector and begin necessary reports."

The sergeant said a polite goodbye and went back to his fellow cop.

Aunt Joan turned toward Jazz with a stern expression that twisted Jazz's insides in a knot like she was still a little kid under her aunt's roof. "I need to talk to you." She said the words under her breath as she brushed past Jazz, clearly intending Jazz should follow her again.

The hunky security guard watched Jazz as she passed.

She gave him a small smile that she hoped didn't look too nervous or desperate.

As soon as they were out of earshot of others, Aunt Joan swung toward Jazz. "You need to help me with damage control." She kept her voice low and glanced around. "We haven't had an accident like this in decades."

"There was the time the kiddy train got stuck on the bridge."

"I mean something this serious." Aunt Joan's eyes flashed. "With injuries that could have been fatalities."

"But you said yourself, accidents happen on rides a lot more often than people realize. Didn't you tell me there are about twelve hundred accidents a year?"

"Yes. But the public doesn't realize that. This could make people feel our fair is no longer safe."

"Okay." Jazz looked at her aunt, trying like always to figure out what the woman wanted from her. She'd never figured it out yet. "So what can I do?"

"You can make sure the security team, staff, vendors—anyone you talk to—understands this was a rare accident that could happen at any fair. It's an anomaly. The Tri-City Fair is perfectly safe."

Jazz nodded. "Got it."

Aunt Joan stared at Jazz like she didn't believe her. "I know how rumors start and gain legitimacy among people who seem to have close access to the truth. If the people who work here spread a false story, that this was intentional or due to some negligence, the fair could be in jeopardy."

"I understand. I care about this fair as much as you do." Maybe even more. It was the only thing Jazz and her aunt had in common. For Aunt Joan, it was her life, her pride and joy. But for Jazz, it was the only place she'd felt special, accepted, and happy. She wasn't going to let anything happen to the fair on her watch. "I'll make sure no one is spreading harmful rumors."

"Excellent." Aunt Joan glanced around one more time, as if checking for eavesdroppers. "I wanted to catch you today. We'd like to invite you to Sunday brunch after church."

The swallow Jazz had been in the midst of stuck in her throat. She coughed, covering her mouth with her hand like her aunt had drilled into her as a girl. "Sorry." She coughed again.

Aunt Joan was inviting her to the house? With her and

Uncle Pierce? Disbelief threatened to choke Jazz again. "Brunch?" It was the only thing she could think to say.

"Yes." Aunt Joan's eyebrows gathered as she watched Jazz like she was being the weird one. "Come at eleven."

"Um." Jazz swallowed back the tickle in her throat. "Okay."

"Good." Aunt Joan stepped around Jazz without so much as another glance and stalked away.

Jazz stared at her retreating figure before letting her gaze travel over the crowded bystanders, the medics, and the smashed Ferris wheel car.

She didn't know which of this morning's events surprised her more. Her Tri-City Fair—the safe haven of her childhood —becoming dangerous or her aunt inviting her to a family meal, voluntarily.

The nerves that tingled in her belly gave her the answer. Definitely brunch with Aunt Joan and Uncle Pierce.

<h1 style="text-align:center">FOUR</h1>

Rebekah let out a low whistle as she preceded Hawthorne through the hallway that opened into a large, open concept space with a living room, fully equipped kitchen, and a white spiral staircase that climbed to the balcony and bedrooms.

Hawthorne smiled at his sister as he moved past her into the living room decorated in a modern style with white furnishings and gray and black accents. "Welcome to my temporary home."

Rebekah's big blue eyes found Hawthorne, the wonder in them reminding him how young she was. Or how old he was. "I've never seen a Floatbnb like this one. Well, only in pics, I guess." She slipped her oversized bag from her shoulder and let it drop on the wood floor. Kicking off her flip-flops, she scurried onto the white shag rug.

She giggled as she curled her bare toes into the soft fabric. "Wow. Is this how you always live?" She whipped out her smartphone from the pocket of her barely there jeans shorts, probably planning to take *pics*, as she called them.

Yep, thirty-one had never felt quite so old until being in the presence of this nineteen-year-old sprite.

He was glad all his personal belongings were tucked away in his suitcase upstairs, so he didn't have to interrupt her frenzy of photos. Which she was probably already posting to her social media accounts in the next five seconds that she tapped on her phone.

"Not exactly." He pressed the button on the espresso maker to start the drink he'd prepped before Rebekah had arrived. "I got a good deal on this rental."

"Uh-huh, sure." She turned her bright eyes on him and hurried to the island in the kitchen where he stood on the opposite side. "The stuff online about you is pretty crazy. You're really famous." And rich, her big grin probably meant. "Don't try to be all humble about it."

He closed his mouth, stopping the response she would probably deem too humble. "I've been blessed to have some success."

"It's so unbelievable you're a writer. I'd love to do something like that."

"I don't think you told me what your major is."

She paused before answering, giving Hawthorne a moment to study her face. Strange that his own sister was so unfamiliar to him. But she'd only been six years old when he'd left.

Her eyes were still the same. Those big blue orbs that could persuade anyone to give her anything she wanted. She'd been the baby of the family in every way. Everyone's favorite. She'd been their energy and hope. The joyous distraction from the tension and rifts that eventually drove them apart.

Her other features, though still framed with baby fat, had developed to create a face he wouldn't have recognized if not for its similarity to their mother's. The small, rounded chin. The oval-shaped face with high forehead. And her glossy blond hair. Rebekah was a very pretty girl. Like a reflection of the photos of their mother when she was young.

"I've switched it up a few times." She gave him a careless grin. "Can't really decide what I want to do, you know? I love art, but that might not pay the bills. And I don't want to work at a grocery store all my life."

"Art, as in painting?"

"Yeah, but digital art mostly."

Of course. "That sounds cool."

"Yeah." She shrugged one slim shoulder under the strap of her fitted tank top. Her smile faded as she dropped her gaze.

Probably remembering why she'd stopped by. The reason he'd come to the Twin Cities.

"Want an espresso?" They could both probably stand to be fortified a little before discussing that. "I can always use a pick-me-up by this time of day." The hazards of being an early riser.

"No thanks." She shook her head. "I can't get past the taste. So bitter." She stuck out her tongue.

He chuckled. "It's not for everyone." And she apparently didn't need the caffeine anyway. He poured himself an espresso and nodded toward the living room. "Let's sit."

"Sure." She hurried over to the sofa, and he followed at a slower pace, sitting in the armchair kitty-corner to her. She bounced her knees up and down in front of her.

Was she unsure how to ask what she wanted to? He took a sip of his espresso. Maybe she wasn't comfortable with him. They were practically strangers, especially from her point of view. Did she even remember him?

A lump formed in his throat, and he took another drink to wash it down. Lowering his espresso, he looked at her. "Did you have something you wanted to talk about?" He'd assumed her text last night, saying she wanted to drop by in the morning, hadn't intended a casual visit.

"Yeah, what have you found out?"

He stifled a smile at her sudden directness and set his cup on the glass coffee table in front of him. "Well." He rested his hands on the arms of the chair. "It has only been one day. I'm afraid I'm going to need a little more time to make progress."

"Oh." Her mouth puckered, so reminiscent of her little-girl pout that he had to squash another smile.

"Sorry. But these things do take time."

"Yeah, I know. But..." She looked away. She pushed off

the sofa and stalked to an abstract painting on the wall.

He waited as she stared at it for a minute. Hard to believe, looking at her skimpy outfit, that she'd grown up at Best Life. But a lot of kids who decided to flee when they turned eighteen were desperate to leave much more than the cult's white robes behind them. He'd been eager to explore a lot of what the world had to offer, too.

She turned to face him. Something glimmered on her cheek.

Was she crying?

His chest pinched.

"It's just…" She bit her lower lip, then let it go. "I've already waited so long." Her voice faded on the last word.

He stood and crossed the room to her but stopped a couple of feet away. He was like a stranger to her. What could he do to comfort her? Not that comforting anyone was his strength to begin with. He hadn't given anyone a hug in… well, ten years or so? And that was a farewell with his last girlfriend.

He cleared his throat. "I'm sorry. It must be very hard."

She sucked in a trembling breath as she swiped away the tears with her hands. "It's been two years since Sam—" She cut off abruptly, as if she didn't want to say the word *died*. "That's too long, you know?" She lifted her gaze to him, her blue eyes shimmering in the pool of her grief.

He nodded.

"It's especially too long to let someone get away with killing him." Her small hands clenched into fists at her sides as she strode back to the sofa but didn't sit. She spun to face him. "Do you still think you can do it? Can you find who killed him?"

He paused, choosing his words carefully, as he'd done when she'd called him to ask if he would come to Minnesota to solve the death—the murder, she believed—of her boyfriend. "I'll do my best to find the truth. I can promise you that. And if that leads me to murder and a killer, then that's where I'll go."

"You're still not sure it was murder." She dropped onto the sofa, whether from defeat or emotional exhaustion, he couldn't say.

He rounded the coffee table and returned to his chair, perching on the edge to be closer to her, better able to catch her gaze when she looked up again. "You asked me to do this because I write crime thrillers—mysteries—and because I was an MP, right?"

She nodded, admitting to what she'd said on that phone call.

"The only way to solve a mystery, especially one in real life, is to approach it without any assumptions. I have to look at all the evidence before I let myself form conclusions or come up with any theories."

She pressed her lips together. "But you know it's not just me, right? His dad swore it was murder, too."

"You have to trust me, Rebekah. I will find the truth for you, okay?"

She stared at him a beat or two. Then she nodded and glanced away.

Compassion filled his chest as he watched the sadness cloak her young face. A nineteen-year-old girl shouldn't have to carry the burden of the tragic death of a loved one. Especially in circumstances like those surrounding Sam Ackerman's death. A death deemed an accident by authorities but believed to be murder by those close to him.

If Hawthorne had read about it in case files while doing research or in the pages of a novel, he'd have thought it was great material for a thrilling plot. But there was nothing thrilling about death—murder or accidental—in real life. Especially when it grieved his sister so much.

"Oops." Rebekah stared at the smartphone she must've picked up while he was thinking. "I gotta go. Work." She jumped up from the sofa and rushed to her flip-flops. She slung the bag over her shoulder as she spun toward him. "Text me as soon as you find out something?"

"Absolutely." He stood to see her out.

Her flip-flops smacked the wood floor as she hurried to the door. "Or even if you don't find out anything?" She threw the question over her shoulder with a glance that seemed to carry a hint of vulnerability. Or maybe fear? Of what, he couldn't say.

"Sure." He slowly closed the door behind her.

He looked at his watch. *4:26 p.m.*

Would anyone get suspicious if he showed up at the fairgrounds when it wasn't his shift? Probably. He'd been up front when he had signed on for the two-week stint as a Tri-City Fair security guard. He'd said he was a thriller novelist, wanting to research the fair. He hadn't mentioned he specifically wanted to investigate a suspicious death at the fair, but no one should be surprised when they learned what he was doing.

Still, he was brand new. He didn't need to make people uncomfortable right out of the gate. He'd wait until his morning shift tomorrow. And remember to start his drive earlier this time. Thanks to Minneapolis traffic, his commute to the Tri-City Fair in St. Paul took far longer than he'd expected when he'd rented the Floatbnb at this location.

He returned to the living room, and his gaze landed on the flipped throw pillow where Rebekah had sat. Maybe he should've admitted that he hadn't been able to start investigating Sam's death today because of the unexpected disaster with the Ferris wheel.

Talk about things that shouldn't be labeled an accident.

He supposed it was normal for the police and fair staff to assume the cabin falling that way was accidental. Rust did cause problems, and the research he'd done when his shift ended yesterday showed the General Manager was right. Accidents with rides happened much more frequently than he'd realized. So maybe this event was an accident, too.

Yet he couldn't help but consider other possibilities. Like a person swapping out good rivets for rusted. Ones the culprit knew would break.

He blew out a breath and grabbed his espresso off the

coffee table, finishing it in one quick gulp as he walked to the kitchen.

He was the one whose brain was abnormal, his imagination always suspicious and overactive. Served him well in fiction writing and military investigations. But he had to remember to keep it in check for civilian life.

He had his hands full with trying to investigate Sam's death. No need to pile up imaginary villains and conspiracies all over the fair.

At least unraveling a mystery wasn't the only thing he had to look forward to at his new security job. He smiled as he rinsed the cup and put it in the otherwise-empty dishwasher.

The memory of fascinating Jazz Lamont filled his mind. If only he'd been able to talk to her after they'd rescued the passenger. But she'd been engrossed in private conversation with the General Manager, which was curious. Perhaps the General Manager recognized she had something special in Jazz Lamont. And then Butch had sent Jazz and Hawthorne out on patrol in separate directions.

He hadn't seen her again during the long shift, even though he'd kept an eye out for her. But the fairgrounds were massive and as crowded as New York City sidewalks most of the time.

He might not see her tomorrow either. If they were even working the same shift again. He could legally base his next series' heroine on her without her permission, so long as he didn't use anything obviously specific to her.

But if he could use her first name, at least, that would be fantastic. And it would be a dream to be able to sit down with her and explore how she'd become such an amazing woman of action and skill. To learn what made her tick, what drove her, and who she really was.

The series would practically write itself.

He just needed to find his heroine again and get her to say yes.

FIVE

"He didn't."

Jazz snorted in response to Nevaeh's statement as she watched the dark road through the raindrops hitting her windshield. "You better believe he did. As if everyone wants to be in his Dating Adventures reels."

Nevaeh's laugh carried through the phone Jazz had on speaker.

"Really, it was like the whole date was supposed to be a way to get him more followers. Which was apparently why he wanted me to throw the glass of wine in his face. While the waitress recorded."

"Sounds so tempting." Nev barely got the words out between laughs.

"Oh, you know it." Jazz chuckled as she switched the windshield wipers to a faster setting. "I'm so done with internet dating. This is like the sixth horrible date I've had thanks to dating sites."

"Yeah, more like eighth."

Jazz tossed a fake glare at the phone in the holder on the dash. "Thanks."

"You're not going to give up on finding someone, are you?"

"I don't know." Jazz sighed. "It seems like a big waste of

time after a date like this. Maybe I should go back to organic."

"Uh-huh, 'cause that worked so well before."

"Hey, I only had two duds—well, maybe three—when I went out with people I met naturally."

Nev laughed. "Okay, I guess the percentages are better. And that's the way I met my man, so I'm a believer."

"Yeah, I'll just sit back and wait to bump into another gentle giant bodyguard. Shouldn't take too long."

"Maybe loosen up your criteria just a little." Nev snickered.

"Fine. He doesn't have to be a bodyguard. Or a giant."

"He still gotta be tall for you."

"Oh, yeah. Non-negotiable." Like the very tall security guard at the fair today.

"You still thinkin' about that hunky hero at the fair?"

Jazz grinned.

"I knew it." Nev could apparently hear the grin over the phone. "Man, I wish I'd seen the guy."

Jazz and Sofia had filled Nev in on the morning's disaster and rescue when she'd arrived for her afternoon shift. But none of them had caught sight of the heroic security guard again.

Well, Jazz hadn't asked Sofia. No need to look like she was crushing on him in front of Sof. "If you had, you'd know it. That's not a face you'd soon forget."

"Oo-ee, dude must be hot. I can hear you swooning over the phone, girl."

Jazz laughed, probably more of a sighing giggle. "Yeah, but it was more than that."

"Uh-huh. Foh sure his character was what grabbed you."

"For real." Jazz had a hard time getting the protest out past another laugh. "He's a terrific climber, and not an ounce of fear. Just saw someone needed help, and he jumped in without a thought for himself."

"Hmm, he might have potential. But I'm gonna have to meet this guy before I can okay him for my bestie."

"Sure."

"Since you've already moved on to your next potential guy, does that mean you don't want a pity party?"

Jazz smiled as she braked for a stoplight and turned right. "Girl, of course I want a pity party." As if she'd ever turn down their tradition of ice cream and a romantic comedy movie after a bad date. "I'll grab the ice cream and be right there."

"Sweet."

"Want chocolate chip cookie dough?"

"Yeah." A hint of hesitation crept into Nev's tone. "Just a heads-up, Branson's here. Okay if he joins us?"

"Oh." Jazz's heart sank with her smile.

"Or he could probably study in the kitchen while we watch the movie." Nev hurried to offer the alternative. "He could totally do that."

It suddenly made sense why Nev had asked if she didn't want the pity party this time. She was hoping to spend time with her fiancé. Which made perfect sense. She couldn't exactly ask him to leave all of a sudden when they probably had plans of their own for a romantic evening.

"No, that's okay." Jazz tried to keep her disappointment out of her voice. "I should've figured you were hanging with him tonight."

"Sorry. I knew you had a date, so..."

Not like Nev would've kept the night clear for Jazz anyway. She and Branson didn't get to see each other often otherwise, between his seminary classes and security job and Nev's work at PK-9. Evenings were their only time together. And they were in love.

It was fine. Jazz was happy for Nev. That's what best friends did. They put each other first. Even when it changed everything.

Jazz pulled her shoulders back and struggled to shove away her crushed expectations as she made another turn. "No problem. Don't worry about me."

"You're disappointed."

Of course, Nev knew Jazz too well not to hear it in her voice.

"Nah, I'd do the same thing if I had a guy like Branson in my life. You know I'm thrilled you have him."

Silence signaled Nev wasn't sold.

Jazz pasted on a smile, hoping it would lift her tone. "I'm the one who pushed you to give him a chance in the first place, remember?"

"True."

"So go ahead and enjoy the time with your man." The realization that had been growing in Jazz's mind for months reached her heart and sank there. This was what it was going to be like from now on.

She really was happy for Nev, but it was already getting so hard for them to do things together just the two of them anymore. That would only get worse—probably impossible—when she married Branson in the spring.

"You won't go home and be sad?"

What could Jazz say? If she told the truth, she'd be the mean friend who guilted her bestie into choosing her over a great guy. But Nev would never buy a lie.

Jazz would be fine. She could get used to being a loner again. She'd been alone for years before coming to the Twin Cities. "Of course not. I have Flash and..." Jazz searched for something convincing to say besides admitting she would feel lonely and—

Wait a second. She'd gotten a notification on her phone right before she'd gone into the restaurant for her disastrous date.

"I have the new Hawthorne Emerson novel." She didn't have to fake the happiness in her voice now. How could she have forgotten? She'd had her favorite thriller author's novel on pre-order, and it had shipped two days before the actual release. If she'd known it was going to arrive that evening, she'd have canceled the date in a heartbeat.

"Ooh, Carson Steele series?"

"Yes!" Jazz nearly squealed with excitement, her evening

looking so much better.

"So I guess you won't mind skipping the pity party." Amusement colored Nev's tone.

"Not a bit." A grin stretched Jazz's mouth.

Nev laughed. "Thought so. But I want to read it right after you're done."

"No promises. I might have to read it twice." Jazz chuckled. But reading it twice was her usual tradition. The first time through, she read super fast because she couldn't wait to find out what happened to Carson Steele, the former Military Police investigator turned private investigator hero of the bestselling series. But then she always read the story again, slower, to savor the poetic prose, the witty dialogue, and all the delicious character details amid the thrilling action.

"A'ight, you have fun then."

"Oh, I will."

They ended the call with a shared laugh. Jazz really lucked out. Give her a Hawthorne Emerson novel over a movie any day. And the story description for *Seconds in Shadow* sounded so good.

Jazz's pulse quickened. She could let Flash outside quickly when she got home, and then start reading.

Some ice cream would be fun, though. And she should fill up with gas, too. She glanced at the gas gauge. Definitely needed a fill or she'd have to fit it in on her way to her morning shift at the fair.

She pulled into the lot of the twenty-four-hour gas station and convenience store she often used since it was only five minutes from her apartment.

The canopy overhead shielded her from the rain as she got out and stuck her credit card into the pump computer.

A breeze whispered across her shoulder, left bare in the white sleeveless blouse she'd paired with skinny jeans and pink heels for her date.

The fine hairs on her arms stood on end.

Something felt off.

She glanced around, stepping to the side to scan the other

gas pumps. The bright overhead lights made it easy to see... and to be seen.

A gray sedan was parked at the next pump over, and a man stood outside the car. He stared at his smartphone while he waited for the gas to pump. Business suit, expensive ride, distracted. Probably not the reason for her sudden edginess.

She kept an eye out as she waited for the pump to fill the big tank of her SUV.

A middle-aged woman left the convenience store carrying chips and a soda. No one else seemed to be in the vicinity.

But Jazz's nerves still tingled. Ready.

Too bad Flash wasn't there. He had much better instincts and would actually be able to pinpoint the danger she could only sense. Or imagine.

Though it wouldn't be the first time she'd been approached by a creep at a gas station.

The businessman pulled away from the other pump as she finished filling her SUV.

She could just go home. She'd already paid. But that would be the first time she'd let danger keep her from living her life the way she wanted. She wasn't about to give up her freedom now, even if her instincts were right.

She peered into the darkness on either side of the convenience store as she crossed the blacktop.

No sign of any movement in the shadows. No sounds.

Maybe the idea of the excitement waiting for her in the Carson Steele novel was enough to put her nerves on edge.

A smile curved her mouth as she entered the store and grabbed the chocolate chip cookie dough ice cream that would pair perfectly with Carson Steele. Though his favorite was mint chip, according to Book Five in the series.

"Have a good night!" She waved at the clerk as she leaned into the exit door, spreading her new-thriller-novel joy to the guy who probably had a long shift ahead of him.

"Thanks." He gave her a small smile back, and she swung away to step onto the sidewalk outside the door.

Strong arms clamped around her.

SIX

You've gotta be kidding me. The thought hadn't even finished by the time Jazz escaped the muscled guy's hold with a shoulder slip. She pushed off his body to gain some distance.

But her back slammed into something else. Someone.

Great. Two thugs.

He grabbed her neck from behind, wrapping his arm around her in a sloppy choke.

She clamped down on his arm and dropped her weight, swinging in a pivot to the side. She flung him down with a quick knee thrust.

He grunted as he hit the concrete hard.

She spun to face the other guy just in time to see him lunge at her.

Something flashed in his hand. A knife.

She dodged to the side, narrowly missing an encounter with his blade.

Time to even the odds.

She snatched the knife from her ankle sheath and threw it at the charging man.

He shrieked as it hit her target—his shoulder. He dropped his own knife to yank hers out of his flesh, letting it fall so he could press a hand against his wound.

The other dude managed to get to his feet, holding the

back of his head where he'd probably connected with the concrete.

This was her chance. She ran at the guy with the head injury. She'd put him in a choke and use him as a shield against his buddy.

But he yelped and turned to run, his pal fleeing ahead of him.

Oh, no, they didn't. Jazz darted to pick up her knife from the sidewalk on her way after them.

"Ma'am?"

She spun toward the male voice.

The clerk.

"Are you okay?" The twenty-something guy cautiously stuck out his head an inch past the glass door he held open in front of his body. "I've called the police."

She peered into the darkness. No sign of the thugs. She was fast, but probably not fast enough. Especially if the engine she heard revving was their getaway car, parked on the next street over.

Sirens sounded in the distance. Great. Now she'd have to spend the next hour telling the police everything that had happened. Probably multiple times.

Disappointment sagged her shoulders as her gaze fell on the ice cream carton that had tumbled from the plastic bag onto the blacktop.

Her date with Hawthorne Emerson would have to wait.

The aroma of corn dogs, cotton candy, popcorn, and some mystery fried food blended in the morning air, making Hawthorne's mouth water. He'd eaten a full breakfast of eggs and bacon before coming on duty at seven thirty, about an hour ago, but his stomach apparently didn't care.

"Hey, Freddie." Hawthorne paused his patrol route by the food vendor whose stand advertised corn dogs, popcorn, hot dogs, and burgers with colorful illustrated signs. "Slow morning?"

Freddie Blain cracked a grin beneath the shaggy mustache that teased his upper lip. "I guess not everyone wants to put hot dogs and burgers into their stomachs first thing in the morning." He rested his hands on the metal counter just inside the large open window. "Go figure, right?"

"Try selling 'em fried cookie dough before nine." The jolly voice to Hawthorne's left drew his gaze to Molly Dreyer, the friendly and sarcastic owner of the food stand across from Freddie's. Molly crossed her eyes and smashed her lips together.

Hawthorne laughed.

"Though I haven't seen the parent yet who can convince their kid cotton candy doesn't make a good breakfast."

"Hey, my food has plenty of nutrition to start the day off right." Freddie leaned forward toward Molly, a gleam in the brown eyes behind his glasses. "Protein is slow-burn energy and essential for health."

"Uh-huh. My fried butter has dairy fats. They protect against cancer."

"My popcorn offers whole grains."

"Try to soothe your conscience much?" Molly smirked at Freddie before swinging her gaze back to Hawthorne. "How you doing, handsome? Now you, I could get used to seeing anytime of the day." She winked as she propped one fist on her rounded hip.

"Don't go trying to rob the cradle, Molly." Freddie laughed as he shook his head.

Molly gave Freddie an exaggerated glare with a haughty lift to her chin. "Some of us are not as far over the hill as you are, Fred Blain."

"Oh, yeah? How old do you think I am?"

She narrowed her eyes at the man as he shifted to the side so his teenaged employee could serve a customer.

"Fifty-four."

Freddie glanced at Hawthorne, crossing his arms over his red apron. "She's good."

"Ha!" Molly flicked back her tightly curled brown hair, the locks barely long enough to brush her shoulder. "And just how old do you think I am?"

"Old enough to know better." Freddie smirked again.

"Ouch." Hawthorne groaned as he laughed. These two were something else. He'd already enjoyed their banter yesterday when he'd introduced himself. He wanted to get a sense of all aspects of the fair for future research, should he decide to use the setting for a book.

But his performance as a security guard would also be improved by cultivating informants, a neighborhood watch, scattered across the fairgrounds. After a little while, they might come to trust him enough that he could ask them about Sam Ackerman's death, too. See if they were at the fair that year and remembered anything helpful.

"We saw you yesterday, scaling the Ferris wheel like you were Spiderman." Molly gave him a light whack on the arm. "Where'd you learn to do that?"

"Online videos."

She laughed. "Oh, go on."

He chuckled and shrugged. "I enjoy rock climbing."

"And being a hero." Freddie looked at Hawthorne with a more serious set to his mouth. "That was a wonderful thing you did. Not many people risk their lives to help someone else. Especially a stranger."

Discomfort started to creep up Hawthorne's neck. Never did like attention. "Well, I wasn't the only one. You probably saw Jazz Lamont up there, too."

"Oh, yes. Isn't she amazing?" Molly's eyes lit. "I've known Jazzy for years."

"Jazzy?" Hawthorne stared at her.

"That's what we called her when she was just a scrawny little thing, running around here with her best friend, Nevaeh. She's here this year, too. Both of them all grown up." Molly sighed, a bit like a mother missing the days when her children were young.

"Jazz grew up here?"

"Mm-hmm. She was here every year back when I was a young thing."

Freddie cleared his throat.

Molly shot him a glance. "A *very* young thing." She smiled up at Hawthorne again. "Jazz spent her summers at the fairgrounds. At least that's what it seemed like. I think she and Nevaeh were allowed on the grounds before the fair started because of Jazz's aunt."

"Her aunt?" Hawthorne struggled to put the pieces together.

"Joan Cracklen. The General Manager."

"Oh. I didn't know they were related." That explained the close conversation Mrs. Cracklen and Jazz had after the Ferris wheel disaster.

"Poor Jazz. She must be upset over what happened yesterday." Molly's chin puckered as she looked down. "She loves the fair more than anything. She always called it her home."

Fascinating. What an intriguing background to grow up at a fair. Hawthorne wanted to see Jazz even more now. He'd been looking for her all morning. The duty roster at the Public Safety Center listed her as working starting at eight a.m.

"Do they have any idea how the Ferris wheel car fell like that?" Freddie lowered his tone slightly as he aimed the question at Hawthorne.

"It appeared to be an accident." Best not to spread his own suspicions around. He didn't have any proof it had been intentional. "I understand fair ride accidents are more common than I'd realized before."

"Maybe so." Freddie didn't look or sound convinced. "But they still shouldn't happen. Not at all."

"I'm sure they didn't let it happen on purpose, Freddie." Molly sent him a chastising glance. "No one wants anyone to get hurt, especially Joan and fair management. It wouldn't do their business any good."

"Doesn't do anyone any good, Molly." Freddie shook his head.

"Exactly. It's just one of those things nobody can do anything about. Though I knew."

Hawthorne swung his gaze to her face. "You knew?"

"I most certainly did."

How could she have known? Unless she'd done something to—

"My cotton candy machine stalled."

Hawthorne's flurry of suspicions screeched to a halt. "What?"

"Yep. It just stalled. First morning, twenty minutes before opening. Terrible omen."

Oh, brother. If only leaving the cult behind meant Hawthorne never again had to hear nonsense about omens and superstitions.

"Good grief, Molly." Freddie said the words Hawthorne held back. "You don't think omens are a real thing, do you?"

"Of course I do. They are real. Like two years ago." She looked from Freddie to Hawthorne. "Neither of you were here then, but a boy died. Right on the fairgrounds."

Hawthorne's breath caught. Was she talking about Sam Ackerman? He worked to keep his features still as she shook her head, her hazel eyes darkening.

"Awful thing. He was only seventeen. He died on the Logboat Adventure ride." She lifted her index finger. "And I knew something bad was going to happen that day."

Did she have evidence the police hadn't known about then? Hawthorne chose his words carefully. "How did you know?"

"My oven broke that morning."

"Oh, Molly." Freddie's exasperated tone matched the feeling rising in Hawthorne's chest.

"Really." She glanced back and forth at the men. "It was a brand-new oven. Mint condition. No reason for it to have problems. But it just broke down. I knew something bad was going to happen after that." She stared at them as if the truth in what she said was obvious. And like she wanted some kind of response.

Hawthorne glanced away to think. "I don't—"

A slim woman with a long, dark ponytail caught his attention. Was that Jazz?

She turned from the dart balloons game, giving him a glimpse of her face as she took the hand of a small child. Not Jazz.

Disappointment sank to his stomach. He'd been doing that all morning, thinking he saw her. Which was pretty dumb. All he needed to do was look for the dog. And glossy red hair. And beautiful features.

Not that he knew what he'd say if he did see her. Any way he could think of to explain he wanted to study her, to write about her in his next novel, made him sound like a creep or a guy with the worst pickup line in history. The last thing he needed was for her to think he was interested in her romantically.

But the ideas for stories surrounding her as the heroine of his new series were taking flight. He'd already jotted down several he'd thought of in the shower that morning.

"Honey, are you okay?" Molly's gentle touch on his arm halted the flow of plot ideas rushing through his mind. Another occupational hazard.

"Sorry." He smiled down at the short woman.

"Were you looking for someone?" Her hazel eyes held too much understanding for his liking.

"Uh..."

"Hey, Molly." That voice.

Hawthorne's pulse picked up speed as he turned to see the woman he'd been looking for.

Jazz Lamont. Her fresh face, smooth skin, shiny red hair pulled back in a ponytail, and those big green eyes were more amazing than he'd remembered. Yeah. She was perfect. For his heroine.

"Jazz. We were just talking about you!" Molly gave the taller woman a side hug with her arm around Jazz's waist.

Her Belgian Malinois panted calmly as he watched the gesture, seemingly used to Molly. Hawthorne had met some military dogs that didn't take kindly to people grabbing their handlers. At least not if they were strangers.

"You were?" Jazz lifted a curved eyebrow as she glanced from Hawthorne to Freddie.

"About five minutes ago." Freddie corrected Molly with a sideways look before he gave Jazz a smile. "Freddie Blain. Manager of the most popular food stand at the Tri-City Fair."

Molly sucked in a breath. "It is not. Mrs. Flover's Chocolate Chip Cookies is the top seller every year. And I'm sure mine does better than—"

"It's called salesmanship, Molly." Freddie gave her a smirk.

Jazz glanced from her indignant friend to Freddie. "Jazz Lamont. Looks like you and Molly are already hitting it off." She smiled at the man. "But what happened to Jim? He's owned this stand for years. Or at least he did back when I was a kid. I hope he's okay."

"Oh, he's fine." Freddie waved off the concern with his hand. "I'm his cousin. He wanted to retire from the day-to-day, but not from ownership. So he owns it, and I manage it now."

"I see. I guess he found the right replacement. Molly would be bored to tears if she didn't have neighbors who give back as good as they get." Jazz grinned at Molly as the shorter woman gave her a saucy glare.

Which lasted about a second before Molly glanced up at Hawthorne with a mischievous quirk to her mouth. "Have you met my friend here?" She switched her gaze to Jazz in time to indicate the question was for her.

"Not officially." Jazz turned her brilliant emerald eyes on Hawthorne.

He smiled, nerves tingling in his belly. Still couldn't think of the best way to ask her. Unless he shouldn't ask her. He'd be giving her a chance to say no. He managed to extend his hand as his thoughts raced. "Hawthorne Emerson."

Her mouth widened into an *O* shape as her eyes grew bigger. And she didn't shake his hand. "You're not a security guard?" Her unexpected question emerged like a strangled accusation.

And he hadn't even gotten to the weird part yet.

SEVEN

Hawthorne Emerson? Jazz's favorite author was standing in front of her?

But it couldn't be him. Here, at her fair. In real life. Looking at her. Waiting for…What was he waiting for?

And what had she just said? Something inane about him not being a security guard.

Heat blazed into her cheeks too quickly to douse. But maybe it didn't matter she'd look like a tomato now. Maybe he wasn't *the* Hawthorne Emerson.

"Are—" The word sounded like a croak. She swallowed. "Are you really Hawthorne Emerson?"

A small smile angled his mouth. "That's what my birth certificate says."

"I think she means, are you the author?" Molly put her hand under Jazz's arm as if she thought Jazz might faint. She might not be too far off, though it'd be the first faint of Jazz's life. "Yes, dear. He is."

"You're him?" Jazz heard her own voice lift to a high, airy pitch.

"Yes, ma'am. I write thriller novels."

"Jefferson Hall and Carson Steele. Carson's my favorite. I love him. I mean, I love you." She stuck out her hand. Had he offered his for a handshake before?

His warm grip slipped around hers. Goodness. His hand was large and strong but gentle. She was touching Hawthorne Emerson.

And she'd just blurted that she loved him. "Your writing, I mean. Your stories. I love your stories." More heat surged into her face. She probably looked more like a beet now. "They're amazing."

Was she pumping his hand too hard? She dropped her hold and yanked her hand back. "You're a terrific writer. My copy of *Seconds in Shadow* came last night. I wanted to start it right away, but..." She stopped before she spilled that she was attacked and all of the weirdness of her life he didn't need to know.

In fact, he didn't need to know any of whatever she'd babbled about. And probably didn't want to. She was rambling like an idiot. "I'm honored to meet you." She firmly shut her mouth. Hopefully, that was a more rational thing to say.

Though deciphering what was rational with a breathless, swoony sensation spiraling through her body might be impossible. How had she not recognized him? Her favorite author in the world?

She tried to casually study his face while Molly said something.

The beard. His photo on the back cover of all his books showed him with a beard. He looked so different without it. Even more handsome, if that were possible. With only the little bit of stubble he had now, she could see the shape of his strong jawline that had been hidden in his photo.

But she should've recognized the eyes. Except that the photo made them look simply blue. They were so much more vibrant in person. The photo didn't capture their electric intensity, their vivid teal color.

The swoony faintness seemed to be increasing. Good thing Molly still had her hand under Jazz's arm.

And Flash chose that moment to brush against her leg.

Probably getting concerned about the weird flood of chemicals rushing through her body.

"I have a question for you." His deep voice seemed to surround her in this dream she must be having.

"You do?"

He smiled. "I was wondering if—"

A boom punctured the air.

It took Jazz a second to be sure the sound wasn't her mind exploding from the realization she was standing in front of her favorite author.

Flash's barks helped. Along with Hawthorne and Molly spinning toward the sound.

Smoke rose from the area of...the Giant Slide?

Jazz and Flash took off, sprinting toward the smoke at the same time as Hawthorne. She pressed the button to activate her coms set. "PT3 to Base. Explosion at Giant Slide. En route to site. ETA one minute." She couldn't see the slide above the cattle barn and horse arena that stood between them, but she knew the layout of this fair as well as she knew her own name. The smoke was from the slide, no doubt.

Hawthorne outpaced her, an advantage to Jazz since he cleared a path through the crowds.

Flash strained at the leash, eager to outrun her and Hawthorne.

Jazz picked up her pace. She swung off into the shortcut around the feed shed and through the indoor horse arena, which would be empty right now.

Sand kicked up around her feet as she and Flash darted across the large arena and flew out the opening at the other end.

The smoke was fading as she locked eyes on the Giant Slide.

It teetered, listing to one side. She forced herself to keep breathing and closed the remaining distance, scanning the area.

"How did you—" Hawthorne ran up behind her as she

slowed. But his question hung unanswered as they stared at the wreckage.

People scattered the grass beside the huge slide where it leaned precariously. Had they fallen off with the explosion?

Other people were at the bottom of the slide, some lying on the pavement and some sitting up.

Crying filled the air. A child calling for her mom.

"S4 to Base." Hawthorne's firm tone duplicated in Jazz's ear over coms. "At scene with PT3. Need nurse and medics. Ambulance. Also crew to stabilize the slide."

"Mommy!"

Jazz homed in on the source of the cry.

A little girl, lying on the grass next to the partially collapsed slide.

Jazz and Flash hurried to the child. "Are you okay, honey?"

Brown hair stuck to tears on the girl's cheeks as she sat up and aimed big eyes at Jazz. "I want my mommy."

"Okay. We'll find her. How about we see if you're hurt?"

"Doggy?" The girl locked her gaze on Flash.

Perfect. "Yes." Jazz smiled. "He's a very nice doggy. Would you like to pet him?"

"Uh-huh."

Flash followed Jazz's cue he was free to visit and approached the girl, gently ducking his head and smelling her face as she put her small hands on his ears.

Jazz carefully palpated the girl's arms and legs, bare beneath her short-sleeved T-shirt and shorts. Some scratches but nothing broken. And no pain response. It would take a real EMT to be sure.

"Hayley!" A woman rushed toward them with her arms outstretched, tears on her cheeks.

"Mommy!" Hayley kept her hand on Flash as the woman reached them.

The mother engulfed Hayley in a gentle hug. "Are you hurt, sweetie?" She pulled back and looked at Jazz.

"I don't think so. Other than some scratches. But—"

Movement caught Jazz's eye. Dark curls, red T-shirt, and a rottweiler mix alongside.

Relief relaxed Jazz's insides as Nevaeh and Alvarez made their way to her.

"Here's an EMT. She'll be able to tell you for sure." Jazz stood, returning Nevaeh's grim nod as she gave her friend room to work.

Jazz walked along the tilted slide to check the other people on the grass. Most of them were on their feet and moving away. A good sign they weren't badly injured.

Marisa DeShae, the onsite nurse, squatted by a victim. Judging from where he or she lay on the grass closer toward the upper half of the slide, the person may have fallen forty feet.

"Everything okay here?" Jazz and Flash paused behind Marisa.

She glanced up from splinting the leg of a boy who looked to be about sixteen. "A fracture, but otherwise, we're fine." She gave a reassuring smile to the guy who grimaced but didn't make a sound. She angled her head to catch Jazz's gaze again. "I canvased the others. One adult with bruised ribs. This leg appears to be the severest injury."

Jazz nodded, not wanting to say more in front of the boy. Never could tell who would sue these days.

A fraction of the tension clenching Jazz's muscles eased as she stepped away, lifting her gaze to the slide. Lucky the injuries weren't worse. The whole side tilted dramatically. Good thing there were short walls along both edges or more people probably would've been thrown off. And it was fortunate this had happened early in the day. There could have been more visitors going down at one time in the afternoon or evening. And if the explosion had happened on the other side, where visitors lined the staircase, she didn't want to guess the number of casualties they'd have.

At least she and Hawthorne had gotten there quickly. Where was Hawthorne? She scanned the area.

Butch Klika, other security guards, and the onsite cops

had arrived and started guiding people off the grass onto the main path.

But no tall, distinctively attractive guy with sandy blond hair.

Weird. Jazz had assumed he would help the injured like she did when they'd arrived on scene. Yesterday proved he wasn't squeamish or cowardly. So where had he gone?

Suspicion tingled at the back of her neck. Two catastrophic accidents in two days. And Hawthorne had been first on scene for both.

EIGHT

Metal plates. A bit of shredded leather, like remnants of a strap.

Hawthorne crouched as he carefully picked his way across the wreckage beneath the highest point of the slide. Which used to be much higher.

"What are you doing?" The female voice made him startle.

He spun around, a smile relaxing his face at the sight of Jazz and her dog. "Hey." Then he registered her question. And the suspicious edge to it. His smile faltered. "I'm checking out the evidence. Trying to figure out what happened."

"Evidence." She glanced from him to the debris on the ground. "You think this wasn't an accident."

Wasn't that obvious? He held back the question that would probably be rude and nodded.

Her shoulders drooped. "I was afraid of that."

Ah. Denial. Not ignorance.

"Bomb?"

He nodded. "Judging from the type of impact and damage, I'd guess dynamite. A small, controlled explosion."

She looked at him, curiosity and maybe a bit of suspicion glinting in her green eyes. "How do you know that?"

"Well, I could say it's because I'm a writer. I've learned a lot in my research."

She still stared.

"But in this case, I investigated some crimes involving explosives when I was an MP."

"That's right. I read it in your bio. Just like Carson Steele."

He smiled. She really was a fan. That should help when he finally got to ask if he could use her as the main character in his next series. "Sort of. I was in the Marines, Carson is Navy."

"Important distinction." She grinned like someone who knew.

"Did you serve?"

She nodded. "Me and Flash." She glanced down at the Belgian Malinois who strained at his leash to reach the nearest fallen post. "Army."

He cringed, earning a musical laugh and brilliant smile.

"Okay, Marine. What happened here?" At least trust had replaced the suspicion in her eyes from a moment ago.

"I think the dynamite was rigged at the top of the tallest support post, not far below the slide itself." He walked a few feet to the remnants of the massive metal post. "You see, only two of the supports were blown at the top, making the lower portions of them collapse, too."

Jazz stared up toward where he pointed at the remaining posts. "And the other support beams took the weight of the slide when it dropped onto them."

"Thankfully. We'll need a crew or the fire department to fortify the slide with more beams."

"You don't want to climb up and do it with ropes?" Jazz sent him a teasing grin.

"Oh, I would. But my weight would probably topple the slide the rest of the way."

She laughed.

Man, she had a terrific sense of humor. Even in situations that would make other people freeze with fear. He'd seen that yesterday, too. Better jot that in his notes on his new heroine.

Jazz started moving through the debris, Flash smelling the ground as he went with her. "I suppose that's what the bomber did." She glanced at Hawthorne. "Climbed up the supports to place the dynamite."

"Maybe. Unless he lowered himself down from above."

"No way anyone could do that during the day. There are twenty-five employees working at the slide at any given time."

"Are you like a walking fair trivia book?" He infused the question with a teasing note.

"Pretty much, yeah." She flashed a smile. "I spent a lot of my summers here as a kid."

Then Molly's intel had been legitimate, not just fair gossip.

"So trust me when I say the culprit only could've set this up at night, assuming you're right about the IED and where it was." She watched her dog as she talked. "Do you think it was timed or remote activated?"

"Hard to say for sure. I'm sure the police lab techs can find out more with a closer examination. I'd guess timed unless the bomber wanted to watch for some particular reason to set it off just then."

"So the question is, why would s—" She stared down at Flash as he pawed at something. "What've you got, bud?"

She squatted next to the dog. "Leave it." She seemed to be staring at some object in the grass.

"Hey, Hawthorne."

He was already walking closer as she glanced over her shoulder.

"Do you have any idea what this is?"

He crouched beside her, and a scent of mild perfume tickled his nostrils. Or maybe her shampoo. A surprisingly soft and feminine scent. He would've expected something bolder, but the surprise of it, the seeming contradiction, was fascinating.

Forcing his thoughts away from her perfume and to the object she seemed to be looking at, his heartbeat stopped.

Then started again at a rush, fueled by the anger that lived in his memories, always ready to be fanned into flame at the slightest provocation.

A gold pin lay in the grass, the unmistakable design he'd hoped never to see again.

"You recognize it, don't you?" Jazz's question was soft.

He glanced at her, taking in the darkening concern in her eyes. He tried to school his expression, though it was probably too late. "It's from the Best Life cult."

"Should I know what that is?"

"You grew up here, right?"

She shook her head. "No. Just moved here like a year and a half ago."

"But you said you spent your childhood at the fair."

"Oh." She looked at the pin and then returned her gaze to him. "I spent summers here when my dad was overseas. And school years. Sometimes." She glanced away, but her closed-off tone revealed the emotion she was trying to hide. "I wasn't exactly in touch with the community."

Sensing this wasn't the time to delve into a clearly painful part of her background—especially since he didn't want to share his either—he moved on. "Well, you can be glad you missed this. They call themselves the Best Life Community, but it's a cult, pure and simple."

"And that's one of their pins?"

"Yeah." He was tempted to pick it up but knew better than to tamper with what could be evidence. He pointed instead. "See the B and L design, interconnected with the sun and moon? Every member of the cult has this pin and wears it on the uniform."

"Uniform?"

"That's what I call it. A required dress code. Everyone wears a white robe."

"That's...creepy."

"Good word for it." His jaw clenched as he stood.

"How do you know all this?" Jazz also rose, but he didn't look directly at her.

The emotions swirling in his gut were probably too visible in his eyes. "I'm originally from the area."

"You are?" The shock in her voice pulled his gaze to hers and gave him something else to think about—her cute, widened eyes and open mouth.

"Born and raised." He gave her a quick smile. "That's not in most of my bios." He'd better change subjects before he gave away more than he wanted to. "Who has access to this spot below the slide?"

Jazz directed her gaze toward the other side where the visitor staircase climbed. "The ground level on that side is staff access only, closed with a fence and gate locking the path to the storage shed. The other side," she nodded to where the victims had fallen to the grass, "people wouldn't normally be able to access without climbing over the fence along the main path at the front."

Another chain-link fence lined the path behind them about twenty feet away from where he and Jazz stood. Only about four feet high, though. Easy for an adult to hop over.

"None of those fences are tall enough to keep anyone out if they want to get over them." Jazz echoed his thoughts. Knew she was smart. "But they'd have to wait until they wouldn't be seen."

Hawthorne nodded and met her gaze. "At night."

"The cult that pin is from—would someone from there want to do something like this?"

He took a breath, pausing a few seconds to think better of the knee-jerk response he wanted to blurt out. He had to stay objective if the cult might really be tied to a crime like this. "It's not their usual style. They profess to be a pacifist community."

He rubbed a hand along the back of his neck, regretting it when sweat coated his fingers. Man, it was getting hot. "But they are against what they call 'worldly' entertainment. And I've seen them act contrary to some of their philosophies for the gain of…certain people and their own interests. The pursuit of spiritual and physical utopia sometimes causes collateral damage."

More heat warmed his body from within. Amazing how irritated he could get just thinking about the cult, thirteen years after he'd escaped. Probably because they hadn't all escaped.

He felt Jazz's gaze on him and glanced at her in time to see her swing away. But not before he caught the curiosity in her eyes. Great. She could probably tell this was personal for him. He didn't need that getting out on the fan sites.

"I'll have Flash follow the trail of the pin's owner and see where it leads."

"He's a tracking dog, too?"

"Military Working Dog. Tracking and patrol. Plus search and rescue."

"I'm impressed." Hawthorne found a bit of a smile again.

"Hear that, Flash?" She smoothed a hand over the dog's side before pointing him back to the pin. Once he smelled it for a few seconds, she gave him a command in what sounded like German.

"Mind if I come along?" Hawthorne trotted after them.

Jazz glanced over her shoulder as she kept up with Flash's eager pace. "Suit yourself."

Perfect. Real life observation of how she worked. With a retired military dog who protected and tracked. This was better material than he could invent on his own.

Flash skimmed his nose along the grass until they reached the four-foot fence where the blacktop met the lawn.

Hawthorne opened his mouth to ask if he should lift the dog over.

Flash sprang off the ground and was over the fence before Hawthorne could blink. Hadn't even needed a running start.

Jazz hopped over the fence herself and Hawthorne followed. Looked like Flash was a fitting partner for his impressive handler.

The dog kept his nose hovering over the blacktop as he followed some trail Hawthorne wished he could see.

More people crowded the wide pedestrian path than before, making Flash have to swerve around moving feet and kids who wanted to pet him.

"Keep back." Jazz voiced the command in a strong voice, her arm outstretched as she hurried alongside the dog. "Stand clear." She repeated the warning several times as she cleared the way for the K-9 to work.

Flash didn't break his concentration once. Not even when a child or two managed to put their hands on fur before he slipped from their reach.

But after a few minutes, he slowed. Then stopped. He lifted his nose into the air. Then he looked up at Jazz, his tongue hanging about a mile out of his mouth.

"Okay, Flash. Good boy." She put her hand on the dog's head and lightly scratched his ears.

"Did he lose the scent?"

Jazz turned toward Hawthorne. "Yeah. The heat on the hard surface evaporates the scent. And there's a lot of contamination here. I'm surprised he could follow it this far. Especially when the scent could be from last night, or even earlier."

Hawthorne followed her gaze back to the slide about sixty yards away. "At least we know the culprit must've approached the slide from the back, avoiding the stairs or anything at the front of the slide."

Jazz nodded. "Even with fewer security guards overnight, an unauthorized visitor could easily be noticed if they were on the stairs or the slide itself."

"Coming from behind and underneath would definitely be safer. But still pretty bold." What kind of person would take such a risk? It was the same question Hawthorne often asked when crafting a character for his novels. Someone with a powerful motive. And something worth the risk.

"PT2 to PT3." A woman's voice came over Hawthorne's earpiece.

"This is PT3, go." Jazz glanced at Hawthorne as she answered.

"Mrs. Cracklen wants to see you at the slide. ASAP."

Was it Hawthorne's imagination or did Jazz's flushed skin pale a little?

"PT2, Roger." Jazz started off at a near jog before she'd finished the words. She must really want to see her aunt.

The subtext of Nevaeh's radio call had Jazz booking it back to the slide. She spotted Nev's big hair and red short-sleeved T-shirt at the left of the slide staircase, in the staff area by the shed.

Aunt Joan stood by her, saying something that probably matched her severe expression.

A man in a gray suit way too hot for the temperature waited behind her. Uncle Pierce. Must be there to visit his campaign booth. She'd seen one set up for his campaign for governor, and the sign had said he'd be there today.

So now Jazz would get to face both of them at once. Just like old times.

Maybe Nev would stick around.

"Well?" Joan's curt question prevented the friendly greeting Jazz was going to try.

"We found evidence of a personal effect behind the slide, and we tracked the owner for a distance over the fence and onto the path. But the scent is too old or not surviving the heat."

"Is that supposed to help?" Joan planted a hand on her hip and glared at Jazz as if this was all somehow her fault. Wondered when she'd slip into the old Jazz-is-always-to-blame routine.

"Of course, that helps." Nev's eyes flashed as she boldly stared at Aunt Joan. "Now you know it wasn't an accident. Maybe the Ferris wheel wasn't either." Good old Nev. She'd always jumped to Jazz's defense whenever she could.

It never helped. Aunt Joan had simply barred Nevaeh from setting foot in their house. But it had always made Jazz feel better. Knowing one person cared.

"As if someone sabotaging the fair is good news." Aunt Joan didn't lose a hint of her ire with the retort.

"Now, Joan." Uncle Pierce placed his large hands on her shoulders. "That's wonderful they found some evidence and were able to determine where the culprit gained access. We do want to know the truth so we can stop the perpetrator, don't we?"

Her expression cooled slightly as she pulled her shoulders back. "Of course." She shifted her gaze to Jazz. "You did what you could. But frankly, we hired you people to make the fair safer, and yet it's been our worst year ever. And we're only on day two."

"That's not Phoenix K-9's fault." Jazz jumped in to respond before Nev could this time. "We don't even know when the culprit set up the explosives."

"That's right, ma'am." Hawthorne's confident voice drew Jazz's attention to the tall man who stepped forward and looked fearlessly at Aunt Joan. "The explosives could have been rigged well in advance with a timing device or to be detonated remotely."

"And how do you know that?" Aunt Joan gave him her classic eyebrow arch, intended to freeze everyone into their rightful places—beneath her.

Hawthorne didn't even blink. "I have training in the area. But I'm sure the police will confirm it with the evidence. And we might find something helpful if we examine the overnight security footage."

"Butch should be doing that." Joan jumped her glance away, probably scanning for the head of security. "There he is." She marched off, and Uncle Pierce followed her, heading toward where Butch stood with another security guard beneath the slide. Looked like they were examining the remaining supports.

"There goes your brunch invite." Nev's quip made Jazz's

mouth tug with a small smile. Even though the truth it carried stung a little.

But humor had always been the way Nevaeh and Jazz coped with life's troubles. It had worked so far. So Jazz gave Nev a grin. "I was so looking forward to the eggs benedict."

Nev laughed.

"You're family?" Hawthorne's voice surprised Jazz, maybe because he now stood closer, next to her with only Flash between them.

She quirked a wry smile. "Hard to tell, isn't it?"

He tossed his head slightly like shaking off an incorrect idea. "All families have their issues."

"Some more than others. Mine is probably messed up enough to be in one of your books." Jazz smiled, but faltered as she heard what she'd just said. "I don't mean my family's full of criminals and murderers like the families Carson Steele investigates. I just mean...we're not close." And no one in her family had ever liked her. But she wouldn't say that out loud. She was probably sounding pathetic enough as it was.

"I get it." He gave her a friendly, gentle smile like he understood and wasn't judging her. Hopefully.

"Wait, Carson Steele?" Nev stepped in front of Jazz to stare at Hawthorne more directly. "Are you Hawthorne Emerson? The writer?"

"Guilty." He didn't look bothered by the attention. He was probably used to it.

"You're Jazz's favorite author!" Nev's voice grew higher and louder as she grabbed Jazz's arm and squeezed her in close. "Oh, my goodness, girl," Nev looked up at her, "you didn't tell me."

A smile stretched Jazz's face at her BFF's excitement. At least Nev was more coherent than Jazz when she'd learned Hawthorne's identity. "I just found out."

"Well, this is pretty awesome." Nev turned a beaming grin on Hawthorne. "Never met an author before. You're my favorite, too, though I don't go quite as crazy over novels as this girl." She hugged Jazz even tighter. "I have to wait for her to read your novels like three times before she'll give 'em to me to read."

Hawthorne's bright eyes twinkled as he watched them. "I'm honored to have my work read by two such lovely ladies."

"Ooh…" Nev winked at Jazz. "Smooth, too. Just like Carson."

"Oh, stop." Jazz pulled away and gave Nev a shove. "You'll have to forgive Nevaeh. This is how she gets when she's starstruck."

Hawthorne laughed—a rich, masculine sound that sent a tickle of heat to Jazz's belly. "I'm sure you're just being kind." His gaze rested on Jazz. "I wanted—"

"Team Leader to S4." Butch Klika's rough voice sounded over coms. "Report to accident location."

He was calling it an accident? Maybe just in case anyone heard their radio chatter.

"That's me." Hawthorne tossed Jazz a parting glance. "Catch you later."

Was that a hopeful note in his tone? Or maybe it was her imagination conjuring an echo of her own hope.

"He was going to ask you out."

"What?" Heat rushed to Jazz's face as she spun to her bestie.

"Totally." Nev's amused gaze locked on Jazz's face. Probably on the tell-tale blush there. A massive grin spread Nev's mouth as she read the signs, her tone lifting with the discovery. "And you were so hoping he would."

"I don't know what you're talking about." Jazz looked away from Nev, but her eyes seemed determined to search for the man filling her thoughts.

"Uh-huh. That's why you can't stop watching him, and your cheeks are the color of Pops' radishes." A soft punch landed on Jazz's upper arm. "Girl, don't try to con your BFF."

"Okay, fine." Jazz gave up the hopeless attempt. Nev

could read her like a book. "But what do you expect? He's my favorite author. A little celebrity crush is normal."

"And the man is super hot."

Jazz arched an eyebrow. "Are you even allowed to notice that anymore, soon-to-be-Mrs. Branson Aaberg?"

"Hey, don't mean I can't admit the facts. He nowhere near as hot as my man, but that goes without saying."

"Not that you're biased or anything." Jazz grinned.

"Don't change the subject. You're single. You can like him. You can go out with him."

"Um, no. He's Hawthorne Emerson."

"So?"

"He's a famous author." Jazz lifted her hands to emphasize the obvious point. "He's a celebrity, New York Times bestseller and all that. He probably only dates supermodels or something."

Nev's features scrunched in her *you're-being-weird* expression. "I don't think it works like that with writers."

"It does when they look like that." Jazz pointed an exasperated hand in Hawthorne's direction.

"Okay. You might have a point." Nev tilted her head to concede. "But in case you ain't been lookin' in the mirror lately, girl, you fit the bill."

Jazz let out a disbelieving laugh. But her heart warmed at Nev's encouragement. Now might be a good time to tell her about the attempted mugging or assault—whatever it was supposed to be—last night.

Jazz had wanted to call Nev after the attack, almost out of instinct, but she'd held back just in time. She didn't want to be the annoying friend who kept getting in the way of Nev's relationship with Branson. They were having a nice evening without Jazz's drama. Branson was in the picture to stay well into the future, hopefully. And Jazz was happy for her friend. So she needed to get used to handling everything alone again.

All the more reason not to bother telling Nev about the incident now. Wasn't a big deal anyway. The police had agreed it was an attempted mugging or assault. Jazz was just glad the thugs had picked her instead of some less-prepared woman alone.

She took a breath and donned a smile. "Before we get too far down this flattery rabbit hole, we should probably go see what Butch wants us to do next. And maybe I should tell him what Flash found, though Hawthorne will probably mention it."

"Sure." Nev and Alvarez fell in step alongside Jazz and Flash as they headed toward the others gathered under the slide. "And I think we should hold a PK-9 team meeting, even though Phoenix is gone."

Jazz tossed Nev a surprised glance. "You think Sof will want to?" Didn't seem like they ever did team meetings when Phoenix was away on one of her mysterious trips. Or disappearances. Who knew if she even went anywhere. Or where she went if she did.

"Now that it looks like this was intentional sabotage, I think we need to meet. We might have to change our protection strategy or something. I'll ask Sof when she comes on shift at four."

Learning the slide explosion was an intentional attack had already changed everything for Jazz. Maybe the Ferris wheel wasn't an accident either.

And that meant one thing. Someone was trying to wreck the fair.

Why, she didn't know. And she didn't care. The Tri-City Fair was supposed to be a place of happiness, joy, safety, and sweet memories for children and families.

No one was going to destroy that. No one.

NINE

Hawthorne bypassed the line of visitors waiting to take the Logboat Adventure ride and opened the chain-link gate that blocked a concrete path. He closed the gate behind him and followed the walkway, but his mind was elsewhere.

The image of the Best Life pin, forever seared in his memory, now blocked his vision. What was it doing on the fairgrounds? Directly under the slide that had just blown up. Well, not exactly. The fifty-year-old slide itself was relatively undamaged. But the supports would need to be rebuilt, and the ride probably closed for the rest of this year's fair. Was that the goal? Why?

Cult members weren't even allowed to attend the fair. It was so-called worldly entertainment and included on the very long, unwritten list of activities and choices banned by the cult. Or, more specifically, by Desmond Patch, founder and leader of the Best Life cult. Destroyer of families. Thief of lives.

The staff entrance door stood in front of Hawthorne, and he halted the maddening train of thought he tried to avoid riding as much as possible. It always led to the same place. A dead end of frustration, sadness, and helplessness.

Hawthorne slipped his ID card into the reader and waited for it to beep and blink a green light. He pushed open the

66

door and stepped into the darkness of the Logboat Adventure ride cave-like tunnel.

Whoever had dropped the pin had broken the cult's rules to be at the fair. Like Sam had. Funny how breaking the cult's rules seemed to go hand-in-hand with trouble. Though *funny* was probably the wrong word for the correlation. Frightening would be more appropriate.

Hawthorne walked along the narrow path that was a few inches below the faux riverbank. The riverbank continued to the middle of the tunnel where it met the manmade river that was bordered by another bank on its opposite side. The skinny path Hawthorne took allowed staff members to get where they needed to without damaging the foliage and rocks of the life-like riverbank.

Laughter and voices echoed in the cave as visitors coursed down the river in boats shaped like carved-out logs.

They passed Hawthorne without paying him any attention. Probably couldn't see him in the darkness where he was.

Dim lights illuminated the river and shore with just enough light to appreciate the display but also keep the atmosphere slightly surprising and mysterious. That allowed for more excitement when they reached the rapids sections of the ride and the dramatic plummet at the end. Though one of the more sedate rides at the fair, visitors wanted some degree of thrill to keep it entertaining.

Hawthorne slowed as he reached the section he was looking for. The curve after the first rapids.

He stopped and watched logboats float past, most holding two or three visitors each. He waited until a few minutes passed and no boats appeared. Should signal the end of this batch of visitors. It would take at least ten minutes for those riders to finish the ride, disembark, and a new group to load up and start. Hawthorne shouldn't need that much time.

He carefully stepped up onto the riverbank display. It was firm but pliable under his shoe.

Real dirt. He had thought it might be concrete or plastic.

He felt the leaf of a plant. Real plants, too. Did that mean the rocks were real and not fake?

He reached the river and stopped. It was wider than he'd expected.

He backed up a step, took a running start, and jumped the water.

He dropped to his knees as he landed on the other bank, trying not to damage the display. There probably was a way the staff accessed this other bank. But he wasn't long on time at the moment.

He was technically allowed in the Logboat Adventure ride staff areas, thanks to his position as a security guard. But he didn't relish the thought of explaining to Butch or anyone else why he was wandering around there. Especially now that someone was apparently sabotaging rides. Didn't need to have anyone suspect him of that.

He looked for the small pine tree, groundcover, and rock configuration from the photographs in the police report copy he'd requested.

There it was. A pine tree short enough to fit under the ceiling that nearly skimmed the top of Hawthorne's head stood near the river's edge.

Green groundcover. And a large rock.

The rock where Sam Ackerman had hit his head and died.

At least according to the police report.

Rebekah had said it was impossible.

Sam had been terrified of water. The boy's father had said the same thing to the press, according to newspaper articles in the days following Sam's death. He never would have gone on the Logboat Adventure ride.

If that was true, then Sam wouldn't have been in a boat, riding down the river, goofing off because of the alcohol the autopsy showed was in his system. He wouldn't have stood up, lost his balance, and toppled out of the boat, head catching the rock that stood at the edge of the water. The conclusions drawn by the police to explain his death wouldn't be true. It wouldn't be an accident.

The thriller writer in him wanted to see the holes. To lean toward Rebekah's claim it wasn't an accident. And believe it was intentional. A murder.

But he'd been an MP too long to approach an investigation with a preferred or foregone conclusion. And that part of him also knew what murder was like in real life. It wasn't exciting and entertaining like a murder in the pages of a mystery or in a movie.

It was horrible. Tragic. More so than an accident because it carried malice and the full horror of intentional evil.

Far better for Sam's death to have been an accident.

The thought was enough to give Hawthorne pause. Should he not have agreed to look into Sam's death for Rebekah? What if he dragged up more pain than she already had? And more pain for Sam's family.

But the only way he'd do that would be if he learned the boy's death was not an accident. And if that were true, he couldn't let a murderer walk around free and unpunished. No, he had to make sure the original findings were true. For Rebekah. And for the sake of justice.

She was so sure it couldn't have happened. Not the way the police had concluded from the evidence they'd found.

Sam had been discovered in this spot, dead. His blood on the rock. A contusion in his skull matched the shape of the rock. His positioning was correct for a fall from the boat if he'd stood up during the ride.

No blood marked the rock now. But, of course, they'd have cleaned that off long ago. Everything else looked the same as in the police photos. Except Sam wasn't in them.

The memory of his still, pale face in the pictures loomed in Hawthorne's mind. Not the first dead face he'd seen. But he never forgot any of them.

He had to be certain the truth had been found. For Sam and the boy's family, who couldn't rest until they knew for sure. Until they could accept it was an accident. Or Hawthorne could find his killer.

Carson leaned over the body, the tragedy of the death wailing in his heart—a soundtrack to spur him on to end the madness.

The victim's hands were positioned to point to three and fifteen in the clock of the killer's mind.

Three fifteen. The numbers floated into place, falling in line with the sequence the previous victims had been positioned to indicate.

Carson straightened, the truth hitting him with the force of a bullet from behind.

There was no serial killer.

And Carson's mistake may be about to cost another life.

A nudge against Jazz's leg dragged her attention from the riveting pages of *Seconds in Shadow*, but she couldn't stop there. She had to turn the page to the next chapter, find out what Carson had realized.

A slobbery jaw slid across her arm.

"Eww, Flash." She gave the Malinois a look with her mouth in a scrunched blend of smile and grossed-out.

He stood next to her favorite armchair in her apartment, staring at her as if completely unaware of how ill-timed his interruption was.

"I was in a really good part, bud." She flipped the book to the back cover, examining Hawthorne Emerson's photo that she'd seen so many times. It was so funny to think of him as Hawthorne alone, not coupled with his last name as she'd always said it before. She could see the resemblance in his photo clearly now. Though, in her defense, he did look drastically different with the beard that hid the handsome lines of his face and features.

She still couldn't believe she'd actually met her favorite author. Worked with him. Climbed a Ferris wheel with him. How crazy was that?

"Pinch me now, Flash."

The Malinois panted as he stared at her, backing up slightly, like he was waiting for her to do something.

"What?" She looked at her watch. *6:40 p.m.* "Oh, my

goodness. I've been reading for nearly two hours? Sorry, bud." She'd meant to go for a run with Flash when she got home after her shift ended at four. But then she'd seen Carson Steele sitting on the table. She couldn't resist at least starting the first little bit.

She should've known she'd get sucked in as usual. And this novel might be the best yet. As she devoured every page, she noticed something funny happening. Instead of the voice she'd always heard in her head as the narrator, she was starting to hear a slightly huskier voice. Hawthorne's voice.

She smiled. Didn't ruin the reading experience one bit.

Flash whined.

She looked away from Hawthorne's photo, which her gaze had somehow locked onto again. "Sorry, Flash. You're right. We need a run." Checking the time again, she stood and hurried to change into her running gear.

It was technically past Flash's dinner time. And hers. But with the trail only ten minutes away, they should be able to finish their run before dark. Dinner could wait until they got back.

Her prediction was right, though barely. The sun set during the tail end of their hour-long run, but the sky didn't become fully dark until she was driving home.

As she slowed and turned into the apartment complex parking lot, her mind was already skipping ahead to throwing a frozen entrée into the microwave and jumping back into the Carson Steele novel as quickly as she could. She'd been turning it over in her mind during the run, trying to puzzle out how Carson knew the series of murders weren't done by a serial killer.

Hawthorne sure was a clever guy.

Jazz found an open stall far from her apartment building. The additional exercise wouldn't hurt.

Flash whined from the back seat.

"I know, we're late on dinner. You'll have to blame Hawthorne for writing such a good book." Jazz grinned at the

Malinois' reflection in the rearview mirror. "You can talk to him about it tomorrow."

Would he be there tomorrow? During her shift again? Maybe she should've checked the duty roster.

Jazz dropped out of her SUV and opened the side door for Flash.

She'd love to tell Haw—

Flash launched a string of short barks.

Jazz hit the pavement just as shots pierced the night.

TEN

Jazz crouched beside the back tire of her SUV, Flash standing next to her as bullets whizzed past.

She put her hand on the K-9's head, indebted to him once again for saving her life.

His strung-together short barks meant one thing. They were about to be attacked. Usually bombs or enemy fire.

She'd learned when they were in service together to hit the deck and ask questions later. Good thing.

She glanced up at the bullet holes in the side door. Those first shots would've hit their target. Her.

No time to figure out why she was being shot at. Just another question that could wait until later.

Right now, she and Flash had to get these guys. Maybe keep them in play until police arrived. If people in the apartments heard the shots and called for help.

The shooters—two of them, she deduced—were using suppressors. But no silencer was actually silent. Hopefully, the noise would be enough to make someone wonder.

Flash had gone quiet without Jazz telling him to. His training kicking in, since any noise could help the shooters find their target.

More shots pierced the night air.

Jazz turned and moved toward the front of her SUV, staying squatted.

Flash inched forward behind her as they rounded the vehicle and darted in front of the neighboring sedan.

They silently crept along the far side of the car until they reached the rear tire. Thanks to the very few lampposts in this farther section of the parking lot, they must not have been seen.

The shooters still fired at where she'd been. Her poor SUV was going to look like Swiss cheese.

She watched for muzzle flashes—very slight, thanks to the suppressors. But enough.

Jazz aimed her Sig Saur pistol and returned fire.

A brief pause. Like they were surprised. Then they fired back, angling their trajectory to her new position.

She shot again. If only they'd shift slightly so she could see what she was aiming at and get a clear hit. But darkness covered where they hid by a big SUV.

More bullets answered her fire.

Sirens wailed. Probably several miles off yet.

The shots stopped. Doors swung open, slammed.

Headlights flared white, almost blinding as the SUV started up and peeled away, tires screeching.

"Guess we scared 'em off, bud." Jazz scratched Flash's ears and stood, pulling out her phone as she headed for where the shooters' SUV had been parked.

She'd have to call Nev this time. Nev would kill her if she found out someone was targeting Jazz and she hadn't shared that info.

Nev picked up quickly, before Jazz and Flash had even made it to the shooters' parking spot. "Hey, girl. Just thinking about you. And your hunky author."

"Hilarious."

"What's wrong?"

Jazz smirked. Even though she felt as relaxed as ever, Nev could read something in her tone. Must come from knowing each other since they were seven years old. "Nothing, really.

I'm fine. Flash is fine. But…" Jazz slowed as she reached the empty parking stall.

"I knew it." Nev's voice tensed. "What happened?"

"Couple jokers decided to take shots at us."

A sharp intake of breath came across the line. "You mean somebody randomly started shooting at you? Where?"

Jazz squatted to see what Flash was smelling. "The apartment. The parking lot. I just came back from my run, and they started firing when I got out of my SUV."

Spent shell casings lay on the blacktop.

Jazz switched her phone to speaker and turned on the flashlight function to shine on the casings.

"They didn't hit you?"

"No. Flash warned me, so I ducked in time."

"Thank the Lord for Flash."

Nev's wording made Jazz pause in her study of the nine millimeter casings. Nev hadn't even been a Christian for a year yet, and she already sounded as churchy as the rest of the PK-9 team's Bible thumpers. Must be part of fitting in with her new crowd.

Used to be Nev had been happy with Jazz as her bestie, as the only peer that really mattered. And they'd always fit in with each other, without having to become anything different than who they were. Without having to believe in fairytales people only used to look good and—

"I'm headed to you now." Nev's pronouncement, backed up with the sound of an engine starting, interrupted Jazz's thoughts.

"You don't need—"

"Don't be crazy. Of course, I need to be there."

"Okay. Police are pulling in now." Jazz rose to her feet as two squad cars turned into the lot, cutting their sirens while the colored lights continued to flash. "I found some nine-millimeter casings. Sounded like handguns with suppressors."

"Definitely planned. I don't like this." Nev's tight tone

said she was taking this more seriously than Jazz was. "I wish Phoenix was here. She'd know what to do."

But would the boss do anything for Jazz? She was still the new kid at PK-9. And she had the undeniable impression Phoenix didn't like her. Maybe didn't trust her either.

"You're definitely coming to stay with me tonight. And until we figure out who's after you and put a stop to it."

"I don't—"

"No choice, girl."

Jazz shut her mouth since two police officers approached her at that moment anyway. She lifted her hand in a still wave, friendly and showing she wasn't a threat.

And for a second, it sank in. This threat had been too close. If not for Flash, she'd have more than one bullet in her now. Probably be dead.

A scarier thought flared in her mind and stuck there— would anyone have cared?

Hawthorne's fingers flew across the keyboard, inspiration flowing like a waterfall as Jazz Lamont chased down a killer.

She stopped the bad guy's flight with a throw of her knife, her accuracy dead-on.

The space ringtone of Hawthorne's phone—the closest he'd been able to find to anything mysterious—sounded just as the villain fell to the ground.

With a groan, Hawthorne angled the steno chair away from his laptop on the desk and checked the phone's screen.

Rebekah.

So much for early morning being the best time to avoid interruptions. He glanced at the computer's clock. *6:00 a.m.* At least he'd managed to write for an hour. An amazing hour. Writing hadn't been that fun in a long time.

The persistent tone reminded him he needed to answer the call.

He slid the icon upward on the screen. "Hi, Rebekah. You're up early."

"Don't get me started." Her tone conveyed both self-pity and fatigue. "Early class." Hopefully, she wasn't driving there, given the way she sounded.

"On Saturday?"

"Yeah. My program offers classes at weird times for people like me who work fulltime."

"I see." He searched for something helpful to say. Poor kid was doing all this adult stuff on her own. Though he and Nathaniel had done the same thing after military service. At least he hoped his younger brother had followed through with joining the Navy and getting an education. "It's great you're putting yourself through school. You won't regret it."

She moaned. "I already regret it."

What should he say to that? What would a girl her age respond to?

A light laugh came over the line before he had to think of something. "Not really. I know it'll be good. I want to make it like you."

"Oh. Great." Sounded like she was driven. That drive to experience all of life and make the most of his freedom had served Hawthorne well.

"What did you find out about Sam?"

Ah. So that was the reason she'd called. And so early. She definitely had the impatience gene, probably inherited from their dad. Their mom had learned never to tell him about anything or ask him to do something until she was ready for him to act on it. Immediately.

On the other hand, Rebekah had been waiting to find out the truth for two years. The thought softened Hawthorne's tone, hopefully not with too much pity, as he replied. "I walked through the scenario and looked at the scene of..." he paused to temper his wording, "the place where they found Sam." He braced himself for any sound of crying or distress.

"And did you find anything new?" Urgency, not tears, tightened Rebekah's tone.

"I don't think so. Not yet. But it was good to see it all myself in person rather than photos. I think the distance from the boat to the location where he hit his head on the rock is very plausible for a fall from standing. It matches his five-eleven height."

"But they only *think* he hit his head on the rock there. I'm telling you, that's not what happened."

"Because he was afraid of water."

"Yes!" The word came so sharply across the line that Hawthorne moved the phone a few inches from his ear. "Not just afraid. Terrified. I mean, he wouldn't even take a bath because he was so freaked out about drowning."

Rebekah did make a convincing case. But there was the alcohol. Maybe she didn't understand how people could change under the influence. He certainly hadn't until he'd left the sheltered confines of the cult. "He was under the influence. That can make people act very differently than they would otherwise."

"I'm in college." Annoyance tinged her voice as she pointed out the obvious. "I know what people are like when they're drunk. But I'm telling you his fear of water was so primal, there's no way he would suddenly want to go on a Logboat Adventure ride all by himself. Maybe if other kids were there, daring him or something..."

She had a point. Such out of character behavior would probably have needed some social encouragement or pressure to happen. But according to the police investigation's conclusions, he'd been completely alone in the boat when he fell.

"I think Randall did it."

That was new. Rebekah hadn't accused anyone when she'd asked Hawthorne to look into the incident. "Randall?"

"Yeah." She didn't say more, as if that were enough for Hawthorne to go on.

"You want to tell me who Randall is?"

"Oh, yeah. Sorry. I'm at school now."

"Do you have to go?"

Rustling, like she was picking up papers or a backpack, came across the line. Then the slam of a door. "No, I'll talk as I walk." Wind noise and voices, probably other students, painted a picture of where she was, walking on the university campus.

"Okay. You haven't mentioned Randall before."

"Didn't I?" She puffed like she was carrying something heavy. Too bad he wasn't there to carry her books for her. Though she probably valued her independence as much as he did. She wouldn't want his help and interference any more than he'd want hers. After what they'd been through, it would only feel like stifling control. "I guess I didn't want to make it sound like I was trying to get back at someone. You know, let you come up with your own answers. Like the detectives on TV and in your books."

She'd read his books? He hadn't thought she seemed like the type to enjoy crime thriller novels. But if his sibling had published books, he'd probably be curious to read them, too.

"What do you mean, 'trying to get back at someone'?"

"Oh, well, he didn't do anything to me, so it wouldn't be like that."

"You're losing me—" He stopped himself before calling her *Becca*, the nickname they'd used when she was little. The name he'd always known her by. But she'd introduced herself as Rebekah when she'd contacted him about Sam. So he'd better stick with that, respecting her choices.

"Sorry. I'm a little out of it. Pulled an all-nighter for this test I have in like five minutes."

And yet she was calling him? She was either a remarkable multi-tasker or a risk-taker who was about to flunk her exam. "Do you want to call me back?"

"No. I mean, I will. But I want to tell you about Randall."

"Okay."

"I should've told you before. See, he was my boyfriend. Well, not really." The words spilled rapidly as her breathing sped up, too. "We went on a date like once—without telling our parents 'cause you know that's not allowed—and I could see how weird and controlling he was right away, so I called it quits. Then he got super weird. Like really obsessive, you know?"

She continued before he could give a response, which she apparently didn't expect or need. "So when Sam and I started going out, Randall freaked and got super jealous and kind of scary."

"How do you mean that?" Hawthorne had to nearly cut her off to squeeze in the question.

"He followed Sam around and got in his face one time. Told him to stay away from me or else."

"Or else what?"

"I don't think he technically said, but it was obvious he meant he'd beat Sam up or something. Randall could get really angry sometimes."

"Do you think he'd ever become violent?"

"I think he killed Sam." Her voice lowered slightly, whether because of the gravity of her accusation or because she'd stepped inside a building, Hawthorne wasn't sure. "I think he followed him to the fair that night, and they probably got in a fight or Randall just ambushed Sam out of nowhere. And then Randall moved him to the Logboat Adventure to make it look like an accident."

"That's an interesting theory." And a plausible one in some ways. At least there was a possible motive for murder.

"You mean you don't believe me?" Disappointment colored her voice.

"Not at all. I believe everything you told me that you know about Randall and Sam is true. But we can't know the truth of the parts you're speculating on without evidence. This is really helpful, though. I hadn't heard of any possible motives for this to be intentional before."

"So you mean you'll look into it?"

"Of course. I promised I'd look into this for you, Rebekah, and I'm going to do that. You just keep giving me any information you remember, and I'll keep following leads, okay?"

"Okay." She sounded slightly appeased. "Well, wish me luck. Gotta take my test."

Given he didn't believe in luck anymore, he searched for a better alternative. "You'll knock 'em dead."

She laughed. "Thanks. See 'ya." The line went quiet as she ended the call.

Knock 'em dead may not have been the best choice of words under the circumstances, but, thankfully, Rebekah hadn't seemed to notice.

Had someone clobbered Sam so hard it had killed him? A rock smash could be matched with or inflicted after a blow to the head from something else. Or a fall against a different hard object, perhaps during an altercation.

Murderous possibilities, always easy to access in the storage vault of his mystery writer's mind, cycled through his thought. Were any of them true in this case?

Only one way to find out—keep investigating. He needed to talk to more of the people who had been there the night Sam was killed and the morning when his body was discovered. Hopefully, Hawthorne would be able to find evidence the police had missed.

They'd concluded it was an accident fairly quickly. They hadn't had as much reason as Hawthorne had now to look harder at the evidence. To consider foul play.

Rebekah's convictions and the first possible motive Hawthorne had learned of ignited a suspicion in the back of his mind. A suspicion she could be right.

And if the boy had been killed, Hawthorne wouldn't rest until he found his murderer.

ELEVEN

"So weird without the boss here, isn't it?" Nevaeh stared at the empty armchair where Phoenix always sat with her K-9 Dagian.

Jazz, sharing the sofa with Nev at PK-9 headquarters, followed the direction of her bestie's gaze. "Yeah." Hopefully, it would be more relaxed. Phoenix tended to bring a sense of intensity to every PK-9 Agency meeting just from her presence. And it was nerve-wracking trying to figure out what the boss was thinking the whole time behind her inscrutable, ever-watchful gaze.

"I keep waiting for her to march into the room with Dag." Bristol Jones grinned as she feigned a glance at the break room door from the end of the love seat she shared with Cora Thomson.

Toby, Bristol's black Labrador, paused in the middle of searching for dropped food on the floor to look in the same direction, as if wondering what Bris had seen.

"I'm hoping she'll return in another week or so." Cora gave Nev her sweet, maternal-like smile, her golden retriever narcotics detection K-9, Jana, sitting on the floor beside the blonde's knee.

"She didn't tell you when she'll be back?" Given how tight Cora seemed to be with Phoenix, it was hard to believe

Cora didn't know more about these mysterious disappearances.

"Not precisely. But her trips usually don't take more than three weeks. She's already been gone for two this time."

"And she didn't say where she went or why." Jazz knew the likely answer, but she couldn't help trying to dig a little. Phoenix had disappeared two other times like this in the year and eight months Jazz had worked at PK-9. Gone for weeks with no warning and no explanation when she'd come back. And everyone on the team seemed fine with that. More than a little suspicious in Jazz's book. It clearly wasn't a vacation, or that would be public knowledge.

"She told me the location this time but not what she's doing there." Cora moved her notebook computer off her lap and set it on the coffee table in front of her. "I can contact her whenever we need her." The note in Cora's tone and the puzzlement in her eyes as she looked up suggested Jazz might be letting her suspicions show a little too much.

But it was so weird that Cora apparently wasn't supposed to share the location with anyone else. What was the big secret? What was the boss hiding?

"I wouldn't worry about Phoenix." Sof lowered into the armchair near Cora as Raksa left her to find the air conditioning vent by his buddy Alvarez.

The German Shepherd and rottie mix sniffed each other before vying for the closest spot to the cool air pouring from the vent.

"She's one *chica* who can take care of herself." Sof's statement drew Jazz's attention to her face. Those dark eyes glimmered back at Jazz. Was that Sofia's way of telling Jazz to mind her own business? She wouldn't be surprised. Sof was the champion of secrets, given that she'd lived under a false identity, lying to the whole team about who she really was until last year.

Well, Phoenix had apparently known the truth about Sofia the whole time. But Phoenix didn't seem to want anyone to know the truth about her. Whatever that was.

"So, temp leader," Nev tossed Sofia a grin, "what's up first?"

"Jazz is."

Sofia's answer jolted surprise through Jazz. Though at least the raven-haired superspy had delivered it with a smile.

"We were so troubled to hear about the shooting last night." Cora's big blue eyes filled with concern as she looked at Jazz. "I'm thankful you and Flash were unharmed."

"Thanks." At least Cora hadn't included the usual *Praise the Lord* stuff. Not that Jazz would've said anything to contradict her or point out a fictional God didn't have anything to do with her survival. Cora was the nicest person on the team and the only one Jazz didn't feel judged by. Jazz wasn't about to ruin that.

"Any idea what led to the attempted shooting? Motive?" Sof watched Jazz closely, but her stare wasn't nearly as unnerving as Phoenix's would be if the boss were there right now.

"I don't know of any." Jazz braced herself inwardly. Nev wasn't going to like this. But if she waited until later to share it, she'd really be in trouble with her bestie. "There was another incident two nights ago, though."

"What?" Nev lifted her dark eyebrows.

Jazz met her BFF's gaze. "Two guys jumped me at the gas station."

"And you didn't tell me?"

"You were busy with Branson."

Nev opened her mouth, clearly about to protest, so Jazz continued.

"And I didn't think it was a big deal." She glanced at the others with a shrug. "I figured it was a random mugging or attempted assault. Those things happen a lot at gas stations these days."

"Sadly, that is true." Cora frowned.

"The police thought it was random, too, so I left it at that."

"You don't mean they actually assaulted—"

"No." Jazz shook her head as she interrupted Nev's horrified question. "I was fine. They jumped me as I came out of the convenience store, so I didn't see them in advance. But I handled them. One guy had a knife. I didn't see any guns. Got one in the shoulder with my knife before they took off."

Jazz shook her head. "They wouldn't have gotten away if Flash had been with me. Right, bud?" She bent over and stroked the Malinois's head where he lay on the floor next to her feet.

"I love how you're so casual about single-handedly fending off two male attackers and stabbing one of them." Bris shook her head as she grinned at Jazz. "Way to go, girl."

A smile found Jazz's face at the compliment from the former cop and explosives technician who could hold her own in a fight, too. "Thanks."

"Okay. Could be random or could be connected." Sof tapped the arms of her chair with her fingers, clearly not as impressed as Bris. Compared to what the former CIA agent had done in her past, Jazz supposed her performance was child's play. "Did you see either of the shooters last night well enough to ID them?"

"No. Too dark."

"I can't believe you didn't tell me." Nev's hurt tone pinged a little against Jazz's heart.

"Sorry." Maybe Jazz should've called her that first night. But she couldn't rely on sharing everything with Nev anymore. Nev had other priorities now. A more important relationship than their friendship. And maybe Nev needed to see Jazz supported that relationship and was okay on her own. "It wasn't a big deal. I handled it."

"With flying colors, apparently." Cora sent Jazz and Nev a smile probably meant to soothe their tension. "Phoenix would be pleased."

Jazz doubted that. The boss never seemed pleased with Jazz or her work.

"I told her about the shooting when I spoke with her this morning."

Jazz watched Cora, her stomach tightening. Would the boss care that Jazz was in trouble?

"She said Sofia should decide how the team will respond to the threat."

Disappointment sank in Jazz's belly. Figured. It was stupid of her to think Phoenix would care enough to cut her mystery trip short and come herself to oversee the protection of Jazz. Never mind that Phoenix was always quick to order security measures for the other team members anytime they were in danger. More evidence Jazz wasn't really one of them, even though she'd been there nearly two years. She was getting the feeling she could be there for ten years and still not be one of them. Story of her life.

"Let's start by looking for motive." Sof's take-charge tone drew the attention of the team. "Do you have any enemies that you know of?"

Jazz shrugged. She'd thought about that last night after the shooters tried to take her out. "Maybe terrorists Flash and I caught in Afghanistan. Or the family of anybody I had to kill over there."

"It seems unlikely they would or could follow you here for a war-related action."

Jazz nodded at Bristol's observation. "Agreed."

"What about your fellow soldiers?" Cora hit a more likely nail on the head probably without meaning to, given her innocent expression.

"They weren't my biggest fans." Not for lack of trying to fit in and get along on Jazz's part. "I don't know of anything they *should* have against me that would make them want to kill me. But some of them were really letting the war get to them. And a few didn't exactly have what I'd call strong morals."

"Go ahead and check into them, Cora." Sof gave the direction like she was already used to being their boss. "See if any are in Minnesota or this area specifically."

"What about someone connected to us?" Nev glanced at Jazz before looking at the others. "Like from a security job."

"Always a possibility, but why target only Jazz?" Sof stood as if she couldn't contain her energy any longer.

"Good point." Bris's gaze followed Sof as she paced behind her chair.

"What are we going to do to protect Jazz?" Nev asked the question Jazz had thought they'd get to much sooner. Or hoped. Would've been nice if someone else besides Nev cared enough to want to keep Jazz safe.

Sof halted and stared at Nev. Had she not thought about giving Jazz protection? Probably not. "That's a must." She shifted her gaze to Jazz. "You're staying with Nevaeh?"

Jazz glanced at Nev. "Only last night."

"Let's make that a longer stay. We wouldn't need to do patrols at your place then. That'll be best since we're already spread thin covering the fairgrounds."

Of course, they wouldn't want to patrol by Jazz's apartment. Forget that Phoenix did that for everyone else on the team the moment they were in danger. What was it Phoenix had said when Nev had been threatened? Something about not tolerating any threat against the PK-9 agency. That apparently only applied to the accepted members of the team. To everyone but Jazz.

"With Nev, you, and your two protection K-9s, the risk should be far too high for anyone to consider attacking you there." Sof continued her justification for not giving Jazz more security.

Nev snorted. "And if they do try, they deserve what they get just for being stupid." She tossed Jazz a grin she didn't return. Nev must not have noticed how differently they were treating Jazz than everyone else.

"Got that right." Bris chuckled along with Nev, though Jazz's bestie gave her a confused sideways glance.

Nev's smile faded as she spoke again. "What about the fair?" She aimed her gaze at Sof. "Should Jazz avoid doing that because of the danger?"

Jazz opened her mouth to put the kibosh on that idea, but Sof answered first.

"The two attacks on Jazz have been overnight, in secluded areas." Sof's dark eyes aimed at Jazz. "I don't think they'll suddenly switch to jumping her in crowded places in daylight."

Even if Sofia was trying to minimize the danger Jazz was in, Jazz liked where she was going this time. "There's no way I'd give up fair security anyway. Not with the fair being threatened."

"But she should at least check in or something, so we know she's okay, right?" Nev looked only at Sof, probably because she knew what Jazz would say to that.

"Good idea." Sof nodded. "Call Nev or Cora every thirty minutes unless you're with one of us."

"You're kidding." Jazz wanted them to be concerned, not make her feel like a teenager who'd been grounded.

A smile curved Sof's lips. "Just for now. Until we can get a bead on who's after you."

"Speaking of the fair," Cora intervened in her sweet tone, probably trying to prevent a confrontation, "their head of security, Butch Klika, called today to request bomb sweeps every morning."

"Hear that, Toby?" Bris glanced down at her explosives detection K-9, who instantly popped up like he was ready to go. "We'll have a reason to get up early again."

Reassurance calmed the tension that had seeped into Jazz's limbs at the reminder of the threat to the fair. Bris and Toby were a spectacular detection team. There shouldn't be a repeat of sabotage using explosives with them on the job.

"It's rotten what's happening this year." Nev's eyes held a mix of anger and sadness as she looked at Jazz. "I can't believe someone's trying to sabotage the fair."

A lump formed in Jazz's throat. "We can't let anything else happen. People will stop coming. Or start pressuring Aunt Joan to shut down the fair before it's done."

"Would that be the worst thing?"

Jazz had to bite her tongue to keep from asking Bristol how she could even think such a thing.

Nev put a hand on Jazz's leg as she answered first. "So much money would be lost. The fair invests a ton of money in advance of the fair to put it on. If they don't recoup that, it could jeopardize future fairs."

"Not to mention all the people who depend on the Tri-City Fair for their livelihood." Jazz couldn't keep quiet any longer. "Vendors, farmers, breeders—there are thousands of people who rely on the fair to keep them afloat, to provide for their families." And then there were the other reasons. The fact that the fair was the happiest place on earth for Jazz, and she was sure she wasn't the only one who felt that way.

The fact that it was home. The place where she and Nev had spent their summers, having adventures together that bonded them like sisters, forever. The place where Jazz had been accepted by the friendly vendors and other staff she'd seen every year. The folks who knew she was the General Manager's niece and treated her with respect and kindness. People who, like Nev, cared about her more than her blood relatives.

"Oh, my." Lines crossed Cora's pale forehead. "There is a great deal at stake, isn't there?" At least the worry on Cora's face meant she got it.

"Does anyone else think it's a little too coincidental that the first attack on Jazz happened the same day as the fair opened and was sabotaged?" Bris scanned the group.

Nev pushed her fingers into her mass of curls. "I wondered about that. When Jazz finally told us about the first attack." She tossed Jazz a glance. Still wasn't going to let Jazz off the hook for not telling her right away.

"You mentioned your aunt." Bris's voice drew Jazz's gaze to hers. "The sabotage at the fair must be aimed at shutting it down, right? Maybe the culprit thinks if they harm you or threaten you, your aunt will give in and close the fair to keep you safe."

Nev nodded. "This could be the setup period where they're showing they mean business, and then they're gonna give Joan a sort of ransom demand."

"Except that it would never work." All eyes turned to Jazz. "Aunt Joan wouldn't care if I was in danger." The words stuck in her throat more than she thought they would. Silly, given that she'd always known her aunt didn't care about her. Her own dad hadn't. Why would her aunt? Jazz swallowed. "Definitely not enough to shut down the fair."

A silence fell. Great. Now they'd pity her. So much for earning their respect and inclusion.

"Even if that's true," Bris's gray-blue eyes held caution as she broke the hush, "the bad guys wouldn't know that."

She had a point. One Jazz hadn't thought of.

"I wonder if Joan has already gotten threats?" Nev looked at Jazz. "I don't think she'd tell anyone if she had."

"True." Jazz met Nev's gaze. "I should ask—"

"I hate to interrupt the momentum of crime-solving minds at work." Humor filled Sof's tone as she rounded her chair and plopped into it. "But as interim leader, I feel I have to give the reminder Phoenix would at this point. Or would've several minutes ago." She smirked. "We weren't hired to investigate, and that isn't our job."

Nev groaned as Sof paraphrased Phoenix's usual mantra. At least until one of the team members was in danger, and the threat was related to a job.

"We do need to prevent the sabotage on our watches." Sof's dark eyes aimed at Nev and Jazz. "I want you both to focus especially on limited access areas by the rides while you're on patrol. I'm going to handle four to midnight myself to make sure we aren't missing anything."

As if Jazz and Nev weren't doing their jobs as well as Sof. Jazz pressed her lips together to avoid saying something that could get her into trouble.

"The culprit is probably coming in after you and the dogs leave." Bris glanced at the three patrol women.

"Which would mean the greatest need is for the fair to tighten their overnight security." Cora made the observation that only increased Jazz's concern. Would Aunt Joan do that? And how was someone getting in overnight anyway? The fair had always gotten by with lighter security overnight because the grounds were locked up tight at that point.

It could be that someone was managing to hide until closing and then only had to get out after they set up their sabotage. Despite Sofia's boast, no single person and K-9 could cover every inch of the fairgrounds before closing. They were too extensive. PK-9 should probably look at putting two teams on for the last shift. If they had another team, like Phoenix and Dag.

But maybe Sofia was right, and someone was accessing the grounds overnight from the outside. It would be tricky, but probably not impossible. Especially with less security personnel on duty then.

What if Aunt Joan wasn't taking the security measures she could because she was getting threats? Maybe concerning Jazz. Didn't seem likely that would faze Aunt Joan, but Jazz needed to find out what was going on. She couldn't sit by and let her Tri-City Fair be destroyed.

If the PK-9 team wasn't going to help, even with the possible connection between the sabotage and the attacks on Jazz, then she would have to start her own investigation.

Someone had to end the threat on the fair before it was too late. Before anyone else got hurt.

TWELVE

"Who did you say you are?"

Hawthorne's security badge and uniform apparently weren't enough to make Jaden Cobb comfortable talking about the morning he'd found a dead body.

"Hawthorne Emerson. I'm security, and I'm also a thriller writer doing research while I'm working here."

A grin split the ride operator's mouth, and he shook his head. "I thought you said Hawthorne Emerson. But I thought there might be more than one of you. Wow. So you're really the guy who writes the Carson Steele books?"

The kid who looked to be about twenty was too young to be in Hawthorne's typical demographic. But if he was a fan, that could help. "Guilty as charged."

"Cool. My mom loves you."

Ah. That explained it.

"She got me started on Carson Steele. I don't read much, but they're really good."

Hawthorne smiled at that. Always great to know his books had turned someone into a reader.

"So you want to know about the kid who died for your books? Are you going to write about that?"

"Possibly."

"They said it was an accident."

"That's what I heard."

Jaden shifted a lever at the control box for the Logboat Adventure ride.

A boat slid into the loading dock where Jaden and Hawthorne stood outside the ride in the humid morning air.

"I don't think I can tell you anything you wouldn't already know." Jaden bent to look inside the boat, then gripped its edge and tipped it toward one side, then the other.

The boat immediately righted itself. To be expected since it was attached to a stabilizing frame and track under the water.

"Did everything look normal when you came to open the ride that morning?"

Jaden straightened and glanced at Hawthorne. "Sure." He shifted the lever to bring up another boat. "Just like this morning."

"Was the staff door unlocked?"

"Nope." Jaden went through the same motions of checking the next boat.

"Did you inspect the boats first, like you're doing now?"

Jaden nodded as he dismissed that boat for the next one. "I always check the boats, then do a quick walk-through inside before we open."

"And that's when you found Sam Ackerman?"

Jaden looked up at Hawthorne, his vanilla skin paling slightly. "Yeah. Laying by that rock. At first, I thought it might be one of the operators. We prank each other some-times. But when I got close...I knew it was real."

"How did you know?"

Jaden swallowed visibly. "All that blood. And the way his eyes were open. Staring nowhere." Jaden gave his head a hard shake. "Freaked me out."

"I can understand that. I'm sorry you had to find him."

"Better me than a paying customer, right?" He gave Hawthorne a shaky grin.

"Good point." Hawthorne smiled. "So you called it in?"

Jaden nodded. "I told security, and they came right away

with one of the onsite cops. Then more cops came from outside pretty soon."

"Were you surprised when they said it was an accident?"

Jaden lifted his shoulders and let them drop as he moved another boat into place. "Not really. Seemed pretty obvious to me. The kid must've been messing around and fell."

"Does that happen a lot?"

"Oh, yeah. We tell people every ride to stay seated, but there's always some joker who thinks it's funny."

"To stand up during the ride?"

"Uh-huh."

"How do you see when they do that if you're only here, outside?"

Jaden met Hawthorne's gaze. "If they do it at the start or the end, we can see. Sometimes people complain after the ride that somebody was standing, or somebody brags about it."

"I see. Have you ever had anyone slip and fall?"

"Yeah, Christy—she's a nighttime operator, been here for like three years—she's seen it all. She said somebody got their pants totally wet because they were messing around and fell in the water."

"Interesting." So Sam standing up wouldn't be implausible. Sounded pretty common.

Jaden bent over a boat and pulled something out. A beer can?

"Are there often things left in the boats?"

"Oh, sure."

"Anything left in the boats that night?"

Jaden plunked the can into a trash bag, then glanced up. "Probably." He operated the lever again. "Oh, I remember."

Hawthorne tried to see the kid's eyes, but Jaden watched the next boat slide into place.

"I found four beer cans in one boat that morning."

"Is that unusual?"

"There's a max of three people allowed in each boat, so yeah. It was weird."

"Did you tell the police?"

"Yeah." Jaden straightened from testing the boat. "But I'd already cleaned all the boats out before I found the..." He stepped back to the controls to cycle the next boat through. "You know. And they couldn't tell which boat the guy had fallen out of, so it didn't really matter."

Unless the four cans meant four people had crammed into one boat? Or three had gone in and somehow moved Sam—maybe already dead—into the ride from a side door? But they wouldn't have staff access. The staff doors were locked from the inside, too.

And that would mean three killers instead of one. If there'd even been a killing at all.

"Thanks, Jaden. You've been a big help."

"Enough to get me into one of your books? Maybe a character with my name?" He grinned at Hawthorne.

"I'll see what I can do." Hawthorne smiled back, but the expression faded quickly as he left Jaden and headed to the Safety Center to get his assignment for the morning. From Jaden's information, it wasn't a stretch for Sam's death to have been an accident. Sounded like plenty of people stood up when they shouldn't and disobeyed ride rules. The beer cans meant people also consumed alcohol while on the ride. That was consistent with the alcohol content in Sam's blood and the theory he was tipsy from its effects.

Maybe Sam was merely a victim of bad choices and foolish behavior.

But Hawthorne wouldn't want to tell Rebekah that conclusion.

And then there was the odd finding of the superfluous number of beer cans in one boat. Maybe meant nothing. And Hawthorne didn't know what it meant if anything at all. But any anomaly was reason to keep digging.

Hawthorne's feet seemed to pick up speed of their own accord as he neared the Safety Center. He wasn't late—his shift didn't start for another ten minutes—but he didn't have to solve the mystery of the eagerness speeding his pulse. He'd seen Jazz listed on the duty roster for this morning.

Hopefully, he could finally ask her to be the model for the heroine of his new series. He felt a little odd already writing about her without her permission. But it was fiction. And he was having so much fun with her character that he didn't want to consider what he'd do if she said no.

He'd simply have to turn on the charm or try bribery or something—because he needed Jazz Lamont in his next series.

THIRTEEN

"Aunt Joan?" The title slipped out before Jazz thought, thumping her knuckles gently against the frame of the General Manager's open office door. Jazz hadn't been allowed to use the title *Aunt Joan* at the fair when she'd spent her summers there.

But she'd been a child then. Hopefully, Aunt Joan didn't think it was too unprofessional now. Unless she still didn't want to own Jazz as family in public—the motive Jazz had always suspected was truly behind her insistence Jazz call her Mrs. Cracklen instead.

Aunt Joan looked up from her desk and waved Jazz in with a raised hand and an expression Jazz didn't like the look of. Even grimmer than usual. Though given the events of the last two days, that wasn't surprising.

Starting right in with pointed questions about the sabotage didn't seem like the best idea anymore. Jazz opened with a gentler question. "How are you doing?"

Aunt Joan arched an eyebrow at Jazz before returning her gaze to the screen of her desktop computer and typing furiously. "I'm not going to give in, if that's what you mean."

Jazz's belly clenched. "Have you received threats?" She stepped into the office, Flash following calmly by her side.

They stopped next to the chair that stood facing the desk as her aunt threw them a distracted glance.

"Threats? No, not yet. Unless you count the wretched sabotage. But the way things are going, I wouldn't be surprised if threats are next."

Jazz blinked at her aunt, the woman still staring at the computer screen as she typed. Then what was she talking about giving in to?

Aunt Joan looked up. "I assume you saw the article in the Gazette this morning."

Jazz shook her head. She did check the news briefly every morning, but the Minneapolis Gazette wasn't one of her regular sources.

"They're suggesting—in light of the evidence that the accidents were intentional sabotage—that the fair should be closed."

Jazz sucked in a breath.

Aunt Joan's gaze went to Jazz, looking directly at her for the first time since she'd entered the office.

"You wouldn't shut it down, would you?" Tension coiled behind Jazz's ribs.

"Of course not." Aunt Joan's answer came without hesitation. "There are far too many livelihoods at stake. People don't realize that." Her eyes shifted slightly like she was scanning Jazz's face. "I'd forgotten how fond you were of the fair. Do you still enjoy it?"

"I love it." Jazz gripped the back of the chair beside her with one hand. "I'd never want anything to happen to this place. It's home."

A small smile, more natural than Aunt Joan's usual smiles, curved her closed mouth. "It seems like only a week ago when you and Nevaeh were getting underfoot in here." Her gaze traveled over the office. "You'd usually come in to ask about lunch, though your faces were already covered with the purple and pink cotton candy you'd convinced one of the vendors to give you." Was that fondness that lifted her tone?

Couldn't be. Aunt Joan had been thoroughly annoyed

every time Jazz had bothered her at the fair. Which was why Jazz and Nev had spent ninety-five percent of their time on their own elsewhere on the grounds, not in the office.

But the gaze Aunt Joan settled on Jazz held something Jazz had never seen aimed at her before. For a second, Jazz thought it was approval. But it couldn't be that.

It was probably nostalgia that had nothing to do with Jazz. Memories of the fair's happiest times. Jazz was happy to share those. "Well, we were very content with cotton candy for lunch every day." She smiled.

And Aunt Joan smiled back. A large, real expression of happiness. But it only lasted a second. "If only everyone understood the importance of the fair the way you do." A frown tipped her mouth as she glanced at the computer screen again. "I've spent all morning answering worried emails, some even from our board members."

She looked up at Jazz. "They thought I might cancel the board's annual tour of the grounds today. Can you believe that?"

Jazz shook her head, for once glad Aunt Joan had a backbone carved out of steel and never let anyone get in her way.

"I've explained to everyone that Butch has increased overnight security, and we've added an explosives detection K-9 to ensure there are no more surprises."

"Good. I saw Bristol and Toby before they left an hour ago. She said everything was clear."

Aunt Joan gave Jazz a blank stare.

"The explosives detection team."

"Oh." Aunt Joan nodded briskly. "Good."

"I'd like to help." Jazz stepped closer to the desk and waited for Aunt Joan to look up again.

She did only briefly. "You're already on the security team."

"I mean, I'd like to help find who's doing this so we can catch the culprit and stop it."

That got her aunt's attention. "How would you do that?" Aunt Joan's brown eyes fastened on Jazz's face.

"Well, we can start with motive. Do you know who would want the fair to shut down?"

Aunt Joan looked past Jazz in the direction of the open office door. Checking for eavesdroppers? When she spoke again, her voice was lowered. "Two years ago, a seventeen-year-old died on our grounds."

Surprise flittered through Jazz's torso. Didn't remember hearing anything about that. Though she would've been far too busy being her dad's caretaker at the time to read any news.

"It was an accident. He fell on one of the rides."

"Which ride?"

Annoyance flashed in Aunt Joan's eyes. "Does it matter? The Logboat Adventure ride."

How would a fall on the Logboat Adventure ride kill someone? There weren't any significant heights to fall from.

"My point is that although his death was clearly an accident, and the police ruled it as such, we were blamed for it by the naysayers in our community."

"There are people in the community who don't like the fair?" The only people Jazz knew of who fit that bill were the ones Hawthorne had told her about yesterday. The Best Life cult.

"Yes. Predominantly the Best Life Community."

So that was who Aunt Joan meant.

"The boy was apparently one of their members."

Whoa. That was weird. Hadn't Hawthorne said the members weren't allowed to attend the fair?

"Desmond Patch made a public statement that the press ran, of course."

"Who's Desmond Patch?"

Aunt Joan raised her eyebrows like she was surprised Jazz was as ignorant as she'd always thought she was. "The leader of Best Life. He's very well known in the Twin Cities."

Meaning Jazz was stupid not to know that. She let the usual inference roll off. "So what did he say?"

"His statement referred to the boy's death as proof that the Tri-City Fair is quote, 'evil and dangerous.'"

"Wow. That's pretty strong." And meant the fair definitely had an enemy. One who just happened to run the cult they'd found a pin from by the Giant Slide.

"Thankfully, everyone in this area knows he's a quack, so he didn't get public opinion on his side." Aunt Joan leaned down and opened a desk drawer. "The boy's father probably did more damage." She straightened with her purse in hand, setting the large bag on the desk.

"More damage?"

Aunt Joan opened her designer bag and reached inside. "He was very upset about his son's death, and he took it out on us in the news coverage." She pulled out a makeup bag and unzipped it. "He said our ride safety was nonexistent and that we were to blame for the accident."

"Did people agree with him?"

"Some public opinion swayed that way, but not enough to harm our attendance at the time. It was close to the end of the season, thankfully." She slipped a compact from the bag and flipped it open, touching up her impeccable makeup. "And he simultaneously claimed his son's death wasn't an accident at all, so that helped."

Helped? It took Jazz a second to realize what her aunt meant. Of course. She meant it helped everyone discount the father's claims the fair was at fault. Aunt Joan always did see everything in terms of how it affected her interests.

At least in this case, Jazz's interests aligned with her aunt's—the continuation and well-being of the Tri-City Fair. And now she knew of at least two people, maybe a whole community, that were against the fair. They could have motive to sabotage it and close it down.

Could that also be related to the attacks on Jazz? She took a breath. Might as well ask. "So you haven't received any threats this year, though? Nothing about your...family or closing down the fair?"

Aunt Joan closed the compact and slipped it into the

makeup bag, returning everything to her purse. "Well, Pierce always gets some harmless threats. That comes with running for political office, especially at the level of governor. But nothing that mentioned the fair."

"Okay. I think I'll look into the cult thing and see—"

"Oh, there is something unrelated I wanted to talk to you about."

"There is?" Jazz wanted to cringe at the hopeful surprise in her tone. Aunt Joan never wanted to talk to Jazz about anything. Well, except to scold or lecture. Maybe that's all she meant.

A rap at the door put Jazz's curiosity on hold.

Aunt Joan's secretary leaned through the doorway. "You said you wanted to go over the numbers before the board members arrive?"

"Oh, yes." Aunt Joan waved her in, giving Jazz a glance. "We'll have to continue this over brunch tomorrow."

So she was still invited. Hope, which Jazz should know better than to allow, flickered behind her ribs. "Do you want me to bring anything?"

"The chef will take care of everything. I look forward to seeing you at eleven sharp."

"Right." Jazz nodded, but Aunt Joan was already holding out her hand to take the folder the secretary quickly offered her.

Jazz didn't envy that job. Though Aunt Joan was being unusually nice today.

And helpful with the information she'd shared.

Jazz pushed through the glass door to exit the building, letting Flash go first as the humid heat of late morning hit her full in the face.

The idea of the fair having two known enemies—or maybe many in the Best Life Community—was hard to grasp.

"We meet again."

Jazz swung back toward the building and the man's voice.

Hawthorne Emerson smiled, the sun kissing his tanned

skin. "Under more pleasant circumstances this time. Unless you don't like the heat."

Her mouth stretched with an answering smile that was probably far too big and eager. "We're adaptable."

He glanced down at Flash, who only panted slightly since they'd just been indoors. "As long as there's air-conditioning, right, buddy?"

And he talked to dogs. Be still her heart.

"I was hoping I'd see you today."

Jazz had to do a double take to be sure he was talking to her and not Flash this time.

His electric eyes looked right at her.

She swallowed. "Really?"

"Yeah. Before anything else crazy happens, I want to ask you something."

Like, would she go out with him? Jazz's heart thumped in her ears. Was Nev right, he was going to ask her on a date?

"Would you let me model my next heroine after you?"

"What?" The word spewed out before she could stop it. Socially inept, as usual.

"Sorry." He cringed. "It's probably a strange question. When I met you on the Ferris Wheel—" He grinned. "Sounds like a line from an old movie." He chuckled and ran a hand down the light stubble coating his jaw. "But seriously, I was blown away."

"You were?" She didn't care how breathless she sounded. Or how dreamily she was probably staring at him right now. Did he mean he liked her?

"Yeah. Your skills, your bravery—you're amazing. Exactly what I need for the lead character in my new series."

His words finally started to sink in. Along with reality. Of a sort. The blip of disappointment collided with an upsurge of excitement as she absorbed what he was saying. "Wait, so you mean you want to write me into your book?"

"Not just a book, a whole series of books. I want you to be the heroine. Well, the model for her anyway. I wouldn't want to do anything to violate your privacy, of course. And that's why I'm asking your permission."

"Yes!" The response burst out of her, followed by a quick laugh. "I'm honored." And flattered, flustered, stunned—and all the other things he didn't need to know.

"Terrific." His handsome smile broadened to kilowatt strength. Goodness.

A shiver tracked down her spine despite the heat starting to create pockets of sweat under her T-shirt.

"I'd like to buy you dinner tonight."

Dinner? A date, too?

"To discuss how you became the way you are, your background. Anything you'd be willing to share that would help me flesh out my Jazz Lamont heroine."

Oh. A business dinner. But with her favorite author, talking all about how he was going to put her in his books? "I'm in."

"Great. You've lived here more recently than I have, so you pick the place. Where do you like to eat?"

Her mind raced through the best options, most of which she'd been to recently on her internet dating flops. The idea of a dinner with Hawthorne going that badly twisted her stomach. "Why don't we do something different?"

He lifted his eyebrows. "I'm game."

"I'm planning to go wall-climbing tonight."

"Perfect. I'm there. You just name the time."

"Seven at Just Climb It?"

"You got it." He held out his hand, and she took hold of it. But the firm handshake her dad had drilled into her faltered, probably turning mushy in the soft, tingly heat of his touch.

He let go at the appropriate time, and she yanked her hand back, hopefully before he noticed she'd lingered way too long. He was going to junk the idea of basing a heroine on her real quick at this rate. Most socially awkward heroine ever.

"Well, we'd better get back to work."

Work. Yes. She nodded and firmed her grip on Flash's leash, not trusting her voice to sound anything but breathy at the moment if she spoke.

"I'll see you at seven."

"See you." She managed to get that much out as she turned around and headed in the opposite direction from the one she'd intended to take. Before she'd been stopped by her favorite author and asked to be the star of his novels.

When Nev came on shift in an hour, Jazz was going to have her bestie pinch an arm as hard as she could. Jazz had to be dreaming.

Though if it were her dream, hunky Hawthorne Emerson probably would've asked her on a real date, too.

What if she thought he was asking her out on a date? Hawthorne cringed as he walked under the Skyride cars that hung suspended from cables above as they carried people from the midway all the way to the other side of the fairgrounds.

Didn't seem like Jazz had thought it was a date, since she'd switched it from dinner to wall-climbing.

Hawthorne rolled his shoulders back. Right. Should be fine.

He'd been so excited when she'd said she would be the model for his heroine that he hadn't thought through what it would sound like if he asked her to dinner.

But she seemed to get it.

He paused outside the midway Skyride building, scanning the people who lined up to board the Skyride and the surrounding crowds at neighboring rides. Hawthorne was beginning to understand why the Tri-City Fair was said to be the largest in the nation. The number of people, especially by two in the afternoon, was astounding. Like walking through Times Square in New York City.

The crowd divided slightly farther up the midway, as if

something was being slowly inserted in the middle of a river and parting the waters.

He stepped to the side of the path and peered above the bobbing heads of visitors. Not the first time he appreciated being taller than average.

Three golf carts slowly drove through the crowds, coming Hawthorne's direction. Was that Joan Cracklen in the front cart?

She came into sharper view as the cart meandered closer, driven by a teen wearing the bright blue T-shirt general staffers wore. The cart halted by the Skyride building, and Joan and three other people got off.

Joan's husband Pierce was one of them, but Hawthorne didn't recognize the other man and woman.

Maybe board members. Butch had warned them the Tri-City Fair board members were going to come for their annual tour this afternoon. Though Butch had said it was more of an inspection, so the security team should be on their toes.

Hawthorne walked closer in case he was needed. Couldn't say he wanted to talk to either Joan or her husband after yesterday. He couldn't believe the way Joan had jumped on her own niece, almost accusing Jazz for the bomb at the Giant Slide. At least her husband hadn't seemed so bad. He'd tried to calm her down.

The second and third carts slowed by Joan and her companions as she held up a hand toward the other board members. "I'm going to take my traditional ride on our beloved Skyride now. It's the best way to see the grounds. Feel free to join me if you'd like or continue looking around on your own."

The occupants of the second golf cart must've decided to stay. Their driver pulled to the side as much as he could amid all the people and let them off.

The third cart continued on at a snail's pace, crawling through the crowds.

Hawthorne eyed the long line out the door of the Skyride

building. He couldn't see Joan Cracklen or her politician husband standing in line for half an hour or more.

Sure enough, Joan led her party to the staff access door at the side of the building, circumventing the line.

Hawthorne smirked. Though he supposed she wasn't getting paid to wait in line at a ride. A job had to have some perks.

"Hey, are you security?" A scratchy-voiced teen boy stopped next to Hawthorne.

"Yes. How can I help you?"

"I think I lost my phone."

"Sorry to hear that." Hawthorne told him the steps to report the phone missing at the Public Safety Center near the entrance. By the time the kid trudged off, Hawthorne saw Joan and the others were about to board the Skyride.

Joan had paired off with the woman board member from her golf cart, and Pierce was deep in discussion with the man as they waited behind the ladies.

Joan helped the woman, a middle-aged lady who appeared nervous, into the enclosed car first and then entered herself.

"Base to S4," the voice of Kerry, one of the dispatchers, sounded in Hawthorne's earpiece as Pierce and the other guy boarded the next car. "Assistance needed with gaming dispute at Darts and Sharks."

"S4, Roger. ETA five minutes." Hawthorne spun away from the Skyride and started toward the booth he'd already had to stop at this morning and yesterday. Took forever to get anywhere on foot through these crowds. But another disgruntled customer who suspected the Darts and Sharks game was rigged didn't seem like enough of an emergency to warrant breaking into a run. Fair games were always—

A cracking boom rocked the ground beneath his feet.

FOURTEEN

"Explosion at the Skyride. Near west midway building. We need medics and rescue services stat." Hawthorne's voice, strong but full of urgency, hit Jazz's ear over coms, pulsing adrenaline and alarm through her veins.

Another explosion? This couldn't be happening.

She whipped around the other direction to head for the midway Skyride building.

"Roger, S4." Kerry responded promptly from Base. "Help is on the way. Describe the damage."

"Approximately four casualties." Hawthorne's radio caught sickening background sounds. People yelling. Crying. "We need more security for crowd control."

"Roger, S4."

Jazz's stomach twisted. "PT3 to Base, we're on our way." She picked up speed, Flash tugging at his leash to go all out. But there was no way in this crowd.

"Out of the way!" The shout she repeated every few seconds helped her and Flash reach jogging speed. Thank goodness they'd been at the History Center not far from the west end of the Skyride. She hadn't heard an explosion, probably because she'd been inside. Could be a good sign it was a smaller one this time.

Though from the casualty report and the intensity in

Hawthorne's voice as he'd called it in, her gut knew not to be optimistic.

The Skyride ropes and dangling pods appeared above. Still. Not traveling like they always were when the fair was open.

A sinking sensation dropped to the pit of her belly.

"Clear the way." Jazz and Flash pressed through people who stood and stared in the direction of the ride.

As Flash pulled her through the front of the crowd, her gaze landed on carnage.

One quarter of a pod dangled from the heavy rope above. Open like a cracked, carved-out bit of eggshell.

Jazz's throat cinched as she lowered her gaze below the pod.

Pieces of metal scattered across the blacktop amid shards of glass and—

Was that…bodies?

Jazz took a step closer, barely feeling Flash's tug on the leash as her eyes locked on the floral blouse on the pavement.

Aunt Joan's blouse.

A gag lurched into her throat. Jazz put her hand to her mouth and moved closer.

An arm crossed in front of her, and something gripped her shoulder.

Her peripheral caught Hawthorne, standing beside her.

"Let me go." She couldn't look away from the blouse. The patches of red that hadn't been there before.

His hold stayed firm, but his voice was gentle. "Her face was badly damaged. You won't ever be able to unsee it if you look."

Like the faces of the two soldiers and six terrorists she'd seen after surviving the ambush. She'd never forgotten those either. He was right. She didn't need more horrors in her head.

She slowly relaxed away from Hawthorne's arm. Weird her reflexes hadn't kicked in and told her to escape his hold instantly. She could have easily. But something about the concern in his voice made his touch feel more like a comforting embrace than—

"My wife." A man shouted. "Is she all right?"

Jazz's gaze sought the location of the familiar voice.

A face pressed through an opening in the pod next to the destroyed one. An unnatural opening—a long split where one wall was broken off almost completely.

"Jazz?"

Uncle Pierce? She'd never heard him sound like that. Anguished.

"Is Joan...alive?" He stretched his hand through the opening like he was trying to reach his wife on the ground below.

Jazz's heart stuck in her throat. She looked at Hawthorne. Maybe she'd misunderstood what he'd meant.

He shook his head slowly.

She looked up, trying to force air into her collapsing lungs. "I'm sorry."

A groan, a sob, wrenched from Uncle Pierce as he seemed to fall back into the pod, swinging it on the rope.

The sound stabbed Jazz's heart.

Another man inside the dangling pod said something Jazz couldn't hear. It looked through the window like he was patting Uncle Pierce's arms. Maybe comforting him.

"I'm so sorry." Hawthorne's words slowly drew Jazz's gaze to him. His brows tucked together, pain in his eyes.

"What happened?"

"I wish I knew. Everything seemed fine. I'd seen your aunt get on the ride with another woman. A board member, I assume."

Jazz nodded. "They were doing their tour today."

"Right." He squinted up at the pods. "I'd just gotten called to help with a dispute elsewhere when the explosion went off behind me."

"Excuse me." The crowd shuffled out of the way as Marisa

pushed through with two more medics. Maybe Aunt Joan had staffed more medics today because of—

The thought cut short with a sharp twist in Jazz's chest. Aunt Joan.

Could that really be her, dead on the pavement?

Marisa and the other medics crowded around her, then one darted to another body Jazz hadn't seen.

"The woman who was in the car with your aunt is still breathing. But she looks to be in bad shape. She must've been farther from the bomb, or your aunt's body shielded her."

Bomb. But there couldn't have been a bomb. Bris and Toby had cleared everything that morning. "Did you see…" Jazz let the question drift. How could she put into words something she didn't even want to imagine? Her aunt being—

"I saw the tail end of the explosion. Everything fell except that scrap hanging there. The car your uncle is in got hit, swung so hard I thought it was going to fall off." Hawthorne lowered his gaze from the pods to Jazz. "I think he and the other man might've been unconscious until you arrived."

Flash whined at her side. Jazz glanced at him, poor guy probably picking up on her anxiety. Or grief. Whatever it was. She'd figure it out later.

She glanced at Hawthorne. "We should get them down. They probably need medical attention. And we don't want another panic situation with any of the passengers."

A flicker of something—maybe surprise?—appeared in Hawthorne's eyes. But he nodded. "Right. I see Butch is here with reinforcements, so we can leave crowd control to him."

The head of security was corralling bystanders with a few other guards, pushing them back to establish a more extensive perimeter.

"Think it'll hold?" Hawthorne's question seemed to come from somewhere far away.

"What?"

"The ride." Hawthorne pointed up at the ropes that stretched out from the building to carry the pods.

"Oh." Jazz blinked away the floral print that seemed to be burned in her mind. She dug her cell phone out of her pocket, tapped to open the camera function, and held it up. She zoomed in on the ropes above the remnants of the exploded pod.

The ropes were darkened, especially the one that had held the destroyed pod, but she couldn't see any signs of fraying. The rope used for the Skyride was an incredibly resilient and strong blend of coils surrounding an inner cable. "I think it will. Let's verify with the operator." She glanced toward the building. Then she needed to call Bris. Pronto.

This couldn't have been a bomb. Not if Bristol and Toby had checked everything.

The fair was supposed to be safe again.

And it couldn't be PK-9's fault, even though Aunt Joan had wanted to blame them yesterday.

The straws she tried to grasp eluded her hold, refusing to distract her from the reality she didn't want to face.

It didn't matter what was supposed to be.

The fair wasn't safe.

And Aunt Joan was dead.

"Are you sure you're okay to do this?"

Jazz glanced at Hawthorne as she finished securing her harness to the auto-belay system. "Having doubts about my climbing skills, even after I beat you down from the Ferris wheel?" Her teasing grin made him wonder if he shouldn't have brought up the sad topic. She seemed to be doing well after the day's events. Surprisingly well.

"I just meant, with everything that happened today, I would understand if you wanted to reschedule this."

"Oh." She frowned, her gaze dropping to the blue floor of the Just Climb It facility.

"Sorry. I didn't mean to bring it up if you were trying to forget for a while."

She looked up again, her mouth lifting slightly at the corners. "I guess I was. Activity is the way I process things. Work off steam." She tested her harness with a tug as she glanced at the forty-plus foot wall. "I'd come alone after a day like today anyway."

"Makes sense." And told Hawthorne a lot about the woman who was going to star in his novels. A woman of action. Processing through activities that would make most people tired just thinking about them made for a fascinating character. "Race you to the top?" He grinned at her.

"You're on." She jumped onto the wall, skipping the first four holds in a move that told him he might be in trouble.

After probably the fastest climb of his life, he lowered from the wall to stand beside the woman who kept impressing him. "Okay, where did you learn to climb like that?"

"My dad started me on it." She smiled, not even sounding winded. She unclipped and walked across the room to the bench where they'd left their belongings. "He wanted a boy, so he taught me everything he would've taught the son he never had."

That explained a lot. But the edge to her tone said she wasn't necessarily happy about that bit of her history. "Including knife-throwing?" He tried to infuse a lighthearted note into the moment.

She narrowed her eyes at him in an overdone way that made him suspect she was teasing. "What in the world are you talking about?" She grabbed a dark green water thermos from the outer pocket of her duffel bag and took a swig.

"Hey, I spotted the extra weapon you carry. Or is that just a special decoration for the fair?"

She laughed, the musical tone that traveled the scale. "Girls love their accessories, you know."

"Uh-huh." He returned her grin as he gave her a quick scan. "You're not packing now, are you?"

"Shh." She stepped closer as she pressed her finger to her lips, drawing his attention to how full they were. "You'll never know. Unless someone gives me cause to use it."

"Ah." His gaze drifted up from her mouth to her twinkling emerald eyes. "So you do have knife-throwing skills."

"A lady never tells." Her smile sparkled.

"Okay. I guess I'll just have to make sure I'm around the next time you need to use that particular 'accessory.'"

She walked back to the climbing wall and hooked up to the auto-belay in a neighboring section.

He followed and clipped in beside her. "So tell me more about Jazz Lamont. You said your dad taught you a lot of skills. Do you do martial arts?"

"Sure." She started to climb.

He grabbed a handhold and hurried to catch up. "What kind?"

"A mix we learned in basic training in the Army. And some stuff I've picked up on my own along the way."

"When did you enlist?"

"Went in at eighteen."

"How many years did you serve?" Why did he sound more winded than she did? Too much time spent at the keyboard, apparently. Or maybe a sign he needed to add cardio to his weight-lifting routine.

"Eight and a quarter."

"Unusual number." He paused briefly to look for his next hold as she increased the distance between them.

"I'd just re-upped when my dad got sick. I got out to take care of him."

Very noble. And sad. But Hawthorne was a little too taxed at the moment to properly respond.

She reached the top and glanced down at him. "Looks like I'm three for three."

He looked up to see her grin as he strained to reach his last, difficult handhold.

"Or four if you count the Ferris wheel."

"I never count." He pushed out the joke as he paused at the top to catch his breath.

"Race you to the bottom."

He was ready for her this time, and he leaned back to belay, hoping his heavier weight might get him there faster.

"Ha." He pointed at her as he reached the ground a split-second before her.

"Tie."

"What?" His teasing disbelief lifted the word.

"You leaned back farther so it looked like you hit first. But my foot touched first."

He narrowed his eyes as she blinked innocently at him. "A little competitive, aren't you?"

"But always a good winner." She winked. "Need another water break?"

He didn't miss the insinuation she'd only taken the earlier break for his sake. He chuckled. "Oh, probably." He wouldn't mind being able to ask her questions without having to race her up another wall at the same time.

He reached the bench first and grabbed his water bottle. "So what made you want to enlist?"

She glanced away as she picked up her thermos. "My dad."

"He wanted you to?"

"Oh, yeah. He was career Army." She returned her gaze to Hawthorne, the spark gone from her eyes. "Not having a son wasn't going to stop him from getting what he wanted."

Career Army. Was that the reason for the pain tightening her features? Maybe the lifestyle? Wasn't easy on kids, from what he'd seen among his Marine buddies who had families. "Did you move around a lot as a child?"

"Sure. Typical Army brat." She took a long drink, looking away again. She lowered the thermos and set it on the bench. "Until my dad figured out he didn't have to take me along at all."

Ouch. Hawthorne hid a wince, not sure if he should ask what that meant.

"But in a way it was better, I guess." Her tone lifted slightly. "That's when I found my first home. The fair." A partial smile lifted her lips, her eyes seeming to gaze far off at something not in front of them.

"He left you there?"

Her glance hopped to Hawthorne's face, as if surprised to see him. "Oh. Not at the fair." She chuckled. "Not exactly. He sent me to live with my aunt and uncle. The mighty Cracklens of Minneapolis."

"Oh. That's nice you had family that wanted to host you."

She laughed, sardonic. "They never wanted to. I'm still not sure how my dad got them to agree to it. Aunt Joan was his sister, so maybe she felt some sense of obligation? But I found Nevaeh here, my best friend. Spent more time with her family than mine. Summers were the best."

A wistful smile played on Jazz's lips. "Nevaeh and I would run all over the fairgrounds, playing games and getting into trouble. The vendors took us under their wings and gave us treats and things. Aunt Joan was busy, so she let us have complete freedom."

Now that was something Hawthorne could understand. Something he'd missed in the latter half of his childhood. The freedom to be a kid.

Sounded like she'd had an idyllic childhood. If he ignored the pain that had been so evident as she told the earlier parts of her story. And the sense of dysfunction and lack of stability that undergirded her tale of even the happy times.

A well-loved child didn't need to escape to a fair with a friend and a bunch of strangers to find belonging.

The best heroes and heroines were often wrought through painful histories. But the real Jazz Lamont wasn't a fictional character. She was a lovely person he found himself wishing he could help somehow. Maybe alleviate some of her pain.

"And now she's gone, too." Jazz's eyes fixed on some distant point again.

It took Hawthorne a second to remember who she'd been talking about a moment ago. Her aunt. "I'm sorry, Jazz."

She drew in a breath and rolled her shoulders back as if trying to rid herself of some burden. The eyes that turned on him were slightly moist. "I should be the one apologizing for dumping so much on you." She gave him a shaky smile. "I have no idea why I spilled my whole life history like that. I'm sorry."

"Don't be. I wanted to know, remember?"

Her brow furrowed as she peered at him. "You're a good listener. I suppose you use that on all your interview subjects for your writing. Like a superpower."

He laughed. "Never thought of it that way, but I wouldn't mind having a superpower." He sobered. "I am sorry about your aunt."

Jazz pressed her mouth into a firm line and looked unseeingly past him again. "She dedicated her life to the fair. In a way, I owe her for making it what it was. And I can't let all those years of work she poured into the fair be for nothing. I can't let anyone destroy it now."

Admiration warmed Hawthorne's chest—that and a little thrill from seeing an ideal heroine come to life in front of his eyes. "What are you going to do?" He felt as if he were asking his character the question, but she was standing in front of him, real as life.

"I'm going to figure out who did this and make them stop."

He would've written the line as *bring them to justice,* but he couldn't ask for more heroic spirit and spunky determination than she embodied.

"After I beat you to the top again." She started for the climbing wall.

He grinned as he followed. She was a perfect blend of serious and tough but fun and playful. Full of life and energy, despite the troubled background that haunted her. "Hey, I was just getting warmed up. Didn't want you to feel badly right out of the gate."

"Oh, is that a fact?" Her laughter said she didn't believe him. "What would you say if I told you I am not left-handed?" She dramatically switched the hand gripping the rope from her left to her right, holding the supposedly useless left appendage in the air.

He laughed so hard at the unexpected movie reference to *The Princess Bride* that she got in one of her jumpstarts again before he'd left the ground.

He pushed to catch up, cutting his previous climbing record to a new personal best, he was pretty sure. But he still touched the floor after her, once again.

She threw him a brilliant grin as soon as he landed.

An odd sensation pinged through his chest. Probably because he was about to have a heart attack. He held up a hand. "I know." He breathed much more heavily than he should need to. "Five out of five."

"Up and down." She gave him a saucy smile. "So is that why you want to use me for a heroine in your novels? Because I can beat you at climbing?"

"Of course. A guy loves getting his ego pummeled as frequently as possible."

She arched an eyebrow. "Something tells me your ego is doing fine."

He grinned. "No comment."

"Really, though. Why me?" She still held a smile, but something else—maybe hesitation—crept into her eyes.

"Because you're so unique."

"You mean weird." Her nose wrinkled in a cute expression he hadn't expected from her. "I don't exactly fit in easily, so you got that right." She turned away, whether to go to the bench because she wanted to or to hide some emotion, he wasn't sure.

He caught up with her by their things. "No, I mean you stand out. In a good way."

She stuffed her thermos into her bag and straightened, turning those amazing eyes on him.

"I've never met anyone like you. Strong with incredible skills, but you still care deeply about things."

Her eyebrows clustered as if she was doubting his words.

"Like how you're determined to find the saboteur who's trying to destroy the fair and killed your aunt." He pushed his water bottle into his duffel bag before returning his gaze to her face. "That's the kind of stuff I usually have to invent for my books."

A slow smile lifted the shape of her lips. "I guess it does sound like something out of a Carson Steele novel."

"You see?"

"So if this were a novel...Or a movie." The twinkle returned to her eyes as she watched him.

"Why do I get the feeling you're about to throw out a plot twist I didn't see coming?"

"Maybe more of a cute trope." She laughed.

He couldn't help the answering grin that found his face. "Not usually used in my genre, but I'll bite."

"Well, this is where I should realize you could help me with my investigation. Help me find the culprit."

"I could? I mean, you should?" He blinked at her.

"Yeah. You were an MP investigator. You have experience."

So that's what she was getting at.

"Want to help me catch a bad guy and save the fair?" She stepped a little closer with an admittedly adorable pleading look on her face. "You could be like Carson Steele in real life."

His mouth twitched at that. He was already investigating one suspicious death for his sister. What was one more? And if the saboteur kept going unchecked, a lot more than Jazz's fair was at stake.

"Carson is quite a bit older than I am..." His tease was rewarded with another nose wrinkle. "But I agree whoever this is needs to be stopped before more lives are lost."

Her eyes widened to an even larger size. "Does that mean you'll help?"

"Absolutely. I'll do whatever I can. Though that might not be much." Especially since he couldn't let a new investigation distract him from finding the truth about Sam. He'd promised Rebekah first, after all.

"Terrific. Thanks." The beaming smile she gave him, along with the light touch of her fingers on his arm, sent a strange, warm sensation through his chest. More helpful research. Now he knew how his characters would react to Jazz Lamont in his story. She definitely had an effect on a person.

Jazz checked her wristwatch. "I hate to cut this short, but I'd better get home to Flash."

Only her dog. Did that mean she didn't have a boyfriend or anyone? He'd have to ask her some other time. For character research.

"Early shift again tomorrow."

"Oh, sure." Hawthorne hefted his duffel bag over his shoulder. "I have some things to take care of tonight anyway." Like heading back to the fair for more investigating. He checked his phone for messages and the time. Only five after nine. He'd have time yet to get there well before the fair closed at eleven. As security, he could get in later, but not without answering questions he'd rather avoid.

Hawthorne held the door open for Jazz as they exited the building.

"Thanks." She smiled, apparently not one of those women bothered by a man holding a door.

He hadn't performed the courtesy as a test, but the research was priceless. Wouldn't have thought such a strong, independent woman would welcome the courteous gesture from a guy. Too old-fashioned and demeaning according to modern opinions, he would've guessed. But Jazz seemed to like it.

Fascinating.

"So you'll need to let me have a rematch soon." Hawthorne fell in step beside her on the sidewalk sin front of the building, the concrete gently lit by lampposts.

Jazz cast him a smile that beat back the shadows. "Sure you'd be up for that anytime soon?"

"Ouch." He laughed. "Hey, I haven't been climbing for a long time. Ferris wheel notwithstanding."

"If you say so. I'm ready anytime." She veered off the sidewalk to walk between two parked cars.

"All right. You're on." He followed her as she aimed for the navy blue SUV she'd arrived in, parked in the next row. "Though I warn you, I'll bring my A game next time."

"Now you have me worried." She tossed a grin over her shoulder that belied the words.

Something beyond her caught his gaze. Something off.

Was the front tire...

"Hey, Jazz."

She paused and turned toward him.

"I don't think you're going anywhere right now." He caught up with her and looked at the right front tire.

It was flattened to the ground.

FIFTEEN

Jazz squatted next to the very flat tire. She ran her thumb over a thin puncture mark. Weird shape. Like a match for her knife blade if she'd stuck it into the tire.

She stood, letting her gaze travel across the parking lot, the hidden pockets of darkness beyond the lampposts.

Was the tire cutter still there, waiting for her to be vulnerable while she changed the tire? That was likely the point.

But how would anyone have known she was there? She always checked for tails. An unbreakable habit from her Army days that came in handy working for PK-9.

"Got a spare in the back?" Hawthorne's question nearly startled her. Forgot he was there.

"Oh." She pulled out her key fob and unlocked the back, walking to the rear of the SUV. The liftgate rose, and she reached inside for the cover that hid the spare.

"I'll get that."

She paused and looked over her shoulder at him. "I've been changing tires since I was six."

"Then it's about time you had a break, don't you think?" He gave her the charming grin that had shown up more than once tonight.

She backed out of the space, ending up much closer to him than she'd expected. She squinted at him to cover the flustered feeling that tumbled in her belly. "Afraid I can change a tire better than you, too?"

"Definitely." The glitter of humor in his eyes, so close to hers, sent a pulse of electricity down to her toes. Was it her or was it super warm outside tonight? That would explain the sparks of heat that tingled between her and Hawthorne.

"Okay, sure." She blurted the response and stepped back in an attempt to halt the mashup of chemicals rushing through her. He was a bestselling author who wanted to feature her in his books. He'd been nothing but professional all night. And sweet and kind...funny, caring. And oh-so easy to look at with his sculpted physique and—

But that wasn't the point. The point was, he hadn't shown any personal interest. Not romantic interest. Not the sparks flying, flame-fueling attraction she'd been battling all evening.

At least she didn't think so.

"Thank you. I'm honored to get to change Jazz Lamont's tire."

She reached for a laugh and her sense of humor, her life-savers tonight. "At least this way, I'll get to tell everyone *the* Hawthorne Emerson changed my flat tire."

His rich laugh lingered as he brushed past her with the spare and jack. "Just no photos on social media, please."

"Aww, really?" She gave her best disappointed teenager imitation, earning another handsome grin as he crouched to remove the old tire.

Jazz's eyes lingered on the contoured muscles beneath the sleeves of his slim T-shirt. They flexed and coiled as he loosened the bolts. Even the muscles of his back rippled through the thin material of his shirt.

She cleared her throat and dragged her gaze away. She'd never realized there was more than one benefit to having a guy change her tire. At least when he looked like Hawthorne Emerson.

She stifled a snort at the thought. Nev would get a kick

out of this story. Though she'd wonder about the suspicious cut in the tire, too.

Jazz's humor faded as she scanned the lot again. Eleven cars were parked there. Just Climb It didn't close until ten, so the vehicles could all belong to climbers inside.

She didn't see anyone inside the vehicles, but a person could easily hide by sitting low or ducking. If she had Flash with her or was alone, she'd go check them out.

But Hawthorne didn't need to know about the strange adventures of her life. He already thought she was weird—or *unique*, as he'd so carefully put it. She didn't want to risk scaring him off either. He seemed comfortable with danger on the pages, but it was different in real life.

He was a former marine. That said a lot. But most people wanted to leave that kind of danger behind when they left the military.

No, she'd solve this puzzle herself. Beginning with how the would-be shooter—assuming that was the intent of this stunt—had found her there. Since she always checked for tails and didn't predictably come to Just Climb It at this time on Saturday nights, that left one other option.

A tracker. Hidden on her SUV, probably. Unless someone had gotten to her things in her locker at the fair, but that seemed less likely.

"Must've driven over a nail, huh?" Hawthorne's question drew her attention to the famous author she really couldn't believe was changing her tire. And especially that he looked so good doing it. His toned forearms dangled over the top of the tire he'd removed and held propped up in front of him.

"Yeah, must have."

"Weird looking nail, don't you think?" His electric eyes pierced her with a stare above the tire rubber.

Her mouth dried. Did he suspect something? She tried to hide her swallow. "What else could it be?"

"I don't know." His head tilted slightly as he watched her much too closely. "But I get the feeling you do."

"Look, I'm gonna be honest with you." Christy Mason threw Hawthorne a glance over her shoulder as she walked on the staff-only path ahead of him. "I don't remember much about that night. I remember a lot more about the next morning, when the police showed up at my apartment to ask me questions."

The narrow path along the perimeter of the Logboat Adventure ride's interior didn't allow for Hawthorne to walk next to the ride operator as she did her closing inspection. Not very conducive to an interview about the night Sam died. But Hawthorne would take what he could get.

The other people he'd questioned tonight, those who had operated neighboring rides and food stands, hadn't remembered anything helpful. No one seemed to have noticed Sam or anything unusual. But they'd also pointed out that they never remembered anyone unless there was something unique about the person. They simply saw too many faces to recall.

Given the number of visitors still there when Hawthorne had arrived tonight, just before closing at eleven p.m., he could see why. He'd thought there would be significantly smaller crowds at closing than earlier in the day, but the number of visitors lingering for a last bit of fun was astonishing.

"That makes sense you'd remember the police showing up." Hawthorne was at least picking up some helpful information watching the young woman's routine for closing the ride. After shutting down the controls and leaving them locked, she'd headed through the staff entrance into the tunnel, where Hawthorne now trailed her for an interior check.

"Are you looking for garbage or people who didn't get out like they should have?"

The dyed stripe of blue in her short, bleached-blond hair glimmered in the soft lighting as she looked back at him.

"Both, I guess." She stepped up onto the shoreline display and retrieved something with her gloved hand. Dropping it in the trash bag she carried, she scanned the area.

"Did you do this check the night before Sam Ackerman was found?"

"Of course. It's required." She grabbed some more bits off the display.

"Right. Did you see anything unusual when you did it that night?"

"You mean like a dead body?" She smirked as she stepped down off the display. "No, I think I would've noticed that. But the police thought I must've missed it."

She headed up the path again, and Hawthorne followed behind. "I was thinking more like something to suggest a visitor hadn't left or a missing boat. Maybe more garbage than usual left somewhere?"

"You mean like extra beer cans?" Amusement was obvious in her tone as she detoured onto the display again. "Jaden gets all hung up on that. But he doesn't work nights. I've seen plenty of visitors get on my boats with more than one can per person." She held up the two cans she found on the shoreline to emphasize her point.

"Do you often see passengers who are intoxicated?"

She snorted. "Oh, yeah. The nighttime crowd tends to be older than the daytime. Fewer kids, unless you count the stupid teens with fake IDs who think they're something as soon as they get a sip of this stuff." She dropped another can into the bag, then returned to the path.

Christy didn't look much older than a teen herself, but given she said she'd worked the fair for five years, she must look young for her age.

"Did you see a teen who fit that description during the evening?"

Christy paused, facing him this time as she crossed her arms and looked away. "The police asked me if I'd seen him. They showed me a photo of the body." Her posture tensed.

"I'm sorry. That must've been difficult to see."

"It's weird in real life, you know?" Her gaze bounced to Hawthorne's face, then away.

"Yes, I know." Most people thought they knew about death and killings, thanks to the saturation of gore and violence on TV and in movies. But the reality was so different. And so much harder to forget.

She took in a visible breath and brought her attention back to Hawthorne. "Nobody asked me about drunk punks that night." She looked up to the right. "Yeah. I actually saw a group of young guys like that. There were like four or five of them together. I remember because they kept trying to hit on me." Her pale lips quirked. "Like they didn't know they were a bunch of drunk slobs. They weren't all super young. The guys trying to pick me up were older, closer to my age then."

"How old was that?"

"Like twenty-one maybe? But I remember thinking they'd brought their kid brothers along 'cause a couple were scrawnier and stayed in the background."

Scrawny teenagers? Could Sam have been one of them? From the autopsy details in the police report and the photos, tall and scrawny would be a fitting description of him.

"Honestly, I had my hands full with that one dude who thought he was God's gift to women." She laughed and put a hand on her hip as the gears of Hawthorne's mind turned.

She probably wouldn't have noticed Sam's face at all. Not well enough to ID him from a photo of a dead body the next morning. While working at the fair, Christy must have seen thousands more people than Hawthorne had seen in his longer lifetime. No way could she notice or retain most of them in her memory.

"Did the guys go on the ride?"

"Yeah. Two times." She rolled her eyes. "I was afraid they were going to stay all night."

"But they didn't?"

"No. Lucky for me."

"Do you know what they did on the ride?"

"Probably drank and threw their cans on the display. I can't really hear what anybody's doing inside. The music is pretty loud."

The music. Both of the times Hawthorne had visited the ride, it wasn't running. He hadn't thought about the loud music that must play all the time when the ride was operational. So the group could've done anything inside and only fellow passengers would have been within range to notice. "Did any of the other visitors complain about the guys?"

"No." She shrugged. "That near to closing, I think everybody's kind of in the same boat." She laughed. "Get it?"

He smiled. "Yeah. I get it."

"Well, I'd better get back to it."

"You've been really helpful, Christy. Thank you." He held out his hand.

She held up her gloved hands, one holding the garbage bag. "You really don't want to do that." She shook her head back and forth.

He chuckled. "Probably right. Thanks."

She gave him a thumbs up before swinging away to continue her pattern.

He backtracked to the staff entrance, his mind clicking through new questions. Had Sam gone to the fair with friends that night? If so, why wouldn't they have come forward after his death? Maybe because they knew his death wasn't an accident.

Hawthorne pushed open the door and stepped into the night air, many degrees cooler than the daytime shift he'd had today.

The crowds that had been there when he'd begun interviewing Christy had finally disappeared. Now only staff members finished up at rides and walked along the wide paths that suddenly looked unnecessarily massive and empty.

Had Christy just given Hawthorne a clue that no one had before now? That Sam maybe wasn't alone. That he may have come to the fair with someone. That someone might know what happened that night.

For the first time, Hawthorne was starting to think Rebekah could be on the right track. He'd never doubted the possibility, but the evidence and police documentation had all pointed to an accident as the most likely conclusion.

Now, the scales might be tipping in the other direction. But the only way to know for sure would be to find out if Sam had been with someone—or multiple *someones*. That would change everything.

"Hey, Brent." Hawthorne lifted his hand to hail a food vendor he'd questioned earlier.

The man in his thirties glanced at Hawthorne as he locked the door of his food stand. "Hey, man. I'm heading out for the night."

"I know. I don't want to keep you. Maybe we can walk out together?"

"Sure." Brent Vaughn shrugged as he swung the strap of a messenger bag over his shoulder and started at a slow pace along the blacktop, his tired posture showing fatigue.

"I just learned from a ride operator that there was a group of four, maybe five, young guys who were drunk that night."

Brent shot Hawthorne a skeptical sideways glance. "That describes a lot of the clientele on a Saturday, man."

"Fair enough. Does that mean you saw a group like that the night Sam died?"

Brent cast his gaze to the starry sky as he trudged along. "I don't know. I could have. But I really wouldn't remember."

Hawthorne stifled a sigh. "Okay. Thanks for your time. Let me know if anything comes back to you, will you? You have my card."

"Yeah. Sure thing."

"Have a good night." Hawthorne lengthened his stride as he waved and headed for a shortcut to the Public Safety Center. Veering behind the Twirling Swings ride and the Torch Rocket ride, he reached the narrow path that wound behind their underbellies. Pretty dark now that the ride's lights were off.

Hawthorne activated the flashlight on his smartphone so

he could walk without tripping over the cords that criss-crossed the blacktop.

How many other people would respond like Brent, with no memory of the group of guys that Christy had remembered? It wasn't likely Hawthorne would find someone who could identify any of them if the staff couldn't even remember the group at all. Especially now, two years later.

He blew out a breath. But he wouldn't give up. There were other ways to find out if Sam had been with a friend that night.

Images of the Best Life commune sprang to Hawthorne's mind. Made him want to shudder.

He'd really hoped this investigation for Rebekah wouldn't require him to go back there. He'd promised himself he would never go back. And that was a promise he still wanted to keep.

But who better than his family to know if Sam was alone or with a friend?

Rebekah had said Sam's mom still lived at Best Life, or at least she had when Rebekah left a year ago.

The police must have already asked Sam's mom that question, though. If she knew then that he'd gone with someone, she would have told the detectives. He couldn't see her hiding that information when the case involved her own son's death.

So Hawthorne probably didn't need to go and talk to her. He couldn't get in anyway. He'd been banned from Best Life since the moment he'd left.

He peeled off the narrow path and joined the wider one to walk the remaining distance to the Safety Center. He gladly abandoned thoughts of the cult to focus on his other mission. Hopefully, Butch would give him permission to view the security footage of the Skyride.

Or maybe Ted Renneth was the supervisor tonight. Either way, he didn't think they'd object to someone willing to spend hours reviewing the security footage leading up to the explosion that had killed their General Manager.

Jazz's face, the stunned horror in her eyes as he'd held her back from the body of her aunt, flashed in his memory, clenching his gut all over again. Didn't think he'd ever forget that sight.

Was the cult responsible for that? No pin had been found this time. They'd hardly leave a calling card unless they wanted the cult to get shut down, which Desmond Patch definitely did not.

And what about Jazz's flat tire tonight? He'd gotten a look at the puncture. The tire hadn't been slashed, but the clean slice looked very deliberate. Like a knife had been used to cut it intentionally. And Jazz had instantly started scanning the parking lot as if she'd suspected someone might be watching. Was she being followed? Harassed? Was it related to the sabotage at the fair?

Hawthorne steeled his jaw. If he found any hint on the security footage or anywhere else that the cult was involved in the fair incidents or endangering Jazz, he'd have all the more reason to revisit his old prison. The place that still held three members of his family captive.

And he'd personally make sure Desmond Patch finally paid for what he'd done.

SIXTEEN

"So someone followed you there?" Nev's full lips pressed into a frown as she watched Jazz across the kitchen table.

"You know I don't miss tails." Jazz sipped flavored decaf coffee from her green mug.

"Then how'd they know where you'd be?"

Jazz reached into her tight jeans pocket and pulled out the pieces of the small tracker she'd disabled. She plunked them on the table.

Nev's mouth dropped open.

"Found it inside the rear bumper."

"So that's what took you so long getting home."

"Well, that and waiting for Hawthorne to change the tire. Then I had to pretend to drive toward home and pull off somewhere so I could look for the tracker."

Nev's dark eyes studied Jazz's face. "You didn't tell him you thought the flat was intentional?"

Jazz lifted one shoulder and took another sip of the hot brew.

"Probably a good idea. How much do we really know about him, besides him being your favorite author?"

"Oh, it's not that I don't trust him." Jazz glanced at her friend. "I just didn't want him to think I was weird or be put off by all the danger we seem to get into."

Nev quirked an eyebrow. "He writes crime fiction." She lifted her mug shaped like a rottweiler head to her mouth. She paused before drinking. "Which could mean he's creepy, actually. You shouldn't just trust him automatically."

"Says the woman who doesn't trust men anyway."

Nev lowered her mug and opened her mouth.

Jazz held up a hand to stop the protest. "Except for Branson. I know." And that in itself was a wonder, given Nev's very good reason for not trusting men. If Jazz had been assaulted the way Nev had, she'd probably steer clear of all men for the rest of her life and be an absolute wreck. Sure was good to see Nev getting her courage back. And to see her so much happier these days. Even if that did mean Jazz had to lose some closeness with her BFF. So long as Nev was happy and at peace, that was the most important thing.

"I think we should ask Cora to tell Phoenix about this." Nev tapped her fingers on the table, making Flash lift his head from the floor and watch her suspiciously. "She might come back early if she knew you're still in danger."

"I don't think so."

Nev leaned forward, her eyebrows drawing together under the blue satin cap that covered her curls. "I don't know why you always think she doesn't like you."

"Because she doesn't."

"You know she act like that with everybody, right?"

Jazz hid a smile as Nev slipped into the Ebonics she only used with her family and Jazz. "You mean like she hates them?"

Nev laughed, leaning back as she lifted her mug again. "She don't act like she hates people. Just like..." Nev cast her gaze to the ceiling, "like she got better things to do than hold your hand."

Jazz narrowed her eyes, though humor twitched her lips. "I don't want her to hold my hand."

"You sure?" Nev grinned.

Jazz stuck out her tongue.

Nev laughed. "Good. 'Cause the boss ain't gonna do

that." Nev took another drink of her coffee and lowered the mug to the table, her mouth pressing into a more serious line. "But she can save your life. She take care of her own. The whole PK-9 family."

The PK-9 family. Another family Jazz wasn't a part of. Same with her biological family, the Army family she was supposed to be able to join, and now the Phoenix K-9 family. There really must be something wrong with her. Or maybe it was a jinx, a curse.

"You'll see when Phoenix gets back. She'll take care of this for you. Make sure you safe."

Like she'd done for Nevaeh? Jazz bit back the sarcastic retort. Though she didn't understand how Nev and the other girls at PK-9 could still act like Phoenix was so perfect at saving everyone when she'd failed to keep Nev from getting kidnapped by the same man who'd assaulted her years before.

Nev had almost been killed, even though Phoenix had known she was in danger and was supposedly taking care of it.

Jazz had been in security long enough to know that no one could prevent every attack or foresee every possibility. Phoenix was human just like everyone else, and Jazz didn't blame her for that. But she didn't get why the PK-9 agents still acted like their boss was superhuman and could fix everything when she'd nearly let Nev die.

"You don't think she'll help you." Nev delivered the words as a statement, not a question.

Jazz stared at the dark liquid in her mug and shrugged. "Doesn't matter. I'm cool on my own." A touch on her hand made her look up.

Nev covered Jazz's hand with her own. "I still got your back, girl."

Jazz dug out a smile. "I know." She turned her hand up to squeeze Nev's.

"And that's why I'm gonna look into this Hawthorne Emerson dude. I know you like him."

Jazz pulled her hand away and wrinkled her nose at Nev, not bothering to deny it.

"You even know how long he's here for?"

Jazz frowned. "No." He'd said he was at the fair for research. Did that mean he'd move on right after the fair ended in only nine days?

"He's probably taking off as soon as the fair is done." Nev's echo of her thoughts didn't help soothe the disappointment pooling in Jazz's chest.

"So? We could have a good time before he leaves." A great time, judging from how well they'd clicked tonight at Just Climb It.

Nev's eyebrows lifted. "That what you want? A fling?"

"Be better than anything I've had for a long time." But the pinch in Jazz's heart contradicted her words. Because it would end the same way as most things in her life. With rejection. Getting left behind.

"How do you know he isn't tied in with these three attacks on you?" Nev leveled a stare at Jazz.

"Only two attacks. One punctured tire."

Nev tilted her head to the side with an exasperated expression that said Jazz should knock it off and answer the question.

"Because I trust him. He's a good guy. Very gentlemanly and…"

"Hot? Fun? Oh, and hot?" Nev ticked off the qualities on her fingers.

Jazz laughed and stood, reaching to shove Nev's shoulder. "Yes. And he wants to put me in a novel."

"Ooh, that gotta mean he solid."

"I'm going to bed."

"Running away, you mean." Nev chuckled behind Jazz's retreating back.

"'Night." Jazz didn't look back as Flash caught up with her in the hallway.

"Sleep tight." Nev's voice called out the traditional last words they'd said to each other since their first sleepover at seven years old.

Jazz's smile faded as she reached the guest bedroom that she'd slept in so much it seemed more like her room than the one she had at her apartment. She sat on the edge of the bed, and Flash jumped onto the comforter.

"Beating me to the best spot, huh?" She scratched him behind the ears, but her thoughts were elsewhere.

The handsome face of Hawthorne, his grin and electric teal eyes, filled her vision. She did trust him. She was a good judge of people, and there was something about Hawthorne that put her at ease more than anyone she'd met before. Other than Nev, when they were seven-year-olds meeting for the first time on the school playground. There was something about him that reminded her of Nev.

No, not of Nev specifically, but of how Nev made her feel. At ease. Understood. Appreciated.

Even though she'd only known Hawthorne for three days, she felt more comfortable with him than anyone but Nev. Probably why she'd spilled her guts and her life story all in one conversation. Or was it two conversations?

She snorted and pushed off the bed, going to the dresser to pull out her pj's.

At least thinking about Hawthorne was a lot more pleasant than trying to figure out who was trying to kill her. The theory someone had only been trying to intimidate Aunt Joan by threatening Jazz was blown now that they'd tried again after Aunt Joan was...

The floral print blouse, Aunt Joan's body on the pavement, flashed before her eyes.

Was she really gone?

Jazz swallowed, leaning her hands against the top of the dresser for a moment. Just for a second, as the reality washed over her. She'd never have another chance to get Aunt Joan to like her.

The face of her dad, pale and lifeless on the stark white pillowcase, rose up in her mind like a flashback from a nightmare.

She'd never have another chance at a lot of things.

SEVENTEEN

"Thanks for meeting me." Hawthorne set the small basket holding his fully loaded hot dog on the picnic table and smiled at Jazz.

As if she would turn down a texted lunch invitation from her favorite author—who also happened to be the most gorgeous guy she'd ever been this close to. She kept that thought to herself and lifted her sunglasses to rest on top of her head—maybe so she could see him better—as she sat down with her corn dog and fries.

Flash panted heavily and dropped onto the blacktop. He apparently wanted to take immediate advantage of the shade under the canopy that covered the cluster of tables between food vendors.

She didn't blame him. The noon sun was punishing today with the humidity.

She swung her backpack off her shoulder and dug out Flash's water thermos. Unclipping his collapsible water bowl from the zipper pull, she filled the dish with water for him to enjoy while the humans ate.

"So you're just starting your shift?" Not that Jazz had been disappointed when she'd seen he wasn't on the morning shift duty roster with her today.

Hawthorne nodded, finishing chewing before he responded.

Looked like a model *and* had decent manners. Be still her heart. She held back her amusement as she took a small bite of her corn dog. Didn't usually eat lunch at the fair at all since finding a salad anywhere on the grounds was impossible, other than in the rabbit pens. She'd tack on another half hour to her run to burn off the fat and calories tonight.

"I switched shifts so I could go to church this morning."

The piece of corn dog stuck in her throat, and she coughed.

"You okay?" Hawthorne's eyebrows pulled together with genuine concern as he watched her.

She nodded and grabbed for her thermos on the table. She took a long swig of water, willing away the color she could feel heating her face. Hawthorne Emerson was a churchgoer? Pretty serious one if he'd rearranged his work schedule for it. Hopefully, that didn't mean he was as extreme as Cora, Bristol, or Sofia. Even Nevaeh was getting there.

A little church could be good. Made some people more moral and civilized. But then there were the people who only went to church to feel better about themselves and look good to others. Like Jazz's family. She tamped down the emotion rising in her chest. Better move off the church topic as quickly as possible. "You'll have burned your lunch break early with this."

"I don't mind." The smile he gave her sent a tingle down her spine. "I wanted to tell you what I found."

She blinked. Did he mean about the flat tire? Had he—

"I spent a couple hours last night going over the security footage from yesterday."

"You did?" Why did that spread warmth through her chest that had nothing to do with the summer heat?

"Yeah. On faster speed so I could get through it all." His gaze caught hers. "I said I wanted to help."

She smiled. "You did." And he'd remembered. About the fair, her aunt's death—things that mattered to her.

His lips curved slowly upward, and a twinkle glittered in his eyes as he watched her.

She was staring. Probably with a dumb, lovesick smile on her face.

She redirected her gaze to the sunglasses he'd set on the table. "What did you find?" Stuffing the corn dog in her mouth, she bit off a ridiculously large piece. Great. Now she probably looked like a chipmunk, cheeks stretched round while she tried to chew the glob of food.

His mouth twitched like he was holding back a grin as he glanced away and picked up his soda cup. "Well, the police have a copy, too, so I'm sure they'll go over it thoroughly. But I did observe some things. Your fellow agent, the explosive detection team..." He paused like he was waiting for her to give him a name.

"Bristol." Jazz managed to mumble the word around the corn dog she was still trying to mash down.

"Bristol. She checked all the cars on the Skyride yesterday morning starting at seven." He took a quick drink through the straw, then set the cup down. "After that, the ride operators at both Skyride docking buildings did a safety inspection on each car before opening the ride at eight."

Jazz finally swallowed the last of the corn dog. "So someone would've had to put the bomb in the pod after the ride opened."

Hawthorne nodded. "Looks that way. The ride operators were on camera during their entire inspection at each of the buildings. They'd have to be really stupid, or incredibly brilliant at sleight of hand, to have placed a bomb in one of the cars while on camera. I didn't see them do or hold anything that looked suspicious."

"What about the rest of the time leading up to the explosion?"

"Only visitors got in and out of the cars. The ride operators physically helped some visitors on and off, but not your aunt. And that would've been too risky of a moment to try to plant a bomb anyway. Not enough time and too many witnesses."

"So the bomb had to be planted by one of the visitors." Jazz took another drink from her water thermos.

"They had the best opportunity. A long ride from one side of the fairgrounds to the other. That would be enough time to plant a bomb and hide it under the seats where the next visitors wouldn't be likely to spot it."

"Then we need to check out all the visitors from eight in the morning until the explosion? That has to be thousands of people."

"Yep." Hawthorne lifted his blond eyebrows. "I never knew how many people could go on a Skyride in a few hours until I watched the footage."

"I know, right?" Jazz glanced at the crowds of people who even now were walking past the tables and lining up at food stands. "I wish there was a way to recognize if any of the Skyride passengers were members of that cult you told me about." She turned her head back toward Hawthorne. "My aunt told me, just that morning, that the guy who leads the cult..." She searched her memory for the name.

"Desmond Patch."

"Right." Jazz pointed a finger toward Hawthorne. "Desmond Patch. He apparently made a public statement condemning the fair two years ago when a teen from the cult died in an accident here. Did you hear about that?"

Hawthorne nodded. "I'm familiar with it, yes. And I'm not surprised about Patch. Like I said when we found the pin, the whole cult is taught to be against the fair." He pressed his lips into a line and glanced away, almost like he was scanning the crowd, looking for something. Was he checking to see if someone was listening to them?

He returned his gaze to Jazz and leaned forward, his forearms braced on the wooden table. "I looked for people from the cult on the security footage." His voice lowered enough that she had to press in to hear him above the noise of the fair. "But I didn't see anyone I recognized."

She straightened. "Recognized? You mean from the pin or their white clothes?"

He paused, his eyes seeming to search her face for something. Then he finally answered. "No, I mean from having seen them before. I—" Hesitation halted his voice for the first time since she'd met him. "I grew up in the cult. Well, from the time I was twelve."

She couldn't have been more shocked than if someone from the crowds passing by had suddenly darted over to slap her. How could that be true? He was a celebrity. Wouldn't everyone know if he'd grown up in a cult? "Are you serious?" The question came out before she'd thought it through.

But his mouth relaxed from the serious line it had held before. Maybe not the worst thing to say, after all. "Sadly, yes. I didn't want to join. I was forced into it, kicking and screaming. I hated every minute I was there."

Jazz stared at him, trying to fathom this normal man—but very successful and brilliant author—having been in a cult. He made it sound like it was all in the past, at least. So maybe he was as normal as he appeared. "Your family left eventually?"

His lips pulled downward in a frown. "No. Not all of us. I got out as soon as I became a legal adult." His gaze lowered toward his hands that he brought loosely together on the table. "My younger brother and my baby sister left after I did, when they each turned eighteen. My other sister and parents are still there."

He flattened one of his hands on the table and seemed to be staring at it. His voice had stayed even as he'd told the facts. But tension radiated off him like the heat emanating from the pavement.

Hawthorne was pretty much an orphan. Like her. Just in a different way. "I'm sorry. That must be really hard."

He took in a breath and straightened, giving her another glimpse of those amazing teal eyes. "Thank you. I didn't mean to dump all that."

She lifted one shoulder. "You were sharing it. And I'm honored you did."

His mouth lifted at one side as he watched her. Was he surprised? Pleased? Or just trying to figure her out?

Either way, they could probably both do with switching to something a little less personal. "You said you didn't recognize anyone in the footage?"

"No. But I wouldn't know all the people at the cult now. I'm sure many have joined since I left thirteen years ago." He lifted his soda cup and took a sip. "The police have a huge suspect pool to deal with." He took another bite of his hot dog.

"Well, they usually want to look at motive, and the cult has that." Jazz tapped her finger on the smooth side of her thermos. "If they're trying to sabotage the fair, a bomb on the Skyride would fit as the next target after the Ferris wheel and the Giant Slide."

"True." Something in Hawthorne's response, maybe the note of hedging in his voice, made her pause.

"You think the motive could be different? Not sabotage?"

"Well..." He wiped his mouth and dropped the napkin on the table. "If this were one of my novels, I might have someone disguise an intentional murder as random sabotage."

Jazz stared at him. "You mean like someone wanting to intentionally kill Aunt Joan? Not sabotage the ride?"

"Or someone with her could have been the intended target. Gretchen Mehl was in the car with her and your uncle and Albert Ferrey were right next to that car. All board members. Plus, your uncle is running for governor. That's another possible motive for him to be the target."

A little thrill buzzed behind Jazz's ribs. It was like getting to see her favorite author in action, creating another fabulous mystery before her eyes. "That does sound exactly like a twist in a Carson Steele novel."

Hawthorne grinned. "Which probably means it's fiction and not likely to be true in real life."

"I don't know. It sounds plausible. They could've known Aunt Joan would go on the Skyride, since she does every year when the board visits."

"But the bomber couldn't have had any way of knowing which car she'd ride in. Or which one your uncle or other board members might ride in. Not to mention the specific timing."

"True." Jazz nodded. "And my uncle doesn't always ride with her. Sometimes he takes a different ride or doesn't even go on the tour. He used to have appointment conflicts sometimes. I remember Aunt Joan fighting with him about it."

"Right. A lot of holes in that theory." Hawthorne smiled.

"I know you could make it work in a book." Jazz grinned. "And I'd love to read it."

"I'll be sure to eliminate all the holes first. And give you credit for helping me." He winked.

Goodness. A bolt of electricity shot through her torso, stopping her heart for a split second before it jumpstarted again. If he really decided to turn on the charm, she would be a serious goner. If she wasn't already.

A beep sounded from her watch, just in time to save her from swooning. "Oops. Lunch break is up." She silenced the alert and bent over to grab Flash's bowl.

"Hey, can I see you again?"

She nearly dropped the bowl as she jerked her head up to Hawthorne. Had he really just said that? To her?

He held up a hand. "Sorry, that came out wrong." A cute little smile curved his lips even as she inwardly willed her pounding pulse to calm down. "I just wondered if I could pick your brain again. You know, find out more about you for the heroine I'm writing."

Right. His books. The heroine he wanted to model after her. His interest was professional, not personal. Her heart rate slowed only somewhat with the reminder.

"I didn't know if you'd be free today? Maybe I could buy you that dinner. I get off at eight."

An idea Nev would no doubt call one of Jazz's devious

schemes formed in her mind. But even if Hawthorne only wanted to meet for professional reasons, that didn't mean a girl couldn't make the most of the situation. "I'll cook you dinner. At my place."

"I can't let you do that. It's too much trouble. And I'm already taking up your time with my research questions."

"Are you kidding me?" She waved her hand at him with a smile as she stood and gathered her trash. "Cooking dinner for the famous Hawthorne Emerson at my apartment will be something I can boast about for a long time." Especially if she managed to romance him with candles and music.

He laughed. "I doubt most people would be impressed."

"You're being modest. And besides, I want to do this as a thank-you for changing my flat tire."

"Which you could've done yourself." He grinned as he followed her and Flash to the trash can.

She shrugged her shoulders and dropped in the garbage. "Like you said, I needed the break." She met his gaze. "Will you come?"

"Yes. And thank you."

"Wait until after you taste my cooking to thank me." She cast him a grin as she hoisted her backpack and slipped her arms through the straps.

He quirked a teasing eyebrow. "Do I need insurance for this?"

"No, but I might require you to sign a waiver."

He laughed, that warm sound that thrilled her to her toes. "Sounds like my kind of adventure."

"Perfect. I'll text you my address."

"See you then, Jazz Lamont."

Something in the way he said the parting words, then turned and walked into the crowd, made Jazz feel like she was in a romance novel, willing her dashing hero to return as soon as possible.

But when she headed the other way with Flash, reality hit her. She wasn't supposed to go to her apartment at all right now. Because of the shooting in the parking lot.

Oh, well. She shrugged off the hindrance and blazed a trail with Flash through the thick humidity and crowding people.

She had to go to the apartment to get the photos for her goodwill visit to Uncle Pierce anyway. She'd just scope it out, clean it up from the way she'd left it, and check all the closets for lurking visitors.

When a girl was going to host the famous Hawthorne Emerson, the last thing she needed was for a hitman to shoot up her dinner.

EIGHTEEN

"Do you remember anything strange that night?"

Dan Harris straightened from pulling a soda can out of the vending machine in the hallway of the Public Safety Center. "No, it was a lot of the usual. Some personal property thefts—phones and things. Lost items. One little girl got separated from her parents, but we found them." The security guard flipped the tab of the soda can and took a swig.

Hawthorne pretended he wanted a bag of chips from the machine, though he'd only come over to interview Harris. According to the old duty roster he'd gotten from Human Resources, Harris was one of three security guards who were there the night of Sam's death and were on staff again this year. "What about a group of rowdy, possibly intoxicated young men?"

"A group?" Harris rested a hand on his hip and leveled a curious look at Hawthorne. "You mean like a gang?"

"No. I don't think so. Just four or five guys who might've been particularly noisy and obnoxious." Hawthorne slipped coins into the machine and pressed the button for the bag of chips. "A ride operator said they gave her a hard time that night. I thought she might not be the only one who had a run in with them."

"You know..."

Hawthorne nearly snapped his head in the guard's direction but forced himself to retrieve the chips calmly before looking at Harris.

"I think that was the night there were some punks like that."

"Less talk, more patrol, men." Butch's gruff voice drew Hawthorne's attention to the head of security. He stood in the doorway of his office, which seemed strategically placed by the vending machine. Perfect way for him to catch any slackers.

"Hey, Butch. You remember that night the Ackerman kid died?"

Hawthorne would have to find a way to thank Harris for the assist. He hadn't been able to think of a way to casually bring up the incident to Butch. But he was listed as having been the supervisor on duty that night. Given his greater expertise and seniority, Butch might be able to shed more light on the events of the evening than anyone.

"Of course. Nobody here will forget it." Butch crossed his arms over his thick torso. "Didn't exactly win our security team any awards."

Harris winced. "Right." He aimed his index finger at Hawthorne. "Emerson here was asking about it."

"Why is that?" Butch turned his dark eyes on Hawthorne, more than a little suspicion housed in them.

Hawthorne didn't blame him. Like Butch had observed, the reputation of the fair's security had taken a hit that night. And Butch probably took heat personally since he'd been the supervisor on duty. But the police investigation hadn't found him or anyone else negligent. And clearly the man had kept his job.

"You remember. He's a mystery writer." Harris smiled at Hawthorne. "Doing research, right?"

Hawthorne nodded, focusing on Butch instead. "I admit I'm intrigued by any suspicious deaths. Never know when they'll end up working as inspiration for one of my novels."

"I don't know much about writers. I'll take your word for

it." Butch's features relaxed into the friendliest expression he seemed to have, still far short of a smile. "But there's nothing suspicious about this death. The police ruled it was an accident. No fault of ours."

"Oh, I know. I read the report." Hawthorne opened the chip bag for something to do that would make him look nonchalant. "I'm just curious. Occupational hazard, I'm afraid. One of the ride operators said she'd been harassed a little by a group of four or five young men that night. I was just asking Harris here if he remembered them."

"Yeah." Harris looked from Hawthorne to Butch. "It sounds like those punks I had to send away from the rifle sharpshooting game. They were mad at the operator. Accused him of cheating." Harris returned his gaze to Hawthorne. "I only remember because I had to deal with them *again* later on at the Skyride. They were hanging out of the pods, disobeying the safety guidelines. They were all pretty drunk."

Confirmation of Christy's story. At least that a group of guys like that had been at the fair. "Can you describe them?"

Harris swiped a hand over his close-cropped black hair. "Man, that was a long time ago. They were young. Early twenties, I'd say. A couple were tall. Others medium height. Midwestern accents like they were from here."

"Anyone younger in the group? Like a teenager?" Hawthorne's breath slowed as he waited for the answer.

"Not that I remember. But I can't say for sure." Harris glanced at Butch. "You remember?"

Butch uncrossed his arms and landed his large hands on his hips. "I never saw them. I recall your report at the end of the night. I was inside pretty much all night that shift. Paperwork. Except when I had to oversee arresting a purse snatcher over by the cattle barns."

Nowhere near the midway or the rides, so it made sense Butch wouldn't have seen the rowdy guys.

"You could ask Barry Greer. He was on that night, too." Butch's suggestion signaled approval Hawthorne hadn't expected.

"Thanks." Barry was next on Hawthorne's list to interview if he could get a shift at the same time as the other security guard.

Butch made a show of looking at his thick watch. "How long is your break?"

"Just long enough to finish a soda." Harris downed the rest of his drink and lowered the can with a grin at Butch. "See you at the circus, Emerson." The guard punched Hawthorne's arm and headed up the hallway.

"Thanks for your help, Butch." Hawthorne met the supervisor's watchful gaze. "Great idea to bring on more security and overlap shifts for more coverage since the incidents."

Butch's features held steady. He apparently wasn't the kind of guy to be flattered by compliments.

"Do you think it'll be enough to avoid more sabotage?"

"You bet it will." Butch's voice dropped lower as his thick eyebrows slashed downward. "I'm not about to let those wackos put me out of a job."

"You mean Best Life?"

Butch took in a rough breath that seemed to grind in his throat. "Who else? The police are finally looking into them, now that somebody died. They'll get what's coming to them."

"I hope you're right." Fire stirred in Hawthorne's belly and traveled up to his chest at Butch's words. Desmond Patch stopped? Hawthorne's parents set free? If only it could be true. Could this be God's way of bringing justice to Patch and the cult at last?

"In the meantime, we need to keep this place locked up tighter than Alcatraz." Butch stared at Hawthorne.

"Ah. So I'd better get out there." Hawthorne gave him a half smile and walked up the hallway, folding down the top of the bag of chips he hadn't touched.

If God was finally going to judge the cult that had robbed Hawthorne of his family, he wanted to be part of it.

"You did not just say you're going to your apartment." Nevaeh's statement, part sarcasm and part dare made Jazz wince.

She turned her SUV into the parking lot of the apartment building. "Come on, girl. Don't make me regret being so honest. I'm calling to check in just like you wanted me to."

"Yeah, while you're driving right into the hitman's trap." Exasperation added volume to Nev's voice that came over the speakerphone.

Jazz glanced at her cell in the dashboard holder as if she could see her bestie that way. But she wasn't about to switch to video at a moment like this when Nev was already ready to give her a tongue lashing. "First off, we don't know there is a hit or any hitman after me."

Nev snorted. "No, everybody gets shot at and jumped every time they go out at night."

"Sof probably does."

"Don't try to distract me." But Nev couldn't hide her snicker that came across the line.

Jazz grinned. "You know I'm right." She slipped out of the SUV and got Flash from the back before Nev could insist she stay away from the apartment. "And I'm here already anyway. It's even daylight." The advantage of long days in the summer.

It was a few minutes after six p.m. but didn't look like evening yet. The sun was shining, clearly lighting every parked vehicle in the lot. "I can see everything, and there's nobody around. I'd say you can stay on the line with me, but you're supposed to be on patrol."

"Girl, Alvarez and I can do this blindfolded."

"And while talking on the phone?" Jazz smiled as she entered the building and went to the elevator.

"Just shut up and tell me when you get to your apartment."

Jazz laughed. "A little hard to do both at the same time."

"Don't make me come there and make you mind, girl."

The mock discipline in Nev's tone kept the smile on Jazz's face.

"Well, you'll be happy to know there's no one in the elevator with Flash and me."

"You sure?" Sarcasm laced Nev's question.

"Flash is sure, so that's good enough for me." Jazz looked down at the handsome Malinois who seemed to grin up at her.

"I should be talkin' to him instead of you."

"Not a bad idea." The elevator doors slid open, and Jazz stepped out with Flash. "Okay, I'm at my apartment." She eyed her apartment door about sixteen feet up the hallway.

"Like literally at your apartment or almost?"

"Um, you do realize I've gone into my apartment hundreds of times without your supervision, right?"

"And how many of those times did you get jumped?"

Jazz rolled her eyes with a laugh as she slowed by the door. "Not enough to—"

Flash let out a rumble at her side.

The door flung open.

NINETEEN

Lucky her apartment door opened inward.

The two men inside had to stand a couple feet back as they swung the door open for the ambush.

Those feet would cost them the fight.

The front guy raised his gun, but Flash launched his whole body into him before he could fire, knocking him back.

The other thug scrambled to avoid being taken down with his buddy and rushed toward Jazz, lifting his Glock.

Jazz's knife had already left her hand. The blade pierced the guy's gun arm.

He dropped the Glock with a squeal and ducked through the doorway, skirting past Jazz.

"Flash, *hier*." She eyed the fleeing thug as he ran down the hallway. Flash would love a good sprint even more than she would.

Flash hurried to answer her call, his eyes filled with excitement as he looked up at her. Nothing like taking down the bad guys. "Flash, *fass*." She indicated the fleeing thug with her hand.

The K-9 tore up the hall, easily catching the thug and detaining him with teeth.

Movement out the corner of her eye caught her attention.

The man Flash had left on the floor of the apartment was

getting up and stupidly reaching for his Glock a few feet away.

"Don't even think about it." She leveled her Sig at him.

Huh. Same guy she'd nailed with her knife outside the convenience store. Nice of Flash to have bitten his alternate arm instead of the shoulder she'd stabbed. And unless her memory was playing tricks on her, Flash's captive in the hallway was his partner from that night, too.

Now maybe she could get some answers. At least about who wanted her dead.

Keeping her gun trained on the guy who gave her a wide-eyed stare while holding his freshly wounded arm, Jazz pulled out her phone.

No sirens or people peeking out from the other apartments, so this fight must've been quiet enough not to wake the neighbors or prompt calls to the police. Looked like she'd have to bring them in herself to take the thugs off her hands.

She glanced at the time on her phone before dialing 911. Great. She still needed to find her old photos and take them to Uncle Pierce before she could possibly get ready for dinner.

But as she put the phone to her ear, she looked past the man on the floor and saw the rest of her apartment.

Her books were scattered all over the floor, her bookshelves broken, table upturned, sofa pillows tossed all over. Irritation flamed in her chest.

"Why in the world did you have to trash the place?" She glared at the thug on the floor. "Did you get bored waiting to kill me? Next time, I'll just give you my schedule. And if you damaged even one page of my Hawthorne Emerson boo—"

The 911 operator picked up, and Jazz filled her in on the situation—once the woman got over her shock that Jazz had a protection K-9 assist in the apprehension of the criminals.

But all the while, Jazz was scrambling to figure out what to do about dinner with Hawthorne. Thanks to the state of her apartment, it looked like she'd have to move the non-date to a restaurant. Hopefully a very romantic, date-like restaurant.

Sometimes this security business sure interfered with a girl's love life.

"Heard you're going to have dinner with my girl tonight."

Hawthorne paused under the Skyride cars overhead and turned toward the female voice behind him.

Nevaeh William's distinctive curly hair and the muscled rottweiler at her side made for a pair that was hard to miss as they walked his way.

He smiled. He could tell when he'd met her earlier that Nevaeh and Jazz must be good friends. Jazz had apparently told her about their plans. "That's right. She texted me a little while ago to switch it to a restaurant. She said her apartment's a mess, but I find that hard to believe. She seems very put together."

"Oh, it's a mess all right." Nevaeh stopped near Hawthorne.

"Really?" He couldn't tell from her peculiar tone if she was joking or holding back some secret.

"Yeah. She got a little..." the woman's big, dark eyes gleamed in the waning light of dusk, "surprised when she stopped by her apartment. She said a restaurant will be easier since she has to run some errands yet."

"Sounds perfect to me."

Nevaeh tilted her head slightly, her curls leaning to follow the motion as she stared at him. "Is this a date?"

Whoa. The woman didn't pull any punches. "Uh." He shifted away from some people who brushed past as he scrambled for the safest answer. An automatic *no* leaped to the tip of his tongue, but maybe that wasn't what Nevaeh wanted to hear. Still, he had to be honest. "No. I only want to find out more about Jazz."

"Right. For the heroine in your new book." Her lips held a line as disbelieving as her expression.

"Yes." He tried a smile. "Honest, that's really all it's about."

"You do this often?"

"Do what?"

"Feature real women in your books." One of her hands slid to her hip. "Take them to dinner and all that." The skepticism in her voice made his behavior sound akin to a serial killer setting up his next victim.

He lifted his hands, palms facing her. "Absolutely not. This is the first time I've ever met anyone I'd like to be the protagonist in a book. First time I've met anyone as impressive and amazing as Jazz."

"Hm." The short sound somehow escaped the woman's sealed lips. Her eyes stayed narrowed as she watched him.

At least Jazz had someone looking out for her. Hawthorne should include a character like that in his series. A close friend to have Jazz Lamont's back and be her confidant. Unless she'd be better off as a loner, having to face all her battles alone.

"Jazz said you switched shifts today to go to church." Nevaeh's unexpected statement jerked Hawthorne's attention from his mental plotting. "True?"

Wow, they must talk to each other a lot. And tell each other everything. "Yes."

"Why?"

"You mean, why did I go to church?"

"Sure." She held his gaze with a look that seemed to threaten some kind of consequence if he answered wrongly.

"Because I'm a Christian, and going to church to worship is a priority in my life."

Her eyes relaxed a fraction at the corners. "Good answer." Then she cracked a startling smile. "I'm a Christian, too."

"Oh. I'm glad to hear that." Did that mean Jazz was a believer? He hadn't expected that.

"Jazz isn't, though."

Too bad. Disappointment dropped into his stomach. She didn't have to be a Christian to be the model for his heroine. But it was sad for her that she didn't know the Lord. He should pray for her.

"Does that make a difference?" Nevaeh's smile gave way to a serious expression again.

"You mean in wanting to feature her in my books? No."

"I mean your interest in her."

"I'm not interested…romantically." For some frustrating reason, he tripped on the word. As if he didn't mean it or felt embarrassed about it.

Nevaeh's eyebrows lifted. Was she insulted or simply didn't believe him?

He kept going, hoping to convey sincerity and confidence. "Not that she isn't worthy of that, of course. I'm just not in the market for that kind of relationship with anyone. But if I were, she would be a great option."

He smothered a cringe. A great option? Not exactly a flattering thing to say about the woman's friend.

"Yeah. She's terrific. But you aren't sticking around here anyway, right? After the fair is over."

"Correct. I'm headed to Boise next."

"Boise?"

He nodded. "Thinking of setting a story there."

"Hey, security." A male voice drew their attention to a young guy hurrying toward them, darting around passing people. He wore a ride operator's yellow T-shirt. Looked like the operator Hawthorne had seen in the security footage of the east Skyride building. Which was near where Hawthorne and Nevaeh were standing.

"I found this by my control box in there." He thumbed toward the Skyride building as he held out a piece of paper with his other hand. "I thought I should probably turn it over to security."

Hawthorne glanced from the guy's tense features to the folded paper. He took it, opening the piece that was about half the size of a normal full sheet of paper.

His gaze fell on typed words.

The evil fair must be closed. Or more will die.

Hawthorne's gut clenched as he skimmed the rest of the page.

A familiar logo and words crossed the bottom. *Best Life Community.*

The police would definitely want to see this. Maybe Desmond Patch's ego had finally driven him far enough for him to be stopped.

Unless they were already too late. Another sabotage or murder could already be set in motion.

TWENTY

Jazz scanned the old mansion as she followed the longtime housekeeper, Mrs. Bates, to the study. Some rich people liked new houses with modern décor. Not the Cracklens. They were old school. Nothing but the classics. Classic, old-world opulence and luxury.

And class. Always class.

That taste was reflected in the interior she knew so well. The marble floor that shined in the foyer beneath a large, low-hanging chandelier. The long staircase that curved along one wall and climbed to the balcony that led to the bedrooms.

The housekeeper led Jazz through the parlor, the library, past the billiard room, and to the study where her uncle had spent much of his time when Jazz was a child. The billiard room and study were the least familiar to her since she'd rarely been allowed in them.

Aunt Joan hadn't wanted Jazz around much either. She'd usually sent Jazz away to her bedroom anytime Jazz dared talk or hang around. But Uncle Pierce had been off-limits completely. Aunt Joan told her never to disturb him. And Jazz had never wanted to. He'd seemed as unapproachable and disapproving as...well, her dad.

The memories of her uncle's grim demeanor increased,

tensing her insides as Mrs. Bates stopped by the closed study door. "You may go in now."

But did Jazz want to? She looked down at the shoebox in her hands, second-guessing her goodwill gesture. It had seemed like a nice idea to give Uncle Pierce some photos she had of Aunt Joan from years ago, when Jazz had been a kid. Aunt Joan may not have been the loving mother figure Jazz had longed for, but she was still family. And she'd taught Jazz some life lessons along the way. Mostly how to sit up straight and cross her legs when wearing skirts.

Aunt Joan was the only sort of mother Jazz had known. Seemed like she should try to honor her memory somehow.

"He's expecting you." Mrs. Bates lifted thin eyebrows above the disapproving gaze Jazz remembered too well. Usually delivered when she'd found Jazz swiping a book from the library or when Jazz had gotten muddy playing in the yard.

"Right." Though he was only expecting her now because when Jazz had shown up at the front door, Mrs. Bates went to check with him before letting Jazz inside. "Thanks."

Jazz took in a breath and stepped toward the door. She could do this. She'd faced real-life combat for goodness sakes. And Uncle Pierce had actually defended the PK-9 Agency the other day in front of Aunt Joan. Maybe that meant he was positively inclined toward Jazz and her work now.

She gripped the knob and pushed open the door. "Uncle Pierce?"

The study looked just the way her vague memory recollected. Though maybe not quite so large. Her childhood perspective had remembered the desk that stood toward the back of the room as the size of a large bed, and the floor-to-ceiling shelves had seemed like giants leaning toward her, ready to chase her from the room.

But in reality, the study wasn't oversized and didn't seem ominous.

Even with Uncle Pierce sitting at the reasonably large desk. "Jazz." He stood and walked around the desk.

She instinctively paused, her reflexes prepping for a threat.

But he smiled.

She could count on one hand the times she'd seen him smile at home. And none of them had ever been aimed at her.

He stopped in front of her with the smile that looked genuine. It was almost warm, actually, with a bit of crinkle at the corners of his green eyes.

She'd sometimes wondered as a child if she'd inherited her eye color from him since no one else in her family had green eyes. But Aunt Joan had explained, with no small degree of irritation, that he wasn't her blood relative and therefore not her real uncle.

"Welcome home."

A breeze could've knocked Jazz over as she stared at him. Had he really said that? And with a kind smile?

The words shot a pulse of warmth through her that ballooned in her heart. If only the sentiment were true.

His smile dimmed slightly as he watched her.

Something in her expression must have shown her surprise or disbelief.

"I know you weren't always as happy here as we would've liked. It was hard for you, being away from your dad, and we didn't always know how to help you with that."

Love and acceptance would've worked. She held in the comeback. If Uncle Pierce was going to start being nice, she didn't want to ruin it by insulting him.

He rubbed the back of his neck with his hand. "I was so busy with work, I'm afraid I didn't do a good job stepping into your dad's shoes and being what you needed."

Was Uncle Pierce apologizing? She fought to keep her mouth from hanging open.

"I'm sorry for that."

Wow. There it was. An apology. Maybe the world would stop turning next.

"Losing Joan…your aunt…has made me see some things for the first time." He turned his head away. "Family is everything." His voice thickened.

Was he about to cry? No way.

He sniffed as he turned and headed back to his desk. "Here I am, going on like a lonely old man. Please," he gestured to the chair on the front side of his desk, "have a seat and tell me what brings you by."

She cautiously walked to the leather armchair and sat. "I thought you might like some old photos I have of Aunt Joan." She scooted forward and set the shoebox on the edge of his desk. "A few of us at the fair with some vendors. And there are others of the time she directed our school choir when Sandra and Crystal were in it."

He reached for the box and opened it, sifting through the photos. A smile lifted his mouth as he brought his gaze up to her. "These are wonderful. Thank you, Jazz." His attention lowered to a photo in his hand. "It's hard to see her. But comforting, too."

A lump formed in Jazz's throat at the obvious weight of grief in his voice. He and Aunt Joan had argued a lot when Jazz had stayed with them, but overall, she knew they were a team. Both career-driven and focused on success for their daughters and themselves. They stuck together more years than most married couples these days. And they'd definitely made something of themselves and their children.

Their daughters must be coming for the funeral. And to be there for their dad. He'd need support. More than Jazz had realized until she saw him.

He was so changed by the loss. Even his posture was different, the usually proud stature slumped now, like he was weighted down by the burden of grief. But maybe the girls were already there, helping with funeral preparations.

"Are Sandra and Crystal here?"

"No. Not yet." He returned the photos to the box and

pressed the lid down. "They aren't sure when they'll arrive. Possibly Wednesday." He met her gaze, a glint of pain in his eyes. "The funeral is scheduled for Saturday. I hope you'll be able to come."

Hadn't thought she'd be invited. But the Cracklens did always like to keep up appearances, so maybe that was why she was being included. She was Aunt Joan's biological family, after all.

"These photos might make a nice addition to the funeral." He rested his hand on the lid of the box. "Sandra and Crystal are considering a commemorative display for Joan. Perhaps they'd like to add a personal element with these." A small, sad smile settled on his face. "Do you have other items, maybe from Lawrence, that we could include? He may have kept mementos from their childhood."

"I don't know. I haven't really looked through Dad's things yet." And she didn't plan to, now at two years after his passing or twenty years later. Much easier to move on and try to forget.

"I'd be happy to help you look." Uncle Pierce's eyes filled with understanding as he watched her. "Though I know how it is with loss. Thanks to this experience." He winced and dropped his stare to the desktop. "Things you didn't think would be hard seem impossible when you lose someone you love."

He focused on Jazz again. "I don't mean to pressure you to do something you're not ready to yet. But it would mean a lot. There might be photos of Joan's childhood or other keepsakes that could be precious to me and her girls."

The pain in his eyes, the desperation to find comfort somewhere, twisted her heart. "Okay."

"You mean you'll let me help you look?"

"Sure. I guess."

"Thank you, Jazz." Warmth she'd never heard in his voice before softened his usually commanding tone. "Let me buy you dinner. I can bring takeout to your place, and we can walk down memory lane together."

Walk down memory lane. Sharing family history with a member of her family. Was that what normal people did? Longing tugged at her heart.

But Uncle Pierce wouldn't want to go to her tiny middle-class apartment. And did he even eat takeout? Nerves shooed away the dreamy spell. "Um, my apartment isn't much. And it's a total mess right now." Thanks to the thugs who'd just trashed it and were now warming the inside of a jail cell.

"No problem." He tapped his smartphone that lay on the desk and scrolled through something on the screen. "Let's make it two days from now. Tuesday at noon. I'll bring lunch." His commanding tone was back, though colored with a friendliness that she didn't remember.

"Okay. I guess that works." Since she had zero social life outside of Nevaeh. And maybe a handsome famous author, if she was lucky. Only problem was her patrol shift at the fair until four. But she could trade shifts with Sof and take the late night. She kept the complication to herself. Uncle Pierce didn't like complications.

"Wonderful." He set down his phone and stood.

She started to stand, too, but he waved her back down with his hand.

"Please, don't leave yet." He rounded the desk and sat on the front edge of it, close to Jazz's chair. "I need to tell you something." His eyes seemed serious and pensive as he aimed them at her. "Did you know your aunt wanted to have you over for brunch?"

A pang shot through Jazz's chest at the memory. The hope it had given her, for a moment. She nodded. "The day after she...died."

He nodded, the set of his mouth sad, as if he were holding back more grief. "She shared with me that since you were living close to us now, as an adult, she felt we should reconnect. She reminded me that family is important and should always be a priority. And with our daughters married and living in other states, I think she hoped you might be able to take their place, a little bit, in our lives."

The lump growing in Jazz's throat plunged behind her ribs and lodged there. Had she really? Maybe that was why Aunt Joan had been so much kinder and reminisced about the fair with Jazz that morning before...

"I admit, I didn't completely understand what she was thinking, though I heartily agreed we should reconnect with you." He looked off to the side. "But now that she's...gone." The thickness returned to his voice. He kept his gaze averted. "I understand what she meant." He drew in a shaky breath. Then he ran a hand over his eyes before dragging his gaze back to Jazz.

Was that moisture lingering at the corner of his eye? Her chest clenched. Poor Uncle Pierce.

"You never know when you'll lose the family you have." He leaned forward and held his hand out to Jazz.

She stared at it. Did he want her to put her hand in his? The idea was beyond her comprehension. She glanced up at his face.

"You cannot put a price on family. And I want to make sure I don't lose any more of mine. Including you, Jazz." He moved his hand slightly closer.

Still not sure if he wanted her to, she reached out her hand and slowly set it in his. He closed his fingers around her hand in a soft, safe wrap like a dad might do with his daughter he loved.

Her heart swelled, even as she tried to tell it to stop. He was grieving. Hurting. He wasn't himself.

And at any moment, when the grief wore off or he got over the shock, he'd return to gruff, standoffish Uncle Pierce who cared only about his blood relatives and his career.

She'd be thrown out in the cold again.

But as he looked at her with the wound of loss and mourning in his eyes, she couldn't worry about protecting herself. No one was there for her when she'd lost loved ones. She couldn't turn her back on Uncle Pierce in the same situation. If he wanted her support, she'd try to give it to him. At least until his daughters came home or he went back to his old self. Whichever came first.

Even as she concocted the pragmatic reasoning in her mind, her gaze fell on his hand holding hers. Emotion she shouldn't indulge swelled in her heart. This must be what belonging felt like.

Maybe she could get a little comfort out of Uncle Pierce needing her, too, while it lasted.

***

"I like your choice of restaurants." Jazz hit Hawthorne with her big green eyes across the candlelit table.

He smiled. But if he'd known the setting of the highly rated Italian restaurant was so romantic, he probably would've picked somewhere else for dinner. "Well, I'm sure it isn't as nice as your apartment would've been." He glanced around at the elegant tables. Couples occupied most of them.

And Jazz had probably known what kind of restaurant this was. That would explain the burgundy dress she wore that highlighted her feminine curves perfectly. She looked stunning. But for a date.

He thought he'd been clear this was business. Research.

Nevaeh's questions cycled in his mind. Had she conveyed his answers to Jazz? The fact he'd said he wasn't romantically interested?

The heat in her eyes as she smiled could definitely be described as romantic. "Believe me, this is way better than my apartment. And I don't get to dress up often, so this is fun."

He forced another smile. "I'm glad." Except for the fact he may have accidentally caused her to think this was a date. "Thanks for agreeing to meet to help with my research." Maybe the reminder would help her remember his interest wasn't romantic.

She reached for her wine glass. "I still can't believe you want to feature me in a book." She took a sip and lowered the glass. "To be honest, with everything that's been going on, this is a nice escape from reality. Though at least nothing bad happened at the fair today."

Hawthorne lowered the fork he'd been winding his pasta around. "Nevaeh didn't tell you?"

"I didn't see her before I came here. She was getting off shift when you did."

Hawthorne nodded. "I was talking to her when the Skyride operator gave us a note he found in the east building."

Jazz's eyes widened. "A note?"

"From the cult. Or at least it looks like it is." He dug out his smartphone from the pocket of his slacks and pulled up the photo he'd taken of the note. He turned the phone, holding the screen toward Jazz.

She leaned forward as she stared at the image. "A death threat? More sabotage?"

"Seems like it."

A flash sparked in her eyes. "Over my dead body."

Hawthorne hid a grin. There was the ferocity of his heroine.

"Where did he find the note, specifically?"

"He said it was tucked into the base of the control panel stand. But that was in the east Skyride building. Far away from the midway where the explosion took place."

"So the police lab techs wouldn't have done a thorough search of that building."

"Exactly. They're doing that tonight, now that the note was found."

"Do you think it really is from the cult?"

Hawthorne paused before answering. He wanted to believe it. He'd jumped to that conclusion right away, fueled by his desire for Patch to be stopped, once and for all. But his reason and logic had caught up with him after his emotions calmed. "Hard to say for sure. On the one hand, it seems pretty dumb for anyone from the cult to use their own stationary if they're behind the sabotage and your aunt's death. But..."

"They're radical enough that they might be that bold?" Jazz's eyes scanned his face as if she was looking for answers there. "Maybe thinking they can't be caught or prosecuted for some reason?"

Hawthorne lifted his fork, catching more fettucine in the tines. "I could see that. Desmond Patch has an ego like you wouldn't believe. That can make some people think they're invincible."

Jazz's lips formed a thoughtful pucker. "I suppose it could also be some member of the cult, wanting to point the finger at Desmond." She lowered her eyebrows. "Though I don't know why they wouldn't just leave instead of doing something so drastic to get at him."

"You'd be surprised. People can get pretty messed up inside that place." And never leave. Even though they should.

Jazz gave him a look that suggested she'd read too much of the thoughts he hadn't spoken. Did she understand somehow? "Let's find out."

"What?"

"Let's go inside." She stabbed some spinach and arugula from her salad with her fork. "I don't know about you, but sitting around waiting for another sabotage attempt doesn't sound like fun. I want to find out if the cult is really behind this. Then we can do something about it."

A grin stretched Hawthorne's mouth. She was really something. "I like the way you think."

"Thank you." She flashed a big smile that sent a jolt through his chest. Like it would do to any healthy male, interested or not. She was a stunning woman. With an amazing personality to match.

Back on task, Emerson. Right. She wanted to go inside the cult. "Unfortunately, I'm not allowed at the commune."

"The commune? Is that what they call Best Life?"

"Yes. That's the community where all the members live together."

"Why aren't you allowed?" She took a bite of the greens.

"It's the regulation for anyone who leaves the cult after living there. They're banned from returning or having communication with any members."

Her eyebrows drew together as she quickly munched her mouthful of salad. She swallowed in a hurry. "You mean you can't communicate with your family there? With your parents and your sister?"

She'd paid attention to what he'd shared with her. Didn't know why that pleased him. Probably because she was the only person he'd shared that part of his background with. Well, the only person since Terry Prentice, the Marine chaplain who'd led him to Christ. "That's right. And they aren't allowed to communicate with me."

"That's awful." The sadness reflected in her emerald eyes showed she meant the words.

"Pretty much." Even more awful was the fact that his parents probably didn't want to communicate with him. Not when Desmond Patch commanded them not to. And not when he'd rejected the rules and community they'd chosen over everything else.

"I'll go in alone then." She took another sip of wine.

"What? I can't ask you to do that."

"You're not asking me to. I want to find out who's hurting my Tri-City Fair. Who killed my aunt. The evidence points to the cult so far, so that's where I'm going."

She sounded so much like the heroine he envisioned for his book. A woman who'd stop at nothing to catch the bad guys and see that justice was done.

"I'd be allowed, right?"

"If you acted like a tourist, yes." An idea sparked in Hawthorne's mind. "Better yet, you could pretend you're interested in joining Best Life. Then they'd even let you make an appointment to meet with Patch."

"Perfect. That's what I'll do then. I'll go and tell them I want to learn more about how to join."

"There's a tour you can take of the facilities."

"They give tours?"

He grinned at the incredulity in her voice. "Yeah. Patch has built the community into quite a corporate success. He and some cult members developed so-called natural supplements and organic foods that are supposed to help people live their best lives."

"And they produce those at the commune?"

"They used to. The products became successful enough to be manufactured on a larger scale elsewhere. So now the community lives off the proceeds of the products and spends their time in the pursuit of their 'best lives.'" He created air quotes with his fingers around the words. "Though truthfully, Patch uses most of the profit himself. Everyone else in the community is sworn to live a moderate life, free of worldly excess."

Jazz quirked an eyebrow. "So he's a con artist."

"You got it."

"Yikes."

"Still want to go in there?"

"Oh, yeah. I've dealt with my share of sleazebags in my life. I enjoy bringing 'em down." She gave him a gleeful smile.

"I bet you do."

"While I'm in there, can I do any investigating for you?" Jazz forked more greens into her mouth.

Investigating. It would be an opportunity to get the information he needed about Sam. Should he tell her? It was a pretty big ask.

"Maybe I could find out how your family's doing or take them a message."

Ah. She meant that kind of investigating. Hadn't thought of that. Probably because he knew it would be fruitless. If his parents wanted to talk to him, cared about him at all, they could simply leave the cult. They'd made their priorities clear when they'd stayed. "That's kind of you to offer. But I have a different favor to ask."

"Oh?" Curiosity lit her gaze.

"You know the seventeen-year-old boy you mentioned that your aunt told you about?"

"The one who died in the accident at the fair?"

He nodded. "That's the one. I'm not sure it was an accident."

Her eyes widened. She leaned forward, resting her hands on the table. "Wait," she lowered her voice, "are you investigating his death?"

"Yes."

"That's the real reason you're here at the fair, isn't it?"

"Yes...But how did you—"

"You're like the real Carson Steele." She straightened as a big grin lit her face. "Of course, you're secretly investigating some crime."

He chuckled. "I don't actually do it that often. Usually, I'm just researching old crimes for inspiration. But my sister asked me to look into this one as a personal favor."

"The sister who left the cult?"

"Yeah. Sam, the boy who died, was her boyfriend when they were both still inside."

"But if he was a member of the cult himself, how could he still go to the fair?"

Hawthorne chewed and swallowed the fettucine that was getting cold, thanks to more talking than eating. "Sometimes the kids figure out ways to bend the rules." As he had more than once. "They want a taste of freedom. And they often have a better sense than the adults do that much is wrong with the culture at Best Life. It's their parents' choice to live under Patch's thumb, not theirs."

"Spoken from personal experience?"

Hawthorne quirked his mouth. Insightful and perceptive, too. He'd have to add those to her list of positive character traits. "Yeah."

"So what have you found out about his death?"

"Nothing concrete yet, but I'd like to follow up on some things that I can only do by getting into the cult."

"Or letting me go in for you."

"Exactly."

She clasped her hands together and let out a low-volume squeal. "I'm going to get to be like Carson Steele."

"A much prettier version." Where had that remark come from? She'd probably think he was flirting. But with her excited smile beaming at him, he couldn't help but voice the incongruity of her comparing herself to the gruff and rugged hero he'd created.

A pink hint of a blush flushed her cheeks in the dim lighting. She dropped her gaze for a second, then flitted her eyes near his face again, as if suddenly shy. "What would you like me to find out for you?"

"My sister told me about a young guy she thinks had motive to kill Sam. His name is Randall Gleams, and he'd be nineteen years old now. He apparently dated my sister and became jealous when she dumped him for Sam. She said he used to work in the gift shop. If you can get him talking about Sam and try to gauge his emotions about him, that could be helpful."

"Okay. Pump the jealous ex-boyfriend. What's your sister's name?"

"Rebekah."

Jazz smiled. "A lovely, traditional name."

He chuckled. "Which doesn't fit her at all. At least at this stage in her life."

Jazz's eyes twinkled back at him. "She sounds fun."

"That's one way of putting it." He shook his head. "She's a real task master with this investigation. Wants me to have it solved yesterday."

"Well, you are the famous Hawthorne Emerson. Carson Steele probably would've had it solved yesterday."

"Not at all." Hawthorne puffed up his chest as if offended. "The book would be way too short."

"Good point." Jazz grinned. "Anything else I can check out for you that would move things along, at an appropriate pace for your plot that I guess we're living out?"

The smile that didn't seem to leave his face much when

Jazz was around stretched bigger. Great sense of humor. Needed to add that to his Jazz Lamont heroine, too. "Yeah. If you can talk to Sam's mom, that would be huge."

"His mom is still there?"

"According to Rebekah. She said his dad left because he blamed the cult, but Sam's mom stayed. I'll try to find out from Rebekah if she knows what dwelling Sam's mom is living in."

"Dwelling?"

"That's what w—" Had he really almost said *we* when referring to the cult? The near slip churned the fettucine that had made it to his belly. "It's what they call the condos the members live in."

"Okay. What do you want me to ask her?"

"Anything she remembers about that day before Sam snuck out in the evening. And especially if he had any friends on the outside, probably kids who aged out and left the cult."

"And if she knows of anyone who had motive to kill her son." Jazz's mouth straightened into a more serious line as her tone firmed.

"Good idea." A niggling sense of something wrong tingled at the back of his neck like a warning. "But, Jazz, do be careful. Nothing at the cult is what it seems. And you could be about to rattle the cage of a killer."

TWENTY-ONE

Phoenix was back. The boss made her entrance like usual, her sandy colored K-9, Dagian, sticking to her side as she crossed the breakroom at PK-9 headquarters without smiles or *hellos* for anyone.

"Welcome back." Cora greeted Phoenix as the boss sat in her favorite armchair, the chair no one else ever used because they knew it was hers.

Phoenix seemed to give a hint of a nod, the bill of her charcoal baseball cap tilting slightly. "What do we know about the hitmen?"

Jazz glanced at Nevaeh, who gave her a small smile. Probably because Phoenix was bringing up the threat on Jazz, despite her claim the boss didn't care.

Jazz had to admit, she was surprised that would be Phoenix's priority first thing out of the gate. But maybe it was an intentional misdirect. What better way to avoid questions about where she'd been for two weeks?

Lines crossed Cora's forehead as she looked at Jazz. "I've been able to keep Phoenix up to date on everything that's been happening with the attempts on your life. Very impressive work in capturing the two men."

"Thanks." Jazz shot Phoenix a glance, but the woman's expression was unreadable, as always. Especially under the shadow cast by her cap. Would've been nice to hear the praise from her, but Jazz appreciated Cora's effort.

"The two men have been identified as a Calvin Crieg and Marty Jenson." Cora switched her focus to Phoenix as she continued. "They both have felony records for assault and armed robbery."

"And yet they're running around loose on our streets." Bris, sitting in the other armchair across the room, pushed out her lips with an exasperated widening of her eyes.

Toby sat up next to her knee and looked at his handler with his tongue dangling as if trying to understand what she meant.

"Gotta love our penal system." Sofia voiced the sarcastic thought as she smoothed her hand along Gaston's ear.

The chocolate Newfoundland water rescue dog sprawled on the sofa with his head resting on Sof's lap and his body hogging most of the other cushions.

Slim Cora had managed to squeeze in next to his tail to sit on the remaining half of the end cushion. "The men sadly are not admitting guilt or giving any indication of having been hired by anyone." Apology filled Cora's tone as she looked at Jazz.

"Good thing we don't need their confirmation." Sof's remark drew everyone's attention to her. "Ramone told me he heard Crieg and Jenson were hired for a hit. They've apparently done low-level hits before. They aren't as expensive as some and tend to be very available on short notice."

Helpful Sof had a source in the local criminal underworld. Ramone, a former arms dealer, had assisted PK-9 more than once with his intel.

"So the creep who hired them isn't in the know himself?" Nev asked the question from the cushion next to Jazz on the love seat. "Like, he's not a crook?"

"Possibly." Sof pushed the fingers of one hand into her gorgeous black waves of hair. "Crieg and Jenson would probably be easy to find through a source with minimal connections to the criminal network here.

Ramone said he didn't know who the mark is or who hired them."

"At least we have confirmation there really is a hit out on Jazz." Bris leaned forward to grab her mug off the coffee table in front of her.

"Or was a hit." Their attention landed on Jazz as she spoke. "I figured it's probably over with now. I mean, I put the hitmen behind bars." She smiled slightly, trying for casual and confident. "That should make the joker who thinks he can kill me give up."

"Or she." Even Nev's lowered eyebrows said she wasn't convinced by Jazz's pitch.

"Okay." Jazz shrugged a shoulder as she lifted her coffee mug to her mouth. "Or she."

"If someone went to all the trouble to find hired killers and pay them to kill you," Bris leveled a serious stare at Jazz, "that person isn't going to quit until you're dead."

Leave it to Bris not to sugarcoat it.

"Good point." Nev touched Jazz's arm as she looked at her. "It's better to play it safe."

Easy enough for them to say. They weren't the ones having to deal with the fact that someone hated them enough to want them dead. But she should be used to it by now. Being disliked was life as usual for her.

Flash shifted against Jazz's ankle, taking some of the weight off his front leg where it lay across her feet.

So what if the surprise attacks weren't over? So what if someone wanted her dead? She and Flash could handle anyone. "Okay. So where do we go from here?"

"We investigate." Phoenix's statement in her deep, emotionless tone nearly made Jazz start.

She'd almost forgotten the boss was there. Though not all the way.

Phoenix's presence gave the room a tense, vigilant vibe that nobody could forget. "Cora."

The blonde nodded to the boss and lifted her open notebook computer onto her lap. "I tracked down all the veterans who served with you in your Army unit, Jazz. There are none in this area specifically. The closest lives in Michigan. A Brad Grayson." Cora's blue eyes lifted to Jazz. "Do you remember him?"

Brad. The company jokester. He'd tried to make her the brunt of the jokes until she put him in his place. Knives were handy for that. She'd earned enough respect to make him leave her alone from then on but hadn't earned his friendship. No one in her unit had granted her that.

She cleared her throat. "Yeah, I remember him. I don't think he'd be any trouble. He was a decent soldier. Obeyed orders. Pretty clean cut."

"All right." Cora nodded at Jazz's assessment. "We'll move him down the list." She cast Phoenix a glance that Jazz couldn't read. Asking for permission or needing to know something?

Phoenix looked at Cora but didn't so much as blink.

Cora seemed to have learned something anyway, as she turned to Jazz with resolve firming her features. "I know you've suffered a great loss in your family, and I want to convey my deepest condolences."

Jazz blinked. Okay. Not what she'd expected her to say. Had Phoenix wanted Cora to do that? Jazz glanced at the boss instinctively, but, of course, couldn't detect anything from her.

"We're all sorry for your loss." Bris glanced at the others, who nodded as they watched Jazz.

An itchy feeling crept up Jazz's neck at the attention. Hopefully, they weren't expecting her to burst into tears or something. "Um, thanks." Jazz shifted her gaze to Nev, a safe landing spot.

Sadness also shadowed Nev's eyes, but at least she got it. Jazz was upset about Aunt Joan. It was awful. But they hadn't been close. Aunt Joan hadn't even loved Jazz. Not like the PK-9 women were thinking.

"I need to ask you a question that may be difficult, and I'm sorry for that." Cora captured Jazz's attention with her earnest tone. "But we do want to find out who is putting you in danger." Cora's tongue slid over her lips before she took a breath to speak again. "Did either of your parents or your aunt and uncle—any family member—have an enemy that might want to harm you?"

That wanted Jazz dead, she meant. After all, that's what hitmen were hired for. But that didn't mean she wanted to chat about her parents in front of everyone. Way too personal and...vulnerable. So she stuck with the safe topic. "Well, we talked about someone wanting to threaten my aunt by going after me. To try to get her to shut down the fair."

"Yeah, but that didn't make sense when they kept trying to kill you after she was dead." Nev gave Jazz a look that said she was surprised Jazz had forgotten they'd discussed that.

Jazz tried to insert the hint in her return gaze that it was a distraction. That Nev should help steer clear of her parents as a topic.

But Nev's eyebrows lowered, and her lips pressed together in a stubborn pucker. Great. She didn't think that was a good idea. Of course, Nev had felt comfortable enough with these women to share her deepest, darkest memories and fears when she'd told them about the assault she'd suffered. And Jazz had been proud of her for having the courage to share and face the pain. The PK-9 team had responded well, rallying around Nev and supporting her like they should.

But Jazz wasn't Nevaeh. These ladies didn't care for her like that. Nev was fun and awesome—she fit in everywhere she went. Jazz was the total opposite. A misfit with everyone. Especially in a tight-knit group of smart, confident, super skilled women who were also mostly all Christians now. One more reason Jazz didn't belong.

"Agreed." Phoenix drew everyone's attention, as she always did when she actually spoke. "We can dispense with that theory." She aimed her gaze at Jazz.

At least Jazz thought that was the direction she was

looking from under the bill of her cap. The feeling of being scrutinized backed up the guess.

"Though there could be someone with a vendetta against you due to family ties. You could also be a means to threaten your uncle in his pursuit of election."

Hadn't thought of that. Could a person mistakenly think her uncle would be bothered if they threatened her? Enough to give up his campaign for governor? It was almost laughable. Although he had acted like he might be starting to care about her a little now.

The memory of his gentle hold on her hand and his kind, almost fatherly smiles yesterday warmed her chest. Maybe he would be bothered if something happened to her. "I suppose they could want to stop Uncle Pierce from running for governor."

"I'll look into it." Cora typed something into her computer. "I don't know that people in his campaign will tell me if he's received threats, but I'll see what I can do. Could you talk to your uncle about the possibility, as well?"

Jazz had to think about that a second. Did she want him to know she was in danger? The warmth in his eyes yesterday as he'd talked about family, including *her* as his family, blocked her vision for a moment. "I remember Aunt Joan said he's gotten what she called harmless threats. She said it was typical for politicians. Didn't sound serious."

Cora frowned. "That is sadly true, I believe. But I'll try digging to see if he's received any the police are taking seriously."

"Did your parents have enemies that you know of?" Sof delivered the variation on Cora's question. Probably because she'd noticed how Jazz had sidestepped it when Cora asked.

"No."

"Father was in the Army." How did Phoenix know that?

Jazz narrowed her eyes. Because she knew everything, Nev would say. And she'd be happy about it.

Phoenix turned her head toward Cora. "Look into his service. Where, when, with whom."

Cora nodded as she typed more notes into the computer.

"Do you have information regarding your mother's history or whereabouts?" An actual question from the boss. So she didn't know everything.

But the reason she didn't know stung deep behind Jazz's ribs. No one knew where her mom had gone after she'd left them when Jazz was a baby. Her dad hadn't known. At least that's what he'd always told Jazz. And she'd never known. Never wanted to know. Why would she want to find someone who'd abandoned her practically at birth?

"No." Jazz hated the thick emotion in her voice. The anger they all wouldn't miss. They'd probably figured out now that her mom had left her, thanks to Phoenix's pointed questions. Nev might be okay with her personal life being paraded in front of these women, but Jazz was not. It'd be different if they loved her like they did Nev. But everything would be different then.

"May I have your permission to try to learn more about her and your father?" Cora's blue eyes filled with compassion as she watched Jazz. Yeah, she'd definitely figured it out. But she was also asking for Jazz's okay. The kindness made tears prick Jazz's eyes. "We only want to ensure your safety as well as we can."

It was what they did for the others on the team when they were in danger. If Jazz had half a brain, she wouldn't prevent the one time they were treating her the same. She nodded assent, not trusting her voice.

Pressure on her knee drew her gaze to Nev, who gave her a gentle squeeze. Courage. Like Jazz had tried to give Nev whenever she struggled with her PTSD. Jazz met her friend's gaze, infusing a *thank you* into hers.

"What about a connection between the fair and the attacks on Jazz?"

Jazz could've hugged Bris for angling the subject and everyone's attention elsewhere.

"I still think it's suspicious the way the first attack on Jazz was the same night as the first sabotage." The former cop moved her gaze over the others like she was looking for agreement. She stopped on a fixed point. Maybe Phoenix? "I know we don't usually investigate when we're only hired for security, but what do you think?"

Jazz swung her head toward the boss, her stomach tightening. If the resources of the Phoenix K-9 Agency could be used to find out who was behind the sabotage, the danger to the fair could likely be ended much sooner. In time to save this season and future ones.

"We'll investigate the fair sabotage and the death of Joan Cracklen. The incidents could be connected to the threat against Jazz."

Hope swelled in Jazz's chest at the boss's declaration. It had taken them long enough to recognize the need to protect the fair, but there was still time. They could find the culprit behind the sabotage and Aunt Joan's death and stop him or her before another attack. "The strongest evidence so far points to the Best Life Community." Jazz couldn't help but blurt out the information in her excitement.

"I've always been concerned about the cult and its influence on people." Cora frowned. "But I didn't suspect any violent tendencies."

"I don't think they've been violent before." At least according to Hawthorne, but Jazz kept her source to herself. "Their leader, Desmond Patch, has spoken publicly against the fair. Called it evil."

Cora glanced at Phoenix a moment before returning her attention to Jazz. "The police are already looking into him because of the pin and the note found last night, but I'll do a deep dive with our resources and see what I can find."

That was definitely an advantage of having the PK-9 Agency on board. They always knew what the police were doing and had connections Jazz still couldn't explain. But if the team was working on this now, she should probably tell them what she was about to do.

"I might be able to find out something, too. I'm going to the cult tomorrow to take a tour of the commune." She caught Nev's surprised stare from the corner of her eye. "I'm going to pretend I'm interested in joining so I can request a meeting with Desmond Patch." She held her breath. Would Phoenix tell her she couldn't do that?

"Were you going to tell us about this?" Nev muttered the question under her breath, hopefully quietly enough that no one else heard.

"Good." The one word from Phoenix loosened the tension clenching Jazz's chest. "Take Sofia or Nevaeh with you."

The pinch came back with renewed strength, squeezing her ribs. How was she going to do the investigating for Hawthorne with one of them tagging along? She couldn't tell anyone about it. Hawthorne had asked her last night to keep it a secret that he was investigating Sam's death and especially that he thought it could be murder.

"I'll go if the timing works with my shift." Nev threw Jazz a glance that said she wanted to hear everything later.

Jazz let out a breath and gave her a half smile. "That sounds good." Especially since the timing wouldn't work. If Jazz needed to, she could probably explain enough of the details to Nev that she'd be okay with Jazz going alone.

"We're switching to a new shift schedule."

Jazz jerked her gaze to Phoenix. Had she picked up on what Jazz was planning?

"Sofia, you'll take the morning shift. Nevaeh, noon to eight. Jazz, four to midnight."

Jazz fought to keep from narrowing her eyes at Phoenix. What was the boss up to?

The others nodded, accepting whatever Phoenix decided, no questions asked, as usual.

Somebody had to ask. "Why the change?"

Even Raksa and Alvarez, lounging on the open carpet past the sofas, looked at her as if they agreed with everyone else that she was weird. But what was actually weird was how no one ever questioned Phoenix. About anything. No one wondered where she disappeared to for weeks at a time. Or why she was so secretive and mysterious. Did anyone know anything about her? She could be a criminal or something for all they knew.

Phoenix waited a few moments—very long, painful moments—before answering. "You're the most familiar with the fair. You should be on duty when the culprit may be attempting to set up his or her next move."

Jazz tried to hide her surprise. Hadn't expected that answer. It was almost complimentary. Like Phoenix thought Jazz would be able to prevent more sabotage or catch the criminal behind it.

"I want you to show me the areas where all three incidents occurred."

All sense of confidence flew out the window, chased away by Jazz's speeding pulse. "You're going to be there?"

"Yes."

Jazz's throat dried to sandpaper. Just what was Phoenix really doing? Did she hope to catch Jazz failing at security detail? Or maybe she wanted to get Jazz alone to tell her she was fired.

And what about Hawthorne? He was probably going back to the morning shift today. She wouldn't see him. Maybe she could call or text him. She'd have to take Best Life's earlier tour she'd seen listed on their website instead of the evening one she'd told him she was going to attend.

Should she hint that Hawthorne could be helpful in the investigation, too? He'd already helped her out with what he'd found in the security footage. "We could loop Hawthorne in to help."

"Hawthorne?" Sof quirked a dark eyebrow.

"Hawthorne Emerson. The author of the Carson Steele novels?"

Blank stares met Jazz's explanation. Well, except Phoenix's stare that never changed.

"Oh, I enjoy those novels." And except for Cora. She smiled at Jazz. "I understand he's with security at the fair."

Now that she thought about it, no one but Jazz and Nev should know Hawthorne worked at the fair. She didn't think

Sof had gotten his name when she'd seen him by the Ferris wheel. So who had told Cora? Jazz glanced at Nev, who gave her a shoulder shrug.

"I've been reviewing the duty rosters."

Jazz let out a slow breath, releasing her vise grip on the handle of her mug. So Nev wasn't spreading rumors about Jazz having a crush or something like that. Good. But she wouldn't have to start any rumors if Jazz didn't stop acting weird about him. She steadied her thoughts. "We've been chatting, since I'm a fan of his novels, and he's been doing some investigating himself."

Sof and Bris exchanged a look that sent a jolt of panic up Jazz's neck. They wouldn't start teasing her about liking Hawthorne, would they?

Jazz hurried to say more before they could. "He has some great ideas. Maybe we can bring him in to help us." She looked at Phoenix.

The boss had brought in men to assist before. She'd even invited Branson into headquarters to help find the person trying to kill Nev.

"We don't need outside assistance." Phoenix stared directly at Jazz as she spoke. Her tone was as passionless as usual, but Jazz couldn't help feeling the words were intended to put her in her place.

Jazz hadn't meant to insinuate the PK-9 team needed help. Phoenix probably only objected to Hawthorne because he was Jazz's recommendation. The guy she was interested in. If one of the other girls had suggested he be looped in, the boss would've agreed to do it. She had let all their husbands and fiancés help, even in the field.

"So if Jazz is with you tonight, I suppose she doesn't have to call for check-ins during that time?" Nev asked the question in a normal, relaxed tone. As if she hadn't seen how Phoenix had just shut Jazz down with no explanation.

"No. Check-ins are not needed at any point. Jazz has proven she can take care of herself."

The observation from the boss herself should've sent Jazz

over the moon. Phoenix finally recognized her skills. This was as close to a compliment as Phoenix ever got.

But it was overshadowed by what Phoenix had also said, disguised as praise. The boss had just stated her reason for not protecting Jazz from danger. And declared that Jazz needed to continue fending for herself.

TWENTY-TWO

"I am so tired right now."

Hawthorne smiled as Rebekah plopped onto his sofa, flinging an arm dramatically out to one side as the other hand covered her eyes.

"Not a morning person?"

A moan was his only response.

"Would coffee or a cinnamon roll help?"

"Yes." She dropped her hand but kept her eyes closed and her head resting on the sofa cushion she'd sunk into.

Hawthorne went to fill a mug for her and grabbed a cinnamon roll from the bakery box on the counter. Good thing he'd stopped by the bakery after his morning run. He dropped the roll onto a plate and carried the goodies to his sister, setting them on the coffee table in front of her. A dose of sugar and caffeine should do the trick.

He went to the armchair on the other side of the table and grabbed the roll and coffee mug he'd already set there for himself.

Rebekah slowly sat up, her gaze landing on the cinnamon roll. She dove for that first, taking a larger bite than he'd have expected from such a slim girl. "Mmm-hmmm." The sigh of pleasure escaped as she sank back into the cushions again.

Hawthorne chuckled.

"This is so good." She dragged her tired gaze up and blinked her blue eyes at him. "You're such a gentleman." The note of surprise in her tone probably should offend him.

Maybe she hadn't met many nice guys. The idea sparked a surge of something in his gut. Protectiveness?

He squashed the feeling. She didn't need an overbearing brother. She'd left the cult to be free, like he had. He wasn't going to steal that freedom from her.

After taking a few long drinks of the coffee and munching more of the cinnamon roll, Rebekah sat up straighter and started glancing around. Caffeine and sugar struck again. "Well, I guess you probably know why I'm here."

He smiled. "I can guess. You'd like to know my progress."

"Yes." She pressed her palms together in front of her chin. "So much."

He brought her up to speed on the investigating he'd done so far, leaving out anything that he feared might upset her too much. He also didn't comment on any of the interviews he related or information he'd uncovered. Better not to indicate any bias or give her false hopes before he was sure of all the facts.

She watched him intently, holding her emotions in and listening silently better than he'd thought she would.

He finished with the story of Dan Harris remembering a group of rowdy young men at the fair that night. Hawthorne added that he'd later talked to Barry Greer, the third security guard on duty that evening, who didn't recall anything unusual.

"You're starting to see it, aren't you?"

Hawthorne paused with the cinnamon roll halfway to his mouth. "See what?"

"That Sam was murdered. It wasn't an accident." Grave earnestness filled the eyes that leveled at him.

He lowered the roll to his plate. "I think foul play is a definite possibility."

She crossed her arms over the light cardigan that covered a blue tank top. "Why don't you want to admit it?"

"Because you asked me to investigate this and find out the truth. I can't do that if I go in with an already formed conclusion in my mind. I have to look at the facts objectively and see where the truth leads me."

Her chin puckered slightly, but she held his gaze. "Okay. Then where is the truth leading you now?"

"Unfortunately, it looks like it's leading me to Best Life."

Vertical lines bunched on her otherwise wrinkle-free brow. "You think BL had something to do with it?"

"Someone there may have."

"You'd go back?"

"If I have to. Sam's mother may have helpful information about that night and if anyone had reason to hurt Sam. She could know if he had friends outside the cult who match the description of the rowdy bunch at the fair."

Rebekah smirked. "She won't know that. Sam wouldn't have told her. It would've been breaking the rules."

"Well, did he tell you about staying in touch with anyone outside the cult?"

She lifted her gaze toward the ceiling. "We had all the same friends since school was so small. There were a few kids in the grade above us who left when they graduated the year before us, and then a couple others from our class left when we did." She pressed her lips together and blinked, as if shooing away tears. "When I did."

Hawthorne stayed silent a moment. Giving her space. But it probably wouldn't do her any good to dwell on the loss. "Can you give me the names of the students who left the year ahead of you? Just the boys."

She shrugged. "Why not?" She set her empty plate on the coffee table and pulled out her smartphone from the large purse she'd set on the floor by the sofa. "I'll text them to you." She rapidly typed on her phone. "I checked with my friend inside, and she said Sam's mom still lives there." Rebekah looked up as she tossed her phone onto the cushion beside her. "Which I do not get at all. It's BL's fault."

Hawthorne nodded. She wasn't wrong. "Do you know what dwelling she's living in?"

Rebekah grabbed her phone again and tapped the screen. "Uh...Twenty-one twelve." She set the phone down. "One of the condos in the West Quarter, you know?"

"Yeah." He'd have to convey that information to Jazz so she could find it easily. "Did you confirm if Randall is still there? I want to follow up on that since you think he had a motive."

"Oh, good. Yeah, he still works in the gift shop." She leaned forward, balancing her elbows on her skinny knees below her shorts. "But they won't let you in. You know that, right?"

"I may have found a way around that. A friend of mine has agreed to go in and take the tour, pretending to be interested in joining Best Life."

"Really?" Her eyebrows crunched as her mouth formed a shape of disgust.

Her expression brought a smile to his lips. That and remembering Jazz's eagerness to play sleuth. "Really. She has reasons of her own she wants to investigate the cult, too."

"She?" Rebekah's eyes lit with a curiosity that triggered warning bells in Hawthorne's mind.

"A work colleague."

"Uh-huh." A grin sprang onto Rebekah's face as she grabbed the mug from the table. "And a very good friend, sounds like."

"A new friend. That's as far as it goes."

"I don't suppose you'd tell me if she was something more." Her smile slowly fell away as she looked down at her coffee. "Do you ever wonder what's happening with the others? Nathaniel and Mary?"

The sadness he'd felt increasingly lately pinched his chest. "Sometimes."

"I wonder if Nathaniel is married or what he's doing." She glanced up at Hawthorne, moisture glistening in her eyes. "I know Mary was engaged when I left. I think that's why she stayed. She's probably married now. Maybe has kids." A wistful, painful smile curved Rebekah's closed lips. "We could have a niece or nephew."

He'd never thought of that. The discomfort behind his ribs twisted a little more.

"I miss them, you know." Rebekah dropped her gaze to the cushion beside her as she ran her fingers in a winding pattern on the upholstery. "Mom and Dad."

Hawthorne's gut clenched as her voice echoed the pain he'd felt at the loss of his parents, the realization he might never see them again. He'd been too angry to feel it when he'd first left and joined the Marines. But four years later when he'd embarked on civilian life, sadness had crept in. A delayed grief.

He cleared his throat. "I know. That's only natural."

"Really?" She looked up at him, a tear tracking down her cheek. "It seems so silly. It's only been two years. And I'm the one who wanted to leave. But I really, really miss them." Her lips trembled. "Sorry." She swiped away the tear and took a deep breath.

He shook his head. "Don't apologize." He stood and went to the kitchen where he grabbed a box of tissues off the counter. He returned and held the box out to her.

A shaky laugh pushed out as she took the box. "Thanks."

"Nathaniel contacted me when he first got out." It was all Hawthorne could think to say to comfort her. He couldn't help her where their parents were concerned. It seemed they would never see the truth, never leave the prison they'd voluntarily moved their whole family into. "He was going into the military. He chose the Navy."

"You haven't heard from him since?"

"No." An uncomfortable mix of guilt and concern settled in Hawthorne's stomach as he sat in the armchair. Should that have worried him? No news could be good news. And the last thing he had wanted to do was crowd Nathaniel.

Hawthorne knew how amazing those first years of absolute freedom were after escaping the cult. He wouldn't have wanted to steal that experience from his younger brother. But Nathaniel had been out for...how many years now? Hawthorne quickly did the math in his head. Eleven.

Much longer than Hawthorne had realized. Maybe he should look Nathaniel up and see how he was doing.

"That's sad. I wonder if he's okay." Rebekah looked at Hawthorne with so much grief that she could have been their mom, staring at Hawthorne when he'd announced he was going to leave.

The similarity sent another spasm of pain through his chest. "I should see if I can find him."

Rebekah nodded. "That would be terrific. I'm really glad I found you. I wouldn't have known how to find you if you weren't a famous writer." She smiled, though not up to her usual bright standards. "I bet you were surprised to get a message from me through your website."

"To say the least." Hawthorne dredged up a smile, too. "But I was very glad."

"Really?" Her eyes widened, cautious hope flickering in them.

"Absolutely. I'm thankful God brought us together again."

She quirked her head. "You believe in God?"

"I do. I believe anything that's true. And there's no denying God is the ultimate Truth."

"Huh. Are you like a Christian?"

He smiled at her wording. "I'm a Christian, yes."

"I can't go there. Not after being taught lies and getting indoctrinated into a big spiritual con my whole life. The God thing is just like another big brainwash."

Hawthorne met her gaze. "I get why you'd think that. I was afraid of that, too. My skepticism kept me from believing in God for quite a while. But then a friend helped me see that because I was so alert to spotting lies, I'd be able to test everything about God and Jesus Christ. So I did. After I encountered the evidence, I couldn't deny God really exists, the Bible is true, and Jesus died for me and rose again to give me eternal life."

"I don't know. I hear other stuff in school. Everybody has a different truth." Rebekah shifted against the cushions and looked away, as if the topic was making her uncomfortable.

Probably enough of that for now. But since she was hurting emotionally, he'd leave her with one thought. "Let me just say this. That loneliness you're feeling, the grief of leaving our family behind because we had to—the only thing that has helped me with all of that has been my relationship with Jesus." Hawthorne caught her gaze in his and held it. "God is our perfect Father, Jesus is our truest Brother and Friend. He can fulfill all your needs and heal what needs to be healed."

Rebekah stared at him for a few seconds, a mass of thoughts seeming to cycle behind her eyes.

It was a lot to think about, he knew. Maybe he'd give her an out so she didn't feel pressured to make a decision about anything now. "I hate to cut this short, but I should get some writing in this morning."

"Okay." She nodded, a look of something like relief relaxing her features as she stood and gathered her things. "Oh." She spun toward him as she slung the strap of her bag over her shoulder. "I was wondering…" She caught her lower lip with her teeth. "Would you maybe want to go see a movie Friday night?"

"You mean with you?"

"Yeah." She lifted her shoulders and glanced away. "Or we could do something else. Just hang out."

He opened his mouth, about to say *yes*. Then closed it. He wouldn't be doing her any favors if he became her crutch while she was vulnerable. She'd end up throwing away her freedom for closeness, for a relationship that could end up burdening and restricting her. She'd regret it later, when she found she'd given up some of the freedom she'd originally sought.

"It looks like I'm going to be working the late shift at the fair." At least that's what he'd managed to switch to for tonight, after he'd received Jazz's text about her change in schedule. "I don't think I'll be free."

"Okay, sure." She turned away, but not before he caught the disappointment in her eyes.

His stomach clenched as he followed her toward the front door. He didn't mean to make her feel badly. But she'd thank him later, when she'd gotten through the fragile, lonely phase and reached the point of cherishing the freedom she would still have if he didn't interfere.

She paused by the door and faced him again. "Did you warn her?"

He gave Rebekah a look that probably communicated his confusion.

"The friend you're sending into BL."

When she put it that way, it made him sound almost cowardly. Or uncaring. Like he was sending Jazz into a dangerous situation. "Warn her about what?"

"About the cult. The brainwashing. You don't think she'll get sucked in, do you?"

"No." The answer came quickly, even instinctively as he pictured Jazz, strong and independent. But doubt crept into his mind. "I think the people who fall for that want to in a way. They're looking for answers and help. She isn't like that."

Rebekah shrugged. "If you say so. I've seen some pretty smart people believe it anyway. There's something kind of weird and creepy there."

She looked away, her gaze seeming to stare beyond the painting on the wall near the door. Maybe at a distant memory. "It's like it feels dark all the time. Like something's watching or hanging on to you, and you don't know if it's human or something...else." She blinked and jumped her gaze back to Hawthorne. "But maybe it wasn't like that when you were there."

It had been exactly like that. Especially in the last year before he'd left. But he had never tried to put it into words like Rebekah had just done.

He'd forgotten that feeling. The darkness and suffocating sense of something evil at work. He shouldn't send Jazz into that environment.

"And if your friend's as cool as you say she is, she'll probably be able to handle it. I'd guess it's a lot easier to shake off if you only visit once."

Unless the sense of evil was a sign of actual danger, maybe even physical danger to anyone hostile. To someone trying to trick Patch or spy on the community.

No, he couldn't send Jazz into danger. He'd have to get ahold of her before the tour she planned to take this morning. He only hoped he wasn't too late.

TWENTY-THREE

"You didn't answer my last text."

Jazz swung toward the male voice, muscles tense.

Hawthorne held up his phone as he walked to her behind the row of cars where she'd parked her SUV.

She breathed again, a smile stretching her face with probably too much obvious pleasure at seeing the gorgeous man she'd been thinking about all morning. "I thought you had to work."

"So that's why you didn't answer me when I said I didn't want you to come here?" A disarming grin quirked his mouth as he stopped a few feet from her at the rear of her SUV.

"I answered the first text where you also said that."

"Yeah, with..." Hawthorne looked down at his phone, "Thanks, but I'm going. Winkey emoji."

She laughed. "I appreciate the heads-up that it could be dangerous. But in case you haven't noticed, the threat of danger doesn't stop me from doing anything important."

"Yeah." His gaze skimmed over her face, his lips still curved in a smile. "I have noticed."

Something about his expression and the way he said the words sent a shiver down her spine. She rested her hands on her hips to give them something to do. "So are you playing hooky?"

"Not exactly." He squinted at her, the sunlight from behind her adding to his allure as it bathed his tanned skin with a warm glow. "I traded shifts with Barry Greer."

"So you could try to stop me from going in?" She grinned.

"Well, not by force, if that's what you mean. I'm not dumb enough to try that." He glanced toward where she usually wore the knife sheath on her thigh. "I'm guessing you're still armed somewhere."

She winked. "Smart man."

He laughed, spiraling another delicious tingle through her. "Okay, but I still don't feel comfortable sending you in alone." He glanced around the lot, probably catching sight of the woman walking to the Best Life building that Jazz kept in her peripheral. He stepped close to Jazz and lowered his voice. "Especially if someone in there is Sam's killer or behind the fair attacks."

Heat from his proximity emanated between them. Goodness, he was so perfectly tall, having to bend his head down toward her when they stood this close. He must be more like six-three or six-four.

Her breathing shallowed as she took in his handsome features, landing on those electric eyes. "Come with me." Her words came out ragged and soft. As if she meant something romantic. Like the ideas spinning through her mind right now.

"What?" His voice sounded a little breathy, too. Was he feeling the same attraction she was? His gaze skidded down her face. Looking for her lips?

She instinctively moved closer. What would it feel like to be kissed by Hawthorne Emerson?

"Uh," he took a quick step back, "I should go with you." He glanced around like he was trying to see the person who'd walked by before. "Right. Good idea."

Was he flustered? Jazz tried to hide the smile that fought to show itself. Sure seemed like he'd felt the sparks, too. She had never seen him uncomfortable before.

She tried to capture his gaze with hers, hoping to rekindle

the connection they'd just shared. Or at least acknowledge it had happened.

His focus darted every which way, everywhere but at her.

Disappointment sank to her belly. Maybe he was one of those guys who took a while to admit his feelings to himself. Or maybe he thought she wouldn't welcome his attention. She'd have to make sure he knew that wasn't a problem. But outside a cult commune probably wasn't the best place. She focused on the mission at hand. "I thought you couldn't go in. That they won't let you in."

"True. But I came prepared." He reached with both hands to his back pockets. When he brought his hands to the front again, they held...a baseball cap and sunglasses?

He whipped the dark blue cap onto his head and pulled the bill low. Then he added the dark sunglasses. "What do you think?" He held out his hands.

At least his playfulness was returning.

She grinned. Somehow the man looked both attractive and mysterious in his disguise. "They might wonder why you're wearing sunglasses indoors."

His teeth flashed with a smile as he removed the glasses. "Maybe I'll keep them handy in case I see anyone I know."

"All right. I guess it could work." And she wouldn't mind a bit having Hawthorne by her side for this adventure. "So what's the plan?"

"We'll go on the tour together. I know where Sam's mother is living, at least according to Rebekah, so I'll peel off when we get close. Maybe you can distract the others if needed?"

She nodded.

"And then I'll need you to see if you can find Randall, hopefully working at the gift shop where you can chat with him."

"Right. I got your description of him, so I should be good. I'll sign up for a meeting with Desmond Patch, too."

"Perfect."

Warmth ballooned in her torso at the look of approval on his face. "Ready?"

"Let's do this." He slipped his sunglasses on as they walked from the parking lot to the Best Life entrance—steel double doors that probably offered security but not much curb appeal.

"Welcome to Best Life!" The beaming woman who greeted them as they stepped inside more than made up for the foreboding entrance. Middle-aged and wearing a long white robe with a hood that fell onto her shoulders, the woman's friendly smile offset the strangeness of her clothing.

"Thank you." Jazz returned the smile and held out her hand toward the woman. "I'm Jazz Lamont, and this is my..." Wait. They hadn't said what she should call him. If she said he was a friend, that might make them stand out as odd from the get-go, visiting a cult together. "Boyfriend. Carson."

The woman shook Jazz's hand as her smile redirected to Hawthorne. "Welcome to you both." She held out her hand to Hawthorne, too, and he smiled as he shook it. Still wearing his sunglasses.

As if Jazz's subliminal hint reached him, he took the glasses off as he released the woman's hand.

"I'm Lavinia, and I'll be your tour guide today." She gestured toward a cluster of people dressed in normal street clothes who stood outside open glass doors that led to a brightly lit room beyond.

"If you want to join the group by the gift shop, we'll get started in two more minutes."

"Thanks." Jazz gave the guide her friendliest smile.

"Shopping, honey. I know where you're going to want to end our tour." Hawthorne clasped Jazz's elbow gently with his fingers as he guided her toward the group waiting under the *Best Life Shop* sign.

Her arm brushing against Hawthorne's as they walked, she caught a spicey scent. Cologne? She threw him a sheepish glance. "Boyfriend was the best I could think of in the moment."

He looked down at her and gave her a cute, secretive smile. "It was brilliant. Less curiosity and questions now. A lot of the people who join are couples. But it will mean a little more playacting than I was thinking we'd have to do."

"I don't mind if you don't." She slid her arm around his waist as they neared the group of people, reveling in the solid feel of his strong and muscled torso.

He glanced at her, surprise glinting in his eyes. And maybe something else. A spark of heat that said he liked the contact as much as she did.

A young man in the group greeted them, and Hawthorne put on a smile as he started chatting with the guy.

The tour began within a few minutes, and she and Hawthorne fell in with the group, walking side by side without much contact for most of it. But the other couples weren't really touching either, so Jazz couldn't use the need to convince observers as an excuse to get cozy again. As much as she'd love to.

She couldn't believe the size of the commune. It looked like a medium-sized building from the front. But the building was actually huge, angling into various wings that formed a giant square with a cutout smaller square in the middle of it. She wouldn't have been able to follow the layout all that well if Lavinia hadn't shown them the artistic rendering of an aerial view of their commune. The image hung in the lobby along with a huge photo of Desmond Patch.

The Best Life leader was much better looking than she'd expected. Distinguished with a bit of gray at the temples of his otherwise black hair, he had a mustache and dab of chin hair that she usually thought looked lame on guys. But somehow it added an air of distinction and confidence to pair with the commanding presence obvious even in a picture.

She hadn't said anything to Hawthorne about the photo once she'd gotten a look at the dark expression clouding his features as he'd glared at it.

But after that moment, Hawthorne had cleared all trace of grimness from his face. He'd soon returned to his normal self, even cracking jokes under his breath to Jazz whenever the Best Life tour guide praised any aspect of the cult or commune.

They slowed as they came to a large window cut into the wall.

"If you'll all stop here, I'd like to show you an important part of our history." Lavinia held up a hand to signal they should halt.

The group formed a loose half-circle around the window as they peered in.

Equipment stood in a room on the other side of the glass. Looked like factory style conveyor belts, as well as microscopes and vials on tables. Did a scientist work there?

"This very laboratory is where our founder, Desmond Patch, created the first product that made our community sustainable and has brought radical change to many lives."

"Radical is right." Hawthorne leaned close to murmur the words in Jazz's ear.

She pressed her fingers to her mouth to squelch the chuckle that wanted to escape.

"You may know of our line of Best Life supplements and life-enhancing products." Lavinia scanned her audience with a smile.

"Because life is worthless without enhancements." He put his hand lightly on Jazz's back this time as he whispered.

She choked back a laugh, even as a marvelous shiver curled up her spine at his touch.

"Well, the first of those bestselling products, the Best Life Booster—a supplement that has revolutionized many lives— was created right here. We keep this room as it was then to remind us of our history and of why we're able to live the fullest, best lives we have now. Because of the success of these products, which have helped change the world, we in the Best Life community no longer worry about worldly concerns like providing for our families. We are fully supported by the meaningful Best Life products so that we are able to focus solely on bettering ourselves and pursuing spiritual peace with the universe."

"I'm sure the universe is thrilled about that." Hawthorne's breath tickled Jazz's ear, and a giggle escaped before she could stop it.

Lavinia and a few other people glanced her way, but they smiled. Knowing smiles that seemed to suggest they thought she and Hawthorne were deeply in love and having a romantic moment.

Perfect. Jazz slid her hand down Hawthorne's arm and found his hand. She entwined her fingers with his as some people asked questions.

Did he stiffen?

She glanced up at him.

If he had been looking at her, he wasn't now. But some people were watching them. Which might be why he put on a smile that appeared a little forced.

Maybe she shouldn't have taken his hand. Everyone was watching. Seemed like a good idea to sell their cover, especially after her giggle.

He didn't pull his hand away as they started forward, and his fingers relaxed, fitted perfectly between hers. His grip was strong, gentle, and warm. She could get used to it way too easily. Get used to being his girl for real. To being a couple.

"And here is where you'll find the heart of our community." Lavinia led them through glass doors into the outdoor portion they'd seen on the map, surrounded on four sides by the massive Best Life building.

Though this section of the commune had looked like a small square on the map, it was huge. A paved path curved through beautifully landscaped grounds and gardens that provided the foreground for many houses.

At least they looked like houses, but Lavinia explained they were multiple dwellings, divided into comfortable condos for families and apartments for single community members.

Despite being nestled in the attractive landscaping, the

houses looked so identical and plain that they reminded her of rabbit hutches. Jazz leaned closer to whisper her thoughts to Hawthorne, but he slipped his hand away.

She glanced at his face, trying to squelch the sting of the connection ending. Good grief. He wasn't her boyfriend. They were only playacting.

But he wasn't looking at her at all. His gaze appeared to lock on one of the gray houses they were passing, set back from the main path.

He leaned closer to Jazz, his fingers lightly brushing her lower back and sending a jolt of electricity down to her toes. "This is her."

Her? Oh. Sam's mother. *The reason Hawthorne is here, dummy.*

She gave him a nod, trying to pretend like the simple closeness and touch from this man hadn't made her lose basic brain function.

"Cover for me?" His teal eyes found hers for a second.

"I've got you." She whispered the reply, then dragged her gaze away from him as she checked on Lavinia and the others in the group. They'd gotten a bit farther ahead, so she picked up her pace, catching up with the group as Lavinia explained about the chosen architecture for the houses and shared how many people lived in the community.

No one seemed to notice Hawthorne slip away.

At least she assumed he had. She wouldn't risk a look. Someone could choose that moment to glance at her, and she'd blow the whole mission.

Mission. Funny how she'd never enjoyed any of her military assignments nearly as much as this one undercover jaunt with Hawthorne.

And so far, there hadn't been any hint of the danger Hawthorne had warned her about. All the people there, even the cult members they passed while on the tour, were so happy and kind. All smiles and friendly *hellos*. She could almost understand the attraction for people who decided to join the community.

It really seemed like the most ideal version of a community anyone could hope for. A family for people who didn't have one. A family you could choose and who would accept you for who you were. A family who would stick with you and be in your life every day. Never reject you or walk out.

Yeah, this place had a definite appeal. She'd have to ask Hawthorne why he'd left. If Jazz had grown up in a place like this, she'd probably still be there. And be much happier.

———

Hawthorne couldn't believe he was back. He tried to ignore the tumult of emotions that nauseated his belly as he made his way on the winding side path to the gray dwelling nestled far back amid the gardens.

Memory after memory had barraged him from the moment he'd entered the commune.

And none of them were good.

Thank the Lord Jazz had been there. Otherwise, he might've punched something or someone. Or broken down in tears in a corner.

He'd forgotten how much he hated this place. How much it had hurt him.

No. The people in it had hurt him.

As if on cue from his thoughts, movement up the path caught his eye.

This path was too narrow to risk passing someone. And he wasn't supposed to be away from the tour group.

He ducked off the path into the vegetation. Pushing through the plants, he squatted under some tall bush with large, floppy leaves.

A man in the BL white robe sauntered down the path. A sound, like muttering, reached Hawthorne's ears as the guy passed by. Probably trying to memorize his assignment from one of his classes. Or maybe muttering the true thoughts he was never allowed to voice to anyone.

Hawthorne waited until the man disappeared from view

before crawling out of hiding. He returned to the path, brushing leaves and probably a few spiders off his T-shirt and jeans as he continued on.

He paused at a signpost along the path. *2112.*

Sam Ackerman's mother should be there, if Rebekah's intel was correct.

He hurried onto the short sidewalk that led to the plain, gray front door. He pressed the buzzer mounted on the wall. Here was hoping the woman wouldn't refuse to talk to him. Or worse, report him as a banned trespasser.

Rebekah had said the Ackermans joined BL when she was ten years old, well after Hawthorne had left. So Sam's mother shouldn't recognize him.

The door opened just wide enough for him to see a short woman in the usual white robe. Her graying hair was pulled back in the braided ring around her head that was the BL standard for women. She landed brown eyes on him. Eyes full of fear.

Maybe because she hadn't expected to see a strange man on her doorstep. And he was breaking the rules, which greatly frightened most BL members.

"Mrs. Ackerman?"

"Who are you?" She pinched the door farther closed.

"Are you Sam's mother?"

Her eyebrows drew together as she stared at him. Hesitated. "Yes."

"I'm so sorry for your loss, ma'am."

The door opened another inch. "Thank you."

"I'm investigating what happened to Sam, and I wondered if I could ask you a few quick questions?"

She glanced beyond the door, her gaze darting to her left, then right. "It's not allowed."

"Please, ma'am." Hawthorne softened his voice. "I think Sam may not have gotten the justice he should have. I just want to hear a little bit about him from his mother, the woman who knew him best. And then I'll leave as quick as I came."

She watched him another few moments.

He waited, not looking away as he tried to interject the sincerity of his concern for Sam into his gaze.

"For a minute." She pulled the door open wider and stepped back.

"Thank you."

She closed the door behind him and stayed standing by it.

The interior of the condo looked almost exactly like the one he'd spent his awful teen years in, though newer and in better condition. Open floor plan with a living room and kitchen, and a closed door that probably led to a small restroom. A narrow staircase rose upward on the left, where it no doubt led to the second floor that housed two or three bedrooms and two bathrooms.

He squelched a shiver of repulsion as he halted his scan and brought his attention to Mrs. Ackerman. "I know you want me to be quick, so you'll need to forgive the directness of my questions."

Her gaze shifted away toward the kitchen. But she didn't respond.

"Mrs. Ackerman, does your husband still live at Best Life?"

That brought her focus back to him. "No. He left right after..." Pain filled her eyes before she looked away again.

"Did he blame Best Life for what happened to Sam?"

She nodded, her lips pressing together as she stared in the direction of the wood-paneled floor. "He blamed everyone." Her voice thickened with emotion. "Desmond, the fair, us."

"Did you agree with him? Do you think Desmond Patch was to blame?"

Her head shot up, eyes widening. "No, of course not. Desmond always does what's right for us. Including Sam." Not a trace of doubt flickered in her gaze, despite how much Hawthorne wanted to see it there.

How were thinking adults so easily fooled by Patch and his philosophies? His empty promises and lies? Hawthorne would never understand it. Or maybe he did understand and didn't like the answer.

Head in the game, Emerson. The reminder brought his mind back to the ticking clock, the seconds he'd probably have before this faithful BL member kicked him out. He couldn't believe she was breaking the rules this long. Must be only for the sake of her dead son.

"I need to know about Sam that day. Before he went to the fair in the evening, was he acting normally? Or in the days before, were there any signs that he was nervous or scared? Had anyone been bothering him?"

"No." She shook her head, then stopped and looked at Hawthorne. "You think someone killed him, don't you?"

"The evidence is starting to suggest that's a definite possibility."

"You sound like my husband."

"But I'm not angry, ma'am. I only want the truth and justice for Sam if the findings were wrong."

"So you say." There it was again. That suspicious glint in her eyes and set to her mouth. Why, Hawthorne wasn't sure. She couldn't know Hawthorne had any reason for a personal grudge against Patch and the cult.

"So there wasn't anything strange in Sam's behavior leading up to that night? Or anyone bothering him here at the commune?"

"No. I would have noticed if there had been." She crossed her arms over her white robe, the collar pulling away to show a glimpse of the gray shirt all members wore underneath the robe. "We were very close."

"I'm sure you were." At least in her mind. Clearly, they hadn't been as close as she thought or liked to pretend.

Sam had snuck out successfully and gotten drunk, doing who knew how many other things that were against cult rules and his mother's wishes.

But Hawthorne would use the opening she'd given him. "Then I'm sure you must have known the name of the friend he was in contact with outside the cult."

"What?"

"The friend who left the cult but stayed in touch with Sam."

"My son would never have done that." Her eyebrows dipped in a disapproving glare as her voice grew stronger. "It is completely forbidden. We don't have contact with those who have turned their backs on our leader and rejected our love."

Her words sliced through Hawthorne's chest with the hurtful power of his mother's voice, the echo of the memory that suddenly seemed as real as the woman standing in front of him.

But it didn't mean anything. They were all taught the same thing. The same lies. The same false idea of what love was.

A pounding at the door yanked Hawthorne from the memory, from the pain.

Before Hawthorne could even think of hiding, Mrs. Ackerman took a quick step to the door and yanked it open.

Two men stood on the threshold, clothed in white.

Hoods up. Black pins depicting an eclipse on their broad chests.

Helpers.

Code for Patch's enforcers.

TWENTY-FOUR

What was taking Hawthorne so long? Jazz had been hanging out in the gift shop for twenty-three minutes. Well, she'd gone to the restroom once during that time so people would be less likely to notice.

Hopefully, it seemed natural for her to still be there, since she'd spent the first part of the time talking to Lavinia. She'd feigned about ten questions to show passionate curiosity and then told the tour guide she thought she wanted to join Best Life.

Lavinia had responded with so much excitement Jazz almost wished she really wanted to join. Like Hawthorne had predicted, the tour guide promptly signed Jazz up for an appointment with Desmond Patch himself tomorrow morning.

After Lavinia had left, Jazz kept an eye on the employees working in the gift shop. Two females worked the counter for the first ten minutes. Then, hanging around for so long paid off.

A guy about five-ten who looked like he could be nineteen relieved the teen girl who'd been talking to customers and restocking shelves. He fit the description of Randall perfectly.

Jazz pretended to browse the Best Life T-shirts as she

waited for the guy to get comfortable. Ambushing him instantly probably wouldn't yield the best results.

She pulled a T-shirt from the rack and read the words printed across the front: *Peace, Love, Destiny. Live your Best Life now.*

Funny that none of the members could wear any of the Best Life merch because of their dress code. But that didn't stop them from selling merch anyway.

Jazz smirked as she hung the shirt back on the rack and turned toward Randall.

He was taking mugs out of a box and setting them on a shelf. Should be something he could do while chatting.

Jazz worked her way slowly toward him, running her gaze over merchandise as she went to look like she was shopping. She slowed by Randall. "Nice mugs."

He didn't look at her or so much as grunt.

Great. "Got any with Desmond's handsome face?"

He turned his head toward her, and his eyes widened slightly. Then a smile cracked his lips.

Perfect. A player. Almost flattering, really, considering she was probably eleven years older than the kid. But she was always told she looked younger than her thirty years. Maybe he thought she was only in her early twenties.

"Yeah. We have some of those." He kept the goofy expression as he looked her up and down.

She gave him a sweet smile back. "Glad to hear it. You look like a smart man. Maybe you can help me."

"Sure." Randall's chest puffed out a bit as he grinned at her and stepped closer.

"I'm thinking of joining Best Life."

"Really?" A red flush colored his cheeks. "Cool."

"But I heard this story about a boy from here getting killed, and it kind of scares me."

His smile dropped as his eyebrows pulled together. "Killed?"

She nodded, pressing her lips together like she was actually worried. "At the Tri-City Fair."

"Oh, that." Randall's shoulders visibly relaxed. "It was an accident. He was stupid. Snuck out and got himself drunk. Then went and killed himself playing around."

"Oh." Jazz tried for an expression of confusion and naïve innocence as best she could. "That's awful. Though I'm glad he wasn't murdered. Did you know him?"

"Yeah, I knew him. A real jerk, but you couldn't tell some people that."

Meaning Hawthorne's sister? Jazz kept the question to herself and searched for the best way to continue pumping the kid.

"Sounds like you had some run-ins with him." She caught her lower lip with her teeth like she was concerned for Randall.

"Nothing I couldn't handle." He bent over and picked up the box of mugs that she was pretty sure didn't need to be set on the shelf at that moment. But it gave him a chance to flex his muscles. Which she couldn't see under the loose sleeves of his robe anyway.

She squelched the urge to roll her eyes. "I can see that." She pretended to admire his arm muscles with the direction of her gaze. "But how did no one notice he wasn't at the commune that night? I learned on my tour that there's a curfew."

"Only for our own good." A defensive note edged his tone. "So we don't become victims of the evils out there. Like Sam. And we can't better ourselves if we're distracted by worldly things outside."

The kid sounded like a programmed artificial intelligence response. But she pretended to buy it. "That makes sense. So you must've been doing something better while Sam was sneaking out, getting into trouble."

"Of course. I was communing with the stars."

"Ooh. That sounds cool." Actually sounded kooky and ridiculous, but she kept her expression open and curious. "All by yourself all night?" Perfect. He'd think she was asking if he had a girlfriend.

Sure enough, his grin slid back onto his face. "It goes until nine thirty so we can make ten o'clock lights out. I was with the other members in our stars alignment course. My ex-girlfriend was there, too. But I'm not seeing anyone right now."

Jazz tried her best starstruck giggle. Sounded more like a strangled frog, but the way the guy's eyes lit, he must've bought it.

She'd have to ask Hawthorne if that timing gave Randall an alibi for Sam's death. She hadn't found out when Sam had died or what time he'd left the commune. If anyone knew.

"So if Sam's death was an accident, why did the news talk about his dad being angry at you guys?"

"Oh, man. He went crazy." Randall glanced around, like checking for listeners. But the shop was mostly empty. The middle-aged female employee chatted with a customer at the register at the opposite end of the store.

"What do you mean? You saw him?" Jazz widened her eyes like she was impressed.

"Oh, yeah. We all did. He attacked our leader."

"No. He attacked Desmond Patch?"

"Yeah. Would've punched him, too, if the Helpers hadn't gotten him off."

"Helpers?"

"The strongest men in our community. They help maintain order."

That didn't sound a bit creepy. Jazz tried to keep the sarcastic thought from coloring her expression. "What did they do to him?"

"Sam's dad? They had to drag him out and forbid him from ever coming back."

"Wow. But you don't think he was right? I mean, that Patch was to blame for what happened to Sam?"

"Oh, no. Our leader only wants the best for all of us. He wants us to live our best life. And he does all he can to help us arrive at our spiritual and physical nirvana."

There he went again. Like she'd pressed the right button to get the programmed answer. Eerie.

"You sure you want to join?" A hint of suspicion crept into Randall's eyes. "You don't seem to think very positively of us."

"Oh, I just don't understand it all. And I've been burned before."

He nodded. "I get that. I have, too. But you'll really like it here if you stay." He gave her what was probably supposed to be a charming smile. "I'll make sure of that."

"Thanks." She managed a friendly expression as she started to put distance between them. "Catch you later."

She let out a long breath as she left the gift shop. Mission accomplished, hopefully. But where was Hawthorne?

She checked her watch. Thirty-five minutes since he'd peeled off to talk to Sam's mother. Had he gotten into trouble?

Seemed hard to believe in a place filled with such happy, friendly people. But something about Randall's programmed responses made her see something different as she looked around now. Saw the people standing in small groups and talking or walking by with books, all in matching white robes. Giving her matching white smiles whenever they saw her watching.

Was it all programmed? Calculated to get people to join the community?

Hawthorne seemed to think there was some danger at Best Life. And he should know. He'd grown up there.

Jazz's nerves started to tingle as the small hairs on the back of her neck stood on end.

What if that danger had caught up with Hawthorne?

Hawthorne twisted his wrist that was tied to a metal rail secured to the wall. The face of his watch was hard to read in the dimly lit room, so he brought his free hand around to press the button for backlight.

Nearly twenty-five minutes since he'd been brought into this room by the Helpers and left there. His cell was a small rectangle. Dark, smooth floor and white walls with minimal lighting like a haunting interrogation room from a TV show. A metal table stood in the middle of the rectangle.

Unless he missed his guess, the Helpers were getting Patch. Which was the only reason he hadn't ditched their hold as soon as they'd tried to escort him from Mrs. Ackerman's dwelling.

It went against the desire of every fiber of his being to acquiesce. To pretend he was as helpless as the scrawny boy he'd been the last time a Helper had pulled him out of class and brought him to a room like this. For *guidance*, they'd said.

Being forced to kneel on a tray of rocks for ten minutes with his hands tied behind his back was hardly guidance. And all because he'd dared to question his teacher's instruction on the importance of obeying the stars and the stars' emissary, Desmond Patch.

When he'd told his parents, his mother had put ointment on his knees. They'd said they hoped he'd learned from the experience. And that Desmond Patch was always right and was teaching Hawthorne the path to live his best life.

Well, Hawthorne was living his best life. Away from Desmond Patch.

And he didn't need to prove he was right anymore. Didn't have to prove he was stronger than those goons and far from helpless. There'd be opportunity for that later. When the time was right.

Now, he would take full advantage of this change in circumstances. He'd landed a private interview with Desmond Patch. And he hadn't even had to make an appointment.

A click sounded. Probably someone unlocking the door.

Light spilled into the room from the hallway.

A shadow filled it. A silhouette he'd recognize anywhere. Desmond Patch.

The cult leader walked into the room with his even, dramatic stride. Then he pivoted in one motion to slam Hawthorne with a stare.

Hawthorne hid the instinctive, inward flinch. A responding surge of anger shot into his chest. How could he still be afraid of this man?

He wasn't. Not consciously. But it was as if the little boy hidden somewhere inside him had suddenly seen the monster from his nightmares and couldn't help but recoil.

But only for a second. Hawthorne, the adult, met Desmond Patch's stare without blinking. All the while searching those charcoal eyes.

Exactly what he'd thought. Calculating, cold, but not one hundred percent confident. Something else lurked far back in that gaze. A hint of doubt. Maybe even fear.

Good. He should be afraid. Hawthorne wasn't a boy anymore. "You know I could sue you till I own your whole fortune, Best Life products, and this property for chaining me up here." Hawthorne pulled on the zip tie for emphasis. "Not to mention the legal charges I'll hit you with first."

Oh, yeah. A definite flicker of doubt in the eyes at that. But then defiance covered the emotion as Patch responded. "You are a trespasser on our private property."

That voice. Smooth as silk and sharp as a blade. "And you even invaded the home of one in our community. A grieving mother. We have the right to help her defend herself and to detain you until the authorities can come to our aid."

"Ah. So you've called the police?"

Patch held his gaze but didn't respond.

Thought not.

"I see you still hold great resentment for me and the love I've shown your family."

Hawthorne swallowed, trying to control the gag reflex Patch was activating. "You don't know the meaning of love."

The man donned a pitying expression, slowly moving his

head back and forth. "You had so much potential. But you always returned kindness and love with resentment and disobedience."

Patch stepped closer. Then he lowered to a squat, his white robe with two wide, red vertical stripes down the front billowing out around him.

An inch closer, and Hawthorne could grab him. Easily put him into submission and make him pay for everything he'd done to their family. But that wouldn't help him find the truth about Sam. And choking the guy out wouldn't exactly be the Christian thing to do.

Love your enemies and pray for those who persecute you.

Yeah. Hawthorne needed more work on following that Bible verse. Maybe after he got justice for Sam.

"I tried to show you the way. The path to your best life was there before you, but you refused to take it. Even when I tried to help you and guide you. You rejected my love. The love of everyone in this community. You rejected your poor mother and father."

Hawthorne tamped down the flame of anger Patch's dig intentionally flamed higher. Did he want Hawthorne to attack him so he could try for an assault charge?

Hawthorne breathed through his nostrils. Had to stay calm. "Is that what Sam did?"

Patch blinked. Good. A genuine reaction.

"Sam Ackerman. The kid who died because he had to sneak out to go to the fair instead of being able to go with his family like a normal boy."

Patch pushed off the floor to stand. "The boy had a rebellious temperament like you do. The evil took hold of him too young." He shook his head with a sorry attempt at a sad expression. "I tried everything in my power to break him free, but he refused to be saved. The stars and I can only guide you to the best life if you are willing. You know that, Hawthorne."

The condescension in the way he said Hawthorne's name, an exact match for the thankfully few times Hawthorne had to talk to him as a boy, still snaked along his spine like a slinking reptile.

"So you decided to punish him, didn't you?" Hawthorne allowed repulsion to seep into his tone. "You followed him to the fair and decided to enact some retribution of your own. Or maybe tried to bend him to your will once and for all."

"I'm surprised at you, Hawthorne." Patch didn't look surprised. His lips pointed upward at the edges in an amused smile. "You were taught enough here to know I do not believe in retribution or violence. I abhor both."

"Oh, right. So I suppose you have an alibi for the night Sam was killed?"

"Not that I need one. But, yes. I was with my wife and other community members in an all-night vigil. Star formation was at its peak, and we knew some in our community would have a chance to achieve the next plane of their journey to epiphany."

"And which wife would that be?"

Patch's mouth twitched. Struck a nerve there. The man had already been on his second marriage when Hawthorne left the cult. Who knew what number he was on now.

"Of course, she and all the members would be your alibi. They'd never cross you."

"We do love each other, that is true. But you know we don't do violence or hurt others."

"Yeah, I've heard the lie."

Patch gave him a sad look, as if he were a doctor pondering a patient who refused to seek treatment for his fatal illness. "I cannot control what you choose to believe. I can only guide you to the truth. It is up to you if you choose to reject it and your best life."

"Oh, but I do know the truth, Patch." Hawthorne glared at the man. "And you do, too. That's why you know how to twist it so well to your advantage. To make lies sound true and the truth sound false. To manipulate people into following you off a cliff if you say 'jump.' I suppose that's why you think you can get away with sabotaging the Tri-City Fair, too. You think you're invincible."

"My, my." Patch met his stare with a blank expression. "You do have an imagination. You were already so hardened and willful when you arrived here. I told your parents they should have joined us sooner so we could have trained you when you were younger."

"So you could've bent me to your will, you mean."

"Then your poor sister followed in your footsteps." Patch continued as if Hawthorne hadn't spoken. "She wanted to be like you, you know."

"Now she's happy and free to live her life. Not exactly what you wanted." Hawthorne smirked.

"She's in danger now. Such great danger."

Hawthorne's muscles clenched. "Is that a threat?"

"I don't threaten, Hawthorne. But I do warn people. To help them."

Hawthorne jerked his bound wrist at a backward angle, snapping the zip tie and launching to his feet before Patch could move.

He stood nose-to-nose with Patch, his own height putting him an inch taller.

Something flickered in Patch's eyes. Fear.

Satisfaction pulsed through Hawthorne. "You should've brought your goons in here with you, Patch." Hawthorne doubted the man even had basic self-defense skills given how much he relied on bodyguards and psychological control. Hawthorne could take him apart so easily.

"If you touch me, many will pay the price. Beginning with your parents."

"Another threat?" Hawthorne gripped Patch's arms, careful not to squeeze quite hard enough to leave bruises, concocted evidence of the physical assault the coward would probably claim to the police. "You may have part of my family in your hold, Patch. But if you want the rest of them, you'll have to come through me."

Hawthorne pushed him just enough to make Patch take a

step backward to catch himself. Then Hawthorne turned, a smile landing on his face as he marched from the room and stalked past the stunned goons in the hallway with a parting wave.

Maybe coming back wasn't such a bad idea after all.

TWENTY-FIVE

"I was about to come in there and rescue you." Jazz put on a smile to cover the concern that had been twisting her stomach for the last ten minutes as Hawthorne walked toward her in the parking lot outside Best Life. "That must've been some chat with Sam's mom."

The grim set of Hawthorne's mouth as he glanced around made her smile fade. Something was wrong.

"Meet me at my car." He angled away before reaching her SUV and headed to the next row of cars, farther from the Best Life commune.

She took a roundabout path to his car, making sure to keep other vehicles between her and anyone's view if they were watching from inside Best Life. That was clearly what he was worried about. But why?

Tension clenched her insides as she neared his black sedan, where he waited by the driver's door.

"Mind getting in?"

She shook her head and went to the passenger side as he ducked inside. She slid onto the leather seat in his obviously expensive car and immediately found his gaze. "What happened?"

"Mrs. Ackerman called the Helpers on me."

"Helpers." The guys Randall had said maintained order.

"Patch's enforcers."

"He has enforcers?"

"Oh, yeah." A muscle in Hawthorne's jaw twitched as he turned his head to look out the windshield.

Her ribs squeezed as she watched him. What exactly did these enforcers do to him? Didn't see any signs of injury. That was good. But there were ways to hurt people that didn't leave marks. She swallowed. "What did they do?"

"Took me to a room where they left me tied up to wait for Patch."

She stared at Hawthorne's profile, shock rolling through her. "But they all seemed so friendly and kind. Like nice people."

"That's the visitor treatment." Hawthorne returned his gaze to Jazz. "They wouldn't get anyone to join if people knew how dark and disturbing they actually are."

"But why would anyone stay if that's what they're really like?"

Hawthorne turned away again. Sighed. "A number of reasons. For one, they don't tend to treat the adults badly, depending on how you define it. The adults could technically leave when they want or report abuses, so Patch handles them carefully. He gives them what they think they want. He just happens to be able to convince them that whatever he says is what they want."

"So they'll put up with things people wouldn't ordinarily?"

Hawthorne glanced at her. "He gets them so twisted around. They believe lies are true and the truth is all lies. He preys on their selfish desires and heightens them by having them spend all their time focusing on themselves. Contemplating every thought and emotion, acting on desires and impulses and prioritizing what's best for themselves above all else."

Hawthorne gripped the top of the steering wheel. "But the irony is they aren't even doing what's best for themselves. Only what Patch has convinced them is best. They're like puppets on his strings, but they voluntarily stay there because he gets them to want that life."

"That's insane."

"Yeah." Hawthorne let out a humorless laugh. "That's the perfect word for it."

Hurt for Hawthorne, for the boy who'd had to deal with all of that, swelled behind her ribs. "How'd you ever get out?"

His eyes found hers, softening slightly. "I was twelve when my family joined. That helped. I was old enough to know what we'd left behind and to see the problems of the cult. Though what bothered me most at that age, of course, were all the rules about what I could and couldn't do."

His mouth curved in a wry smile. "But being old enough to question my parents helped me see things more clearly than they did. I worked hard to convince them to leave every year until I was eighteen. I don't know if they ever thought my attempts were anything more than teenage rebellion."

He ran his hand over the light stubble on his jaw, weariness settling on his features.

Jazz longed to reach over and rub his shoulders or just hold his hand and tell him she was there for him. But they weren't a real couple.

"Some family, huh?" He glanced her way with that same crooked smile that did nothing to hide the pain in his eyes.

"We can't pick our family."

Something in her tone must've given away the hurt tightening her throat. He tilted his head slightly and watched her. "Have your own family problems?"

"Mainly a lack of family, I guess." Her turn to look out the windshield at the quiet parking lot.

"I just dumped all my baggage on you. Don't hold back." His attempt at humor brought her gaze back to him.

"My dad died two years ago. It was just him and me growing up, except when I'd stay with my aunt and uncle instead. None of them ever liked me. Not my dad, Aunt Joan, Uncle Pierce. Even my cousins hated me."

Silence hung between them as she looked out the passenger window, not really seeing anything but a jumble of sad memories.

"Did you ever get to see your mom?" Hawthorne's question came to her soft and gentle, like a comforting touch.

"No." Jazz brought her gaze to his. "She left when I was a baby. I have no memory of her."

The muscles at the corners of his eyes and mouth twitched like in a flinch. For her sake. He did care.

The proof of it pumped her heart faster.

"I'm so sorry." Sincerity emanated from his eyes. "I'm sorry about your family."

He gave the smallest of nods. "I guess we have that in common, too."

So he'd noticed they had things in common. Almost like he was keeping track.

Her pulse skipped a beat. Maybe they could be each other's family.

The urge to say the thought out loud pushed at her lips. But she stopped herself. Too much, too soon. He'd think she was proposing. Perfect way to scare off a guy, especially one used to traveling and never settling down.

She'd have to be patient. Wait until he cared for her even more. Until he wanted to stay with her. Or maybe take her along on his travels.

Right now, she'd do everything she could to continue to impress him and prove her worth. Like with the info she'd learned from Randall. "I did find out some interesting things from Rebekah's jealous ex."

"You saw Randall?" Hawthorne's eyes lit, electrifying the teal color so much that Jazz had to fight to keep a clear thought in her head while under the spell of those mesmerizing orbs.

"Yeah. He was in the gift shop like your sister said."

"Perfect. Did he talk?"

She smiled. "A lot. He seemed to take a liking to me, so I was able to question him pretty naturally."

A grin showed off Hawthorne's teeth. "Of course he did. What's not to like?"

Jazz's pulse fluttered. But she tried to stay nonchalant. "I know, right?" She flicked her hair back over her shoulder, earning a chuckle from Hawthorne. "I tried to check for an alibi the night of Sam's death. Randall said he was with others at the cult until nine thirty. Would that give him an alibi?"

"No. The autopsy put time of death between ten p.m. and midnight. But the investigation concluded he must have died during the last ride of the night at the Logboat Adventure, which would mean just before eleven."

"So Randall could've snuck out after his weird stars class."

"Yeah."

"I have a hard time imagining he would've, though."

Hawthorne lifted his eyebrows slightly. "Why is that?"

"I get that he was mad at Rebekah and Sam, and he obviously thinks Sam was a jerk, but he's also totally in love with the cult. He spewed out these programmed answers anytime I pushed the right button."

Amusement curved Hawthorne's mouth as he watched her.

"So I can't really see him having been able to think independently enough to buck the cult and his beloved leader. He'd have had to break so many rules and be somewhat clever."

"Sounds like a good assessment. You're probably right, he's at the bottom of the suspect list."

Jazz nodded. "He did tell me something helpful, though. He said Sam's dad attacked Desmond Patch."

Hawthorne angled toward her. "Attacked him?"

"That's what he said. Sam's dad apparently had to be dragged out of the commune and was banned from coming back."

"Huh." Hawthorne rotated forward and rested his hands

in a loose hold on the steering wheel. He looked ahead through the windshield.

"Are you thinking what I'm thinking?"

He turned his head toward Jazz. "That Sam's dad has a motive to sabotage the fair and put the blame on Patch?"

"Exactly." She pressed her lips together. "We've got to find Sam's dad."

"Sam's mother doesn't seem to know where he is."

"I'll ask Cora to track him down for us."

Hawthorne gave her a questioning look.

"She's the communications and tech specialist at Phoenix K-9 Agency. She's a whiz at research and finding people nobody else can."

"Okay, great." Hawthorne didn't look as happy as his words sounded. A faraway expression coated his eyes.

"You've thought of something else, haven't you?"

He redirected his gaze to Jazz, seeming to come back to the present. "I was just thinking. If Sam's dad has such a volatile temper, I wonder if Sam could've inherited the same tendency."

"What if he did?"

"Could've led him to fight. With Randall or anyone else."

"Like the other young guys he might've been with at the fair?"

"It's still only a theory. I don't even know that Sam was in that rowdy group. But it's the best lead I have so far."

"What about Desmond Patch? You saw him?"

"Oh, yes." Hawthorne turned back to the wheel and clamped it harder this time.

"Do you think he could be behind any of this? Sam? The sabotage?"

"I definitely wouldn't put it past him to have made an example of Sam." Hawthorne kept his grip on the wheel as he threw Jazz a glance. "He favors harsh discipline with kids."

She winced inwardly at the implications. Had Hawthorne suffered from such so-called discipline as a child?

"But…" His hands loosened their hold and lowered to the bottom of the steering wheel. "He's smart. Very smart. He wouldn't declare to the world he sabotaged the fair if he was really behind it. Unless his sense of invincibility has become so great as to make him believe his own lies."

"It's a possibility. Sometimes even genius leads people to insane actions." Jazz touched Hawthorne's muscled shoulder. "I have a meeting scheduled for tomorrow. I'll stay on him."

Hawthorne's brow furrowed.

Jazz had thought that would please him.

"I don't think you should be alone with him."

"But it was your idea."

"Before."

"Before what?" Her heart rate sped faster. Did he mean before he'd realized he cared for her?

"Before I saw him again. And his goons."

Oh. Disappointment slowed her pulse.

Hawthorne met Jazz's gaze, intensity in his. "It's not a safe place."

She stared back. "Most places aren't. Never bothered me." As quick as a reflex, she had her knife out of the ankle sheath and in her hand. "Future heroine in your books, remember? I got this." She winked.

A grin took over his handsome face as his posture relaxed, and he looked from the knife to her. "How could I ever forget? Desmond Patch had better watch his back. Jazz Lamont might be the one to take him down."

TWENTY-SIX

Jazz had never been so uptight on a patrol in her life. Terrorists hidden in the desert wilderness had nothing on Phoenix Gray.

The boss and her equally silent K-9 Dag had accompanied Flash and Jazz since nine thirty. Meaning Jazz had survived two hours so far with only her and Phoenix. Two hours for the boss to observe how Jazz did patrol. And probably note everything she thought Jazz was doing wrong.

But the boss hadn't said anything critical yet. She'd said almost nothing at all. Not even when Jazz had shown her the sites of the sabotage.

At the Skyride, Phoenix had only asked if Jazz had seen which portion of the exploded pod was left and how much of her uncle's pod had been damaged.

She hadn't remarked on anything. Hadn't given Jazz a clue to what she was thinking.

But Jazz was sure she *was* thinking. A lot. She just didn't like Jazz well enough to tell her anything.

That made two of them. Jazz didn't trust Phoenix either.

So they walked the fairgrounds in silence for most of the time.

Jazz checked her watch as they took the curve of the main path that led to another section of rides.

Flash's panting sounded loudly next to Jazz, thanks to the absence of the usual fair noises.

The music from the rides had ended about thirty minutes ago when the operators started closing them down for the night.

The attendees of the country music concert had left around that time, as well. They should all be out by now, though they wouldn't have been in this sector of the grounds anyway.

Dag kept his mouth closed at Phoenix's side. Probably not allowed to pant like normal dogs or he'd ruin the mystery.

Jazz stifled a chuckle at her own joke. She kept her gaze moving at the same time, not about to be caught slacking by the boss.

Phoenix set a steady pace, slightly quicker than Jazz's usual patrol speed but not too fast. The woman's posture had stayed confident and strong, not showing a moment of tiring after two hours of walking.

Jazz had expected nothing less. She couldn't deny Phoenix was in perfect physical shape. Toned and slim without an ounce of weakness or softness aside from her feminine curves. Jazz had wondered more than once what Phoenix did for workouts. But she wasn't about to ask a personal question of the boss.

She could ask the question that had been burning on her tongue all night. The boss wouldn't object to her wanting to know information that could help their investigation, would she?

Jazz took a breath and risked it. "Did Cora find anything on Sam Ackerman's father?"

Phoenix didn't so much as glance her way or pause her movement, clearly not as startled as Jazz was that she'd initiated conversation. "Gary Ackerman. Fifty-one. Caucasian, brown on brown. Location unknown."

"She can't find him?" Surprise lifted Jazz's voice. Cora could usually find people within hours.

"Not yet." Phoenix seemed to increase the pace as she

talked, still not looking at Jazz, her head slowly rotating side to side as she scanned the surroundings. "He ended a lease on an apartment in Wisconsin three months ago. The last use of his credit card. No trail since."

"Oh. Too bad."

"We'll find him." Phoenix's trademark confidence. Nothing seemed to shake her certainty about everything. An admirable quality if it wasn't so unnerving. And suspicious. As if she'd figured out a way to rig life. To cheat it.

"Cora learned Desmond Patch has a criminal history."

Jazz cut Phoenix a look to see if she'd been reading Jazz's mind.

The boss kept her gaze moving, checking for threats without a pause or indication of anything amiss. "He was arrested for vandalism as a college student during a protest rally. He was an active member of the Students for the Environment Society."

The radical environmental group that had spawned the Twin Cities river dam bomber that Bristol and PK-9 had caught before Jazz joined the agency. Yikes. "So he's probably not a peaceful pacifist like he claims." Which would totally fit what Hawthorne had told Jazz about the cult leader.

"He's a viable suspect for the sabotage and your aunt's death. He's taken credit for violence in the past, when he felt it was for a worthy cause."

Jazz would need to tell Hawthorne as soon as she could. They'd bumped into him earlier on patrol, but their conversation had been brief. Jazz didn't blame him for not wanting to stick around with Phoenix eyeing him in her intimidating way from under the bill of her charcoal cap.

A rumble interrupted her thoughts. Dag.

Flash almost instantly added his own growl.

Jazz peered in the direction of their gazes.

A tree and grass.

Phoenix picked up her pace, her attention locked somewhere ahead and to the right.

The Logboat Adventure ride was around that corner.

Jazz lengthened her stride to keep up.

They rounded the corner where the tree had blocked their view.

A shadow moved in a doorway. The staff entrance of the Logboat ride.

"Hold it." Phoenix's cold voice would've stopped Jazz in her tracks. Especially accompanied as it was by two K-9s' warning growls. "Step out, slowly. Hands where I can see them."

The shadowy figure shifted, coming into the light cast from the lampposts along the main path.

"Freddie?" The word popped from Jazz's mouth as the food vendor stepped into view, his hands lifted in front of him.

"Fred Blain." How Phoenix knew who he was, Jazz couldn't guess. But like Nevaeh always said, the boss seemed to know everything. "Step over here." Phoenix angled her head toward the main path as she kept her hand on her hip. Close to her holstered Glock.

Freddie's eyes were wide as he stared at Phoenix and slowly followed the narrow offshoot that led away from the staff entrance. He stopped on the main path, about six feet from the women and their K-9s.

"Are you carrying any weapons?"

"Weapons?" Genuine shock overtook his features at Phoenix's question. "Oh, my goodness. No. I don't own any weapons." He started lowering his hands, probably involuntarily. Poor guy looked scared to death.

He'd been so friendly with Hawthorne and Jazz. She knew anyone could be guilty of anything, but it didn't seem likely Freddie was violent or the killer she and Hawthorne were looking for. "What were you doing here, Freddie?"

His gaze jerked to her face as his hands lowered completely. "Molly visited Christy here tonight, and she thought she dropped her reading glasses somewhere on the path."

"From the staff entrance?"

He nodded. "She and Christy left together that way at closing."

Jazz fought to keep from narrowing her eyes at him. Better to keep an open and non-judgmental expression. Especially to compensate for Phoenix's stony silence. "It's well past closing now, Freddie. Why are you still here?"

"One of the kids royally messed up the count for the night, so I had to redo it twice myself. But I'd promised Molly I would look for her glasses before I left. She said she had to get home to watch *Murder She Wrote*."

Sounded exactly like Molly. Jazz glanced at Phoenix. Would the boss think it was a false alarm, too?

"You're free to go." Phoenix's deep voice projected command through her sheer lack of emotion. "Be sure you leave the grounds immediately."

"Of course." Freddie glanced at the boss with widened eyes as he turned and hurried off in the right direction to reach the fair's main entrance. Poor guy probably wouldn't sleep a wink tonight.

"Not sure you had to spook him so much." Jazz wanted to snap the criticism back as soon as it escaped her mouth. Irritation must've given her the courage. To be stupid. Phoenix could fire her in a second.

The cap turned in Jazz's direction, bringing the stare that was probably impossible to read if Jazz could see it in the shadow the bill cast over the woman's eyes. She suddenly flicked on a flashlight Jazz didn't know she had and shined the blinding beam on the closed staff access door. "Do you know where he was?"

"The Logboat Adventure ride." Don't tell her Phoenix thought Jazz didn't know her way around the fair.

"Where Sam Ackerman's body was found."

"You okay?" Hawthorne glanced at Jazz as he walked with her out the main entrance of the fair at the end of their shift.

He gave Barry a wave over his shoulder as the guard swung the gate closed behind them, then returned his attention to the redheaded beauty.

She was awfully quiet tonight. Not full of her usual spunk and smiles. "I guess I should've asked you for more details about Sam's death. I didn't realize he was found at the Logboat Adventure until Phoenix told me. I don't even know how she knew." Jazz muttered the last words as if to herself.

"Yeah, sorry. I guess everything's been going so fast, I didn't share all the information with you. He was found there, but Rebekah and Sam's dad don't think he died there. They think he was killed somewhere else and moved."

Jazz turned her big eyes on him, and something thumped in his chest.

Couldn't be his heart. He wasn't emotionally involved with Jazz. He couldn't be.

"What do you think?"

He swallowed, his throat suddenly tight. "I was skeptical at first. I know how strong the desire is for people to make sense of their loved one's death. But there is the fact that Sam was so afraid of water he'd refuse to even take baths."

"Oh." Her eyebrows rose as she stopped on the sidewalk outside the fairgrounds, turning to face him. "That does make it unlikely he'd be on that ride."

"Autopsy showed he was intoxicated, so that might've overcome his fears. That was the detectives' theory at the time."

"But you don't buy it." She was starting to read him well. Or maybe it was that intelligence he'd admired in her from the beginning.

"Well, the ride operator that was on that night showed me her closing routine. She does a thorough inspection of the entire interior of the ride. I don't think she'd have missed Sam's body lying there."

Jazz glanced down at Flash who sat next to her leg, looking a little weary from his long shift. "So that would back up the theory he was killed elsewhere, then moved after the ride was closed."

"Exactly."

"Who could do that? Are you saying someone with staff access would've had to do it? Someone who works at the fair?" The way Jazz's features contorted showed how horrifying she found the idea. Of course, she would. The fair was like her home.

"Could be. But I think it's just as possible that someone else could've found a way to hide and wait for the ride operator to leave before putting Sam in there."

"But how could someone else get in?"

Hawthorne lifted his shoulders. "Picked the lock? I don't think the police had reason to check for that. Or tried different rides until they found one that had been left unlocked by accident. If Sam was killed, it doesn't seem like a very well-planned crime. More like an unplanned murder that made the killer have to punt the best he or she could."

"So you think any visitor could've done it." She pressed her lips together. "Or a vendor."

Hawthorne nodded. "I was sorry to hear about Freddie, too. He's a nice guy. Or at least he seems to be."

"Yeah. He's new this year, so I suppose I shouldn't feel so disloyal for suspecting him. I think it's because Molly's taken such a liking to him. And he reminds me a lot of his cousin Jim who used to come with the food stand. He was a great guy. Always nice to me and Nevaeh." She glanced toward the parking lot. "I guess I'd better get going, or Nev will wonder what happened to me."

"The two of you share your apartment?"

"No." She turned away from him with the hasty reply. "I'm staying at her house just for...fun." Jazz stepped off the sidewalk onto the blacktop.

"I'll walk you to your car." He fell in step beside her, Flash on her other side.

Jazz shot him a glance, her eyebrow quirked.

"Though I know you absolutely do not need my protection."

She smiled at him and moved a bit closer, letting her arm brush against his. "Doesn't mean I don't want it."

His pulse picked up speed as heat flared in his belly. A natural reaction of any red-blooded male. Didn't mean he was losing control of his emotions. Or that he had to act on any of the attraction he had to admit he felt for this woman. Like when she'd surprised him by putting her arm around his waist and taking his hand at the commune.

He should've pulled away instantly. But he'd had to keep their cover, which he knew was the only reason she'd initiated the touches anyway. Trouble was, the longer he'd kept the connection with her, the more he had started to like it. Way too much.

Kind of like now. It felt pretty good—almost natural—to walk her to her car.

Good grief. He could throttle himself for the romantic sentiments. He didn't even like to include romance in his novels, let alone his personal life. It was after midnight, and he was clearly feeling the effects of fatigue. He needed to wrap this up.

"Do you think Freddie was up to something, being by the Logboat ride?" Jazz was apparently doing a better job focusing on something other than their proximity.

Hawthorne cleared the thickness out of his throat. "I don't really know. It is strange. From what I've seen, the vendors usually close as quickly as they can at eleven and head straight out."

"But his excuse could've been legit." Hopefulness laced her tone.

"True. And, honestly, I'm not sure what he could've been doing related to Sam at the Logboat Adventure. It's two years too late to tamper with any evidence. But sabotage? That's a real possibility."

"Phoenix seemed to think it could be related to Sam's death." Jazz turned into the row where her SUV must be parked. "Though I'm not sure how. She just told me it was where Sam was found. Like it was important." Jazz cast him a glance. "She never really explains any of her riddles."

"Not too surprising. She seems very..." Hawthorne should be able to find the perfect word to describe Phoenix Gray, given he used words for his profession. But Jazz's boss somehow evaded his search for the perfect descriptor. "Enigmatic." Best he could do for someone he couldn't figure out, let alone describe. At least not from a first meeting.

Jazz's musical laugh floated in the cool night air. "That's perfect. Most people say 'intense' or 'intimidating' after they first meet her."

He nodded. "Those work, too." He gave her a smile as they slowed by the rear bumper of Jazz's SUV. "I assume she must be more relaxed around the agency with people she knows."

"Nope."

"Oh?" Intriguing. His writer's imagination started to percolate.

"You're curious about her, aren't you?"

He pushed his hands into his pants pockets and shrugged. "She does seem mysterious."

"She is that. She'd probably make a better heroine for your novels than I would." She looked away, but he caught the disappointment in her voice. Like she expected to get dumped for someone else.

"Not at all."

That brought Jazz's attention back to him in a quick jump. Her eyebrows lifted.

"I don't think a heroine based on her would be relatable enough. A little mystery and a few secrets can go a long way. A lot can be too much."

"Too much, huh?" Her smile flashed in the shadows that competed with the light from the nearby lamppost. "Then I'd better be sure to tell you everything about me so you can choose how much to keep secret."

"I'd like that." His gaze locked on hers, dipping into the

pool of her emerald eyes. Until he realized what he'd said—how it sounded. "We'll need to have another interview so I can get more facts…for the character." He still couldn't pull his gaze away from those hypnotic eyes. Maybe because of the way they were fixed on him. Like she couldn't look away either.

A car door slammed.

They both startled and jerked back. He hadn't realized how close they'd been standing to each other. He twisted to look toward the noise.

Only Dan Harris getting into his sedan to leave. Hawthorne had thought Dan had the overnight shift. Must've gotten him confused with someone else.

"Well…" Hawthorne turned to Jazz, rubbing his hand across the back of his neck while he tried to get his ragged heart rate to settle down. "Thanks for telling me about Patch. Not surprising he has a criminal background."

"Yeah. I'm glad I have the meeting with him tomorrow. I'll let you know what I find out."

"If there's even a hint of danger or anything off, text or call, and I'll be there as fast I can."

"Thanks. But I've got it, remember?"

"Right." He grinned. "I keep forgetting I'm talking to a thriller heroine."

"Dangerous thing to forget." Her eyes twinkled as she laughed.

"Yes, it is." Almost as dangerous as forgetting to keep his guard up and keep his distance. Women didn't usually worm their way past his defenses. He was in and out too quickly for that at any location. Especially since he'd become a Christian, he wouldn't go in for short flings, and he knew he was better off single. Meant to be single.

He couldn't let a woman even as special as Jazz interfere with what he knew was best. Having a spouse would limit what he could do. And he could end up like his parents, tied down to someone who would up and decide to do something insane like join a cult. And he'd be trapped. Or she could suddenly change personalities, reject God, turn out not to be a real Christian at all. He'd seen it happen to friends.

Jazz wasn't even claiming to be a Christian, so what in the world was he getting all worked up about?

He was going to tell her about the names Rebekah had given him of guys Sam could have stayed in touch with outside the cult. But the urge to get while the getting was good welled up inside him. He could tell her later, if the leads amounted to anything.

"Well, have a good night." He spun on his heel.

Her faint, surprised, "Goodnight," reached his ears as he kept walking away. Running away was more like it.

But isn't that what the Bible told him to do? Flee from temptation?

His quick flight landed him by his car in fifteen seconds when it probably should've taken him twenty. He unlocked the driver's door and slid in behind the wheel.

Something white and square caught his eyes, stuck to the windshield.

He paused. A hasty move to get out of the car right away could be just what someone wanted. Reaching for the paper without checking his surroundings would make him vulnerable to ambush.

He checked the side and rearview mirrors. Nothing but quiet parking lot, dotted by the ten cars that remained there for the overnight security guards.

Hand going to his holstered Glock, he slowly stood, checking in all directions.

An engine started.

Jazz's SUV pulled straight ahead through the empty stall in front of her and drove at an angle across the parking lot to leave.

Hawthorne reached for the paper on the windshield.

Blank.

He turned it over.

Typed letters stared up at him. *Curiosity killed the writer. Go somewhere else for research. Or it's The End for you.*

TWENTY-SEVEN

A crash smashed through Jazz's dream, jolting her upright in bed.

Flash sprang to his feet, snarling, and raced out of Nev's guest room.

Jazz snatched her Sig from its holster on her nightstand. Rushed after him.

A large blur nearly crashed into her in the hallway.

Alvarez. The K-9's barks stung her ears as he sprinted past.

Pop-pop-pop.

Shots. Near the back door. An AR-15?

Nev dashed up behind Jazz in her pajamas and satin cap.

Jazz stopped, gave her a look. All they needed to communicate the plan. Jazz would lead high, Nev would follow low. They hurried forward, weapons ready.

Snarls and barking. The intensity meant Flash and Al were charging to attack.

More pops cracked through the house.

If whoever it was hurt Flash...

Jazz pressed forward around the corner to the kitchen, trying not to let her rising emotion force her to rush into an ambush.

Yells and screams brought a smile to her face. The boys had caught their targets.

Jazz and Nev cleared the kitchen quickly and hurried to the short hallway that led to the mudroom by the back door.

She hit the mudroom fast, confident of what she'd find.

Flash had a man's arm in his jaws, pinning the squealing thug to the floor near a fallen AR-15.

Al controlled another guy, latched onto the man's hand and pulling hard.

Jazz glanced at Nev who stood a few feet from Jazz's side and aimed her gun at the intruder closest to her.

Nev nodded.

"Flash, Alvarez—out." Jazz kept her Sig aimed at Flash's prey as the K-9s released their holds and returned to their partners. "Good job, boys. We'll take it from here."

"Got zip ties on you?"

Jazz didn't take her eyes from the men to answer Nev. "Contrary to popular belief, I don't sleep with them."

Nev snorted. "Too bad. I'll cover while you get some."

"Roger."

With a gun in hand, two K-9s, and six feet between her and them, Nev's PTSD shouldn't be triggered if Jazz left her alone. Especially now that Nev was doing so much better coping.

Commanding Flash to stand guard, Jazz dashed to her room, grabbed zip ties from her backpack, and returned in seconds. She had the men's wrists tied behind their backs shortly after.

"What do you think?" Jazz gestured to the gaping dark opening that revealed the night outside. The crash that had woken them had apparently been the thugs kicking in the door, which now lay on the floor. "It's seamless indoor/outdoor access."

A cool breeze drifted in, along with the sound of crickets.

"Yeah, so chic." Nev rolled her eyes. "Cover them while I call everyone." Nev lowered her Sig and disappeared, reemerging soon with her cell phone.

She wasn't kidding about everyone.

Jazz moved to sit on the short bench along one wall while Nev phoned Phoenix, the police, and then Branson. At least all the calls were short.

And so was the wait for the first arrival. Which both Nev and Jazz predicted would be Phoenix.

Sure enough, the boss beat the police. One of the greatest mysteries about Phoenix was how she managed to never get a speeding ticket. Then again, Sof seemed to avoid them, too, even though she raced through the streets like a stock car driver. Some people had all the luck.

Phoenix walked up close to each thug where they sat on the floor, wrists tied behind their backs.

They looked none too comfortable, thanks to their bite wounds.

She crouched in front of one, then the other, staring into their faces until they looked away. She was so creepy, she even freaked criminals out. Not sure that said anything good about Phoenix Gray.

Sirens seemed to sound the end of Phoenix's silent interrogation of the intruders.

Nev went to open the front door and came back with a couple uniformed police officers and Sof, who must've arrived at the same time. She'd brought Raksa with her, and the German shepherd gave the bound thugs a warning growl as soon as he looked at them. Good judge of character.

Sof glanced at the kicked-in door, then smirked at the bad guys. "Little overconfident, don't you think? Next time, try not announcing your arrival."

"And pick an easier target." Nev added the critique as she swung her gaze to Jazz and winked.

Jazz smiled. So awesome to see Nev's spunk and courage back in full force, even after facing her worst nightmare. But she'd survived. And nearly a year later, she was thriving like she hadn't for years. No denying the PK-9 team and Branson had been good for her.

"Ma'am?" A tall policeman stopped by Jazz. "I'll need to get your name and your take on what happened here."

"Sure."

As Jazz described the night's events, Nev did the same with a different officer on the other side of the small room.

The rest of the PK-9 team members filed in as Jazz and Nev finished their accounts.

A couple EMTs also showed up and managed to work their way through the crowd to reach the injured men.

"Let's go to the living room." Nev pointed back up the short hallway as she glanced at the PK-9 team. Though not all of them were there. Phoenix had disappeared again. "I'll put on coffee."

"No, I'll do that." Cora touched Nev's shoulder as she gave her that maternal, concerned gaze that was pure Cora. "You and Jazz sit down and rest." She cast the look at Jazz, too. "We'll take care of everything."

Nev smiled. "Thanks." She caught up with Jazz and looped their arms together. "Guess we get to take it easy now."

"I won't fight it if you don't." Jazz grinned.

"I never refuse the royal treatment."

"Uh-huh. You remember you still have this on?" Jazz touched the edge of Nev's satin cap.

"And Branson's coming." Nev's eyes widened as a note of alarm infused her voice. "Though he wouldn't care, you know."

"Oh, I know." Jazz smiled. It would only be a few seconds before—

"I'm just gonna pop in the bathroom."

"Of course." Jazz laughed.

Nev pushed off of her with a grin, leaving Jazz to enter the living room alone.

But Bris was the only one there.

"Where is everyone?"

Bris tucked her hands into the pockets of her navy blue

PK-9 windbreaker. "Sof went outside to find Phoenix. Something about checking the premises for evidence."

"Nevaeh?" The deep voice of Branson Aaberg preceded his giant body through the front door. He glanced wildly at Bris and Jazz. "Where is she?"

Jazz held up her hands in a calming gesture. She hoped. The man looked like he was ready to attack someone. "She's fine. She'll be out in a sec."

"Branson?" Nev burst from the hallway like a ball out of a cannon, her arms outstretched.

Branson caught her in his muscled arms and smushed her against his chest. "Thank God you're okay." He buried his face in her mass of curls and closed his eyes.

It was kind of over the top, these head-over-heels lovers. But a lump formed in Jazz's throat anyway. And a hint of envy curdled in her stomach. She'd probably never have a man in her life who cared about her that much.

Unless…Would Hawthorne act like that if he knew Jazz had been in danger? There was no denying the electrifying chemistry between them in the parking lot tonight. Or last night, since it was now technically morning at nearly three a.m.

He'd had a hard time walking away from her. At least for a moment. She'd been pretty sure he had felt as drawn to her as she had to him.

"You two love birds going to let each other go long enough to catch your breath?" Bris brought Jazz's attention back to the present and the brunette's amused smile at the lovey-dovey couple. "Or at least to talk about what happened?"

Nev leaned back with a smile that didn't hold a trace of shyness or embarrassment. "Where's Phoenix? I figured she'd want to do a debrief or something."

"Outside with Sof." Jazz shrugged. Just like Phoenix to disappear without explanation to anyone.

"We're back." Sof flashed a grin as she entered ahead of Phoenix through the front door, their K-9's with them.

"Did you find anything?" Cora appeared from the hallway, carrying a tray of chocolate chip cookies—the prepackaged variety Nev kept on hand that Cora must've dug out of the cupboards.

"Black SUV parked a block away behind some trash bins." Sof stalked to the tray and grabbed one of the miniature cookies. "Stolen plates."

How did they run the plates so quickly? Without the police even being out there with them? Jazz itched to ask. But she'd just look dumb or like she was challenging Phoenix. The boss had probably phoned one of her mysterious police sources. Or maybe Agent Nguyen, her buddy at the FBI.

"We'll have the police search the vehicle interior and see if there's anything helpful." Phoenix stood near the closed front door with her feet in a wide stance, Dag sitting beside her leg.

Must be nice to be able to tell the police what to do. Though Jazz still wondered how Phoenix seemed to have that kind of power over...well, everyone.

"I'd like to know who these characters are, and why they broke into Nevaeh's house." Branson guided Nev to the sofa with a hand on her back. "Do you know what they were after?" He looked toward Phoenix.

"Jazz has a hit out on her." Nev lifted her adoring gaze to Branson as he sat beside her, filling nearly all the rest of the sofa with his large frame.

"And you didn't tell me that?" Surprise, but no irritation, shaped his voice.

Nev lifted one shoulder under the red terry robe she must've thrown on when she went to the bathroom. "It was Jazz's business." She glanced at Jazz.

Glad to know Nev didn't tell Branson absolutely everything. Jazz hadn't been sure. Now that they were about to get married, she knew Nev would want to share everything with him, and she'd wondered if that would include the private conversations Jazz and Nev had kept secret since they were seven. She should've known Nev wouldn't go that far.

"Well, now it's our business, too." Branson put an arm around Nev's shoulders. "I'm going to stay on the sofa here until I know you're out of danger."

Nev opened her mouth to protest, but Jazz beat her to it.

"I'll just leave."

Everyone's attention swung toward Jazz.

"Seriously. I'm obviously going to go back to my apartment. Or a hotel or something. I'm not going to keep bringing hitmen to Nev's door."

"You're welcome to stay with me at my house, Jazz." Cora's offer sent a jolt of surprise through her. Did Cora really want Jazz to stay with her? The woman was one of the sweetest people Jazz had ever met. She probably took in every stray, needy person she came across. But Jazz wasn't that needy.

"Thanks, but I'll be fine. I have Flash."

"Oh, no, you don't." Nev pushed off the sofa to stand, glaring at Jazz. "You are not going off somewhere to die alone." She planted fisted hands on her hips. "We can handle this together. We just did."

Jazz's mouth quirked as amusement interfered with her desire to be firm. "I hadn't really planned on dying, but…"

Nev relaxed her arms with a chuckle. "Good. Then you'll stay?" She glanced down at Branson, then returned her gaze to Jazz. "We'll need a chaperone anyway if this big bodyguard insists on sleeping on the sofa."

"Oh, yes. We can't have you sullying your Christian good girl reputation." Jazz rolled her eyes with a smile.

"Glad that's settled." Bris perched on the arm of the love seat that faced the happy couple. "But if we want it to be temporary and not have another night like tonight, we need to figure out who's behind this."

Cora nodded, standing near the coffee table as she transferred her gaze to Jazz. "I've been looking into the family ties, and your father's background appears clean. Lawrence

Lamont had an impeccable service record, as I'm sure you know. He seems to have been well-liked and highly respected by his fellow servicemen that I've spoken with, as well. No one knows of any enemies he could have had."

Impressive that Cora even talked to friends of Jazz's dad. She'd known Cora was thorough but not that thorough.

"So I'm afraid I haven't found anything useful yet. There is one possible anomaly that I needed to request more information on, and I'm waiting for that to come through."

"An anomaly?" Did Cora mean about Jazz's dad or something else?

"More of a curiosity at this point. I'll keep you informed as soon as I know more." Cora's mouth pinched. Was she holding something back? She'd said she was going to look into Jazz's mom, too. But Jazz wasn't about to ask. Not in front of all these people. And probably never at all. She'd already been rejected enough.

"Nothing from Ramone either." Sof walked closer to the love seat. "I'll check with him again now that a new pair of goons were hired."

"How did they even know I was here?" Jazz voiced the question that had been bothering her since they'd captured the hitmen. "I check for tails. There haven't been any. And I'm checking for trackers, too. Every time I take my SUV anywhere." She braced herself for someone to challenge her ability to find the tracker or spot tails.

"They likely watched your apartment until they concluded you weren't staying there." Phoenix finally spoke again, still standing guard by the door. "They would have then checked the addresses of your known associates from the agency."

A sinking feeling trickled downward to Jazz's stomach. "Which would've led them to my SUV in Nev's driveway." She should've thought of that and parked her SUV in the garage instead of Nev's pickup. Now she probably looked like an idiot to Phoenix…again.

"Do you think it's safe for Jazz to stay here?" Cora turned her blue eyes on the boss.

Jazz was wondering the same thing. The bad guys knew she was there. And even though they'd been caught, they could've first passed along the info to whoever had hired them. No way was she going to put Nev in danger, no matter how much her BFF insisted Jazz stay. Nev had been through enough hard times.

"With Nevaeh, Branson, and two protection K-9s, the results of any attack will likely end the same way." Phoenix's cap turned in Jazz's direction, like she was fixing her gaze on Jazz. "It's safer here than elsewhere alone."

But Phoenix didn't offer her own home for Jazz to stay in. She'd invited Cora in and let her stay at her house overnight when Cora's life was in danger. As far as Jazz could learn, no one else on the team had ever seen Phoenix's house. Everyone knew the boss had done that because she thought it was the safest place Cora could stay.

And Cora was her favorite. No one on the team seemed to know why, but they all knew it was true. Jazz just wished she knew what it took to be Phoenix's favorite. Or simply to get on her good side.

Phoenix clearly didn't want to get involved with Jazz's protection at all. By the time their impromptu meeting disbanded, Phoenix still hadn't even set up nightly patrols outside Nev's house. Wasn't that the norm when someone on the team was threatened? She'd done it for everyone else.

But not for Jazz. No matter how hard she tried, Jazz would never be part of the agency that Nev called a family.

Didn't matter. If Jazz was right about Hawthorne's feelings for her, and if Uncle Pierce really meant all he'd said, she might have a real family of her own soon.

TWENTY-EIGHT

"Welcome." The infamous Desmond Patch rose from behind his desk as soon as his assistant led Jazz into the office.

The room was large and richly decorated in a classical style similar to Uncle Pierce's home study.

Jazz would've expected something more minimalist and bare, given the white uniforms of the cult members. But the apparent contradiction made her realize that despite the tour she'd taken of the commune, she still didn't know any concrete details about what the cult taught and believed.

Her survey of the space was quickly cut short by Desmond moving toward her with a graceful stride, extending his hands. He smiled warmly as he reached her, keeping his hands out as if expecting her to take them.

Apparently, people who wanted to join the cult had to get touchy-feely awfully fast. She could do hand contact to keep her cover. Anything more than that, and she might have to introduce her knife to this party.

But he only took her hands in a gesture a man might do with a long-lost sister. And the warmth in his almost-black eyes looked genuine. No creep factor at all.

"Please," he swung an arm toward the little seating area where a wingback chair, shorter armchair, and sofa were gathered, "let's sit and talk awhile."

Jazz passed in front of him to take a seat on one end of the sofa, some of the tension relaxing its hold on her insides.

"Jazz Lamont." He gazed at her with a friendly smile as he lowered into the wingback chair, his red-striped, white robe draping onto the armrests. "Such a unique name for an especially beautiful woman."

Ah. There it was. Flirting?

And yet, nothing in his eyes glinted or seemed ogling. He kept his gaze on her face with more of a paternal expression —caring and sweet. How he pulled that off, she couldn't imagine.

"I understand you're interested in joining our little community."

She nodded. "I just have some questions I'd like answered first. So I can be sure it's right for me."

"Of course. That's wise and understandable." His mouth shifted into a soft line that complimented the understanding in his gaze. "Please, ask anything you'd like to know. I hope I can give you answers that will bring you peace."

She started with softball questions about the housing, how many members there were, and the like. Easy stuff to put him at ease before she challenged him.

She watched his reactions and expressions closely as he responded. If Hawthorne hadn't told Jazz this guy had enforcers who'd locked him in a room, Jazz wouldn't have believed Desmond Patch was anything other than what he appeared to be—a warm, intelligent, charming man. Whose good looks and distinguished demeanor probably didn't hurt him with the ladies either.

Granted, the massive wingback chair he sat in seemed a little throne-like with his tall posture and air of authority. But he did a good job laying on the charm to offset any sense of domineering.

He didn't give any hint of snake oil salesman either. Even when going on about the benefits of Best Life. No matter how outrageous the requirements for membership in his community were.

"So I would have to sign over all my financial assets before I could join Best Life?"

"That's a common misconception." He returned her hard-hitting serve with a relaxed lob. "You'd be choosing to leave your worldly goods, those things that caused you the most stress and worry in life, in the hands of others so you would finally experience true freedom. The freedom to live the rest of your life without a care in the world and to have the time you've always wanted for other pursuits."

She'd overlook his twisty way of getting everyone's money for now. "What other pursuits?"

"Attaining your best life."

"I'm a little confused about that part. How do we attain our best life? How do we even know what that looks like?"

He nodded slowly, tenting his index fingers against his chin as if thinking about the answer—to a question he'd probably been asked a thousand times. "No best life is identical, just as no human is completely identical to another. But through years of practice, study, and proven results, I can say that I have discovered the process that will enable every person to attain their best life for themselves."

Yeah, that didn't sound far-fetched at all. Jazz kept her expression full of curiosity as she watched the man. "What does that involve?"

"We study and commune with the stars, the celestial beings that have been in existence far longer than us and have much to teach us. We provide courses of study for all of our community members, free of charge, to learn from the wisdom of the ages and the skies."

Desmond watched Jazz with a steady gaze as he had during the whole interview. "Those who dedicate themselves to the path of the stars and self-discovery will attain their epiphany and achieve their best lives."

The dude was beginning to sound as programmed as Randall. But at least his gaze didn't go blank and distant like the boy's. Desmond managed to look like he genuinely believed what he was saying. Passion even filled his voice as if he honestly cared about the cause of people achieving their best lives. And really believed in all that astrological hogwash.

But Jazz was about to gag if she had to keep pretending to buy it. Desmond Patch may be one of the most convincing con men she'd met, but what he said didn't make any sense. It was too unbelievable.

"I can see you still have doubts."

Got that right.

"And I can see that for you, your best life would mean being surrounded by people who love you."

Her breath caught. How did he know that?

"The pursuit of the best life I spoke of, learning from the stars and leaving worldly cares behind—we do that together, Jazz." His mouth curved in a closed smile that carried so much sweetness and understanding that it caused an ache in her chest. "I, too, know what it is to search for a family. For people who will love you for who you are. Forever."

He leaned forward, his dark eyes gripping her. "That is what your best life will be here, Jazz. *We* are your family. We are the people who understand you and love you like no one else."

With every word, Jazz's pulse thumped a little harder and faster. Hope ballooned around her heart, increasing the ache there as he held her in his gaze.

"I can see how special you are, Jazz. You belong with us. That is why you haven't found your home yet. Why you've always been rejected and hurt by everyone you've given your heart to."

How could he know? Tears pricked her eyes as she stared at him, still unable to look away.

It was like his dark eyes were piercing her soul, seeing all her pain and wounds laid bare. And he wanted to heal every one of them.

"Join us, Jazz." His voice deepened and smoothed even more. "Give us the opportunity to prove our love to you. I promise you will not be disappointed." He stood and moved closer to her, reaching down to lift her hand from her lap.

The touch, though warm and almost paternal, broke the spell.

A spell was what it had to be. Or something like hypnosis.

Wow. Hawthorne had said Patch was charismatic, but this was ridiculous.

The man had taken her nearly to the point of tears by spitballing guesses that could've been accurate for ninety percent of the human population. Everyone had been rejected by people they'd loved. Lucky guess for him that Jazz had tasted the pain of rejection more than most. He might've managed to buy her soul and gain all her financial assets with that tactic.

The man was more than a con artist. He was a magician. A magician who stole and used up lives, from what she'd gathered from this meeting and Hawthorne.

But he wasn't going to get hers.

She blinked to clear away the moisture and resisted the urge to pull back from the thumb caressing her hand in an increasingly less paternal way. She looked up at him with what she hoped was an innocent expression. "Thank you. That helps a lot."

She bit her lip and extracted her hand to brush her hair behind her ear. "But I'm still a little concerned about some things I've heard in the news."

"Indeed?" He chose a new spot to sit. Right next to her on the too-small sofa. The position brought his face close enough that she could see he had some wrinkles to go with the gray streaks in his black hair. He had to be at least twenty years older than her, but that apparently wasn't going to stop him from trying to get cozy. He must think he was charming, too.

She pretended not to see through his player move and faked a concerned expression. "I've heard the police are looking into Best Life in relation to the awful things happening at the Tri-City Fair. I heard they think someone here might be involved?"

A flicker sparked in his eyes before he doused it. Guess he hadn't seen that topic coming. "Someone found a Best Life pin at the fairgrounds, but I explained to the police that those pins could be in the possession of anyone who ever stayed here, even for a brief time."

Did Desmond know Jazz was the one who'd found the pin with her K-9? Could he have hired hitmen to silence her because of it? He'd have enough money, given how he somehow managed to convince everyone who joined the cult to hand over all their financial assets. And he'd have a lot at stake if it was proven he was behind the sabotage and her aunt's murder.

"No one in the Best Life community is guilty of any violence, I assure you. Violence is the antithesis of everything we stand for." Said the man with enforcers who held people hostage and, if she'd read between the lines of Hawthorne's words correctly, treated kids roughly.

She nodded, pretending to believe him. "I'm only concerned because…well, my aunt. She was the one who was killed in the explosion at the Skyride."

"Oh, Jazz." The creep used the excuse of her grief to take her hand again, this time between both of his.

She fought the urge to pull away or break his arm.

"I'm so sorry. That is truly awful. This is the kind of thing that we can help you through. If you'll let us."

"Even though she died at the fair? I heard you don't like the fair." Jazz injected her voice with a thickness that suggested tears, rather than accusation. "That you think it's bad or something."

"Every individual must make their own decisions about what is best for them, but I personally believe that fairs and other worldly sources of entertainment are dangerous. They perpetuate evil, and naturally, evil things happen as a result. I'm sure you see that in what happened to your aunt."

Jerk. To use her aunt's death as an object lesson was

pretty low. But he apparently thought petting her hand would make her miss the disgusting tactic.

"I'm sure you're right." She somehow forced a smile. She should really be in the running for an Oscar with this performance. "Does anyone ever get bothered by having to follow all the rules, though? I understand there are a lot of them here."

"No, not rules, Jazz." His smile was more condescending now as he dipped his head like that helped him see her better. "Guidelines to seek and attain your best life. As I said, I know how to get you to where you want to be. It's up to you to choose the best life for yourself. Some people, sadly, don't realize how happy they would be if they'd simply follow the proven path I've laid out for them."

Jazz swallowed the bitter taste pushing up her throat. She'd had enough of this conman's gimmicks and definitely enough of his hand holding. She could be allowing the touch of the person who was trying to have her killed. Though the first attempt on her life was the night before the pin was found, the day of the Ferris wheel sabotage.

But maybe she'd seen something or someone she hadn't realized was significant that morning. She'd never seen this joker before. His height and handsome, uniquely distinguished face would not have been something she'd miss or forget. Not that he would've risked being spotted at the fair.

She scanned her memories from that morning before the Ferris wheel car had fallen. She and Flash had caught the purse snatcher. Her pulse sped as a new possibility took shape in her mind. Could the teenager have been a diversion? "Do you have a family? A wife and children?"

At least that got the man to slide his hands away from Jazz. But he covered with a smooth smile. "I do have a lovely wife, yes. No children yet, I'm afraid." Which at his age probably meant he didn't want them.

"Oh, that is a shame." She stood and lifted her purse strap to her shoulder. "I have to run, but thank you for your time. The community does sound like a wonderful family."

She practically choked on the lie, but it was for a good cause. "Before I commit, can I talk to some of the members? I know you said they'll love me like family, but I'd like to see what kind of people they are for myself first. I'm sure you understand."

"Of course." He smiled. "As you leave, ask my assistant, Sarah, for an appointment to speak with some of our members."

"Oh, it doesn't have to be so formal." She waved a hand to dismiss the trouble. "I just wanted to chat with a few people I see on the way out. Keep it organic and simple."

"That's a lovely idea." He put his hand on her shoulder as he guided her to the closed door that led out of his office. "But not every person in our community is at the right stage in his or her journey to be questioned without harming them. We protect our members. Which you will benefit from when you join us." He gave her a broader smile and took her hand again as he opened the door. He lifted her hand to his lips. He wasn't going to kiss it was he?

She slipped out of his grip before she could find out. "I'm sure I will. Thank you so much." She walked away, thanking her own lucky stars that she still had her sanity and wits intact. Seemed like not everyone could say the same after an encounter with Desmond Patch.

"The midnight sun." Hawthorne walked out from the far side of Jazz's parked SUV as he spoke the line he hoped Jazz would remember.

The gorgeous redhead paused her step for only a second as she spotted him, a smile showing off her perfect white teeth. "Never shines on me. Carson Steele's code line to make sure his buddy hadn't been swapped with his double?"

Hawthorne grinned and leaned back against the closed liftgate of her SUV, crossing his arms over his T-shirt as he grinned. "Seemed the best way to be sure you didn't get brainwashed in there."

He glanced over her shoulder at the Best Life commune that stood a good distance away from where she'd parked in the large lot. Far enough that no one should see him talking to her.

"Aren't you afraid you'll blow my cover?"

He peered at her from behind his sunglasses. "More afraid of the brainwashing."

Jazz stopped a few feet from him and wrinkled her nose. "Think I'm that susceptible, huh?"

"I think Patch is that tricky."

Jazz moved closer and lowered herself to perch on the thick rear bumper. She looked straight ahead instead of at Hawthorne. "Came closer than I'd like to admit. He's really good." The regret and surprise in her tone twisted his gut a little.

Hopefully, the experience hadn't been too painful. Maybe he could alleviate any disappointment in herself by sharing more of his experience. "He is an expert at persuasion and mental control. He didn't target me with his persuasion because I was only a child. But I watched him do it to my parents and other adults in the cult."

Hawthorne lowered his weight down to the bumper next to her and stretched his legs out in front of him. "I always thought they were stupid not to see through what he was doing, how he was manipulating them. But now that I'm older, I understand it a little more. He knew how to find their weaknesses and exploit them. Always in a way that made it look like he understood them, saw them like no one else. And that made it seem like he was the only one who could give them the deepest desires of their hearts."

"You described it...perfectly." Jazz turned her head toward Hawthorne. "That's how he almost got me. For a second."

He couldn't help but get caught in those emerald eyes that gave everything away. Shock, longing, and vulnerability he hadn't expected to find in tough, heroic Jazz Lamont. "I'm glad it didn't take." His throat thickened around the words.

"Thanks to you and your warnings about him." She sighed. "It must've been so hard. Growing up there."

He pulled in a deep breath, his hands going to grip the bumper on either side of his body as he looked down at the blacktop, chest clenching. "The worst years of my life, for sure. The hardest part was seeing how quickly my parents changed. And with them, my whole family, our lives. I was a kid, so I didn't like having more rules, but it was so much more than that."

He reached up to run his fingers through the intentionally ruffled hair on top of his head, probably messing up the gelled style. But he didn't care at the moment. "They became robots, programmed by Patch to do his bidding. After a few months, I never got to talk to my mom or dad ever again." Emotion caught his voice. He paused, trying to push back the sadness before it became even more obvious. "It was like talking to Patch instead of them. They were shells of the parents I'd known."

Hawthorne felt Jazz's touch on his shoulder before he saw it coming.

A gentle hand, softly comforting and supporting through the contact. "Did they try to brainwash you, too?" Her question was quiet, her voice colored with so much empathy that a lump clogged his throat.

He cleared it away before attempting to answer. "They tried through the school they have at the cult. Everything is carefully designed to indoctrinate the children into the cult's philosophies and lies."

He let go of the bumper and ran his sweaty palms down his jeans, sunshine pouring heat from the sky. "I was so angry that I think that helped keep me from believing what they taught us. And I had the evidence of the cult's destructive power on my parents." Hawthorne turned his head to meet Jazz's gaze.

The compassion in her eyes hit him hard, slipping past his defenses again to knock on the walls of his heart.

He looked away, grabbing at what he'd been going to say before he could be tempted down an emotional path he shouldn't take. "I realized later, it was really the grace of God that created the circumstances which kept me from buying Patch's teaching."

He let the statement float between them. If she wasn't a believer, as Nevaeh had said, he was curious to see how she'd respond to the concept of God's grace.

"You sound like some of the agents at PK-9."

He glanced at her to catch the smirk on her lips.

"Are you a Christian, too?"

Too. As if she had more Christians than she wanted in her life. Well, good. Maybe God was already working on her. "I am. A chaplain led me to Christ when I was in the service."

"Led you." No missing her sardonic tone.

"Did I say something funny?"

"I just don't know why you'd want anything you have to be *led* to. It's like being forced to follow someone you don't want to, just like Patch got your parents to do." She swung a hand toward the commune for emphasis.

Hawthorne nodded. "I see your point. It could sound like that. But what I mean by *led* is more like someone showing me the better path that was there all along, but I hadn't seen it before. Someone helping me realize what I didn't know I wanted until I saw it. Does that make sense?"

She threw him a skeptical glance, then looked away. "Still sounds too much like Patch for my taste."

"I didn't have to be dragged or forced by any person to become a Christian. And I didn't have to be conned or manipulated either. But I also didn't want to be a Christian."

She brought her gaze back to his face at that, surprise lifting her eyebrows.

"I didn't want to be reconciled to God and forgiven of my sins until *God* changed me from the inside out. He had to change me so I could begin to want what I hadn't known I most needed."

"That sounds really confusing. And still a little like echoes of Patch."

"Maybe in some ways. Evil and lies are often most convincing when they masquerade as poor imitations of the truth. What better way to get people to accept a twisted, destructive fake instead of the real thing?"

"I've seen plenty of imitations of Christians in my lifetime. My dad said my mom was a churchgoer. Aunt Joan and Uncle Pierce never missed a Sunday except when they were traveling or on their yacht."

Hawthorne winced. A negative history with people who claimed to be Christians wouldn't help Jazz want to come to Christ. "Anyone can go to church. That doesn't make them Christians. What about your co-workers? Nevaeh?"

Jazz pressed her lips together. Hopefully an indication he'd pointed her in the right direction. But she lifted her wristwatch to eye level. "I should head out. Lunch plans." She stood and turned toward him. "But I made an appointment for Thursday to interview some members of the cult."

A twinge of something like worry pinged behind his ribs. "You sure you want to come back here?"

"No. But I do want to figure out who's behind the sabotage before they strike again." She grinned. "Be sure to tell me the code for next time so you can confirm they haven't brainwashed me when I get out. Maybe 'Venice has never been charming.'"

"You really do know Carson Steele."

"Already read *Seconds in Shadow* twice. Kept me up when I should've been sleeping."

He couldn't help the big smile that stretched his mouth wide. "You liked it?"

"Let's put it this way. I thought *Midnight Sun* would always be my favorite. But not anymore." She flashed a meaningful smile. "This one is your best yet."

That mixture of relief and elation he always felt when a

reader loved his stories seeped through his chest. He should've said *thank you* or something charming. But he stood there like a dope just long enough for her to brush past him, dropping a parting, amused whisper in his ear.

"Don't look so surprised."

As she backed out her SUV and drove off a moment later, he managed to step away and wave.

Trouble was, he was surprised. By how much more her compliment meant to him than any starred review he'd ever received.

And by how his heart lurched as she disappeared into the distance. As if it wanted to follow her wherever she went and never look back.

TWENTY-NINE

Jazz watched Uncle Pierce closely for any sign of disdain as she set out her inexpensive plates and budget flatware.

Of course, the food itself was in plastic takeout containers. From Isabella's, one of the most expensive Italian restaurants in the area.

Flash had barked when Uncle Pierce first arrived, but now he was being quiet in her bedroom where Jazz had left him with his favorite chew stick. He wasn't a jumper or anything, but Jazz had him tucked away when Uncle Pierce came anyway, knowing how he disliked pets. He'd always said cats and dogs were too dirty and unruly to have in a civilized home.

"This is perfect." Uncle Pierce smiled and dished out the carbonara onto their plates.

It was so surreal. Uncle Pierce in her apartment was strange enough. She'd scurried straight from Best Life to the apartment and spent the next two hours cleaning it from trashed to spotless. She hoped. But it was still an older apartment, and the age showed if a person looked closely enough.

The fact Uncle Pierce had brought takeout made the experience even more unbelievable. He also hadn't seemed disapproving at all so far. Not of the apartment, her green blouse and dark skinny jeans she'd thrown on before he'd arrived, or the food.

"Thanks for agreeing to meet for lunch, Jazz." Uncle Pierce poured water into his glass from the pitcher she'd filled with plain old tap water. "And I appreciate your willingness to host." He gave her a gentle smile, the one he'd adopted when she'd stopped by his house.

So strange for him to look at her with kindness. Aunt Joan's death must have really shaken him. Changed him. "Your aunt wondered about where you were living."

"She did?" Jazz halted the progress of lifting her glass to her mouth.

"Yes. She mentioned it." He glanced around the small dining nook that opened to the living room and front door. "It's a very nice apartment. It suits you." He did a good job not letting any note of criticism slip into his voice. He had to be thinking it. Her whole apartment was smaller than the foyer at his house.

"But the real reason I wanted to come was to see you, Jazz."

She spooled fettucine on her fork, afraid to look and see insincerity in his eyes that would puncture the warm bubble of hope forming around her heart. She'd told herself his kindness and sweet words when she'd visited him with the photos had been driven by grief. He hadn't been himself.

By now, she was sure he would've returned to the Pierce Cracklen he'd always been—driven politician, ruthless businessman, exacting husband and father, cold and disinterested uncle.

"I meant what I said at the house. I know I probably surprised you."

Jazz pushed the pasta into her mouth and slowly chewed, still avoiding his gaze. *Surprised* was the understatement of the year.

"But I meant every word. Joan's death has made me see so many things I missed before. I took her and my daughters for granted. I took you for granted."

She looked at him then, bracing herself for what she'd see—evidence to contradict his words.

But real emotion filled his eyes. Sincerity and something like...loneliness. Or was it need? "Without Joan and my daughters here, you're all I have. You're the family I took for granted. I don't want to do that anymore." He set down his fork and held her gaze. He sighed. "I can see you don't completely trust me and what I'm saying."

She leaned back and reached for her glass for something to do. Heat crawled toward her face. "It's not that." But it totally was. "It's just...a lot to process."

He nodded. "Because I didn't pay much attention to you before." He reached his hand farther across the round table and spread his palm against the wood. "I am sorry for that. I'm sorry for what I missed." He glanced away. "I was too caught up in work, campaigning, providing for my family."

He brought his gaze to her face, regret deepening vertical lines at the edges of his mouth. "I want to make it up to you. And I'm hoping the timing is good for both of us."

"The timing?"

"Yes. We're both alone, in a sense. But we have each other. I know I didn't reach out to you when Lawrence died." He dabbed at the corners of his mouth with the paper napkin, then lowered it to his lap. "Now that I've lost Joan, I understand what it feels like. And I'm all the sorrier that I didn't support you in your time of loss."

She shrugged. "It's all right." She hadn't expected anything different from the uncle and aunt who'd never given her support at any stage of her life.

"No, it's not. I'd like to make it up to you now, if you'll let me. Tell me how you're doing with your father's passing. It must have been very hard to lose him."

Jazz blinked. No one had ever asked her that. And she'd never thought Uncle Pierce would be the one to do it. "I... guess." Was it hard? Probably not in the way he meant.

The slow progress of the kidney failure, the caretaking for so long—that had been hard. Her dad's disapproval and complaints with everything she tried to do for him—that had been difficult.

After the memorial service and cremation he'd dictated that he wanted, she'd realized what was the hardest thing. Not that he was gone. But that she'd subconsciously been hoping all the caring and loving of her dad would pay off in the end. That he'd make some declaration of love or even approval on his deathbed if not before.

That was the hardest part. He'd died still making sure she knew she wasn't good enough to be his daughter. Not good enough for his love.

"I know Lawrence could be…difficult. I suppose that gives you mixed emotions about his passing."

Such an accurate assessment from Uncle Pierce startled her.

Understanding softened his features. Did he know what her dad had been like? Did he understand?

Her heart squeezed.

"You mentioned you kept some of his things. Like those photos you brought over. Does it help to look through them, to remember him?"

"I…don't know." She waved a hand toward the hallway to the right. "I keep them in my guest room. There are a bunch of boxes of things. I should probably go through them sometime and see what I can get rid of."

"My offer still stands to help you. I'll have to do that with Joan's things yet." His mouth pulled into a deep frown, and his brow furrowed slightly. "When I'm ready." He lifted his focus to Jazz. "Perhaps we can help each other with that task. I'd be happy to start with a box or two now, if you're up for it."

Go through her dad's things? Her chest squeezed. It was one thing to quickly find the shoebox she knew she'd stored photos in from her childhood. Totally different to go through his belongings, medals, mementos. She might even find something about her mother in there.

Her stomach lurched. "No." The response came out

sharper than she intended. "I mean," she made a show of looking at her watch, "I have to get ready for work." In several hours, but he didn't need to know that.

"Oh." His eyebrows dipped with what looked like disappointment. "I'm sorry to hear that. Maybe another time."

"Sure."

"Do you think you could come to the house for dinner one evening? I could have the chef cook us a fabulous meal." He smiled. "You can tell me what your favorite dish is, and I'll be sure it's on the menu."

The genuineness of his smile smoothed away the tension in her chest. "I'd like that."

"But not tonight?"

"No, I work late."

"Well, I'll keep asking until we find a time that works. I want to have you in my life, Jazz. We're family."

Family. The way he said the word, all warm and certain, surged a burst of hope through her. Could Aunt Joan's death finally bring her the family she'd always longed for?

She tried to stay skeptical, to protect her heart. But Uncle Pierce's approval and acceptance seemed too genuine to deny.

It was the kind of thing she'd dreamed of getting from her dad. Maybe, all this time, she'd just been looking in the wrong place.

"The works and extra bacon, please."

Freddie chuckled at Hawthorne's familiar order. "I could've bet on that one." He turned around and relayed Hawthorne's and Jazz's orders to the teenagers at the grill inside his food stand. Then Freddie scooted to the side of the window and leaned toward them as they stepped out of the line of customers. "Just between us, the bacon is what keeps us in business." He grinned.

"I believe it." Jazz laughed, that lovely sound Hawthorne still hadn't figured out how to capture in words in his book.

But right now he needed to focus on taking this opportunity to try to find out more about Freddie, since the man seemed to want to chat. "Jazz and I were talking about your cousin Jim. He must've retired out in Oklahoma?"

"Yeah, that's right."

"Is that where you're from, too?"

"No. I was an Army brat. Lived in six different states and Germany by the time I was eighteen."

"I can relate." Jazz gave Freddie a smile.

"Dad?"

She nodded. "Yep."

"Mine, too."

"Where do you call home these days?" Hawthorne tried to interject the question as casually as possible.

Freddie straightened. Did that make him uncomfortable? "Not sure yet. I've enjoyed traveling with this job, managing Jim's business."

"I get it. I'm a fan of the nomad life myself."

Someone said something behind Freddie, and he turned around. Then he swung back, two paper baskets cradling hot dogs in his hands. "Here you go." He handed them over with a joyful smile that didn't look wary or any different than his normal friendly demeanor. "Enjoy."

"Thanks." Jazz smiled as Hawthorne handed over her hot dog, and they started for the tables shaded under the canopy.

Flash panted heavily by her other side. Poor dog looked like he could use a good, long drink. The heat and humidity were a nasty combo again today.

"Here I thought you had suggested we meet for dinner just to see me." Jazz slid her basket onto the table and swung the backpack off her shoulders, glancing at Hawthorne just long enough for him to catch the teasing twinkle in her eyes.

He grinned as he sat down and took off his sunglasses. "Men can multitask, too, you know."

She straightened from pouring water into a foldable bowl

for Flash. "Really? I didn't know that." Her laugh seemed to ripple through the air and into his chest, awakening feelings he had no business entertaining.

She lowered to the bench across from him, her mouth straightening into a more serious line. "If there's anything to find about Freddie," she glanced toward the food stand as she lowered her voice, "Cora will uncover it."

"Good. Because I couldn't find anything online. No criminal record that I could see. No current residence or phone number."

"Maybe he travels a lot." Jazz lifted her hot dog to her mouth and paused. "Like you." She bit off a large, messy chunk of the ketchup-laden hot dog. Some ketchup smeared onto her cheek.

Hawthorne couldn't help but smile at the cute sight.

"What?" She mumbled the word around the hot dog she chewed.

"You just have a bit of..." He pointed toward the spot.

"Oh." She lowered her hot dog and picked up a napkin, pressing it to her mouth on the wrong side.

"No." He leaned over the table, reaching closer to her face. "There." His heart thumped in his chest, willing him to touch her skin. Caress the cheek that looked so soft and smooth. He jerked back. "About an inch to the left of your mouth."

If this were a novel, he'd have his hero give in to the temptation. Have a romantic moment with his love interest. But this was real life. And Hawthorne wasn't in a romance. He didn't want to be. And that's not where God wanted him to be either. He was meant to be single. To use his freedom to seek closeness with God and do the work He'd called Hawthorne to do. Getting tied down would only interfere with that. Probably lead him astray from God.

"Do you ever get tired of it?"

"Of what?" He'd gotten so lost in his self-directed lecture that he had to scramble to remember what Jazz was referring to.

"Traveling. Never settling down anywhere." She'd wiped the ketchup off her face just fine. So much for all those trope scenes in books and movies where no woman could clean off her own face.

"Not at all. I love seeing the world and being able to find settings for my books in person. No better way to do research."

"I can see that. The settings in your books are so rich. Like another character."

He smiled. "Thank you." He took a bite of his hot dog, stretching his mouth around the mound of toppings.

Jazz munched more of her dinner, too, so Hawthorne glanced at Freddie's food stand. Hopefully, the vendor would leave soon. Hawthorne had gotten off patrol at eight p.m., and it was eight fifteen now. Last night, Freddie had stayed until close, but that didn't seem to be his typical pattern. He'd come in later yesterday and had told Hawthorne he would have to stay until close because his usual closer was sick. Today, he was probably back to his normal hours.

"Have you ever thought about settling down one day? Maybe having a family?"

Hawthorne's chest tensed as he looked at Jazz. Why was she asking? He'd been afraid she would have picked up on his...attraction to her. Maybe this was a good time to try to clarify he hadn't meant anything by that. "No. A marriage and family wouldn't be a good fit for my work, my lifestyle. I need to be free to pick up and go whenever the need or idea hits me."

Her lips curved up slightly at one corner. "You sound like Carson. You really fooled me in *The Killer's Corpse*."

Book Fourteen, the most recent installment before his newest release. He'd surprised a lot of people with that one, including himself. Mostly by the fact he'd included a romance at all. He hadn't done that with Carson before. But it was a good way to create higher emotional stakes.

"I really thought he was finally going to give up bachelorhood for Valentine Edwards." Jazz shook her head as if she still couldn't believe it. "She was such a perfect match for him. And it seemed like he loved her near the end."

"He did have feelings for her." Hawthorne reached for his soda cup. "But Carson values his freedom above everything else." He took a long sip of the cool drink, checking on Freddie again. Maybe to avoid Jazz's gaze.

"And you?"

Hawthorne reluctantly met her stare. But it would be better to make things clear now than let her get attached and expect something he couldn't give her. "I like freedom, too."

She rubbed her thumb on her thermos. "So you've never been tempted? Never met a girl special enough to catch your eye?" Something in the way she threw in the second question, her darted glance away, the flush in her cheeks, made him hold back the flippant denial he was going to give.

And he couldn't honestly say he hadn't. That would be a lie. Because he was looking at the woman who was that special. "Well...maybe once."

Her emerald eyes lit on him, widening slightly as a smile curved her lips.

He shouldn't have said it. Shouldn't have looked at her the way he was now, probably revealing too much of his growing attraction for her. Not after all that work to clarify he didn't want a relationship.

But the way a flame blazed in his torso at the pleasure and heat in her eyes told him his feelings didn't care about clarifications or boundaries.

"Have a good night, you two." Freddie waved from outside the canopy as he shouted to be heard above the crowd noise and the music from nearby rides.

Jazz returned the wave with a smile as Hawthorne immediately gathered his soda and remnants of hot dog.

"You're going to follow him, aren't you?" Jazz's perceptive gaze locked on Hawthorne.

"I am free at the moment." He grinned.

"Too bad I'm working 'til midnight." Her frown switched

to a smile, and she waved him on. "Good luck. Give me a call if you need backup."

"Thanks for dinner." He threw the words over his shoulder as he hurried to drop the trash in a bin and make sure he didn't let Freddie get too far ahead. He might've already given the vendor too big a lead in such a thick crowd of people. Maybe he should've asked Jazz to bring Flash for the first leg. He could probably track Freddie.

Hawthorne used his height to advantage to see above the people he weaved through.

Freddie was unfortunately pretty average looking with nothing to make him stand out in the crowd. But Hawthorne knew which exit he'd be headed for—the staff door by the main entrance that provided a quicker way in and out by avoiding the lines.

Hawthorne kept his stride long but not too fast. Wouldn't be good to get ahead of Freddie. Although Hawthorne was off shift. If he did see the man, it wouldn't be suspicious for Hawthorne to be leaving at the same time.

With that excuse in mind, he picked up his pace. If he passed Freddie without spotting him, he could simply wait outside the gate until he saw the vendor leave.

But as Hawthorne neared the gate, the crowds cleared slightly.

And Freddie's dark hair with receding hairline caught Hawthorne's eye. Red polo T-shirt, tan khakis. Glasses and mustache. That was Freddie.

Hawthorne slowed, keeping Freddie in view as the vendor went through the staff exit as predicted.

Since more visitors were entering than leaving at the moment, Hawthorne slipped out through the main exit instead, allowing him to maintain more distance without losing sight of Freddie.

He kept one row of cars between him and Freddie as he watched to see where the vendor had parked.

Freddie eventually stopped by a light blue sedan and unlocked the driver's door.

Hawthorne sprinted away. His car was parked in another section of the lot too far away.

Sweat dripped from his face by the time Hawthorne reached his car and jumped into the sweltering oven it had become. He started the engine and turned the air conditioning on full blast as he drove as fast as he thought he could get away with toward the section of the lot where Freddie had parked. Too fast, apparently, given the way his brakes slipped as he slowed for a turn.

Freddie would probably use the west exit out of the lot, since that was closest to where he had parked.

Hawthorne took the shortest route to catch the vendor at that exit. Hopefully.

As he reached the west exit, he strained to see past other cars slowing to get in line.

A light blue sedan caught his eye. Two cars ahead.

"Thank you, Lord." He let out a breath as he pulled into the row of vehicles waiting for cross traffic on the street to clear.

He kept his attention fixed on Freddie's car as the blue sedan reached the front of the line, then turned onto the street.

Hawthorne tapped the steering wheel, his pulse picking up speed. The traffic could stop him from tailing Freddie if the car in front of him didn't turn soon.

The next car pulled out, and Hawthorne drove forward, braking for a truck passing by on the road.

The brakes slipped again. Great. He was probably going to have to take the car to a garage and have it looked at. Brake pads must be getting worn down. He had driven it nearly across the country to get to the Twin Cities.

He accelerated hard as soon as the truck passed and darted out onto the road. Freddie shouldn't be too far ahead.

He pressed the gas pedal harder than he technically should for the speed limit. But if Freddie were guilty of sabotaging the fair, Hawthorne could learn a lot by following him. Who knew what the man would do if he didn't think he was being watched? Maybe he'd pick up more supplies for his next sabotage attempt.

Light blue caught the corner of Hawthorne's eye in the lane to his right. Only a few cars between them. Perfect. Hawthorne could hold his position, but then he might not be able to turn quickly if Freddie did.

Sure enough, Freddie slowed at a green light ahead, his right blinker flashing.

Hawthorne jerked to look over his shoulder and darted in between two cars to fit into the right lane.

He pressed the brakes to slow for the turn.

The car didn't slow.

He pushed the brake pedal harder.

Nothing.

Freddie turned off onto the cross street.

The car in front of Hawthorne darted through the intersection just as the light turned red.

But Hawthorne didn't stop.

He couldn't. His brakes were gone.

THIRTY

Hawthorne darted around a car slowing in front of him as his muscle memory took over, implementing techniques learned in his Marine tactical driver training.

His gaze pushed ahead, spotting vehicles and obstacles that he needed to avoid.

The gas pedal could be as useful as brakes in some situations.

Like now, when he was about to crash into the back of a minivan.

He hit the gas and swerved into the oncoming lane, then sped back into the right lane in front of the minivan.

He took his right foot off the gas and used his left foot to pump the brakes hard, several times.

There. The dual braking system started to respond, giving him a weaker brake from half the system.

If he could slow enough, he could use the emergency brake to do the rest. But if he tried it at the speed he was going now, he'd lose control.

Didn't help that vehicles kept getting in his way.

And that he'd just reached a hill. That he was going to go down.

The height at the top of the hill gave him a birds' eye view

271

of the traffic ahead. Three cars in front of him, then a brief gap before the oncoming traffic would reach him.

He hoped.

His car slid down the hill, gaining speed.

The rear of the pickup truck in front of him came up fast.

He darted around, letting the plummet give him the speed he needed to pass the pickup, then the two cars ahead of that.

The oncoming semi gained speed faster than he'd hoped.

Great time to drive ten miles over the limit, pal.

Hawthorne glanced over his shoulder, watching for the split-second he cleared the front car.

There.

He darted back into the right lane as the semi driver blared the horn.

If only an uphill would follow, but the road laid out flat instead, letting Hawthorne's car keep its speed.

He pumped the brakes again, getting a little help from half the braking system.

A chain-link fence on the right bordered what appeared to be an industrial property. Looked like the best assist he was going to get.

He kept pumping the brakes as he neared the fence.

He angled the wheel just enough to send his car over the curb, onto the empty sidewalk where he could line up the passenger side with the fence.

As gently as he could, he aimed his car toward the fence.

A scraping sound made him grit his teeth. His car would never be the same.

He angled away, then back to the fence, letting the scrape of metal on metal slow the car until he could safely apply the emergency brake.

The car finally stopped.

And Hawthorne breathed.

Thank the Lord he hadn't hurt anyone.

He pushed open the driver's door and stood, adrenaline

still coursing through his veins. No way was that from worn brake pads.

He dropped to the grass between the sidewalk and the fence and pulled his smartphone from his pocket. Turning on the flashlight function, he shined it under the car.

Sure enough. The brake lines had obviously been cut and were wet with splattered brake fluid that should've been on the inside.

Pulling back from the car, he got to his feet. Who would want to tamper with his brakes?

The author of the threatening note from the night before? Someone from the cult? Maybe he'd shaken up Patch as much as he'd hoped. Pushed the conman to do something about the threat Hawthorne presented. Patch could've had someone leave the note on Hawthorne's car, too. Intentionally using Best Life stationery to send a clear message.

Hawthorne had left voicemail messages with two of Sam's friends whose names he'd gotten from Rebekah. He hadn't been able to find a number or location for the third one yet. Maybe Hawthorne was getting too close to the truth about Sam, and Patch or someone else wanted to stop him.

But what if he wasn't the only target? Jazz's flat tire hadn't been an accident either. The knife-sized cut made that obvious. What if the same person who'd just tried to frighten or kill him was after her, too?

She'd tried to brush it off as nothing that night. Did that mean it wasn't the only harassment or attack she'd experienced?

Hawthorne awakened his phone's screen and looked up the local police non-emergency phone number. He'd let the police investigate the damage to his car, but first thing tomorrow morning, he needed to talk to Jazz.

As tough and independent as she was, he needed to know if she was in danger. Because if she was, he would do everything in his power to protect her.

———

"Oh, here it comes. The meet cute coffee spill." Nev pointed at the screen as she stuffed more popcorn into her mouth.

Jazz laughed when the predicted moment unfolded in one of their favorite romantic comedies. They'd seen the movie about a hundred times, but it was even more fun to watch now that they'd memorized every line.

She reached into the popcorn bowl she and Nev shared on the sofa between them.

Alvarez was conked out on the rug a few feet away, but Flash kept an eye on the TV screen fixed to the wall and barked every time a doorbell sounded in a scene.

Grabbing a handful of the buttery popcorn, Jazz grinned. "Aww, I love this part. Look at his face."

Nev nodded. "Mm-hmm. You know he love her, girl. From first sight."

She and Jazz let out an exaggerated, swoony sigh at the same time, then broke into laughter.

Jazz had so missed this. These girls' movie nights. Hanging with her BFF, just the two of them, relaxed and safe in their affection for each other.

She'd been surprised when Nev had suggested a movie night as soon as Jazz got home after her late shift at the fair. It had already been twelve thirty a.m. then, but Nev had said they'd better take advantage of the moment. Branson wasn't going to be back to camp on the sofa until three in the morning after his security job shift was done. And he'd apparently told Nev he'd feel better if she stayed awake and alert until he was there to protect her anyway.

Jazz hadn't needed more of an excuse than that to hang with her best bud. She could sleep in tomorrow since she would be taking the late-night shift at the fair again.

Even if she'd had to take a morning shift, she wouldn't have missed this. It was just like old times. The best of her old times with Nev. This was what had gotten her to move to the Twin Cities when Nev had asked her to. If only things hadn't changed, and they could still enjoy life together like this.

The jazzy ringtone of her phone contrasted with the movie's soundtrack. She scanned the end table by the sofa and the coffee table in front of them. "Where'd I put it?"

Nev stopped the movie with the remote. "Um." She glanced around. "Oh. I've got it with mine." She turned to her right and pulled the decorative pillow out from beneath her arm. Their two phones had inexplicably ended up nestled together there. Nev tossed Jazz her cell.

"Thanks." Jazz caught it and checked the screen as it rang again.

Phoenix? Jazz mouthed the word to Nev as she pressed the button to answer.

"Meet me at the Forever Home training center at six thirty a.m." Phoenix's command hit Jazz's ear before she could even say *hello*.

"Forever Home?" The name sounded vaguely familiar, but Jazz couldn't place it.

"The shelter and training center where Alvarez and others were rehabilitated."

Oh. Jazz had heard something about a woman who had helped Phoenix train Alvarez and Toby. Maybe Raksa, too. She couldn't remember the details. It didn't seem like the PK-9 team talked about the place or the trainer much. "Why do you want me there?"

She probably shouldn't ask. Everyone else went with a no-questions-asked policy with Phoenix. Like they were all afraid of her. But if Phoenix was going to spring an early morning meeting on her with only a few hours warning, she should at least be able to know there was a point to it.

"Marion Moore has added an outdoor training field where Flash can test and refresh his takedown and agility skills."

That did sound cool. The facility Phoenix usually rented for them was pretty small and had limited equipment. Especially for a dog like Flash, whose exceptional athleticism meant he was rarely challenged by average setups. "Okay."

"I've messaged you the address." Through the encrypted app PK-9 used, Jazz assumed.

"I'll see you tom—"

All sound from the other end cut off before Jazz could finish.

"Bye to you, too." Jazz muttered the sarcastic farewell as she lowered her phone and gave Nev the look of annoyance she'd rather aim at Phoenix.

"What?" Nev had shifted so her back leaned against the arm of the sofa and she fully faced Jazz, legs crossed under the afghan her grandma had crocheted.

"She wants me to meet her first thing in the morning. Six thirty. At this Forever Home place."

"Ooh." Nev widened her eyes.

"What?"

"Nobody gets to go there."

Jazz gave her a skeptical stare.

"I mean, adopters must since Marion Moore adopts out dogs she rescues. Phoenix got Al and Cannenta from there. But I don't think even Cora has been there." Nev fingered a twisty curl of her hair as she looked toward the ceiling. "Bris maybe mentioned going there once to touch up Toby's detection skills. But she's the only one I know of besides Phoenix."

"That's...very sus."

Nev shifted the popcorn bowl she'd conveniently moved to her lap and shoved Jazz's leg with a blanketed foot. "It is not."

"What's wrong with the place? Is that where the boss's dead bodies are buried?"

"You crazy." Nev held up a kernel of popcorn between her fingers and aimed it at Jazz before letting it fly.

The kernel harmlessly bounced off Jazz's soft Henley and fell to the red fleece blanket covering her legs.

"Phoenix goes there a lot, right?"

Nev shrugged. "I dunno." She pushed popcorn into her mouth.

"But she never takes anyone with her."

Nev held up a finger, so Jazz corrected herself.

"No one but Bris, apparently. So why in the world would she call me in the middle of the night and say I have to meet her there? She doesn't like me, so it can't be good."

"You always think she don't like you. But this proves I'm right."

"About what?"

"That she just treatin' you the way she treat everybody. I told you she don't act no friendlier with anybody else."

"Then why is she singling me out for this?"

"It's an honor. Maybe she likes you best."

"More like she plans to do something weird there when nobody's around to see."

Nev snorted. "Girl, you been reading too much Carson Steele. The boss ain't no serial killer."

"How do you know?" Jazz crossed her arms over her shirt.

"You for real?"

"Sort of." Jazz lowered her arms. "I mean, what do you really know about her? What do any of you know? She's always so secretive, and nobody knows why. What's she hiding? Don't you want to know?"

"Not really." Nev fingered the popcorn without picking any up. "We all got a right to some secrets."

"Not when she knows everyone's secrets but doesn't want anyone to know hers."

Nev narrowed her eyes as she watched Jazz.

"What?"

"I'm just surprised."

Jazz knew that tone and the shift to more formal language. It was the lead-in to something she was not going to like.

"I didn't think you'd be so sensitive, what with your Army training and all."

"I'm not sensitive."

"Uh-huh." A sarcastic version of the affirmation that

meant Nev didn't believe it. "You're only suspicious of the boss because you think she doesn't like you."

"That's not true. Anyone who isn't so awed by her as you and the team would be suspicious."

"You know what I've noticed about the boss?" Nev tucked her fingers into her curls. "She seems to expose people's insecurities without having to do or say a thing. People just bring their insecurities with them, and their hangups make them either hate her or be like...drawn to her. It's like her superpower."

"So you're saying it's my fault she doesn't like me?"

"Course not. I'm just saying she can help you with those insecurities if you'd let her."

Jazz pressed her lips together to keep in the retort she wanted to throw out. That she didn't have PTSD like Nev. But she wouldn't risk hurting her best friend. "I know she helped you. But I haven't been through trauma or anything."

"You been through stuff."

Jazz fiddled with a pilled bit of fabric on the blanket. "Nothing like you."

"Doesn't mean the boss couldn't help you anyway."

Jazz lifted her gaze to Nev. "Pretty sure she doesn't want to. And I wouldn't want help from someone who keeps so many secrets. Does anyone even know who she really is? I mean, she could have some really scary skeletons in her closet."

Nev smushed her lips together and turned her head away. Then she brought her dark gaze back.

Jazz braced herself. She knew that look. Nev was about to tell it like it was. Or at least how she thought it was.

"Have you ever thought that maybe you put up walls with people?"

Jazz stared at the image on the TV, the couple frozen in their romantic moment.

"Like maybe you're afraid they'll reject you, so you reject them first."

"Of course not." Jazz jerked her gaze to Nev, hurt

squeezing her ribs. "I don't push people away. They just don't like me. You know I'm not like you, popular with everyone."

"That's not true." Nev leaned forward over the popcorn bowl. "You would be popular, and everybody would love you, if you'd let them."

"So you *are* saying it's my fault." The hurt migrated to Jazz's voice and pricked at her eyes. "I thought you always had my back."

"I do." Nev pulled away as if Jazz had struck her. "You know that."

"Sure." Jazz clenched her jaw to keep from crying. "That's why you don't want me to like Hawthorne either."

"I didn't say that. I just don't want to see you get hurt."

"And you're so sure I'm going to. That he's not going to like me because no one does."

Nev lifted her hands in exasperation. "I'm afraid you're going to fall in love with a guy who's going to leave. A guy who doesn't feel the same."

"Plans can change." Jazz tilted up her chin as she looked away. "And I think he does like me. A lot."

"Fine." Nev picked up the remote and twisted to face the TV. "Then go ahead and like the guy."

"I will."

Nev played the movie, and they watched the rest of it in silence.

Jazz had encouraged Nev to like Branson and supported her when she'd found love. Why couldn't Nev do the same for her?

Nothing seemed to go right anymore. Except for Hawthorne.

The hero in the movie said something sweet to the heroine, a lovesick light in his eyes.

But Jazz heard Hawthorne's voice instead, saw his handsome face, his amazing eyes aimed at her, filled with love and acceptance.

If things continued with Hawthorne like she hoped they

would, she'd finally have the happiness she'd been looking for all her life. She couldn't wait.

THIRTY-ONE

Jazz raised her eyebrows as Phoenix and Dag veered toward the older, two-story house instead of the large building with a sign that read: *Forever Home*.

Jazz followed with Flash, but her nerves tensed. This whole setup was so weird—Phoenix bringing only Jazz somewhere she didn't bring most of the PK-9 team.

And now she was leading Jazz to a house that looked very lived-in, judging from the tricycle and toys on the front porch.

Phoenix didn't take detours. So why was she going up to someone's personal home instead of to the kennel where the sound of dogs barking echoed through the walls? Or out to the grassy property where it looked like fences partitioned off sections that held agility equipment.

Jazz kept her questions to herself as she followed the boss. But she wasn't going to be caught unaware if Phoenix was setting up some kind of trap. Even if it was an emotional one to lay all her insecurities bare, like Nev had suggested last night.

The front door swung open before Phoenix reached it.

"Phoenix." A woman of medium height with dark brown, wavy hair appeared in the doorway, a sweet smile on her face. Like the kind a person would give a long-lost friend.

Not the usual response people had to Phoenix.

"Come in." The woman stepped back, and—another shocker—Phoenix and Dag walked in.

Jazz followed, counting on Flash to give her warning if Phoenix had set up some kind of ambush to test their skills.

Squeals jerked Flash's attention to two small bodies tumbling past. He pulled at the leash, wanting to chase the boys who couldn't be more than three or four.

"Phoenix!" Another boy, maybe about five or six, and a girl who looked the same age shouted the boss's name in unison from the kitchen counter. They smeared what appeared to be blue paint from their hands onto the cushions as they slipped off the bar stools they had sat on.

"Hold on." The brunette's voice held more gentleness than scolding as she pointed at them. "Wash first."

They groaned as they scrambled around the counter to a sink where they suddenly grew in height. Probably thanks to a short stool or something.

"You'll have to excuse all the chaos. It gets lively around here sometimes." The brunette turned a smile toward Jazz, letting her see the other side of the woman's face for the first time.

Jazz tried to keep her expression blank as she took in the scarring that puckered and marred the entire left cheek. The poor woman.

"I'm Marion Moore, Director of Forever Home and mother to these tykes." She waved toward the children, the smile not leaving her face as she extended her other hand toward Jazz. "Though it feels more like I'm a ringmaster at a circus most days."

Jazz shook the woman's small hand. "Glad to meet you. You're a dog trainer, too, I understand."

"I try to be. I think the dogs teach me more than I teach them." Marion's gentle demeanor and laidback friendliness had such a warming, welcoming effect that Jazz's tension relaxed.

The two fingerpainters rushed over to Phoenix and Dag,

then braked abruptly one foot away as if they'd been trained to do so. "May we pet your dog?" The girl asked the question as the boy leaned forward, clearly anticipating the answer.

"You may." They shot toward Dag, who sat perfectly still and solid, as always.

"Slowly." Marion smiled at the children as they reached out their hands in closed fists to Dag.

Jazz chuckled. They'd clearly been taught how to safely approach a strange dog.

But Dagian looked like he was only tolerating a ritual he knew was completely unnecessary.

The kids then petted Dag, but quickly shifted their gazes to Flash, who was eying them just as eagerly.

The children turned big eyes up at Jazz. "May we pet your dog?" The boy asked the question this time.

Jazz smiled and nodded. "You may."

They approached Flash much more slowly as their mother looked on. Flash nuzzled their fists with his nose, probably hoping they had treats hidden in their small hands. They giggled and stepped closer to rub his furry neck.

"I see he's very comfortable with children."

"Oh, yeah." Jazz smiled at Marion. "He's pretty rock solid about everything. Except cats. He wants to chase them, I'm afraid."

Marion laughed. "Well, we don't have any cats here. Yet. My oldest, Marnie, is working on that." Marion looked at Phoenix. "She and Joe are waiting for us out—"

"Phoenix." The male voice jerked Jazz's attention to the bottom of the staircase across the small living room. "Good to see you." A thickly built, bearded man walked toward them, carrying a baby that looked tiny nestled against his large chest. Marion's husband? His dark brown skin and black curly hair explained where some of the adorable kids had gotten their black curls and brown skin tone that didn't match their mom's ivory shade.

The guy stopped by Jazz, giving Flash an assessing gaze.

Probably trying to make sure the dog was safe. Good thinking.

He pulled his attention up to Jazz's face and extended a large hand. "Eli Moore. I get to call this beautiful woman my wife." He gave Marion a wink as Jazz shook his hand.

Marion blushed like a newlywed.

Jazz squelched a smile as she returned Eli's firm handshake. "Jazz Lamont."

"Here to see the new additions, right?" Eli gave Jazz a close look that was a bit like the assessment he'd aimed at Flash. But his body language seemed friendly enough, and a glint of humor lit his eyes.

"I guess so." Jazz glanced at Phoenix, who was in silent mode as usual, though she watched their interactions.

"We've worked hard on the expansion, so I hope you like it. But speaking of work," he turned toward his wife, "I'd better get going." He dropped a kiss on the infant's small head. "Though I hate to leave this one." Then he stepped closer to Marion and swooped to land a sudden kiss on her lips. "And especially this one."

Oh, brother. Jazz barely stifled an eyeroll. This couple could be in the movie she and Nev had watched last night.

Scratch that. Nobody was that romantic. Especially not after as long as these two must've been married to have all those kids.

But her cynicism didn't keep a bit of envy from pinching her chest as she watched the loving couple exchange the baby, briefly embracing the child and each other as they said goodbye.

Marion tucked the still-sleeping infant against her shoulder and looked into the kitchen where a taller boy Jazz hadn't noticed before was going to the refrigerator.

"LeBrae, you're in charge."

The kid waved an acknowledgement that must've satisfied Marion, since she turned to smile at Phoenix and Jazz. "Shall we? Marnie is probably wondering what's taking us so long."

Phoenix gave a nod, and Marion led them out the front

door into the bright sunlight and thickening air. If it was that warm at only six thirty in the morning, today would be a scorcher.

They walked along a gravel path to the building Jazz still assumed was a kennel, given the loud barking of several dogs coming from within.

Her deduction was confirmed when she followed Marion and Phoenix inside. A large, open space held about twenty runs, most of them filled with dogs.

"Would you like a quick tour?" Marion turned her brown eyes on Jazz.

"Sure."

"If that's okay with you." Marion looked toward Phoenix, who returned her question with a silent stare. "Great." Marion launched into explaining the facility as she led them around, as if Phoenix had actually given her an answer. Maybe she had a knack for reading Phoenix, like Cora. Or she'd learned to do whatever she wanted unless Phoenix stopped her.

Jazz smirked at the thought.

Marion gave a brief history of the twelve-year-old shelter, which she'd expanded into a training and rehab facility for the dogs she rehomed. "Phoenix has given many of those dogs homes and purpose in life by partnering them with the ladies at the Phoenix K-9 Agency."

Jazz nodded. "I heard you trained Toby and Alvarez?"

"Yes." Marion smiled. "Such sweet dogs."

"And Cannenta, right? She's my friend's dog."

"Oh, yes." Marion caressed the baby's back with her hand as she walked. "Cannenta came from our training program with inmates at the prison. Such a blessing to help dogs and humans bring healing to each other. How is Cannenta?"

"Great. Living the dream. And she helps my friend a ton."

Marion's smile broadened. "Wonderful." She opened a door that led from the kennel to another large space she explained they used for training and adapting dogs to household environments.

She looked around the empty room with a frown. "I told Marnie and Joe to wait for us here. She was going to work with Kippie." Marion looked at Pheonix.

"The training field."

"Of course." Marion nodded like Phoenix had given her the answer and moved toward another door Jazz guessed would take them outside.

After walking about a half-acre along a gravel driveway, they reached a chain-link fence that bordered an open area of grass containing training obstacles and agility equipment. Must be what Phoenix had wanted to show her.

A skinny girl and a stocky boy stood in the middle of the grassy area while a short-haired, brown and white dog sprinted around them in circles.

The girl swung a pole away from her body that was attached to a string with a ferret-like stuffed toy on the end of it.

Flash pulled toward the toy as Phoenix opened a gate to let them into the yard.

"Flash, *lass es*."

The K-9 worked hard to restrain himself at the *leave it* command.

Marion glanced at Flash, then the kids. "Marnie, that's enough. Our guests are here."

The girl lowered the toy, letting the hyper mix grab the fake ferret in its mouth.

As Phoenix, Marion, and Jazz approached with Flash and Dag, Marnie stood in front of the dog and commanded it to drop the toy in a confident tone.

The dog obeyed, and Marnie tossed it what Jazz assumed was a treat from the pouch on her hip.

"Put the leash on him, Joe." She threw the order at the boy as she turned toward the newcomers. "Phoenix." Her small mouth spread into a smile, and she squinted up at the boss. The girl looked to be eight or nine judging by her size, but something in her brown eyes suggested she was older. Or maybe it was the way she seemed happy to see Phoenix but didn't shout with excitement like the children in the house. "I knew you were here before Mom told me."

Her glossy, straight black hair, olive-toned skin, and Asian features were a puzzle. Didn't look like she could be a child of Marion or Eli.

Stranger still was the slight movement Jazz caught on Phoenix's face. The boss's lips lifted the tiniest bit at the corners in the almost-smile Jazz had only seen Phoenix give Cora. Once. "Well done."

And a compliment from the boss? Jazz looked from Phoenix to the girl and back again as the two watched each other.

"Hiya, Phoenix." The boy brought the bouncy dog toward them on leash, his Hispanic features and coloring making Jazz all the more curious. Were some of the kids adopted? Marnie had called Marion her mom.

"See the ladder we added?" The boy Jazz guessed to be eight years old pointed toward a ladder angled upright against a steep ramp that sloped downward on the opposite side. He looked up at Jazz. "Mom says your dog can climb that." The eagerness in his voice, like he couldn't wait to watch, made Jazz smile.

"Oh, yeah. No problem."

The boy's eyes widened, and he threw a hopeful look at his mother.

"Yes, Joe, you can stay. But I need to talk to Marnie."

"Why?" The girl's black eyebrows lowered.

"I told you to wait for us in the training center, Marnie. You disobeyed me again."

"Only because I knew Kippie would have more room out here. You said you wanted to try him on the weave poles and the ramp. I did that before we played with the flirt toy. So you wouldn't have to get it done later."

Jazz squashed an amused smile at the girl's tactic of making her rule-breaking sound like she'd done her mom a favor. Smart kid.

"It's still disobedience, Marnie. You know that." Marion's

voice stayed gentle as she put one hand on her daughter's shoulder. "Now you'll have to go inside and help LeBrae with the little ones until we're done out here."

Anger snapped in the girl's eyes as she stepped away from Marion's touch. "That's not—" Her voice suddenly cut off as she jerked a glance toward Phoenix.

Jazz hadn't heard the boss make a sound.

But Marnie stared at her for a second, her features scrunched with fury. Then she spun and walked at a quick clip out of the yard. Though her coiled posture suggested she'd prefer to stomp or kick something.

"I don't suppose you have time to talk to her while you're here?" Marion sent Phoenix a hopeful look.

The boss? Talk to a kid?

Phoenix gave a short nod. "Later."

Marion sighed, apparently relieved. "Thank you." She turned an apologetic gaze on Jazz. "Sorry you had to witness that."

"No problem. You have a big family."

Marion smiled. "That's a very nice way to put it. Thank you. Many people have other choice words when they see us with seven or more kids."

"More?"

Marion nodded. "We've been privileged to adopt, give birth, and provide a home to some still in foster care. So the number can change, but we're always a family built on love, as Eli likes to put it."

A family built on love. A lump formed in Jazz's throat. How different her life would've turned out with a mother like Marion. And a dad like her husband. Sounded like they accepted and loved everyone.

"But you aren't here to meet my family. You're here for Flash to see our new training facilities." Marion supported the baby as the infant shifted slightly against her shoulder. Then she walked Jazz and Phoenix through the training layout of obstacles and agility challenges, explaining how it would function as a place for all the PK-9 Search and Rescue dogs to keep their skills fresh.

Marion took them to another section of land farther out and gestured toward the extensive acres they'd fenced in to have a controlled area for Dag, Flash, and any other tracking and SAR dogs to train.

"Phoenix, I think we'll shift our cadaver training to the east section there." Marion pointed at an area that included the edge of a forest. "There are more trees there for varied terrain, and we'll get a different set of scents by changing location."

Jazz didn't register much of Marion's continued explanation. She was stuck on the first part. Cadaver training? Was that one of the secrets Phoenix was keeping from the team?

Jazz turned to the boss and opened her mouth before she lost her nerve. "Did you get a cadaver dog?"

Phoenix stared at her for a silent moment. "Dag is the cadaver dog."

"Oh." Jazz dropped her gaze to the sandy colored dog who finally panted in the heat as he sat by Phoenix's leg. "I never heard he scents cadavers, too."

Marion looked from Jazz to Phoenix, then back to Jazz. "We've been training him for the past six months. He picked it up very quickly, as he does with everything."

So it was a new thing. Did anyone else on the PK-9 team know? Jazz cleared her throat and ventured another question. "Why are you training him for cadavers?"

"We'll be able to expand our services for clients." At least Phoenix didn't look annoyed with the questions. Though she never showed any emotion anyway.

Jazz didn't buy for a second that was the only reason she wanted Dag to be able to find cadavers. Though she had no idea what the real explanation could be. Unless Phoenix had literal skeletons buried in her closet. Wouldn't Nev be surprised.

Marion interrupted Jazz's train of thought with the suggestion Flash try the equipment right then.

The poor dog had been fidgety ever since the kids in the house had gotten him excited. And seeing the flirt toy had only amped him up more.

They returned to the agility equipment where Joe still waited to watch. Jazz unclipped Flash's leash and ran him through the obstacles, letting him show off his insane athleticism.

After a while, Marion's baby awoke and started to fuss. Marion headed inside, telling them to stay as long as they wanted.

But Phoenix told Jazz to leash Flash, and they headed back to their vehicles in the driveway, Joe following along.

"We'll need a photo of Freddie Blain." Phoenix startled Jazz by speaking as they neared her white van, and Joe angled away to continue to the house.

"Did Cora find something about him?"

"Not yet. No trail to find." Phoenix stopped at the rear of the van but didn't make any move to open the double doors.

"So no criminal record then."

"No record at all."

Meaning, Freddie didn't exist? Or he'd been careful to stay off the grid somehow. Jazz kept the thoughts to herself. Phoenix would probably keep any answers she had secret anyway. "I can get a photo of him tonight when I'm on patrol."

"Sofia or Nevaeh will attempt to get one in the daylight today."

Jazz nodded. "He might not come in until noon or after if he takes another late shift."

"Cora has a narcotics job in the afternoon. Her response to photos may be delayed until she's finished."

"Okay. Keep me posted." The words popped out before she thought. Did Phoenix keep anyone posted? Maybe Cora. But certainly not Jazz.

"I guess I'll head out." Jazz gave an awkward wave before she thought about who she was waving to and went to her

SUV parked a few feet from Phoenix's van. As she stopped at the rear and opened the liftgate, she glanced toward the boss.

But she wasn't by the van anymore.

She and Dag had disappeared.

Jazz pressed her lips together. So creepy how she could do that.

Was she going to talk to the girl, Marnie, like she'd hinted to Marion she would? What could Phoenix say to a young girl that wouldn't just frighten her?

Jazz shrugged and closed the liftgate after Flash jumped in. She hurried to the driver's door to start the air conditioning before poor Flash overheated inside the SUV.

Since Phoenix likely wouldn't keep Jazz informed about Freddie, maybe Jazz should call Cora after her narcotics job was finished to hear what she'd discovered as soon as possible.

A little progress in finding the person trying to destroy the fair would go a long way toward calming the warning in Jazz's mind that had been growing louder every day. The warning that said the danger to the fair and the threat to her own life were far from over.

THIRTY-TWO

Excitement pulsed through Hawthorne's veins as he knocked on the door of apartment number 128. The same buzz he always got when a book's plot came together or he thought of the perfect twist or hidden clue to throw in.

Two of the names Rebekah had given him for Sam's friends that had left the cult, the two young men he'd been able to leave voicemails for, had called him back. They had both moved out of state as soon as they'd left the cult and had alibis for the night of Sam's death. Not that Hawthorne had asked them outright, but the course of conversation had revealed the information he'd needed. Including the address of the elusive other friend.

The second guy Hawthorne had talked to—Kal Fine— explained he had kept in touch with Sam briefly, and he knew Sam had been in contact with their mutual friend, Ezekial Thorston. Kal also knew where Ezekial lived.

Hawthorne knocked again, his pumping pulse slowing. Was Ezekial not home? Maybe he worked mornings.

Shuffling on the other side of the door surged anticipation through Hawthorne.

The door opened a few inches. "Yeah?" A young, thin guy who looked about the right age to be Sam's now twenty-year-old friend blinked tired eyes at Hawthorne. His neck-length hair was tousled like he'd just rolled out of bed.

At seven in the morning, it was early enough for that to be reasonable. "Hi. My name is Hawthorne Emerson. I got your name from Kal Fine. He said you'd be willing to talk to me about Sam Ackerman?"

The door opened another inch as Ezekial stared at him. "You a reporter?"

"No. I'm Rebekah Emerson's brother. She asked me to find out what happened to Sam."

He swung the door open enough to show his rumpled T-shirt and plaid shorts. "Rebekah." His mouth angled in a sleepy grin. "She was always cool. How's she doing?"

"She'll be a lot better if I can tell her I spoke with you about Sam. Can I come in, Ezekial?"

The kid ran his fingers through his shaggy hair. "Call me Zeke." He turned and walked away, leaving the door wide open.

Taking that as an invitation to enter, Hawthorne stepped inside and closed the door behind him. The apartment looked fairly new but was as cluttered and messy as a stereotypical bachelor pad, complete with pizza boxes and takeout containers piled on the kitchen counters.

Hawthorne veered through the kitchen and into the adjoining living room where Zeke flung himself onto the navy blue sofa.

"Look man, I want to help and all that." Zeke laid his head back on the upholstered cushion and closed his eyes. "But I gotta be at work in like an hour."

"Okay. I'll be quick." Hawthorne scanned the two armchairs cluttered with papers and discarded clothing and thought better of trying to sit. "Did you go to the fair with Sam the night he died?"

"Sure." Zeke didn't even lift his head. As if what he'd said wasn't a revelation that would've changed the entire investigation of Sam's death.

"Why didn't you tell the police you were with him?"

"'Cause it wouldn't have made any difference." Zeke lifted his head and squinted at Hawthorne. "Oh." A disbelieving half-laugh puffed from his mouth. "You think I mean—no, I didn't see him…die or anything. I wasn't with him all the time."

Could be true. Could also be a lie. But the former seemed more likely given how easily and quickly Zeke had admitted to being with Sam. If he'd tried to hide that fact for two years because he'd murdered Sam or witnessed a killing, why tell Hawthorne now?

"When weren't you with him?" Hawthorne kept his tone free of suspicion.

"Uh…" Zeke tipped his head back again and blinked at the ceiling.

"Why don't you walk me through that night."

Zeke tilted his head to the side to look at Hawthorne without lifting off the sofa. "All of it?"

"At least the high points."

Zeke dragged his head off the cushion and leaned forward, bracing his elbows on his knees and resting his chin in his hands. "I met him at the fair like we'd planned. He'd sneaked out while the nut jobs were having one of their star-communing parties. Then we just hung out."

"Doing what?"

"You know. Going on rides, hitting the games, following girls. Whatever."

That didn't account for the group of four or five guys Christy and Dan remembered. "Did you meet up with anyone else there?"

"Not really."

Hawthorne's ears perked at the wording. "You mean you met people, but maybe someone you'd rather leave out of it?"

Zeke lowered his arms and leaned back again, not looking at Hawthorne. He blew out a sigh. "Maybe."

"Look, Zeke. I'm not a cop. Telling me doesn't mean your friend will get into trouble." Not necessarily, at any rate.

"Don't you think we should know what really happened to Sam?"

Zeke slowly swung his head toward Hawthorne, peering at him around the hair that fell over one of Zeke's eyes. "You don't think it was an accident?"

"No. I don't." The threatening note and cut brakes had seen to that. No one beside Jazz knew he was involved in investigating the fair sabotage outside his capacity as a security guard. The attempt to frighten or kill him had to be about Sam. Everyone he'd questioned knew he was looking into the boy's death.

"Man." Zeke pushed back his hair, running his hands along both sides of his face. "Okay. I had a friend at the gas station where I worked who was twenty-one. He said we could hang with him and his buddies so we wouldn't need fake IDs to have a good time."

So that was how Sam had managed to get alcohol at only seventeen years of age. "Did you and Sam drink much?"

He swore by way of affirmation. "We were kids. And it was Sam's first time out of the cult on his own. I stopped that kind of thing after my DUI, though. I don't touch the stuff anymore."

"Glad to hear it." The more crucial questions pressed against Hawthorne's lips, but he fought to keep from shooting them out too quickly. Timing and pacing was everything, as in one of Carson Steele's interrogation scenes.

Hawthorne stepped closer to the back of a short armchair and braced his hands on it. "Tell me what happened later in the evening. You said Sam wasn't with you the whole night. Was he away from you several times?"

"Nah. We were pretty tight. And the other guys were our ticket to a good time, so we stuck with them."

Remembering Christy's account of the young men at the Logboat Adventure ride, Hawthorne ventured one of the big questions. "Did Sam go on the Logboat Adventure ride with you and the others at around eleven?"

"We went on it. Don't know what time it was."

"I thought Sam was afraid of water."

Zeke smiled. "Oh, yeah. I forgot. After that many drinks, trust me—he was a whole new Sam."

So Sam had gotten over his fears temporarily thanks to alcohol. Did that mean an accidental death was possible?

Zeke pushed up from the sofa and shuffled past Hawthorne to the kitchen. He paused by the island. "He begged me not to say anything. Didn't want the older dudes to know he was scared, you know?" He gave a single laugh. "Funny. I'm nearly their age now."

Hawthorne closed some of the distance between him and Zeke, stopping at the edge of the tile that bordered the small kitchen. "So when did Sam leave? When wasn't he with you and the others?"

Zeke flipped open a pizza box and pulled out a slice that had probably sat there overnight or longer. At least the piece didn't appear to have mold on it yet. "Just at the end, I think."

"The end? Do you remember what time?"

"Nah." He took a large bite of the pizza.

"But it was when you were leaving?"

"No." He mumbled the word around the pizza. "The rest of us stayed after. Like until the fair closed down."

Hawthorne's pulse picked up speed. "Sam wasn't with you then?"

"Nah." He stuffed more of the slice into his mouth, as if he had no idea he'd dropped another bombshell.

Hawthorne battled to keep his tone calm. "Where did he go?"

"He went to get a smoke." Zeke waved the remainder of the pizza slice through the air as he talked with his hands. "They don't let you smoke anywhere but at these marked areas."

"Sam had brought cigarettes?" He certainly wouldn't have gotten those at Best Life.

"He bought 'em at the grocery store at the fair. You know,

the one behind the beer gardens?" Zeke shoved the crust end of the piece into his mouth.

"Do you remember which designated smoking area Sam went to?"

"Uh…" Zeke reached in the box for another slice. "I remember we were in line for the SkyPlunge ride, so the spot at the midway, I guess."

A witness to a location where Sam had been. This was incredible. "Okay, so Sam went to smoke and then what happened."

Zeke paused with the pizza by his lips. "I don't know."

"What do you mean?"

He shrugged and bit off a chunk. "I never saw him again." The garbled words were still clear enough to hit Hawthorne deep in the gut.

"You didn't think that was strange? Didn't you look for him?"

"No. The guys didn't want to wait in line with things about to close, so we went to a different ride farther up the midway. Then a couple of the older dudes found some chicks, and my friend and I hit a few more rides. Then it was closing time. I figured Sam found something better to do. I saw a hot chick headed to the smoking spot when Sam said he was going to get a smoke. I figured he was chasing her, and he must've gotten what he wanted, you know?" Zeke grinned around the piece of pizza as he shoved the rest in his mouth.

Rebekah wouldn't like the sound of that. And Hawthorne didn't buy it. Because sometime after that, Sam had ended up dead.

"Did you see anyone else in that area?"

"Dude," Zeke leveled a stare at Hawthorne as he munched the pizza in his mouth, "like hundreds or thousands of people."

"But you noticed the girl. Anyone else you noticed?"

"A few more girls, but they weren't going to smoke. Security guards. They'd been all over us the whole night. Kept making us move on whenever somebody thought we talked too loud or something. I think they were tailing us after the one dude started a fight with that cheat at the air rifle targets."

The security guards probably had followed them, and rightfully so. Sounded like Zeke and his pals had made a significant nuisance of themselves. Enough that Dan Harris still remembered them two years later. "Could you see Sam in the designated smoking area from where you were in line?"

"Uh…" Zeke closed the pizza box. "Not really."

"And you never saw him again after that."

Zeke pushed his fingers through his hair and shook his head. "Never."

Except for the killer Hawthorne was now certain existed, he was pretty sure no one else had seen Sam after that either. Not alive.

Gravel kicked up behind Jazz, skimming her calves beneath her three-quarter leggings as she sprinted up the steep incline.

Flash outpaced her and ran ahead, clearly enjoying the freedom to test his speed on the quiet wooded trail.

They'd passed some walkers about two miles back but otherwise had the trail all to themselves. She brought her wrist toward her face to check her watch. Almost seven thirty. The time when Hawthorne's text had said he'd meet her at the lookout he would drive up to from the other side of Elk Horn Trail.

Her heart rate double-timed. And not because of her fast pace or the climb.

She could already picture it—hunky Hawthorne standing with her on the lookout, checking out the view. But mostly enjoying gazing at each other.

He hadn't said in the text why he wanted to meet. Just that he had something to tell her. Could that something be that he wasn't going to leave after all? That he'd fallen for her?

Her throat tightened at the possibility. Which wasn't helpful for running.

Flash circled back to her to check in as usual, then sprinted ahead up the incline like it was nothing.

"Show off!" Jazz managed to call, finally feeling short of breath.

Just before he would've been out of sight, Flash stopped. He spun toward Jazz and barked, charging at her.

She braked, staring at Flash, expecting him to stop and signal what was wrong. "Wha—"

He flew off the ground, launching himself into her chest.

The wind whooshed from her lungs as she fell backward.

Just as the ground exploded.

THIRTY-THREE

The distinctive blast yanked Hawthorne back to his Marine Corps days. That sound. The damage and havoc it wreaked.

Explosives.

Jazz was supposed to be on that trail. Close.

Hawthorne took off, sprinting away from the lookout onto the three-foot-wide trail.

Barks, like those he'd heard right before the blast, came from somewhere around the curve ahead.

A black and tan body whizzed into view.

Flash.

The dog locked his stare on Hawthorne and barked repeatedly.

"Where is she, Flash?"

The K-9 spun and took off.

Hawthorne raced to keep up, tearing around the curve bordered by trees on both sides. He frantically scanned the path ahead as it straightened.

Jazz.

He froze. Staring.

Her body lay on the ground.

His heart stopped. Was she dead?

Barks answered the horrible question. Flash wouldn't be getting help if she were dead. Would he?

Hawthorne pushed his legs forward, fear of what he might see up close holding him back.

Chunks and splinters of wood mingled with scattered piles of dirt on the ground.

A slim tree lay across the path, blocking his access to Jazz. Its trunk was splintered and cracked.

He jumped over it as Flash must have done, adrenaline hitting his bloodstream and overcoming his trepidation. "Jazz!"

He jogged to her.

Flash stopped barking as Hawthorne neared, whining with a single wag of his tail.

Hawthorne stopped next to—

Jazz raised her hand off the ground.

"Jazz." Hawthorne's heart lurched, and he dropped to his knees beside her. She was alive.

She braced her elbow against the ground as if trying to sit up.

He slid an arm around her back and helped her. His chest squeezed at the sight of the small, bloody cuts that scratched her cheek and forehead. "You probably shouldn't move."

But she drew in her legs to stand anyway. Stubborn woman.

He kept his arm behind her back and lifted her to her feet. Then without another thought, he pulled her into an embrace, cradling her against his chest.

He couldn't help it. She could've died.

So that's what he said as he caressed her silky hair with his thumb. "I thought you might be dead."

She leaned her head back and brought her gaze up to his. Something shimmered in her emerald eyes. Tears? Was she hurt?

"I'm sorry." He loosened his hold around her, lowering his hands to gently brush down her arms. "Are you injured?"

She shook her head, watching him with what looked like wonder. Maybe her head injury had left her a little confused.

His hand went to her face, cupping her cheek as his

thumb neared one of the red marks. "Your face is scratched. Are you sure you aren't hurt anywhere else?"

"Pretty sure." Her gaze didn't leave his.

She was breathtaking. Twigs in her mussed ponytail and scratches and dirt smudges on her face couldn't do a thing to diminish her stunning beauty. Or the effect she seemed to be having on him.

A well-timed whine from Flash drew Jazz's attention to the dog. And reminded Hawthorne he'd better rein in his emotions. She was okay. And he was still romantically unavailable.

"Thanks for saving my life, partner." Jazz crouched face-to-face with the K-9 and rubbed his head and ears with both hands. "Again." She pressed a kiss on top of the dog's head, then stood, looking in the direction of the damage on the trail. "That was close."

He couldn't have picked a better heroine. She'd nearly been killed, and she was as calm and cool as ever. "What exactly happened?"

"I don't think it was a land mine since Flash warned me before either of us triggered it. Probably a buried IED."

A run-of-the-mill homemade bomb. Not very friendly.

"Had to be remote detonated since nobody would know when I'd be here. Unless it was meant for someone else." Her tone said she didn't consider that a realistic theory. She shot her gaze to Hawthorne. "Did you see anyone at the lookout?"

"One hiker was headed onto this trail as I arrived." Hawthorne recalled the man in jeans, boots, gray T-shirt, and baseball cap. He'd only seen the man from the back. "At least I assumed he was a hiker."

"He was coming down this way?"

"Yes." Hawthorne clenched his jaw as he looked past the wreckage the explosion had left on the trail. "And I bet I ran right past him on my way to you. He probably hid off the trail."

"Flash and I will find him." She turned toward her K-9 but swayed.

Hawthorne reached for her and braced her arms. "Hold on. You're in no condition to go anywhere. And I guarantee he's already gone. He wouldn't be hanging out to wait for the rescue squad and police."

"But Flash can track him." She pressed her hand to her forehead as if it hurt.

"Maybe. But you can't right now." He tried to guide her in the other direction. "Come sit down and rest for a bit."

"Don't be ridiculous."

"Is it ridiculous to want to take care of you?"

She dropped her hand, allowing him to see her eyes. Her brows lowered as she peered at him. "I don't know. No one ever has."

The lonely shadow in her eyes felt like a kick to his gut. He didn't know how to respond. What to say or do. He'd already said too much. Implied too much.

He tried for a smile. "Then enjoy the moment. And sit down before you fall down, will you?"

She gave him a mock glare and lowered to sit on the gravel and dirt path, Flash moving in close to nudge her face with his nose.

Hawthorne pulled out his cell phone and called emergency services in case no one elsewhere in Whitlow Park had reported the sound of the explosion.

"We can't just sit here." Jazz looked at Hawthorne as he ended the call and dropped to the ground a few feet from her.

"We can, and we should. The lady on the phone said I need to keep you still and quiet until the ambulance gets here and they check you out."

"Who made her the boss?"

He grinned at her ready humor, even in the face of near death. "I don't know how to answer that."

"Thought so."

"But I do have the answer to the question I wanted to ask you."

"What was that?"

"I was going to ask if that 'flat tire,'" he made air quotes with his fingers around the mythical label, "was the only incident like that you've had happen lately."

She stared at him a moment.

Was she going to deny what they both knew to be true? She'd tried to pass it off as nothing before.

"Now you know."

Good. She trusted him enough not to hide that she was in danger. But the confirmation of what he'd suspected affected him more than he had anticipated. Someone wanted to hurt Jazz. Maybe kill her.

A rush of something he couldn't identify rolled through him in a hot wave, seeping into his muscles and limbs. "Why didn't you tell me? I could've helped. I could have…" His voice trailed off as the thought finished in his mind. *He could have protected her.*

Is that what the strange feeling was? Protectiveness?

He'd never felt it like that for anyone before. Maybe a hint of wanting to give Rebekah some brotherly advice recently. But not this powerful, almost angry emotion that made him want to shield Jazz from danger and take down anyone who'd even think about hurting her.

Man. He needed to leave. Maybe sooner than he'd planned. He was starting to care about her way too much.

And she was starting to look at him like she knew. As if she saw how much he cared.

He had to fix this. Had to make it clearer he wasn't in the market for a relationship. But in a way that didn't hurt her.

Because the hope he'd accidentally given her was written all over her lovely face.

He looked away and cleared his throat. "I wondered because I've been getting some of the same treatment."

"You have?" Surprise lifted her tone.

"Threatening note, and then my brakes were cut last night."

She sucked in an audible breath. "Were you hurt?"

He couldn't help but look at her again when she asked the question with concern squeezing her voice. "No. I'm fine. But —" He stopped just short of saying he was concerned about her. He'd made enough of that kind of mistake for one day. "But I'm thinking whoever is going after me could be the same person after you."

"Oh." Something passed in her eyes. Doubt? Or maybe she was simply processing the idea.

"It seems likely to be someone who doesn't want us to get any closer to finding the truth."

"But about the sabotage or Sam?"

"I don't know." He kept his gaze from meeting hers. Easier to feel less and show less if he didn't look at her so much. "Whoever it is could know you're helping me investigate Sam's death."

"You mean someone from the cult." She paused, but he didn't give in to the temptation to glance her way. "Maybe Randall? Or someone who found out I'd asked him about Sam? He doesn't seem like the kind of guy to keep his mouth shut."

"If it's about Sam, the person is right to be worried about what we'll find. I just talked to the friend Sam was with at the fair."

"You're kidding."

The excitement of having more of a trail to follow thrummed through Hawthorne's bloodstream. "I have a last known location on the fairgrounds now. And more reason to believe Sam wouldn't have gone to the Logboat Adventure ride alone. Even drunk, he'd only gone on the ride earlier because of peer pressure. And he hadn't expressed any plans to go back."

"That's wonderful."

"I'm going to visit the smoking area where Sam was last seen. From what his friend told me, Sam had planned to return to his pals. But he never made it." Hawthorne finally allowed himself a glance in her direction. "I hope you and Flash can help me search the area. Hopefully find something.

It's a longshot for evidence to still be there. But getting the lay of the land and playing out possible scenarios could lead to a breakthrough." He smiled. "I might finally be able to solve this case."

"That would be...great."

He caught the wistfulness in her voice that he now realized had been there in her previous comment, too.

Sirens sounded in the distance, likely from the ambulance or police headed their way.

But it was too late for the kind of rescue Hawthorne probably needed most. Someone to extract him from the situation he'd gotten himself into.

A hint of sadness settled around Jazz's mouth, but the hope he'd read on her face before was still there.

Guilt swelled in his throat. He'd better solve Sam's murder fast.

He needed to get as far away from Jazz Lamont as possible in the next day or two if he could get out of his security contract. Because there was no way he could give her the relationship he was starting to suspect she wanted.

And he was afraid, given the emotion in her eyes that he didn't dare define, he was going to have to break her heart.

THIRTY-FOUR

Who'd have thought nearly getting killed could feel so good? Jazz smiled as she leaned back into the cushions of Nev's sofa and propped her feet up on the coffee table, holding a mug in her hands.

Hawthorne cared for her. Maybe more than cared.

Her pulse fluttered as she remembered the deep concern in his eyes as he'd touched her cheek and asked if she was hurt.

A shiver tracked down her spine at the memory of the way he'd held her in his strong arms, squeezing almost too tight as he pressed her against his chest, like a person did when they'd nearly lost someone they...loved.

Nev had interrogated Jazz about Hawthorne almost as much as the explosion when Jazz had returned home. Probably because Nev could see Jazz's swoony feelings written all over her. Jazz guessed she was beaming. Wasn't that what a woman in love did?

She frowned.

If only Nev had been supportive and happy for her. Not that Nev had said much. She hadn't needed to say anything with her grim expression broadcasting her thoughts so loudly. Jazz didn't see why Nev—

The ringtone from her phone drew Jazz's gaze to the device on the coffee table. The paramedic at the scene had told her not to use electronics for twenty-four hours since she had a mild concussion. But talking on the phone should be fine, as long as she wasn't staring at the screen.

The caller ID *Pierce Cracklen* appeared on the screen.

She grabbed the phone as she set down her mug. "Hi, Uncle Pierce."

"Jazz, hello." His tone sounded pleased, like he was happy he'd reached her. "I wasn't sure when you were working today."

"Not until the late shift."

"Are you all right? You sound tired."

Was Uncle Pierce coming to know her that well? The possibility brought a smile back to her face. "Yes, I'm fine." Should she tell him what had happened? The unfamiliar urge startled her. She'd never wanted to tell her aunt and uncle anything about her life as an adult. But that was before Uncle Pierce had started to like her and care.

"Are you sure? It sounds like something is wrong. Are you sick?" Worry pinched his voice.

"No, no. I'm not sick." She couldn't have him calling a doctor or rushing over himself. "I have a mild concussion, that's all."

"A concussion? How did you get that?" His concern was almost palpable. And it went straight to her heart. Probably into the hole left by parents who'd never cared.

She told him about the bomb on the trail, how the explosion would've killed her if not for Flash.

"I'm coming to your apartment right now. You shouldn't be alone." The protective ferocity in his voice reminded her of Hawthorne.

Was this real? Did she really have two men in her life who cared about her now? One who was becoming the father she'd never had and the other...

But her uncle's words sank in, halting her delightful

thoughts. "I'm not at my apartment. I've been staying with a friend for the last couple days."

"Oh. Before what happened today?" His confusion came clearly across the line.

She should tell him. "Yeah. This wasn't the first attack, so I left my apartment to try to throw whoever's trying to kill me off the trail."

"Kill you?" A mixture of anger and shock raised his voice. "Jazz, why didn't you tell me? I could help keep you safe."

Wow. He really did care about her now. Things were looking up.

"Have you told the police?"

"Yes, they're involved. But no one's been able to figure out who's behind the attacks, beyond the thugs I caught."

"I had no idea, Jazz. I'll have my people investigate. And I'll contact the security firm I'm using during my campaign to have them give you protection."

The gesture warmed her from the inside out. So this was what it was like to have a real dad. Someone to protect her. To make her feel loved just by showing his concern. "Thanks, but I have good security already."

"You do? All right." He paused, like he was thinking. "I suppose you're trained for this kind of situation. But I...I can't lose you, too."

Jazz's throat tightened.

"Not after Joan. You remind me of her in some ways, you know."

Jazz tried to swallow as tears pooled in her eyes. No one had ever compared her to a family member. Not at all. As if she'd never really been related to any of them.

"You're strong and determined. And you love the fair so much." He paused. Was that a sniff? Was he crying, too?

She didn't try to stop the tears that fell down her cheeks.

"She would be as proud of you as I am."

Jazz's heart squeezed so hard she thought it might burst. He was proud of her? "Thank you." She pushed the words past the thickness in her throat. "That means a lot."

Uncle Pierce took in a breath that sounded a little shaky. "The reason I called was to ask you something. The girls are coming home tomorrow, and I wondered, would you sit with us at the funeral on Saturday?"

If Nev had been there, she would've said she needed to scrape Jazz's jaw off the floor. Jazz had never been more shocked in her life. He wanted her to be publicly recognized as a member of his immediate family? Alongside his two perfect daughters?

"Um…" She cleared her throat. "Sure?" The answer ended more like a question. Mostly because she still couldn't believe she'd heard him right.

"Wonderful. I'm so pleased." And he sounded pleased. As if he wore a smile as he spoke. "But I don't want to wait until Saturday to see you again. And I'm sure the girls will want to get reacquainted."

That, Jazz seriously doubted. His daughters made Cinderella's wicked stepdaughters look like sweethearts.

"Will you join us for brunch on Friday at the house?"

Jazz paused. Since Phoenix had her working late nights at the fair now, she should be able to make that. Maybe she could even bring Hawthorne along and introduce him to her family.

The idea sent a thrill through her that fueled her answer. "Yes, I'd love to."

"Excellent. But please call me anytime you even think you're in danger. I want to be there for you, Jazz. I mean that."

His words were like something from the dream of her aching heart. If it was a dream, she hoped it would never end.

"Hey, Emerson."

Hawthorne paused in his walk past the cattle barn and looked back.

Nevaeh Williams marched toward him with her K-9. The agent's expression didn't look friendly.

Hawthorne tried not to inhale too deeply as he waited the couple seconds it would take for her to reach him. The odor of manure and wood shavings wasn't his favorite.

Nevaeh stopped a few feet away and leveled a challenging stare at him.

He tensed automatically, though he had no idea what he could've done to her without knowing.

Her dog looked up at him with a panting grin that suggested he thought Hawthorne was less of a problem than Nevaeh seemed to at the moment.

"I thought you said you weren't 'in the market' for a relationship." She thrust her fingers into the air more like knives she wanted to stab him with than air quotes.

Oh, man. Not another interrogation about Jazz. He hadn't figured that one out to his own liking yet.

He swallowed, his throat suddenly dry. "I'm not."

"Then why, exactly, does my best friend think you're in love with her?"

"She—" The reply got stuck, as if his throat had decided to shut down completely. "She does?" The squeak that escaped the second time wasn't much better.

"Yes, she does. And she wouldn't if you hadn't led her on."

"Whoa." He lifted his hands, palm out. "I did not lead her on." The protest rang weak in his own ears. Could he honestly say he hadn't?

"So you mean you do love her?"

The question made sweat drip down his forehead. Or maybe that was thanks to the direct sunlight they were standing in. But the sun had nothing to do with the way his heart thumped hard against his ribs. As if it wanted to give an answer his brain knew was wrong. Wanted to say he did love Jazz Lamont.

"I..." He ran his tongue over his lips. "I never meant to convey that." Why didn't he just say *no*?

Then Nevaeh would stop giving him that weird look she'd switched to the moment he hadn't instantly answered. Slightly raised eyebrows and a tilted head. As if she was surprised by something she'd just realized.

Irritation sparked in his gut, and he wiped the sweat off his forehead with his hand. "I never meant to mislead anyone. Does she…" No, he would not ask if Jazz loved him. Not even to calm his pulse that took off at a sprint the moment he pondered the question. "I hope she doesn't really think I feel that way about her."

"Are you still leaving? Going to Idaho?"

"Yes."

"When?"

As soon as he possibly could. He bit back the desperate response. "When my commitment is fulfilled with the fair." Which meant he'd have to make it over another week yet. Maybe he could avoid working shifts with Jazz. Though all the shifts overlapped somewhat. Maybe he could ask for desk duty or something.

"Commitment." Nevaeh watched him like one might a bug under a microscope. "Have you ever been married?"

"No." He probably should've made an effort to keep the horror that rolled through him out of his voice.

Her eyebrows lifted farther. "Ever been in a long-term dating relationship?"

He narrowed his eyes, not keen on where she was going with her line of questioning. "Look, I appreciate that you're protective of your friend. It's great Jazz has someone like you. But that doesn't mean I need to share all the details of my personal life with you."

"That would be a *no*." The woman smirked as she crossed her arms over her red T-shirt. "Afraid of commitment?"

"More like I'm wise enough to know the dangers of it."

"Dangers?" Disbelief stretched her flattened lips wider.

"Being trapped in a lifelong commitment is one of the most dangerous things there is. You never know how the other person will control you or what they'll force you to do.

You completely lose control over your own life. You lose your freedom." He shut his mouth before he unloaded more. Her crack about him being afraid chafed at his pride, and he'd said too much. Been too annoyed.

He opened his mouth to apologize.

"Hey, guys." Jazz's raised voice jerked his attention past Nevaeh to see Jazz hurrying toward them at a quick clip, Flash straining at his leash as if he'd like to move faster.

More heat surged up his neck, headed for his face. Hopefully, Jazz wouldn't notice. Though he shouldn't have to feel guilty or embarrassed. What he'd said was correct. And he had every right to choose a single life of freedom over marriage. The Bible even condoned that.

"You're not going to believe this." Her breath came in uneven pants, which had to be more from excitement than her quick pace. He'd seen her level of fitness in action. "I just heard from Cora."

"About what?" Nevaeh watched Jazz with widened eyes.

"Freddie Blain. Though that isn't his real name."

"It isn't?" Nevaeh stepped closer to her friend.

"No." Jazz shook her head. "But that's not all." She pulled her phone from her jeans pocket and tapped the screen.

Hawthorne frowned. Should she be using the device yet? He'd thought her boss wasn't being cautious enough when Jazz had shown up and said Phoenix Gray cleared her to work. Jazz had said something about Phoenix recognizing Jazz had reasons she wanted to be there and that Phoenix liked her agents to be tough.

"When Cora got to the office after her narcotics gig, she got a look at the photo you sent earlier." Jazz threw a glance at Nev. "Then she sent me one of Sam Ackerman's dad, Gary Ackerman."

"Why?" Nevaeh asked the question on the tip of Hawthorne's tongue.

Jazz lifted her phone and extended it toward Hawthorne first, the screen facing him.

He stepped in closer to see the image, shading it from the sunlight with his hand.

It couldn't be.

Gary Ackerman was Freddie Blain.

THIRTY-FIVE

Jazz lingered in bed after her alarm had gone off. She felt for her phone on the nightstand and lit up the screen, checking the news as she always did briefly before starting the day.

The national news was as depressing as always, so she swiped past that to reach local coverage.

A picture of Gary Ackerman, alias Freddie Blain, featured at the top of the headline article. No surprise his arrest had made the news, given how much the press had been following the events at the fair. Hadn't been pretty seeing the police surprise Freddie at his food stand and cuff him.

The look on his face had kept her up for a while last night. Shock. Hurt.

Jazz had almost felt guilty, given her part in the whole thing. The PK-9 Agency was responsible for his arrest, since Cora had been the one to tell the police his true identity, prompting the arrest for sabotage and the murder of Aunt Joan.

But right after his initial shock, Freddie—Gary—had become angry instead, shouting that the police were letting the guilty get away with murder. Poor man had been seriously messed up by the death of his son. It was like his life ended when his son's had.

Jazz had spotted Hawthorne talking to Gary briefly before

the police put him in a squad car. But she hadn't heard what they'd said. And she hadn't been able to catch Hawthorne after that, thanks to the detectives questioning them about Gary, too.

"You awake?" Nev appeared in the doorway, her curls freed of her satin cap but the rest of her still clothed in the tank top and cotton shorts she wore as pj's. She carried two mugs of something steaming in her hands.

"Coffee?" Jazz slipped out of bed and hurried around it, her hands stretched toward Nev. "Knew I kept you around for a reason."

Nev swung the mug away from Jazz's grasping fingers. "What's the magic word?"

"Um, please?" Jazz pasted on an exaggerated smile.

"And 'thank you,' but that will do, I guess." She put the mug in Jazz's grip with a grin.

"You've been spending *way* too much time with your nieces and nephews." Jazz took a sip of the hot coffee, not minding the little burn as it slipped down her throat.

"I let all the dogs out, and they're back in, chowing down breakfast."

Jazz gave Nev a grateful smile. "I figured, since Flash didn't wake me before my alarm for once. Thanks."

"Did you see the news?" Nev's mouth formed a straighter line as she looked at Jazz.

"Yeah. It's hard to swallow. He seemed like such a nice guy."

"Been there."

Jazz tensed, hoping Nev wouldn't wander too far into her frightening memories.

But Nev's expression was calm. Didn't look like she was going to have a PTSD episode. Even though Jazz knew she must be thinking of her own attacker who'd also played nice before revealing himself to be a monster.

Nev drank from her mug, then lowered it. "Cora texted. Phoenix got to watch the detectives question Ackerman last night."

Jazz walked to the end of the bed and sat down. "Did he admit anything?"

"No." Nev went to sit beside Jazz. "Cora said he kept insisting he only used the false name so he could investigate his son's death and find the person he thinks killed him. He apparently didn't break any laws by using the name Freddie Blain. He really is Jim Morris's cousin, so he didn't put his fake ID on tax documents or anything like that. Cora didn't think the police would be able to hold him beyond seventy-two hours."

"Did he offer any names? Who he thinks killed Sam?"

"I guess he mentioned Best Life, the cult, but I don't really know what he said about that."

"It's really sad."

Nev angled toward Jazz. "You sound like you don't think he's guilty of the sabotage. And Aunt Joan."

"I don't know. He could be." Jazz ran her finger along the mug in her hands. "Aunt Joan said he was super angry after Sam's death and blamed the fair." Jazz blew out a breath. "Maybe he could've blamed Aunt Joan personally since she was General Manager at the time."

Nev nodded. "He could've killed her on purpose because he thinks she let his son die."

"Hard to imagine. But at least if he did it, the danger would be over now."

"What does Hawthorne think about Gary as the culprit?"

Jazz shortened her sip of coffee and swallowed before answering. "I don't know. I didn't have a chance to talk to him after the arrest." She grabbed her phone off the bedspread. "I'll text him. He gets up early, too." She smiled as her pulse pumped a little faster. "You know, we really have a lot in common."

"I talked to him yesterday."

Jazz glanced at Nev. "You mean after Freddie—I mean, Gary—was arrested?"

"No, earlier. About you."

Jazz's stomach clenched. Though she shouldn't be

surprised. Nev was protective in the extreme. And, for some reason, she'd decided Hawthorne wasn't right for Jazz. So of course, she'd go poking her nose where it didn't belong.

Nev folded her leg onto the bed to face Jazz more fully. "Do you love him?"

Good thing Jazz hadn't been drinking her coffee at that moment. She might've spit it out. But the answer came quickly, shooting from her heart to her mouth. "Yes." The realization of what she'd already, secretly, known to be true filled her with warmth from her belly to her chest and outward to all her extremities. She didn't have to look into a mirror to know her smile was beaming. "Yes, I do love him."

Nev looked away. "That's what I was afraid of."

The happiness spreading through Jazz halted as if it hit a hard wall. "I don't understand why you don't like him."

"It's not that I don't like him."

"Then why can't you be happy for me? I was happy for you with Branson."

"It isn't the same."

Jazz pushed off the bed and stalked a few steps away. "Yes, it is."

"Jazz, Hawthorne isn't right for you. He doesn't want to commit to one person, let alone one location."

Jazz jerked toward Nev, irritation sparking. "Did he tell you that?"

"He told me he's never had a long-term relationship and that he doesn't want to get married."

Jazz crossed her arms and turned away. "Tons of men say that until they fall in love with the right woman." She heard Nev approach her from behind.

Nev put her hand on Jazz's bicep. "But he doesn't even believe in marriage. At least not for him. He says a lifelong commitment is one of the most dangerous things. He called it being trapped."

The words stung, even though Jazz refused to believe they were true. Nev was probably taking them out of context to make Hawthorne sound worse. She spun to face Nev. "Why were you even asking him about all that?"

Nev's thick eyebrows lowered as her voice raised. "Because I'm worried about you. We watch out for each other. Always."

"It doesn't look like you're watching out for me." She glared down at Nev. "It sounds like you're trying to ruin the one good thing that's happened to me."

"But it's not what you think." Nev lifted her hands out from her sides in a frustrated motion. "Did you know he's a Christian? Even if he suddenly decided he wanted to get married, he wouldn't marry you because you're not a believer."

"Oh, great. I wondered when it would turn into that. An 'us' and 'them,' and I'm not in the 'us' anymore, right?" The truth of her own accusation pierced Jazz's heart.

Nev shook her head, the anger in her eyes softening. "It's not like that. I just mean he wouldn't want to marry someone he doesn't agree with on the most important things, and you shouldn't want that either."

"Don't tell me what I should and shouldn't want, Nevaeh." Jazz brushed past her to the bed. She crouched beside it and pulled her suitcase out from underneath, flopping it onto the bedspread.

"What are you doing?" Surprise laced Nev's voice, but Jazz didn't look at her as she stalked to the dresser along the wall.

"What does it look like? I'm going back to my apartment. Where I should've gone a long time ago."

"Jazz, don't do that. The danger to you might not be over yet."

"Sure it is. Haven't you heard? They arrested Gary. He was probably trying to kill me because he thought I knew he knocked off Aunt Joan and sabotaged the fair."

"You don't know that. And you don't sound like you believe it."

Jazz shot a glare in Nev's direction. "I do know that it

doesn't matter. We're not on the same side anymore. So it's past time for me to go back to my own place."

"I can't believe you're doing all this because of a guy." Nev's voice tightened, stretched with emotion. "You don't get it. He is *leaving*." She emphasized the last word as if Jazz were an idiot. "He told me himself he's going to Idaho as soon as the fair is done."

Jazz gritted her teeth as she threw her clothes into the suitcase.

"He just said that yesterday, Jazz. Knowing you hasn't changed him at all. It hasn't changed that he's leaving you."

...leaving you. A prick of pain stabbed Jazz's heart as Nev's last two words echoed in her ears. She kept packing. Held her voice level as if she wasn't fazed at all. "I know he's leaving when the fair ends. I told you that before. If he still wants to go when it's over, I'll go with him."

"Jazz." The pain in the one word nearly drew Jazz's gaze to Nevaeh. "You wouldn't. We've always dreamed of living in the same town. Being together all the time."

Jazz closed her eyes, pressing her fists into the stack of T-shirts she placed in the open suitcase. That had been their lifelong dream. A dream put on hold only because of her dad's plans for Jazz's life, the military service she was supposed to do, then his unexpected illness that led her into a different kind of service for him.

When he'd passed and Jazz came to the Twin Cities, even getting to reunite with Flash thanks to the job at Phoenix K-9, she and Nev had finally been able to start living their dream. And it had been a wonderful dream. Until she woke up.

"You wouldn't really leave me, would you?" Nev's question, her pained whisper, surged tears to Jazz's eyes.

Jazz turned toward her friend, the person who'd been the most like family she'd ever had until now. "You already left me, Nev." A tear escaped and coursed down her cheek, the wet drop clinging to her chin. "For Branson."

Nev opened her mouth, her eyes glinting like she was going to protest, switch back to fight mode.

Jazz lifted a hand and spoke to stop her. "No, Nev. I am happy for you, but it's changed everything." She bit her lip to hide its quiver as Nev met her gaze, dark eyes melting into softness as moisture filled them, too. "I only want to find someone like you did. Someone to love me. And I think I have found him. Can't you please just be happy for me?"

Barks from the front of the house made her start. Flash and Alvarez.

"Hey, boys." Branson's deep voice carried easily to the bedroom, and there wasn't another peep from the dogs who both loved the man. He must be returning from his early morning workout. "Nevaeh? You here?"

Jazz watched her friend, hoping she'd say something. Say she supported Jazz with Hawthorne. That she understood and wanted Jazz to be happy. That she loved Jazz just as much whether she was a Christian or not. And that she'd always love Jazz and support her no matter what decisions she made and who she chose to spend her life with.

But Nevaeh didn't say any of those things. She pressed her lips together, swiped away the moisture on her cheeks, and walked out.

Jazz stared at the empty doorway, barely hearing the sounds of the happy couple greeting each other as she reeled from the rejection. Her best friend. Her sister by choice. And she'd sent a message without words that she was done with Jazz.

Swaying, Jazz turned in time to sink to the bed next to her suitcase. Her chest stung, right where Nev had torn out a chunk of her heart.

Flash rushed in, his tail wagging as he jogged around the bed to Jazz and rubbed his wet chin on her lap.

"Just you and me again." But as she spoke and gently rubbed Flash's ears, hope slowly returned. She had Uncle Pierce and Hawthorne. Two men who had shown they cared about her. One her real family and the other the man who'd hopefully want to become her family someday.

She smiled as the ache in her chest dulled. Getting to her feet, she went to the dresser to grab the rest of her things. "Come on, Flash. We need to get ready for the adventure of a lifetime."

———

The screen of Hawthorne's smartphone lit, catching his eye.

He grabbed it off the desk beside his keyboard, eager for some excuse to stop trying to eke out words for his Jazz Lamont book. No flying fingers on the keyboard this morning. Probably thanks to his conversation with Nevaeh last night about the woman who'd inspired his heroine.

Rebekah's name flashed on the screen, and he slid his finger across the glass to answer. "Rebekah, hi."

"How could they arrest Sam's dad?" Her tight voice cut across the line.

Oh, boy. She must've seen it on the news. Should he have told her first? It'd been too late last night to call or text.

"That won't help anything. It won't help us find Sam's killer." Desperation pitched her tone higher than normal.

He tried to think of something calming to say. "It's not as bad as you think. They won't be able to hold him unless they have some evidence he did the sabotage. They were acting on the discovery of his fake identity, probably hoping it would lead to a confession or more evidence. But they'll have to release him if neither of those happen."

"He's not going to confess." Indignation strengthened her voice. "He didn't do anything. He would never have killed that woman, the manager. And he wouldn't have put other people in danger."

"I appreciate you want to think well of him, Rebekah. But how do you know that for sure?" Hawthorne had to keep an open, objective mind. Even though his gut was telling him Rebekah was right.

"I just know. He's Sam's dad. They're good people."

Hawthorne didn't respond to that emotionally based judgment. But the panic was starting to infuse her tone again. He had to try to tamp that down if he could. "I talked to Gary last night, and he swore he was only there to investigate Sam's death and find the killer."

"See? That's exactly what I'm saying."

Hawthorne tapped a key on the keyboard with too little pressure to depress it. "He also told me his theory that someone killed Sam and hid the body until after closing, then moved the body to the Logboat Adventure ride." Which exactly echoed the theory Hawthorne had been favoring, as well.

"Yeah. That must've been the way it went down. Can't you prove it somehow?"

"I'm going to try." Examining the smoking area where Sam had last been seen would hopefully reveal something new. Or something helpful, at least.

"But, Rebekah, we do have to consider Gary could be lying about his innocence. He has a strong motive because he blames the fair and Patch for Sam's death. Sabotaging the fair and blaming it on Patch would be the perfect revenge."

"No. I don't believe that."

Hawthorne could almost hear her head shaking in denial on the other end of the line.

"I hate that he's in jail. If we can find the person who murdered Sam, we could get Gary out of there right away." A slam, perhaps from a car door closing, sounded in the background. "Maybe I can help. Maybe if I go to the fair, I'll see something that only somebody close to Sam would notice."

"There's no need for you to do that." And much safer if she didn't, given how dangerous the fair was. Especially when someone was targeting Hawthorne and Jazz because they were investigating Sam's death. The last thing he needed was for a killer to go after Rebekah, too. "I have it covered. What I learned from Zeke changes everything. Now I know where Sam was last seen, and I'm confident that will lead me to what really happened. And who was involved." He might be overrepresenting his confidence level a tad. But he had to try to keep Rebekah from accidentally putting herself in danger.

"If you say so." She sounded somewhat appeased, but not convinced.

The temptation to tell her about the risks and more strongly caution her not to go to the fair pressed against his closed lips. But he had no right to limit her freedom.

She'd left her family behind to secure that freedom, as he had. To rob her of that would be to strip her of the most valuable possession she had.

No, he wouldn't try to control or limit her choices. He'd simply have to find Sam's killer before his sister tried to take matters into her own hands.

THIRTY-SIX

"Hey, Cora." Jazz's greeting came out softer and weaker than she'd intended. Probably thanks to the tightness of her throat and dryness of her mouth.

She'd turned over her decision in her mind a hundred times on the drive to PK-9 headquarters. But she knew it was the right one. She had to be ready to leave with Hawthorne. He was her future. She'd never belonged at Phoenix K-9 anyway. No matter how hard she'd tried.

The self-reminders rapid-fired through her brain as she forced her legs to carry her to Cora's desk just inside the front entrance.

Jana came out from behind the desk to greet Jazz, her swishing tail and friendliness only making what Jazz had to do harder.

Cora smiled up at Jazz, no hint of suspicion in her innocent blue eyes. But there was a trace of a question. Had she asked Jazz something?

"Sorry." The heat of a blush surged into Jazz's cheeks as she straightened from petting Jana. "Did you ask me something? I was...distracted."

Cora kept her sweet smile. "I only said hello to you and Flash." She looked down at Flash, standing on leash next to

Jazz. Then she lifted her gaze, and fine lines crossed her forehead. "Is something wrong, Jazz?"

Cora always was perceptive about people.

Though Jazz wasn't exactly doing a brilliant job hiding her tension either. "Not really." She tried to force a casual tone, but her own ears told her she'd failed. She took a breath. Better just rip off the bandage. "I need to put in my two weeks' notice."

Cora blinked. Then her eyes widened as she watched Jazz for agonizing seconds. "Do you mean notice of resignation?"

Something like guilt clogged Jazz's throat. She shouldn't have to feel guilty. People left jobs all the time. "Yes." She swallowed. "You need two weeks, right?"

Cora tapped something on the keyboard of her open notebook computer that sat to her left. "I believe so. It's never been a question before."

Meaning Jazz was the first employee to ever leave PK-9. Great. Just went to show how much of a misfit she was. The only one who wasn't accepted there, who'd never managed to be well-liked enough to be happy.

Cora's eyebrows pinched together as she examined something on the screen. "Yes. Two weeks' notice is required." She brought her gaze back to Jazz. "Are you sure you want to leave?"

Jazz nodded, tightening her muscles against the sadness in Cora's voice. "Yes."

"I'm so sorry, Jazz." Cora's words socked Jazz right in the growing balloon of guilt in her belly. Cora didn't have anything to apologize for. She'd been the most welcoming person at PK-9. If they'd all been as loving and accepting as her, Jazz probably would've been able to belong there.

"I thought there might be something troubling you. I should have tried to help." Regret shaped Cora's features. "Can I help you in some way now?"

This was harder than Jazz had thought it would be. She hadn't meant to make Cora feel bad. But the problem wasn't something Cora could fix. It wasn't really something anyone could fix. Jazz just didn't belong at PK-9. And didn't even belong with her best friend anymore, apparently.

The memory of Nev turning away from her and leaving without another word fueled Jazz's resolve. She finally had a better option than staying where she wasn't wanted or wandering through life alone. She had Hawthorne and an uncle who loved her. She could travel with Hawthorne and keep in touch with Uncle Pierce, visiting him whenever she could. Especially at holidays and birthdays, like normal families did.

Yes, this was definitely the right decision. "You're so sweet, Cora. Thank you. But I don't need help. I'm okay." Jazz managed a smile. "This is the best decision for me right now. I plan to travel soon and try other things."

"Oh." Sadness still sloped Cora's mouth. "Well, I hope that goes well for you." She looked at the computer screen again.

Probably the moment Jazz should make her escape. She didn't want to risk caving under misplaced feelings of guilt and Cora's kindness. "Thanks for taking care of it for me. I'd better get going." She started to turn toward the doors.

"Jazz, wait."

Jazz tensed and rotated back.

"I'm sorry. I wanted to double check to be sure. But in order to officially submit your two weeks' notice, you'll need to talk to Phoenix."

"What?" Jazz's stomach twisted.

"Yes, I'm afraid it's in the contract you signed."

"You're kidding." Jazz stalked around the desk, Flash following her sudden movement.

Cora leaned back in her chair so Jazz could see the contract she'd pulled up on the computer screen.

There it was in black and white. Any employee wishing to terminate employment needed to meet in person with Phoenix Gray before notice of resignation could be submitted. Jazz narrowed her eyes. Wasn't that just like Phoenix to have one last trick up her sleeve. A secret hidden away to trap Jazz at the end.

Though a vague recollection started to surface in Jazz's mind. That she might've noticed the clause but hadn't cared when she signed. From Nev's description of the work environment and her great love for all the agents at PK-9, Jazz had thought she'd stay forever.

She dropped her gaze to Flash, who was enjoying petting from Cora. As Jazz looked at the screen, instinctively checking to make sure the requirement was still listed there, her gaze caught on a notecard on top of a thick stack next to the computer.

Beautiful calligraphy filled the card. *But now thus says the Lord, He who created you, O Jacob, He who formed you, O Israel: "Fear not, for I have redeemed you; I have called you by name, you are mine." – Isaiah 43:1*

"Is that from the Bible?" Jazz stared at the words.

Cora took a second to answer, probably looking to see what Jazz was talking about. "Oh, yes. Those are my Scripture memory cards."

Jazz turned her attention to Cora. "You're memorizing that?"

"Yes." Cora smiled. "All the verses in the stack."

"Why?"

"Because I want to have God's Word hidden in my heart, so that I know what is true and what is not. So that I have His comfort and promises with me wherever I go. I never want to forget that He loves me or forget the proof that He loves me."

The proof that He loves me. It sounded like the way a woman talked about the man she loved. Cora was married, and her husband, Kent, clearly adored her. But she still wanted to believe that a distant, probably made-up being loved her? Seemed weird when she had the real, sure love of a man she could see and touch.

"Here's another favorite of mine." She pulled the next card out of the pile and read from it. "For God so loved the world, that he gave his only Son, that whoever believes in him should not perish but have eternal life."

"Is that talking about Jesus?"

"Yes, it is." Cora set the card on the desk and angled her blue eyes up at Jazz. "Jesus Christ, the Son of God, who died on the cross to pay the penalty for the sins of His children and give them everlasting life with Him."

"Is that what Christians believe?" Jazz hadn't heard it put quite like that before. Never really heard an explanation at all.

Cora nodded. "It's why we follow Christ. Because He redeemed us, and we belong to Him."

That must be what Hawthorne believed, too. Would that keep him from wanting to be with Jazz, like Nev had said? Only one way to find out. Cora would never give a misleading answer for personal reasons.

"Is it true Christians aren't supposed to marry someone who doesn't believe the same as they do?"

Cora pressed her lips together in a thoughtful expression. "If you mean that the other person is not a Christian then, yes, that is true. God directs us in His Word that we should not be unequally yoked, not bound to an unbeliever."

Then Nev hadn't made that up to get Jazz to stop liking Hawthorne. Jazz started around the desk.

"Jazz?" Cora's voice stopped her again. "Phoenix doesn't believe Gary Ackerman had anything to do with the attacks on you."

For once, Jazz agreed with Phoenix on something.

"We're still trying to find a possible motive or likely suspect. Do you know much about your father's military service in Iraq?"

Jazz shrugged. "He won some medals, so I guess he did all right. Didn't you say his record was impeccable?"

"Yes, it seems to be." Cora folded her arms over each other on the desk. "However, there is one incident Phoenix wanted me to look into more deeply. I feel I should warn you that what I find could be...difficult."

Jazz stepped closer to the desk from the front side as her stomach clenched. "What do you mean? What is it?"

Cora straightened. "I don't want to give details until I'm sure of the facts. Speculation is never a good idea. Phoenix likely wouldn't want me to say anything yet. I'm waiting to hear from her Army contact, who I hope will give me the details I need to know the truth."

Great. More of Phoenix's ideas and orders. "Fine. Maybe I'll be gone by then anyway."

"I did find some concrete information that I wonder if you'd like to know." The hesitation in Cora's tone added a twist to Jazz's stomach. "It concerns your mother."

Jazz stopped breathing. Had Cora found her?

"I know this is an understandably painful area for you. I will keep what I learned private and not share it with you unless you want to hear it. But you may want to know this."

Jazz forced herself to breathe. She could handle it, couldn't she? She had a man who liked her, maybe loved her. And she had a supportive uncle who seemed ready to be a better father to her than her real dad had been. They could help her through meeting her mother or learning she was a homeless drug addict. Whatever it was. "Go ahead. Tell me what you found."

Sympathy pooled as unshed tears in Cora's eyes. The first sign Jazz should've said no. "I'm sorry, Jazz. Your mother passed away ten years ago."

THIRTY-SEVEN

Maybe Jazz shouldn't have gone ahead with these interviews of Best Life cult members. Her mind was only somewhat present for most of them, her attention occupied by the news Cora had given her.

Her mother had been dead for ten years. Which meant that for twenty years of Jazz's life, her mother still hadn't wanted her. Hadn't even wanted to meet her.

The old, deep wound of the rejection she'd received at birth seared as if it'd been sliced open again.

But dwelling on it wouldn't help. That had never helped. Forgetting was the only thing that helped. And doing all she could to make sure she never felt that kind of rejection again.

Like finding Sam's real killer for Hawthorne so he'd see how useful Jazz could be for his work and his life. And proving her worth to Uncle Pierce by finding the person who had killed Aunt Joan and was trying to destroy her beloved fair.

She tuned in to the woman who sat in front of her across a table in a small, brightly lit room decorated like a classroom for children.

The woman, her dark hair pulled back in the braided up-do all the women wore at the cult, smiled as she wrapped up one of the scripted answers the other two members before her had also given Jazz. At least this one delivered it with more gusto.

"One more question, if you don't mind." Jazz forced a smile. "Do you feel safe here at Best Life? Or have you ever felt the community is too punitive or frightening in any way?"

The woman looked up at an angle for a moment.

Jazz's attention sharpened. The others had spewed out a response she'd assumed was rehearsed. But she'd still asked, since it seemed like the best way to get at whether or not Patch and others at the cult were more sinister than they liked to pretend. Jazz's money was still on Patch or another cult member for Sam's death and the fair sabotage. Every time she returned to the commune, she became more aware of the eerie feel of it. Like menacing, sinister danger was lurking just out of sight.

"I would say no, but I remember there was one time that I felt that way."

Jazz tried to keep her features from showing her surprise. Was the woman going to admit something bad about the cult?

"For a little while, a man stood outside our commune nearly every day, and he would follow us when we went out."

Okay. That wasn't the kind of confession Jazz had hoped for. But she should see where this trail led. At least she was getting an unscripted answer. Maybe she could leverage that for more off-script intel. "He followed you, specifically?"

"No, not only me. Any of our members who left the building. He didn't seem to care if they were male or female, young or old. He even followed Desmond and his wife." She lightly touched her fingers to her chin. "Although, I don't think she was his wife then." She smiled. "They were courting at the time."

"When was that?"

"Let's see." The woman folded her hands together on the table. "It would have been about two years ago." A frown reshaped her lips. "I remember because my daughter used him as a reason to leave Best Life when she turned eighteen and graduated that year. Though the man stopped soon after she left."

"Stopped?"

"Yes. He wasn't there one day, and I don't think anyone has seen him since."

"Did Desmond get a restraining order or file any charges against him?"

"No. Some members approached him about that, but he said the man hadn't broken any laws since he waited on the city-owned sidewalk and never harmed anyone he followed." The woman smiled again. "I think Desmond didn't want to do anything because of who the man was. Desmond is like that. Always very kind and tolerant."

Because of who he was? Jazz locked on to the hint of something significant. "Who was the man?"

"Oh, didn't I say?" The talkative cult member blinked innocently at Jazz. "He was the ex-husband of Desmond's new wife."

Possibilities sparked in Jazz's mind as she absorbed the information. An angry ex-husband intimidating Patch and the cult. That signaled motivation for sabotaging the fair and blaming it on Patch.

And it had happened two years ago, timed with Sam's death.

But how did the two connect? Maybe they didn't connect at all. She didn't know, but her gut told her she was getting close to the person behind Aunt Joan's death and the sabotage. Maybe even the person who was trying to kill her, though she didn't know how that could be related to an angry ex-husband.

She needed the mind behind Carson Steele's brilliant crime-solving skills. She needed to talk to Hawthorne.

Hawthorne made his way through the crowds to Molly's food stand where Jazz had texted she would meet him before her shift started. His stomach recoiled at the smell of the deep-fried foods Molly specialized in.

"Hey, sugar!" Molly waved from inside the stand.

Hawthorne forced a smile and kept his distance. Not exactly in the best form to talk to the perky woman right now. Not with his insides knotting themselves.

He'd have to clarify things with Jazz. Nevaeh had made it clear Jazz had the wrong impression. Apparently thought he loved her. He hadn't thought he'd shown that much emotion.

But if Nevaeh was right, then he had to straighten everything out before this went any farther and Jazz got seriously hurt.

"Hawthorne." Jazz's warm voice behind him made his pulse jump.

Only because she'd startled him. Or because he was nervous about talking to her. Couldn't be anything else.

An undeniably gorgeous smile spread her mouth wide, and her emerald eyes lit with a twinkle that threatened to undo his resolve to set her straight the moment he saw her.

Maybe it could wait. He swallowed. "Your text said you had something to tell me?"

"Yes." She stepped closer and touched his elbow as she angled away and pointed toward the tables under the canopy. "Let's go over there."

"Lead the way." He paused to let her go first, which also got her to pull away from him as she headed for the seating area with Flash.

She paused to wait for him by a table, and he picked a side and sat down.

But instead of sitting on the opposite side of the table as she usually did, she joined him on the same bench. Not inappropriately close, but close enough to make him feel boxed in. And drawn to her at the same time.

An image of what it would be like if they were a couple

popped into his mind—him scooting closer, putting his arm around her shoulders.

Absurd. He was only going to send her the wrong message again if he didn't regain his focus. He was apparently caught up in some sort of infatuation.

And why not? She was an amazing woman. One of a kind. But he knew these desires and feelings wouldn't last. And he knew that when he was thinking clearly, his strongest desires were for freedom to live as he chose and work for the Lord independent of attachments to others who would try to control him or lead him astray.

Jazz shifted to face him as much as the bench would allow. "When I interviewed the Best Life members today, one of them told me something very interesting."

"Oh?" He had a hard time mustering even basic curiosity while fighting the internal battle for control.

"She told me that two years ago, a man started waiting outside Best Life for anyone who came out. He'd follow members, including Patch and his wife. Though she maybe wasn't his wife yet then. I got confused on the timeline there."

"He's had three wives, so it is confusing."

"Really?" Jazz's eyes widened as her mouth shaped into a smirk. "Somehow that doesn't surprise me."

He wanted to smile with her. To enjoy her sense of humor that had clicked with his from the first time they'd met. But maybe that would send the wrong signal, too.

She seemed too excited to notice his lack of response as she jumped back into her story. "Anyway, it turns out this stalker guy was the ex-husband of Patch's new wife."

"Her ex-husband?" That *was* interesting.

"Yep. Talk about passive aggressive, right?"

"Or aggressive, aggressive." Hawthorne didn't know anything about Patch's current wife. Maybe he could try to find her previous husband.

"I had thought Patch might be behind the sabotage, but now I'm thinking this ex-husband could be our man. He has a strong motive to incriminate the cult if his wife left him for Patch."

"You're right. And he could've chosen the fair as his means to do it because it's the only place Patch publicly denounced in the press."

Jazz nodded. "Exactly. We should look for the ex-husband. How do you think we can find out who he is?"

"I'd start with the record of Patch's most recent marriage and get the wife's former surname from there. Then..." Hawthorne suddenly realized what he was doing—partnering with her again. Helping her with her quest to find the culprit behind the fair. He'd said he would, but he had technically fulfilled that obligation already with the other things he'd done for her. Anything more now could be confirmation in her eyes that he...loved her.

He smothered his natural desire to track down the truth and the bad guy. "Isn't that something your agency can find out for you?"

The happiness in her eyes went out as fast as a candle doused with water. "I'm not with them anymore."

"What do you mean?"

"I mean, I don't work there anymore." She pushed her shoulders back and glanced away, but she didn't appear to be actually watching the passing visitors. "Well, I put in my two weeks' notice."

"Oh." That was a surprise. He hadn't realized she was unhappy at the agency. Or maybe she was planning to move or do other work? The questions he wanted to ask hopped to the tip of his tongue. But he bit them back. Showing too much interest could be misinterpreted.

"It's for the best." She smiled again, but it didn't quite reach her eyes. "And you know how we can track down the ex-husband anyway. We'll find him...together."

The way she said the last word made his muscles clench. And made him think Nevaeh had been exactly right about Jazz misunderstanding his intentions.

He needed to put a stop to this right now. "It's a great

discovery." He forced himself to meet her gaze, though his gut clenched at what he might see there next. "But I really need to focus on solving Sam's murder, so I can fulfill my promise to my sister and get out of here next week." There. He couldn't have been plainer and clearer that he was leaving, so of course she would know he didn't intend to date her or anything close to that.

But the disappointment he'd braced to see on her face didn't show.

Her closed lips shaped into a small smile. Almost a satisfied smile. Did she want him to go?

"I knew you'd have to leave, and I completely understand that." She reached over and covered his hand, resting on the table, with hers. "You're a brilliant writer. You need to travel wherever the ideas take you and do your research like you've always done it. I won't make you choose or pressure you to stay." Her smile beamed full and wide. "That's why I quit the agency. So whenever you need to leave, I'll be ready to go with you."

Go with him? His throat started to close, and her hand felt like the warning alarm for the walls closing in around him from all sides. The walls of a cage.

"You can't." The protest popped out louder than he intended as he yanked his hand away and pulled his legs free to stand behind the bench.

She blinked up at him. "But I can. I'll just finish up my two weeks. If you need to leave before then, I'll follow you right after I'm done."

"No, you don't get it." He tried to tamp down the panicked edge to his voice. "I don't want you."

A visible wince pinched her features.

That had come out harsher than he'd meant. He tried for a calmer tone, but still firm enough that she'd know he was sincere. "I'm sorry if you got the wrong idea about my interest in you. I never meant to mislead you."

She stared at him without moving, as if she was in shock.

"I tried to be clear that I wanted to get to know you only

for the purpose of basing my heroine on you. I never meant to imply anything else. And I was always clear I was leaving."

With every word he said, more pain clouded her beautiful eyes.

Guilt pressed hard against his ribs. But it wasn't his fault. "I told you marriage and a family wouldn't fit with my lifestyle."

"But I wouldn't stop you from traveling and moving whenever you want." Her eyebrows scrunched together, her voice taking on a strangled, pleading quality. "We'd do it together."

She would stop him. Stop him from having the freedom to live his life on his terms, without anyone controlling him or owning him.

"I have to do what's best for my life, and you'll see someday that this wouldn't be best for you either."

Moisture shimmered in her eyes.

"I'm sorry." He whirled away and stalked out from under the canopy, into the hot sunlight. If only it would burn away the memory of wreaking pain and devastation on the most amazing woman he'd ever met.

THIRTY-EIGHT

Jazz stared out the windshield of her SUV parked in the dark lot of some diner. She was living out the dramatic heartbreak scene in a rom com. But knowing that didn't stop Jazz's heart from feeling like it was breaking into a million tiny shards that cut her inside as they fell.

Flash whined from the back seat, either worried about Jazz or wondering why they were sitting there instead of going home after their patrol shift at the fair.

Home. Like she really had one.

She looked at the dashboard clock. *12:45 a.m.*

There was no way she'd go back to Nevaeh's. They were pretty much finished. That much was clear.

And Jazz didn't feel up to going to her apartment where thugs or other such surprises could be waiting for her. Awfully suspicious how Phoenix and the agency had been able to help everyone else when they were in danger, but when it was Jazz—nothing. The attempts on her life just kept coming and Cora and Phoenix—the whole team—didn't do a thing to stop them.

Whatever. She would move on from them, too. Enough of trying to please people who didn't want her.

"You don't get it. I don't want you." Hawthorne's words cut deeper every time they echoed in her memory.

Tears tumbled down her cheeks, and she blotted them with a tissue, soaked from all those that had come before.

Why did everyone reject her?

No. Not everyone. Uncle Pierce cared about her. He'd made that clear. He wanted to protect her and support her like his own daughters. And Aunt Joan had even wanted to get closer to Jazz before she was killed.

Aunt Joan. The sabotage.

Jazz reached for her phone she'd left in the cupholder. She'd completely forgotten to try to find the ex-husband of Patch's wife.

If he turned out to be the culprit behind the sabotage and Aunt Joan's death, it would bring such comfort to Uncle Pierce. He'd have closure, knowing her killer was caught and justice was served. And that Jazz was protecting Aunt Joan's legacy by eliminating the threat to the fair.

He would probably love Jazz even more if she could do that for him and Aunt Joan.

Her gut told her Gary wasn't their man. Maybe she just didn't want to believe it. But it made more sense that he was simply trying to find his son's murderer.

And Patch's stalker—the jealous ex of his wife—sounded much more like the type of guy to exact that kind of revenge. Violent, targeted, vindictive revenge.

If Jazz could find out who he was and somehow get the evidence to prove he was the culprit, then she could give Uncle Pierce the news, and they could put all this behind them. Start getting to know each other without the grief and danger.

Her biological family was her only real chance at being loved and accepted. She'd forgotten that when her family rejected her for so long. She got desperate for substitutes. Nevaeh, PK-9, and now Hawthorne.

But she didn't need any of them. She had real family that cared for her and loved her now. Uncle Pierce.

She would stay and build a life with him. Be his comfort when his daughters left him after the funeral to return to their own lives while he had to find his way without Aunt Joan.

Jazz would be his shoulder to cry on and help him through. She'd support his campaign for governor and maybe take over his security to be sure he was protected.

The plans for her new family of two were like a salve that covered and soothed the wounds in her heart that Hawthorne had inflicted. That this whole day had inflicted, starting with Neveah.

But there was happiness in store for Jazz yet, with Uncle Pierce.

First, she needed to find out if the police had the right guy behind bars. Or if Patch or his crazy stalker were the real culprits.

She lifted her phone and woke the screen. A notification appeared. A voicemail message from Cora.

Jazz's finger paused over the notification. She was quitting the agency, leaving them behind. She didn't need to march to the beat of Phoenix's orders anymore. She'd check the message after she finished the more important task of finding her aunt's killer.

Jazz swiped the notification off the screen. Then she navigated to a court records search website and typed in *Desmond Patch*.

Hawthorne turned his head against the pillow to see the alarm clock on the nightstand.

12:55 a.m.

Five minutes later than the last time he'd checked. Maybe he should get out of bed since he apparently wasn't going to be able to sleep.

The pain in Jazz's eyes and the echo of his own, unnecessarily hurtful words wouldn't leave him alone. Neither would the guilt contorting his belly.

He'd only been trying to tell her the truth he had failed to make clear before—that he wasn't looking for a relationship. And he did need to stay focused on fulfilling his promise to Rebekah and then leaving as planned.

He wasn't good husband material anyway. That much was clear from the way he'd handled communicating—or not communicating—with Jazz this whole time. And especially today. Or yesterday, technically, given the time on the clock.

She probably realized now, after he'd told her he didn't want her, that she shouldn't want him. She was likely moving on already, realizing he was an insensitive jerk who wasn't worthy of her.

And that was for the best.

The painful twist in his chest didn't match what was supposed to be a positive train of thought. It was good Jazz would get over him now. He couldn't have become attached to her anyway—even if he'd gone crazy and wanted to do so against his better judgment—because she wasn't a Christian.

Why did that thought feel like desperation? Like grasping at straws to assuage his guilt. Or an attempt to distract himself from the disturbing stirrings of regret within.

Good grief. He pushed to sitting and dropped his legs over the side of the bed, pulling off the light sheet.

If his priority was getting out of there, he'd better get to work on that goal rather than lie in bed obsessing over something he couldn't change. And shouldn't want to change.

He'd examined the designated smoking area at the midway while on patrol, sans a K-9 or Jazz to offer their keen senses and insights. Still, looking at the spot in person had helped him visualize the circumstances better.

If Sam had gone there on his own, he could have talked to other people also there, or he could have smoked alone. The area was a small grassy patch with one park bench and an ashtray fixed on top of a stone pedestal.

Seemed like Zeke should've been able to see Sam the whole time he was there if Zeke had been in line for the SkyPlunge ride as he'd said. But given that Zeke had apparently been drunk and enjoying the company of his pals, he probably hadn't cared to notice.

Hawthorne knew from personal experience that young guys that age had plenty of other things on their minds than watching out for the safety of their friends.

So Zeke and his other buddies had grown tired of the line and decided to move on. There had probably been plenty of girls for Zeke to be distracted by, as well.

Sam would've been at the smoking spot for a while, until he finished his cigarette.

Or until someone attacked him. Maybe it had begun quietly, a verbal challenge or argument between two males under the influence.

But if a violent altercation had broken out, wouldn't people have noticed?

That thought had led Hawthorne to consider another theory. Maybe Sam had left the smoking area and went somewhere nearby. Maybe a girl lured him away or someone else had approached him.

Adjacent to the smoking area stood a small building with indoor bathrooms. A maintenance shed was also nearby, but it was gated off for staff use, locked with a padlock that required a key.

If Sam had been lured somewhere close, there weren't many choices that would've been private enough to hide a fight. There was a patch of blacktop behind the restroom facilities that was slightly off the beaten path, but also a distance from the smoking area.

A person would have to leave the smoking spot, cross the wide blacktopped path full of visitors, and oddly stand by the pipes and plumbing that connected to the restroom facilities in the unlit area behind the building.

Would Sam do that while smoking a lit cigarette he wanted to finish? Not unwillingly, coerced or pressured by an attacker. Which meant that couldn't be the likely explanation for how he was killed.

The trouble was, after Zeke had left for other parts, Sam

could've gone anywhere. No one would have recognized him and known to come forward with the information later.

Hawthorne couldn't calm Rebekah's impatience with another dead end. He had to find something more.

Like the information Jazz had told him about Patch and the ex-husband of his wife.

Thanks to the need to straighten things out with Jazz, he'd completely forgotten about what she'd found. She'd said the cult stalker had been around two years ago.

He hadn't missed the significance of the timing. Seemed like a long shot to think the ex of one of Patch's wives could be connected to Sam. And yet, maybe it wasn't such a stretch.

Sam had been at the cult then. If the stalker was around before his death, had Sam interacted with him? Been followed by the man?

Hawthorne stood and went to his computer on the desk, waking it from sleep. Sitting down as it came to life, he navigated to the internet browser and looked up family court records.

He found Patch's more recent marriage record and scanned it for the wife's name.

Brenda Klika.

Hawthorne froze.

Butch's last name was Klika. Maybe it was a more common surname than Hawthorne thought. Or maybe she'd used her maiden name, rather than her previous husband's surname.

He quickly clicked through to divorce records and searched for Brenda Klika.

The divorce listing popped up on the screen.

Brenda Klika had divorced Butch Klika. Two months after Sam Ackerman's death.

The pieces fit together in Hawthorne's mind as he leaned back in the chair, staring at the screen.

Butch had supervised security the night Sam was at the

fair. He'd been stalking people at the cult, furious with Patch and his soon-to-be ex-wife.

Had he recognized Sam from obsessively watching the commune and following the Best Life members? He could've waited until Sam was alone at the smoking area and approached him.

Then what? Butch started a fight?

Hawthorne ran his fingers and thumb down the stubble on his chin. But why would Butch attack Sam personally? Maybe his anger had grown out of control, and he wanted revenge on the cult anyway he could get it. Butch wasn't exactly the friendly or gentle type to begin with.

If he'd attacked Sam in the open, he could've been seen. Butch must have managed to get Sam behind the restroom facilities nearby. But how?

There were still unknowns, but enough fit into place. Butch would have had the key to access the storage shed. A shed where he could've hidden Sam's body until the fair closed.

Then, since he had full knowledge and control of the security detail that night, he could've easily waited until no one was near and moved the body across the grounds to the Logboat Adventure ride.

A mixture of satisfaction and grim determination pulsed energy into Hawthorne's limbs. He should call the police. Even without solid evidence, he was sure they'd want to know about a new suspect with a powerful motive for the fair sabotage. If Patch had lured Butch's wife away from him, Butch would hate Patch enough to craft a plan that would incriminate Patch for terrorism, shut down his cult, and land him in prison.

Hawthorne wouldn't mind it if that had been the result, but justice was more important than seeing Patch put away. And justice for Sam might finally be possible if Hawthorne could convince the police to look at Butch as a murder suspect. Maybe the detectives could get Butch to confess if he knew he was already going to prison for Joan Cracklen's death.

Hawthorne went back to his nightstand to grab the phone he'd left on the silent setting for the uninterrupted sleep he'd intended to be enjoying right now.

When the screen lit, the symbol for a voicemail message caught his eye. He tapped to see more details. Left at eleven thirty p.m. From Rebekah.

His gut clenched before the message hit his ear.

"Hey, I'm going crazy just waiting around not doing anything. I never wanted to go to the fair after Sam. Thought it would be too hard, you know? But I realized when we talked that I should be the one to come here. I knew Sam best. I can figure out where he was. What he really did that night. I've gotta try." She paused, and he heard something in the background. Music from one of the rides. The Spin and Roll. Her voice lowered slightly as she continued. "I'm staying here when they close."

Hawthorne gripped the phone tighter, not believing his ears.

"I'm going to hide somewhere so they won't know I'm here. I'm sure I can find something. Figure it out. This is where somebody killed Sam. I'm going to prove it."

The line went dead.

Hawthorne's breath caught. He'd glanced at the duty roster before he'd left, mostly verifying when Jazz was working. But he'd seen the overnight supervisor's name.

Butch Klika.

Rebekah was there alone. Now. With Sam's killer.

THIRTY-NINE

Butch was the angry ex-husband?

Jazz pressed her hand to her forehead and stared unseeingly through the windshield as the shock faded and the facts became clear. It made so much sense, like at the end of a Carson Steele novel when the truth suddenly seemed so plain, like she should've seen it all before.

Butch had free access to all parts of the fair, all the staff-only areas. He knew the ins and outs of the fair after working there for fifteen years. He could go anywhere without raising suspicions. He could even control which areas would have security when.

Aunt Joan had never said anything negative about Butch, and Jazz didn't remember ever seeing them argue. Didn't seem like Butch had a motive to kill Aunt Joan. But maybe she'd simply been collateral damage like everyone initially thought. The unfortunate victim of bad timing, putting her in the pod that Butch had chosen to explode for sabotage. That he would then blame on Patch.

It would be a very satisfying way to get revenge on the man who'd taken Butch's wife from him. If Butch's plan worked, it would destroy everything Patch had built—his business and the cult. And land Patch himself in prison.

Jazz should call Nev.

The instinct hitched in her heart before her mind caught on. Nevaeh wasn't an option anymore.

Pushing aside the pain of remembering she'd lost her best friend, Jazz naturally jumped to Phoenix K-9 next. Cora would usually be the one she'd call to give information if she didn't go through Nevaeh.

Stupid habits. She'd gotten more used to being at PK-9 than she'd realized. She thought of calling them before the police every time. Because that's the way Pheonix had wanted it.

Well, she didn't answer to Phoenix anymore. Didn't have to earn her approval.

Looked like she'd be calling the pol—

A ringtone sounded, pulling her gaze to her phone where she'd laid it on her lap.

Uncle Pierce's name appeared on the screen.

The first happiness she'd felt in hours surged up inside her as she lifted the cell. She so needed to hear his loving, approving voice right now. "Hi, Uncle Pierce."

"Jazz."

The quiver in the one word sent a chill down her spine. Something was wrong.

"I've been taken hostage. By the head of security at the fair. Butch Klika."

"What?" Not Uncle Pierce. Fear wrenched her stomach. She couldn't lose him. "Where are you?"

"The fair." He paused. "He's watching me right now and has a gun." Uncle Pierce's voice became more rigid and controlled, like he was saying only what Butch told him to say. "He wants you to come right now, if you want me to live."

"I'm on my way." Jazz turned on the ignition and hit the gas almost before the SUV had started.

"He says no weapons and no dog. If he sees either, he'll kill me immediately. Please, Jazz, do as he says." Panic pinched Uncle Pierce's plea.

Jazz's chest pinched, her pulse speeding as she fought

back tears. She never cried in dangerous situations. She never even felt nervous. She'd been trained, knew what she could handle. Fear had never been her problem. Why now were her fingers trembling on the steering wheel while her stomach tied itself in knots? "I'll get you free, Uncle Pierce. Don't wo—"

"Go to the east side employee's entrance." Uncle Pierce spoke quickly and robotically, like he'd been prodded to say more. "Enter code six zero six two. Go to the History Center. Jazz, be—"

The line went dead, cutting him off.

Had he been going to tell her to be careful?

Her heart squeezed behind her ribs. His life was in danger, he was being held by a kidnapper, and he still thought of her. If she'd doubted that his change to a loving uncle was possible, she was more than positive now.

A tear escaped and tumbled down her cheek as she raced on the mostly quiet streets to reach the fair. Lucky she hadn't gone far, thanks to not knowing where to go.

Within five minutes, she spotted the east entrance ahead. She pulled into the empty, small parking lot, running through the scenario and options in her mind as she'd done the whole drive there.

Clever of Uncle Pierce to make sure she knew Butch had a gun. Though that would have been safe to assume since he wore one as security personnel.

If that was all he had for weapons, she should be able to beat him without a problem. But if he held the gun on Uncle Pierce in the right way, things could get trickier.

Jazz turned off the ignition and grabbed her Sig that she'd pulled out of the holster so it wouldn't dig into her hip while she sat in the car. She tucked it into her waistband behind her back and pulled the holster off, dropping it onto the floor in front of the passenger seat.

She reached for her backpack on the seat and pulled out the dark green PK-9 windbreaker. Didn't exactly want to show team spirit at the moment, but the jacket would help cover her gun, and the lower nighttime temperature shouldn't make it too sweltering to wear.

Her knife was still strapped to her thigh. A little too obvious.

She took off the sheath and put it on her ankle, hidden under her jeans.

Flash whined, drawing Jazz's gaze to him in the rearview mirror.

She turned toward her partner, and he pushed forward so his head fit between the front seats. "Sorry, bud. You can't go along this time." A lump slid into her throat. "I can hide my other weapons, but I can't hide you."

He whined again and angled his head toward her as he panted heavily, clearly not liking the idea.

"I'm sorry. But I'll be back before you know it." She pushed herself up in the seat to press a quick kiss to his forehead, then swung toward the door and hopped out.

She closed the door as quietly as she could. The east entrance was too far from the enclosed History Center for Butch to hear her arrive, assuming he was in that building, but she didn't want to grab the attention of the other security guards. Their efforts to help, or being seen by Butch if he wasn't at the Center, could cost Uncle Pierce his life.

She couldn't risk that.

She'd handled much tougher assignments and even ambushes on her own. Taking down a single armed opponent by herself wouldn't be a problem.

No sign of movement or flashlights showed through the chain-link fence on this side of the fair as she approached the entrance.

Of course. She should've thought of that before.

Butch wouldn't be able to get away with a kidnapping at the fair if there were other guards around. He must have doctored the duty roster to clear the area where he wanted to play.

Well, it was going to be game over for him very soon.

Jazz punched the security code into the keypad at the small gate and entered.

The fair was eerily quiet. No colorful lights from the midway. No fun sounds and music. No voices or laughter.

Jazz kept an eye out for surprises as she hurried quietly up the path, making her way by the direct route to the History Center.

But once she was close, she veered off the path and cut behind the Skyride building to come around to the side entrance. Hopefully, Butch would expect her to enter the History Center by the main door.

If not, she'd still take him down. It just might be a little messier and take a bit longer.

But she would take him down. Uncle Pierce was not going to get hurt. They were still going to have their future together. The two of them would form the loving family she'd dreamed of.

First, she simply had to free Uncle Pierce from a killer.

Jazz stopped by the side entrance and flexed her fingers, taking in a slow breath to ease the unfamiliar tension between her ribs. She'd leave the gun behind her back in case Butch spotted her first. Didn't want him shooting Uncle Pierce because she hadn't respected his demand for no weapons.

She turned the knob on the metal door and pushed it open.

Didn't squeak or make a sound. Perfect.

The building was dark. The only illumination seemed to come from two large overhead lights attached to each end of the long building. Probably the only lighting that was usually left on overnight.

Shadows and dim light touched the exhibits that interrupted the otherwise open space, providing some cover for Jazz.

She crouched and silently weaved through the exhibits, scanning the open spaces for any sign of Uncle Pierce or Butch.

Her heart beat more erratically the longer she went without seeing anyone. Had Butch moved Uncle Pierce elsewhere?

She stepped around an old sleigh of some kind and checked the shadows beyond.

Something lay on the floor. A thick shape that tapered downward as it lengthened to what looked like legs.

Uncle Pierce? Dead?

The thought nearly choked her. She'd seen plenty of dead bodies. But she was not ready to see his.

She glanced around, making sure no one was there before giving in to the urge to move closer.

The shadows shifted as she approached.

A body for sure. A man's.

No. Grief pushed up her throat. It couldn't be Uncle Pierce.

A sound behind her.

She spun toward it, whipping out her Sig and aiming.

At Uncle Pierce.

Horror collided with disbelief as her brain struggled to make sense of the scene.

A girl, a teenager, whimpered from under the arm Uncle Pierce had wrapped around her neck.

And he held a gun to her temple.

FORTY

"Lord, please protect Rebekah." Hawthorne whispered the prayer in the silence of his car, pressing the gas pedal as far as he dared without attracting the kind of attention that would only slow him down.

He looked at the GPS he'd activated on his phone to calculate how many minutes away he was from the fairgrounds. Still twenty-five.

He smacked the wheel with his open palm.

Regret and guilt more bitter than he'd ever felt gnawed at his insides. How could he have let this happen?

Rebekah had taken matters into her own hands because he hadn't been able to solve Sam's murder fast enough. And now she could be in the hands of the killer himself.

Hawthorne had almost called the police the moment he'd learned Rebekah was at the fair. But he'd realized just in time the mistake that would be.

The police would contact fair security when on their way, probably have them look for Rebekah.

But security at the fairgrounds tonight was in Butch's control. He might even be the one who'd answer the call from the police. Then he'd find Rebekah for sure, if he hadn't already.

"Please, God. Please don't let him find her. Keep her safe. Protect her."

Protect her. His own words echoed back at him and stabbed his conscience. Because that was exactly what he should've done.

His better instincts had tried to tell him to give her some help and guidance. Protection. But he'd tossed them aside because it seemed to violate the greatest possession in his own life—freedom.

Rebekah wanted freedom, too. That much was clear in the fact that she'd left her family and all she'd known behind to set out on her own, make her own decisions, craft her own life. Who was he to stand in the way of that when he'd done the same?

He couldn't steal the freedom she'd given up everything to have by being an overbearing control freak.

But as he pictured her at the fair, possibly running from a killer, maybe already caught by him, and—

No. Hawthorne tightened his fingers around the wheel. That couldn't happen. He couldn't have made that big of a mistake.

Despite his excuses, there was no denying it was a mistake. A catastrophic one.

Rebekah was only a kid, completely alone in the world. And she'd come to him for help. Not only help with Sam's death.

He'd heard it in the way she'd spoken of their brother, wondering if Hawthorne ever talked to him. In the story she told of her doubt she would've been able to find Hawthorne if he hadn't been an author with a website. And in the glistening tears in her eyes when she'd admitted she missed their parents.

Had she wanted him to be involved in her life? To care enough to check her freedom a little with his concern for her safety and well-being?

She had asked him if he'd go to a movie or hang out with her. He knew he'd disappointed her when he had said he was too busy. But hadn't it been better to help her preserve and enjoy her freedom instead of relying on him—a brother who would be gone in two weeks?

He swallowed, slipping the car into the right lane to catch the exit ramp off the freeway.

The burn in his chest from his searing conscience gave him the answer to his own questions. And to another he hadn't formed into words, even in his thoughts.

Why? Why had he left her vulnerable?

He'd told himself he was staying out of her life to give her freedom. But the truth smacked him in the face so hard he winced.

He hadn't gotten involved because he wanted to guard his *own* freedom. It was for him. So he didn't feel tied down, didn't have to watch out for anyone but himself. So he wouldn't have to set aside what he wanted to do or how he wanted to live for someone else.

He'd done the same thing with Jazz. The look on her face that he'd never forget flared in his memory—the palpable sting of rejection. Who knew the full extent of the damage his words and actions may be having on her.

But at least refusing to risk his freedom to care about Jazz hadn't sent her into danger. Like Rebekah.

He could've tried to get closer to Rebekah like she'd wanted. Could've invited her over or hung out with her instead of only seeing her when she wanted news about Sam. He could have told her about the way guys tend to think and the dangers of dressing too scantily. He could have asked her if she was careful not to walk to her car alone at night. If she knew any self-defense.

He could have tried to get to know her, learn who she really was beyond the girl who grieved her boyfriend's death. They could have done fun things together.

He should have told her about Christ and salvation through Him.

Now it might be too late. For all of those things.

Hawthorne's heart felt like someone was squeezing it in a vise, trying to crush it completely.

Dear God, please don't let my mistake cost Rebekah her life.

He still had his freedom. But what would that be worth if keeping it sacrificed his sister?

"Uncle Pierce? What are you doing?" Jazz's voice came out weak, strangled by the horror filling her lungs.

He smiled, still holding the suppressor-equipped gun to the poor girl's head. It wasn't his new smile, the one that was warm and gentle, full of approval and love.

No, it was the old smile. The condescending smile that meant she'd better get out of his way if she knew what was good for her. "I thought you might have grown into a reasonably intelligent person. What does it look like I'm doing?"

Jazz stared at him, her mind as frozen as her body. She couldn't figure it out. Who was the girl he was threatening to kill? And who was the man on the ground who still hadn't moved?

She couldn't make the leap from her uncle's desperate call, saying he'd been kidnapped, to the scene unfolding in front of her. "Where's Butch? Or is he not even here?"

"Oh, he's here. Behind you."

The man on the floor. She didn't dare turn her back on Uncle Pierce to confirm it. "Is he dead?"

"I certainly hope so. That was my intention when I choked him that long."

"You choked Butch?" The man was thickly built and muscled, though not as tall as Uncle Pierce.

"I was in the Army, too, remember? They taught us those things even back in my day." A coldness seeped into Uncle Pierce's eyes.

The girl in a hold he could turn into a choke at any moment became paler by the second as tears streaked her cheeks. Whoever she was, Jazz had to get her away from him.

"Okay." Jazz held up a hand, palm out. "Why don't you let the girl go, and we can talk about whatever is going on here."

"Let the girl go? Come now, Jazz. You know I'm not stupid. She's the only reason you haven't tried to take me down already. Isn't she?"

That and the fact that shock seemed to be seeping into every inch of Jazz's body, shutting down the function of most of her limbs with a numbing sensation.

This had to be a mistake, some massive miscommunication. Her uncle was not a criminal. He didn't kill people.

He was her future. Her family. The only person who accepted her and loved her.

She wasn't losing that. She couldn't.

"Uncle Pierce, this doesn't make sense. This isn't who you are. Just tell me what's wrong, and we can fix it together. Whatever it is, I can help you get through it."

"You?" A sardonic laugh popped from his mouth, echoing in the large building. "That would be ironic, to say the least, considering you've been the problem from the beginning."

He shifted the girl to the side slightly, as if to have a clearer path to level at Jazz the fiercest glare she had ever seen. "You're the reason I'm in this mess. I have to do this because of you. I had to do it all because of you."

The words would have hurt more if they made sense. But they seemed to be the ravings of insanity. "I don't understand."

"No, you never understood, did you? But you would have someday. When you came across the evidence in Lawrence's things."

Dad's things…Was that why Uncle Pierce had wanted to go through them with her? But she still had no idea what he was talking about. "What evidence? Of what?"

His eyes narrowed. "I should have found a way to get rid of you years ago. The moment Lawrence dumped you with us so you could be a threat hung over my head. Instead, I let him force us to take care of his brat he didn't even want."

The truth stung, pricking her eyes with hot moisture. But

she blinked it back. She'd never heard the part about being a threat. About Uncle Pierce and Aunt Joan being forced to take care of her.

Evidence in her dad's things. The realization of what he must be talking about rolled through her in a freezing wave of shock. "Blackmail." The word popped out without her meaning to say it.

"Yes. Pernicious, relentless blackmail." Uncle Pierce's mouth twisted with pure hate. "That's the kind of man Lawrence was. Didn't matter we'd served together, been friends once. Whenever he needed something, I had to supply it. Money, childcare, schooling. And if I refused, he would threaten to expose me."

"But what could he have had to blackmail you with?"

"You'd like to know, wouldn't you?" Uncle Pierce sneered. "So you can use it against me, too. You won't get the chance." He jerked a nod in the direction of the body behind her. "That's what happens to people who try to blackmail me now."

"Butch was blackmailing you, too?"

"No, my dear." He spoke the endearment in a tone of pure ice. "I killed him so he could not."

"How would he know what my father knew?"

"He didn't. He knew what I did here." Uncle Pierce glanced up toward the ceiling and dropped his gaze to the right, as if encompassing the building.

Did he mean the fair? Her breath caught. "You were the one who sabotaged the rides?"

"Well, not all of them, no. I'll have to give credit to Butch for the first incidents, and for the inspiration for how I could get rid of my little problem."

The first incidents. The last one was…Aunt Joan.

Jazz's heart leaped into her throat, nearly gagging her. "You…killed…Aunt Joan?" She could barely force out the words.

"Yes." That horrible, hateful smile curved his closed lips

again. "Amazing how easy it was. A simple IED in that giant purse of hers."

"Why?" The question emerged as a near whisper, from the depths of her stinging heart.

"I already told you. Because of you."

"That doesn't make any sense."

His smile faded. "I didn't think so either. But she didn't think I should have you killed."

"Have me...*You're* the one who hired the hitmen?"

"All the good it did me." He stared at her, that hatred flashing in his eyes. "Joan was so sure we could talk things out so I wouldn't have to take such a step."

The Sunday brunch. That was why Aunt Joan had suddenly invited Jazz to brunch. Maybe why she'd acted friendlier the day she died, too.

"She had never liked you, so I was quite taken aback by her sudden desire to protect you. Very inconvenient."

"Inconvenient?" A small spark of anger flared in Jazz's chest. "You killed your own wife because she wanted to save her niece from being murdered by you, and you call that *inconvenient?*"

"Very." He snapped the reply with a glare. "It meant I needed to get rid of her, too, and that gave the fool over there," he cast a glance toward Butch, "the idea to blackmail me. And now we end up here. Where I have to do away with you myself —something I should have done from the beginning, apparently. And this unfortunate girl." He squeezed the girl's neck tighter, and she clutched at his arm with her fingers.

Maybe Jazz could at least help her out of this. "Who is she?"

"I have no idea." He lifted his eyebrows with mild annoyance. "But she showed up here right as I dispatched Butch, so I have no choice but to eliminate her, as well. I suspect she must have been here in connection with Butch somehow. It will add more validity to the theory the police will no doubt arrive at. That Butch killed the girl and you because you discovered he was the culprit behind the sabotage and my dear wife's death."

He gave Jazz a sickening smile that dropped as quickly as it appeared. Then he dug the suppressor deeper into the girl's head. "Now, lay down any weapons you're carrying, or I'll blow the girl's head apart right here."

FORTY-ONE

Raindrops pummeled the windshield as Hawthorne flipped the wipers to a higher setting, trying to see the dark road before him.

The GPS on his phone, propped up in the dashboard holder, reported he still had ten minutes to drive before he'd reach the fairgrounds. And even when he'd arrive, he wouldn't know where to find Rebekah. The fairgrounds were massive. It could take hours to find her.

Especially if Butch had...

His heart lurched into his throat, seeming to jam it so he could barely breathe.

No. His mistake couldn't lead to that. Not Rebekah...dying.

But the possibility was all too realistic in this scenario he'd let unfold. All because he wanted to make sure he didn't lose the freedom he'd sacrificed so much to gain. Handy thing that protecting Rebekah's freedom meant he didn't have to give up any of his hard-won autonomy.

Distant thunder rumbled as he had to stop for a red light. Frustration rose inside him. Everything in him told him to run the light, but he couldn't risk being delayed even more by a well-meaning cop.

The pause gave him a moment in which his own thoughts circled back, their echo reaching his consciousness.

Freedom he'd sacrificed so much to gain. Hard-won autonomy.

Had he sacrificed anything for his freedom? Sure, he'd left his parents and family. Had to venture into life at a young age and make his way alone. Didn't have anyone to support him through trials or celebrate his victories.

But that was all exactly what he'd wanted. He hadn't wanted to stay with parents who chose to pursue their own best life at the expense of the well-being of their own children.

Oh, no. Dismay exploded in a cold rush that coursed through Hawthorne's torso. He'd become his parents. Or maybe he'd always been that way. Far more like his parents than he'd recognized.

The realization cut him to the core. He'd made a god out of freedom—his freedom, his wants, his desires. And his love of independence and freedom had only grown since he'd left the cult. He never even got involved at any church, excusing his lack of engagement with the fact he'd be moving on again. But was all the traveling really just a way to keep his life the way he wanted it? Under his control, independent, and free of relationships that would mean he'd have to sacrifice his own desires for someone else?

For the first time, the truth of how he'd been living became clear. And jolted him like he'd been struck by a bolt of lightning. Because it was wrong. Dead wrong. Sinful.

He had even tried to excuse his avoidance of relationships by claiming he'd been called to singleness. That might be true, but being chosen to live as a single person didn't mean he wasn't supposed to be in non-romantic relationships.

And he couldn't know if God meant him to be single the rest of his days. It only seemed that way because he was still single. And, most of all, because he'd always *wanted* to stay single. The very idea of being married made him claustrophobic.

He didn't want to belong to anyone, be owned by someone, be obligated to someone. That would give the person so much control over how he could live.

He wouldn't be a slave to anyone. Not after the cult.

Wasn't it good to want freedom? After all, one of Hawthorne's favorite Bible passages—one he'd memorized when he'd first become a Christian—said, *For freedom Christ has set us free; stand firm therefore, and do not submit again to a yoke of slavery.*

Another foggier memory rushed forward, as if awakened by the retrieval of that verse from the storage vault of his mind. Chaplain Terry had shown Hawthorne other passages about freedom and slavery, too. There was one Hawthorne hadn't liked the sound of, but he couldn't recall why.

Hawthorne kept his gaze on the wet road as he tapped his phone's screen to wake it up. "Find the Bible verse about being slaves of sin."

The computerized voice of the phone answered within a few seconds. "But thanks be to God, that you who were once slaves of sin have become obedient from the heart to the standard of teaching to which you were committed, and, having been set free from sin, have become slaves of righteousness. Romans chapter six, verses seventeen through nineteen."

Slaves of righteousness? He'd forgotten the Bible used that language to speak of what it meant to be a Christian, to follow Christ. Because it wasn't just following Him, was it? It was also belonging to Christ.

The computerized voice startled Hawthorne as it spoke again. "But now that you have been set free from sin and have become slaves of God, the fruit you get leads to sanctification and its end, eternal life. Romans chapter six, verse twenty-two."

Slaves of God. The phrase reminded Hawthorne of something Terry had tried to teach him at the beginning of his Christian walk. There'd been so much to learn and try to comprehend, this truth must've gotten lost. Probably because it was the part Hawthorne hadn't wanted to hear.

And part of him still didn't want to hear it. But he'd grown enough as a Christian for ten years to know he had to accept everything God said in His Word, not pick and choose only the parts he liked.

His preferences were still driven by sinful desires so much of the time. He wanted to be his own master, to do only what made him happy. Like his parents. And like Adam and Eve, the first sinners in the Garden of Eden.

Hawthorne wanted to be in charge. When he'd been pushing people away, fearing they'd jeopardize his ability to control his life and do what he wanted, he'd also been setting a boundary for God. In essence, he'd been telling God there were lines He couldn't cross. Parts of Hawthorne and his life that he wanted to keep just as they were, under his own control.

But Christianity didn't work like that. Life didn't work like that.

Whether or not Hawthorne liked it, God was in full control of Hawthorne's life. No matter how many boundaries he set, trying to keep God out of it.

Conviction settled heavily and uncomfortably in Hawthorne's gut.

"I'm so sorry, Lord. I got so focused on myself, I didn't realize how selfish I'd become. Didn't see I'd made an idol out of my idea of freedom."

The other verse Hawthorne had loved enough to memorize sprang to his mind.

So if the Son sets you free, you will be free indeed.

That passage was still true, too. No matter how much Hawthorne thought he was free once he escaped the cult, he'd been a slave of Satan and sin.

Until Christ set him free. To be a slave to Jesus Christ instead, yes. But only in Christ could true freedom be found.

Hawthorne knew that, but he hadn't lived it. Without recognizing it, he'd voluntarily submitted himself again to a yoke of slavery like his favorite verse said. That slavery was his selfishness.

His desire for freedom became the top priority dictating all his choices, making him reject Jazz and keep his sister at arm's length. He'd become a slave to his own desires for freedom and doing whatever he wanted. Which ironically meant he wasn't free at all.

"Please forgive me, Lord. And show me how to live out the freedom I have in you, the freedom to reject my selfishness and choose to serve you instead. The freedom to be in relationships and sacrifice my own desires for others. Remind me how much better it is to be a slave of Christ, living in obedience to You, than to be a slave to my own selfishness."

He knew from the promises of Scripture and his own experience that living for Christ instead of himself would yield much greater happiness and joy than the selfishness he'd been living for in recent years.

But what about the people he'd hurt along the way, thanks to his bullheaded focus on his own wants and his fear of relationships? Like Jazz. The memory of the hurt in her eyes stung like a stab wound in his chest.

She would probably never forgive him, even enough to let him be her friend. He'd completely destroyed any possibility of telling her about Christ, too. Why would she want to listen to him about God when he'd been such a pathetic example of how a Christian should live?

The voice of the GPS told him to take another turn. Good thing, since he'd been too preoccupied to notice the intersection he should've recognized coming up.

Rebekah was the one who might pay the biggest price for Hawthorne's mistakes. But with the reminder that he needed to serve God, not himself, Hawthorne was ready to do anything for his sister.

He only hoped he wasn't too late.

FORTY-TWO

A tremor shook through Jazz's body as rain soaked every inch of her clothing, including the PK-9 windbreaker. But the rain had little to do with the way her body was shutting down, a cold chill creeping through each limb until she felt numb all over.

Uncle Pierce stepped onto the loading platform of the Flying Dragon ride. It was the spot where the ride operator usually stood to ensure passengers were secured into the long gondola by the cushioned metal bars that were supposed to encase their arms and waist, along with a seatbelt.

Funny thing, Uncle Pierce wasn't concerned with safety. He'd held his gun on the girl and threatened to shoot her to get Jazz to climb into the seat compartment for two.

Now he bent over the girl in the seat next to Jazz and tied the teen's hands behind her back with pre-cut rope sections he'd apparently brought for the purpose. He'd forced the girl to put duct tape on Jazz's mouth and tie her hands in the History Center, threatening the terrified hostage with the gun until she had tightened the knots to his liking. He'd repeated the same tactic before Jazz slid her feet into the compartment for her legs in the ride, having the girl tie Jazz's ankles together first.

"This is ironic, don't you think? You're going to die at the Tri-City Fair. The place you and Joan loved so much. Maybe there will be some comfort in that for you." His amused grin didn't suggest he cared either way.

It was a good plan, really. The thought came to Jazz's numb brain, devoid of emotion. Kill Jazz and the girl, whoever she was, in a way that looked like another act of hate against the fair. No doubt Uncle Pierce's idea was that the police would think Butch had put them in the ride without being strapped in so they would die, and he could blame it on the fair and the cult.

But the police would find Butch's body. An autopsy would show he'd been choked to death. They would look for a killer.

Judging from Uncle Pierce's gloved hands, and the fact he'd put his hostages on a ride close to the History Center, he was planning to leave without a trace. Get away with another killing without anyone ever suspecting him of the crime.

If Butch had invited Uncle Pierce there to blackmail him, the security supervisor must have shut down the cameras in Sector Three in addition to not scheduling any patrols in that area. Uncle Pierce was smart enough to have figured that out. And realized it meant he could get in and out without anyone knowing.

Except Jazz.

"I guess this is goodbye." Uncle Pierce took a step back and leveled a stare at her. The smile was gone, but in its place was that look of loathing that shook Jazz to her core. "Thirty years too late." He spun and hopped down from the loading platform, disappearing into the sheets of rain.

Lightning lit the sky, allowing her to glimpse his form as he went somewhere closer to the ride on the ground below. Probably going to the controls.

Thirty years. The duration of her life.

A crack of thunder shook the ride. But her life was already crumbling beneath her.

The man she had thought was her ticket to the happiness she'd always longed for hated her. So much that he wanted her dead.

Bile slid up her throat. She swallowed it back before it reached her duct-taped mouth and choked her. How could this be happening?

She'd trusted him. Believed him when he said he wanted to get to know her, that she was family. Thought he accepted her. Loved her.

She'd thought he was claiming her as his own.

It wasn't supposed to end like this. She was supposed to go with Uncle Pierce and finally have a family she belonged to.

But he was playing her. Like the criminals she'd dealt with time and again in her line of work. How had she missed the signs?

She had let him play her like a fiddle, conning her into believing he loved her only to reject her like everyone else in her life.

How could she have trusted someone like him? Someone who murdered Butch without a thought. A man who killed his own wife without even the smallest bit of remorse. And now he was going to kill his niece and an innocent girl.

That was the kind of family Jazz had. She shouldn't even want to belong to a family like that.

Then why did it feel like her heart was being ripped from her chest?

Maybe because it had already been wounded so much. By Hawthorne saying he didn't want her, Nev turning her back, the PK-9 team never accepting her.

Who was Jazz kidding? It hadn't started with them. Her heart had never healed from her dad's rejection either. The constant reminders all her life that she wasn't good enough for him to love. It was the same whether he was home and ridiculing her for everything she did wrong, or he was over-seas, gladly leaving her with an aunt and uncle who disliked her as much as he did.

And she'd never healed from that first, possibly worst rejection of all. The one that happened before she could remember but was most deeply embedded in her soul. The mother who didn't want her.

Even she was gone now. Dead. No possibility of an idyllic reunion someday. No chance she'd realize her mistake and want to see her daughter. Want to love Jazz and be part of her life.

The dreams Jazz had never labeled, never recognized in her own heart, imploded all at once, like whatever they'd been built on gave way. The pain of their destruction seared through her body from her stomach to her chest, shooting from there through her arms and legs.

She sucked in air through her nose, closing her eyes against the anguish.

She thought she'd always been alone. But she hadn't tasted utter, stark, desolate loneliness until now. She had absolutely no one. And no hope of someone she could belong with in the future.

Her own family had refused to claim her as their own. No one else ever would.

Nev's sweet face, her dark eyes filled with hurt, rose in Jazz's memory and blocked her vision. *"You wouldn't really leave me, would you?"* Nev's voice reached her ears—the agonized whisper as she'd asked the question.

Had Nev thought Jazz was rejecting her? Horror at the possibility squeezed Jazz's ribs hard enough it seemed they would crack.

Jazz would never do that to someone else. She knew what it felt like.

But the look on Nev's face, in her eyes, had said differently.

Jazz's stomach churned, sending more nausea upward.

Nev had said Jazz pushed people away first so they wouldn't reject her.

Jazz swallowed hard as she saw it for the first time. Nev was right. And Jazz had pushed Nev away, too. The one person who'd been the closest to family Jazz had ever had. The one person who had accepted Jazz. Loved her.

Nev had been talking about the PK-9 team and Phoenix when she'd said that about Jazz putting up walls. Would those ladies have wanted to be her family? Could Jazz have belonged with them if she'd let them get close to her?

It was her fault.

The awful realization nearly choked her with grief. Maybe she could've belonged in this city, had something like a family, if she hadn't pushed the team away. And she'd put the final touch of doom on the whole thing when she'd stupidly pushed even Nev out of her life. What had she been thinking?

The answer came quickly. She'd wanted the real thing with Hawthorne through a marriage or with Uncle Pierce, her actual relative.

She sure was an idiot to think she'd ever find belonging with either of them.

And now, thanks to her own foolishness, she was totally on her own. No help from PK-9 or Nev to get her out of this mess. Because Jazz had cut them out. She had thought she could handle the situation herself, and she'd already burned all her bridges with PK-9 and Nev by the time Uncle Pierce texted.

Thanks to the way Jazz had rejected them, they wouldn't want to help her now even if they knew the bind she was in.

Another thunderous boom quaked the sky, shaking the ride more than before.

No, that wasn't the thunder. The ride had started. It was beginning the slow swing that would stay horizontal with the ground at first, then lift higher and higher until the upswing turned the long, dragon-shaped gondola vertically and then upside down.

Jazz and the girl would probably fall out at vertical, given that Uncle Pierce had put them in seats at the front end.

Jazz peered down through the rain, trying to see Uncle

Pierce. At least it had taken him a while to figure out how to operate the ride. Not that it mattered. No help would come.

A whimper beside her caught her attention.

She looked at the girl in the seat next to her. The girl's straight blond hair was darkened, soaked, and plastered to her head. She puffed air through her nose like she was struggling to breathe, probably thanks to the panic that reflected in her eyes.

Poor kid. Jazz hadn't even been able to get her name or find out what she was doing there. How had she gotten involved in this mess?

If Jazz hadn't been so blindsided by Uncle Pierce being the real kidnapper, she probably could've freed the girl. And herself.

But the shock had numbed her brain as she'd tried to process what was happening. And the few times she had thought of using her knife or martial arts on him later, she couldn't do it. She couldn't hurt her own uncle, her only living family member.

What a moron. Everything was lost, and she was still trying to hang on to some hope. Some dream that she could belong with Uncle Pierce someday if she kept him alive. When would she get it?

No one wanted her. She would never belong with anyone.

Even as she reminded herself of the truth, her heart squeezed in protest and a rebellious hope at the back of her mind said it couldn't be true.

Was she really so desperate that she'd rather believe she had a chance with a murderer than believe no one would ever want her?

Yes, she was. She knew because she didn't care that the gondola was swinging wider and higher. She knew because she didn't care she'd fall to her death soon, and it would all be over. She'd rather have that than keep living this painful, lonely life, unwanted and unclaimed by the world.

The world. What was it Cora had said in that quote from

the Bible? It was one Jazz thought she had heard at church when her aunt and uncle had taken her. And seen on billboards sometimes. Something about God loving the world so much that He gave His Son to give people eternal life.

Did that mean He might love Jazz? She wasn't even sure He existed, so it was a pointless question.

But her mind worked to recall the other Bible quote anyway, the one she'd seen written in Cora's perfect calligraphy. The one that had creeped her out in a way.

She tried to remember why as the gondola swung high enough for her stomach to lift a bit on the downward plummet.

That was it. The quote had said, *You are mine.*

She didn't know why she'd thought that was creepy. Wasn't that exactly what she wanted? Someone to love her so much that they wanted to claim her as their own?

She tried hard to picture the other words swirled on the notecard. *Fear not,* then something about being redeemed, and...*I have called you by name.*

What was left of her broken heart ached at the words.

Cora often called God her father. What would it be like to have a father to call Jazz by name and claim her as his own family? It would be...heaven.

I want that. Her lips tried to form the words before she remembered they were taped shut. Could she talk to God without speaking? She hoped so, because with the gondola swinging higher, this would be her last chance.

God, if You can hear me this way, can You tell me if I can be Yours? Can You call me by name and want to keep me and love me? I want to belong to You. Forever. I want to be loved by You like Nev says You love her and take care of her. Nobody else wants me, God.

Hot tears tumbled from her eyes, mingling with the rain that already soaked her cheeks. *Nev says even if we've messed up, You'll forgive us if we ask and believe in You.*

So I'm asking, God. I pushed everyone away who might've loved me because I was scared. I was stupid and wrong. And now I'm paying for it. And this poor girl beside me is paying for it.

I'm so sorry, God. Will You please forgive me?

Wind blew stronger in her face as the gondola swung upward.

I'm probably about to die. I want to go to heaven and be with You, because Nev says You love perfectly. She says You're like the best Dad anyone could imagine, and You never let Your kids go. I should've listened to her before. It didn't seem real.

But you said, "You are mine." Please, let that be true for me, God.

A bolt of lightning split the sky, touching down somewhere in the distance.

The roll of thunder followed within a second.

Was that God answering?

Nev would've snorted if she'd heard Jazz ask that question out loud.

Jazz didn't really think it was. But a feeling inside drew her attention instead. The pain situated in her chest, where her heart had shattered into a million pieces, started to lessen.

Something shifted within, then a rush of sensation seemed to pour into her, as if the rain that had soaked her body from the outside was now flowing through her. The sensation reached even her fingertips and toes.

And it left her feeling like she never had before. She couldn't describe it.

But she knew she was different. And she knew, through a warm confidence that seemed to be rebuilding her heart, that God had heard her. That He'd said *yes*. He'd said, *You are mine* to her, Jazz Lamont.

The wonder of it made her forget where she was for a blissful, achingly beautiful moment as tears of joy ran with raindrops down her cheeks.

Then a wail from the girl beside her brought Jazz back to feel the vertical rise of the gondola and the pull of gravity, tugging her upper body forward.

The gondola plunged back down, lurching her stomach into the air.

One or two more swings upward, and she and the girl

would fall. There was no way they would survive the head-first drop from their height onto the metal supports below.

If Jazz could get her arms in front of her, she could grab her knife at her ankle and cut their ropes so they could try to climb down somehow. But there wasn't enough room in the small compartment to attempt the challenge of pulling her long legs between her arms so her wrists would be in front.

Unless help came, this was going to be it for her and the girl.

And help wouldn't come.

She'd seen to that when she'd pushed away Nev and the PK-9 team, not telling them anything about Uncle Pierce's call. They couldn't come even if they wanted to.

And even Nev, with her new Christian values, probably wouldn't be able to forgive Jazz for wanting to leave her. Hopefully, someday, Nev would remember how much Jazz had loved her and try to forget how things had fallen apart at the end.

Jazz would dearly love to have seen Flash and said good-bye. Someone would find him in the parking lot. He was probably barking now, wondering where she was and wanting to get out.

Grief caught in her throat. But Nev would take care of him. She wouldn't let any bad feelings she might have for Jazz keep her from caring for Flash.

Clinging to that comfort, Jazz clenched her calves tighter to the seat, trying to stop the pull of gravity as the gondola climbed even higher.

She and the girl barely stayed in.

Jazz tried to breathe as the gondola plummeted toward the earth.

One more swing, and they'd be done.

I guess I'm going to see You pretty soon, God. The thought didn't scare her the way it would've a few minutes ago.

It actually felt like it could be a good thing. That it might feel like coming home to be welcomed by the dad she'd always dreamed of.

Jazz closed her eyes as the gondola began another upward ascent. And she remembered His promise. *I have called you by name. You are mine.*

FORTY-THREE

Hawthorne strained to see through the pouring rain that pooled on his windshield as he turned into the north parking lot by the fairgrounds.

Going through the front gate wouldn't be a good idea since he couldn't possibly convince the guard on duty there that his supervisor was a violent criminal. At least he couldn't do so in a few seconds, which were all he would be able to afford before searching the grounds for Rebekah.

He looked at the massive fairgrounds. "Lord, where do I start? She could be anywhere."

A flash of lightning illuminated the sky.

Movement caught his attention. A vertical, dark shape climbed upward. It looked like the outline of a dragon.

The Flying Dragon ride was running?

He leaned toward the windshield, the wipers clearing a portion of glass for him to see through. But with the lightning gone, he couldn't see that far, and the ride's usually green and orange lights weren't lit.

Nothing should be operating this time of night.

Hawthorne's jaw clenched. He had no idea if or how the ride could be connected to Rebekah's whereabouts, but it was an anomaly, and that's what he had to look for.

The Flying Dragon was on the east side of the fairgrounds. He could drive all the way around to the east parking lot and entrance. But getting out and running, taking some of the shortcuts he'd found while on patrol, would probably get him there quicker. And it would enable him to keep his eyes peeled for Rebekah and Butch as he went.

Not wasting another second on deliberation, he jumped from his car and dashed through the rain to the north entrance. It didn't usually have a posted guard at night but was covered by cameras and locked.

Using his keycard, he got through the unmanned gate quickly and jogged up the narrow path that connected to the main one.

Rebekah didn't know the fair well. From what she had said, she'd never been there in her life. So it wasn't likely she would have deviated from the main thoroughfare.

Unless someone had forced her to.

The thought spurred his feet faster, and he picked up speed, scanning the rides and booths on both sides of the path.

If he hadn't seen the Flying Dragon in motion, he'd head straight for the Logboat Adventure ride. That's likely where Rebekah would have thought to go first, looking for clues about Sam's death.

But the Flying Dragon shouldn't be operating. And his gut said there was something very wrong in the fact that it was.

Sweat broke out on his forehead as he pushed faster, reaching the east side of the grounds.

Another lightning streak brightened the sky. He stopped and looked up, trying to spot the Flying Dragon above the food stands in front of him.

The same dark dragon rose high in the air.

Wait. Something small and white toward the top of the gondola caught his eye before the sky went dark.

Was that a person? Rebekah?

Adrenaline surged through his limbs. He took off at a sprint, praying all the way.

Jazz clenched her muscles, bracing for the upward movement of the dragon to carry them past vertical until they were upside down. And fell to their deaths.

A muffled scream came from the girl beside her.

If only Jazz wasn't tied, she could reach over and comfort her. But if she were free, she could save them, too.

At least Jazz wasn't afraid anymore. Not of dying alone or living alone. Because either way, she had God now. She belonged to Him, her Father. Forever.

The gondola climbed higher.

She held her breath.

It stopped climbing.

Jazz's insides froze. Was it malfunctioning? That would probably only kill them in a different way. Unless they managed to survive with injuries instead of tasting death.

It reversed, dropping quickly down like it had after the other swings, surging Jazz's stomach up toward her chest with the fall.

She stared straight ahead, trying to prepare for the next swing and imminent death.

But the dragon settled at the bottom. Slowing…stopping.

"Welcome back." The female voice jerked Jazz's gaze to the loading platform on the right.

Sofia?

Jazz stared at the woman's beaming smile that shone in the darkness, the hood of her black rain jacket covering most of her wavy hair.

"I'd ask if you enjoyed the ride, but it's probably more fun if you can yell and all that." Only Sof, and maybe Nevaeh, could joke at a time like this. But if Jazz's hands weren't tied right now, she might just hug the woman for it.

Sof leaned over to remove the duct tape from the closer girl's mouth first and untie her hands.

Just as well. With the mix of shock and joy tumbling

through her, Jazz was pretty sure she wouldn't be able to talk anyway.

"Jazz?"

The sound of Nev's voice instantly sprang tears to Jazz's eyes.

Jazz searched for her best friend, looking past Sof as she helped the girl from the compartment and off the loading platform.

Nev's black curls were visible first before she sprang around Sof and clambered into the compartment next to Jazz.

Nev ripped the tape off Jazz's mouth, glistening tears falling from her eyes to join the sprinkles of rain on her cheeks.

Jazz barely noticed the sting of the tape, her gaze locked on the love and forgiveness in her precious friend's eyes. "Nev." Her dry throat croaked on the word. She swallowed quickly and kept going. "I'm so sor—"

Her apology was lost in the tightest hug Nev had ever given her. And Nev was known for her breath-sucking hugs.

Jazz's tied arms yearned to hug her back. But she savored the hug anyway. The love behind it.

This was belonging, too. How had she lost sight of that?

"I am *so* thankful you're okay." Nev spoke the words next to Jazz's ear, still not letting her go.

More tears flooded Jazz's eyes. "Thank you." She managed to get the whisper out past the lump growing in her throat.

"Hate to break this up." Bristol's voice came from somewhere behind Nev, but Jazz couldn't see her past Nev's cloud of curls. "Now that Nev stopped this monster, we've gotta get the other ones."

Uncle Pierce.

Jazz jerked back. "Quick. Untie me." She twisted toward Bris as her phrasing fully registered. "Did you say *ones*?"

Nev spoke before Bris could as she started to undo the knots. "I can't believe Butch was the one behind the sabotage. And your own uncle was trying to kill you. I knew Pierce was a rotten dude, but I—"

"Wait. You know?"

Nev glanced up as she worked on the knots. "Just since Cora told us when she said to get over here."

So that's what had brought the PK-9 team there, just in the nick of time like always.

Amazement filtered through Jazz's exhausted system as her wrists split apart, finally free. "I don't know how Cora or Phoenix figured it out. But I'm glad."

"Are both monsters here?"

Jazz pulled her legs out from the compartment and grabbed the knife at her ankle. "Butch is dead and Uncle Pierce is getting away."

"Dead?" Shock lifted Nev's tone.

"No time to explain. We have to catch Uncle Pierce." Jazz sliced through the rope around her ankles and stood up quickly.

Too quickly.

Nev reached an arm around Jazz's back to steady her as she wobbled, her legs numb and tingly. "Do you know where your uncle went?"

"I assume the east gate where he came in. He must've parked his car over there. Maybe not close to avoid any trace he was here."

Nev still held an arm around Jazz but twisted her head to see behind. "Bris, tell Phoenix Butch is dead, and Pierce is fleeing the scene by the east gate."

"Roger." Bris jumped down from the loading dock.

"Phoenix is here?"

"Sure." Nev gave Jazz one of her *you-crazy* looks. "We all came. As soon as Cora got the intel on the sus past your uncle shared with your dad, she hacked the GPS on Pierce's car. She found it near the fairgrounds, so we knew he was here. Phoenix figured you'd be, too."

Uncle Pierce and Jazz's dad had a suspicious—

Another rumble of thunder shook the air, but a bark cut through it, darting straight to Jazz's heart.

Flash.

"Is Flash here?" Jazz shifted her legs, and Nev let go, climbing out of the gondola so Jazz could follow. Her circulation working again, Jazz scooted past Nev to see her boy, looking up at her from the ground below.

The handsome Malinois let out another excited bark as he watched her from Cora's side.

"Flash!" Jazz hurried down the steps from the loading dock and dropped to her knees in front of her partner. She rubbed his ears and neck, the warmth of his fur caressing her wet hands. "I really needed you here, bud."

"He let us know you were here as soon as we arrived." The smile in Cora's voice drew Jazz's gaze up to her. "He was barking nonstop in your SUV."

"Good boy." Jazz scratched his ears again. "You knew I shouldn't have left you behind."

"Praise the Lord you're safe. I was praying for you." Cora's blue eyes held nothing but grace and compassion, even after Jazz had put in her notice.

"How did you know I was in danger?"

Cora's lips curved in a gentle, closed smile. "There are different kinds of danger. I was praying for the spiritual one."

Wow. Had God been watching out for her even before she'd believed in Him? A smile found Jazz's face. "It worked."

Cora's eyes widened and her eyebrows lifted.

"Hey." Nev grabbed Jazz's shoulder from behind and leaned in, interrupting Jazz's chance to tell Cora what had happened with God. "Phoenix sent Sof and Bris on the main path to cover from here to the east gate. If Pierce is somewhere along the way, they'll find him."

"What if he's already at the gate or outside of it? I don't know how long we were in the dragon after he left."

"That's our job." Nev glanced behind her, and Jazz turned to see Phoenix and Dag.

The boss seemed to look at Jazz, but it was hard to be sure through the extra darkness cast over her eyes by the bill of her cap. She hadn't bothered to put up the hood of her black rain jacket.

Jazz's stomach clenched. Would Phoenix blast her for quitting? For getting into this jam?

"You know the fair best." Her deep voice was steady and emotionless as always. "Get us to the gate before he reaches it."

No scolding. No anger. Just empowerment. Maybe Nev was right about Phoenix, too.

Jazz nodded. "Yes, ma'am." She grabbed Flash's leash and threw Nev a glance. "Follow me, team."

She took off around the side of the Flying Dragon, running onto the hidden path that wound behind and under rides and would cut minutes off the race to the gate.

If Pierce had already gotten through, she and Flash would keep going, beyond the fair and as long and far as it took to catch him.

FORTY-FOUR

Hawthorne slowed his sprint as he neared the Flying Dragon.

A person stood in the rain wearing a light-colored jacket.

As he got closer, he spotted another figure, sitting next to the path. A dark hooded jacket was thrown over the person's shoulders.

Both people looked small and slim. Women?

Thunder roared as he stopped close to them, gaze locking on the person sitting down.

It looked like…yes. "Rebekah?"

She lifted her head, and he knew for sure. Rebekah's round, sweet face and big eyes.

She got up and sprang into his arms, hitting his chest hard.

Hawthorne held her tight, all his regret, guilt, and worry melting away as the desire to protect and cherish this girl swelled in his chest. "Thank you, Lord."

"Amen." The comment brought Hawthorne's attention to the woman who stood a few feet away, watching them with a soft smile.

"Did you save her?"

"No. Well, not alone. I'm with the Phoenix K-9 team."

Rebekah pulled away slightly, and Hawthorne kept one arm around her as she stayed tucked into his side.

"Phoenix K-9 is here?" Hawthorne's heart hiccupped. Did that mean Jazz was there, too?

"Yes. All of us. I'm Cora. The others are on their way to catch Pierce Cracklen before he leaves."

"Jazz's uncle?"

Cora nodded. "I believe he's the one who tried to kill her and your sister."

A surge of anger shot through him. Righteous anger, he hoped. No one could do that to his sister and get away with it. "Where'd they go?"

"Jazz went that way." Cora pointed toward the faint path by the Flying Dragon that he could barely see in the rain-soaked darkness. "I believe it's a shortcut Jazz knows to reach the east gate as quickly as possible."

Hawthorne ducked his head toward Rebekah. "Can you stay with Cora until I get back?"

Rebekah nodded against his ribs, slowly lowering her arms from around his torso.

"I'll be right back. I promise." His reluctance to turn away surprised him. God must already be preparing his heart for the relationships he wasn't going to hide from anymore.

But another relationship called to him. With a beautiful redhead, who happened to be going after the bad guy Hawthorne wanted very badly to take down right now.

He headed for the obscure path, hoping it would lead him to the villain and the heroine. And, Lord willing, a happy ending.

Jazz glanced over her shoulder as she darted under the supports of another ride.

Nev and Alvarez jogged close behind.

Phoenix and Dag followed them, though the ease of their movements made Jazz suspect the team could probably outpace them all if they wanted to.

"Where's Cora?"

"She stayed with the girl." Nev breathed hard as she answered. "Who is she?"

"I don't know. Pierce said she showed up when he was killing Butch, so he kidnapped her. Used her to hold me off."

"Nice."

Jazz knew Nev meant the opposite, though the sarcastic tone was lost in her heavy breathing.

Jazz pushed harder. They were close now. Just a few more seconds.

There.

She broke through onto the main path, the east gate to her left.

She stopped in front of it.

The gate was closed. No sign of anyone approaching from the main path. Should they stay and wait for him? Or had he already escaped?

Flash growled, then barked. The Malinois faced his ready stance toward the gate.

"Got it, bud." Jazz threw a glance at Nev and Phoenix as she went to the gate.

"Wait a sec." Nev stepped closer, pulling a gun from behind her back instead of her holster. "You took off so fast, I didn't get to give you this. Sof left one of her guns for you to use."

A laugh tumbled from Jazz's lips. Sof and her portable arsenal. Jazz took the Glock from Nev's hand.

"We got your back, Jazz." Nev's words landed in Jazz's heart, sparking more tears again. Good grief. She and Nev needed to have a long chat after this was all over, so she could say all her *sorrys* and hopefully get over being so emotional. Though maybe she'd always be emotional about almost losing Nev.

Flash's growl brought her back to the task at hand, and she hurried to open the gate. She stepped through, watching her peripherals, though she doubted Pierce would be waiting to ambush anyone.

He'd be desperate to get away as fast as he could.

Flash rumbled, a sound echoed by Dag and Alvarez. The K-9s stared in the same direction.

Toward a shadow that suddenly moved.

FORTY-FIVE

The east gate was open as Hawthorne approached, pulling his sprint to an abrupt halt.

A rumbling sound filtered through the opening. Not loud enough to be thunder.

A dog?

Hope squeezed his chest. Flash and Jazz?

Not wanting to spook them or interfere with their effort to catch Cracklen, he walked to the gate as quietly as he could.

The falling rain broke around the outline of three women and their dogs. One of them stopped and faced him.

Phoenix, judging from the cap.

He held up a hand in a still wave, hoping she'd recognize him.

She must have because she rotated forward again and followed the other two women. One wore a red jacket, and the silhouette of her head shaped in a mass of what could only be Nevaeh's curls.

His gaze hopped quickly to the third person. Tall, slim, and decidedly feminine. Jazz.

He walked through the gate, following them at a distance as he scanned the dark night.

They appeared to be going toward the hedges that

bordered the small parking lot all the way to where it met the road.

"Freeze!" Jazz's shout seemed louder than the lightning as it broke through the air.

A shadow—no, a person—moved in the corner where the hedge changed direction. The person stood. Ran.

Nevaeh took off with Alvarez, headed toward the road but angling to the left, probably to catch him if he tried to turn that direction.

Phoenix stopped and stood still, her dog mimicking her actions.

A shot fired from the shadow. Sounded like a suppressor on a Glock.

But Jazz didn't return fire. She walked slowly to where the shadow had disappeared into the sheets of rain. Was she frozen because he was her uncle? Maybe she didn't want to shoot him, despite what he'd done.

Hawthorne had no such compunction. And he wasn't about to stand there and watch Jazz get hit. He pulled out his Glock and hurried forward.

Another pop split the air.

Hawthorne ducked, but Jazz kept walking.

Pretty sure Cracklen would be running, though stopping to shoot behind him was undoubtedly slowing him down. Hawthorne couldn't be sure how much, since he couldn't see the man through the pouring rain and darkness.

If he was still moving quickly, he'd get around the straight, long hedge that ran west and east, and he'd turn right or left at the road.

Nevaeh was covering the left. Hawthorne would get the right.

He climbed over the north-south, five-foot hedge that met with the longer one closer to Jazz. The branches scratched more than he'd expected, but he managed to leave the some-what damaged hedge behind and moved through the thin stand of trees.

He scanned the long hedge leading to the road as he went,

searching for any sign of Cracklen on the other side of it. Though if the man was crouched low, Hawthorne probably wouldn't see him above the five-foot hedge.

"Flash, fass!" Jazz's voice, strong and commanding, pierced through the night.

Movement above the hedge caught Hawthorne's eye.

What—

A silhouette moved above the hedge, like something flying over it.

Lightning lit the sky, letting Hawthorne see clear as day.

But he couldn't believe what he saw.

Flash flew, literally flew over the hedge, his feet stretched out in front of him and behind him. How he stayed suspended in the air for so long, Hawthorne couldn't fathom.

But the Malinois kept soaring, all the way to the end of hedge that had to be at least twelve feet long. Then he dropped out of sight.

Loud snarls echoed.

Jazz sprinted past the hedge on the other side, and Hawthorne took off in the same direction, headed for the road.

He dashed out between trees, coming around the end of the hedge.

Jazz stood near Flash, the K-9 biting down on Cracklen's left arm as he moaned. "You're not taking my dog from me, too."

Hawthorne's gaze caught on the knife hilt sticking out of Cracklen's right shoulder. Jazz must have thrown the knife to stop Cracklen from shooting Flash.

Jazz glanced at Hawthorne, her eyebrows raising before she glared down at Cracklen again. "Flash, in ordnung."

The dog immediately let go and assumed a watchful position a couple feet from Cracklen.

"You're right, it is ironic. It all ends for you at our Tri-City Fair." The triumph in Jazz's voice was weakened by the emotion Hawthorne saw glistening in her eyes.

The sight of those unshed tears cracked his heart.

And he suddenly knew. He loved this woman.

His fear of being trapped must have been powerful indeed to have stopped him from knowing it before. Because now his heart felt like it might explode with love for her, with the desire to go to her, hold her, and comfort her until a smile replaced those tears. To tell her he was sorry for rejecting her. To tell her how very wrong he'd been to push away the person he had the feeling could change his life forever in the best ways possible.

"We'll take care of him for you." Sofia and Bristol appeared seemingly from nowhere, and the petite raven-haired woman pulled Cracklen's arms behind his back, none-too-carefully, to tie his wrists with a zip tie. She hauled him to his feet and pushed him in front of her. "March right back into the fair. Don't try to get clever or my K-9 will eat you for a late supper."

"Thanks, Sof." Jazz gave Sofia a smile that looked much weaker than her usual one.

"We got your back. Not that you need it." Sof gently punched Jazz's arm with a grin, then herded Cracklen toward the fair, her German shepherd and Bristol staying with her.

Jazz stared at the concrete sidewalk where Cracklen had lain.

Rain mingled there with the blood from his wounds, washing it away.

Was she in shock? "Jazz?" He took a step toward her, not wanting to startle or crowd her.

Flash walked to Hawthorne and swished his tail as Hawthorne leaned down to give him a quick pet. At least Flash forgave him. That was a good sign.

"Jazz, are you all right?"

She finally looked at him, but the humor and vibrance in her eyes seemed dimmed. No wonder. She'd been through a lot, though he didn't know all of it yet.

She nodded, but the way she crossed her arms over her open, soaked jacket said she was in need of comfort.

Would she let him give it to her?

He slowly took another step, then another.

Her eyes stayed on him, but she didn't back away or speak.

So he closed the remaining distance between them, his arms outstretched.

She fell into them, fitting against his chest as perfectly as she had after the explosion on the trail.

She shivered against him, her hands gripping the front of his jacket next to her face.

He stretched his arms farther around her back, trying to give her all the warmth and solace he could. And he didn't mind a bit the way the contact sent sparks of heat through him, too.

Questions about her uncle swirled in his mind. Why had he tried to kill Jazz and Rebekah? Why was Jazz even at the fair tonight?

But he tamped down his desire for answers and focused simply on holding her instead. On being there for her for as long as she'd let him.

The rain finally slowed and dwindled to a light sprinkle as they stood there.

Jazz pulled away and stepped out of his arms, sniffing as if she'd been crying. Her face, already wet from rain, didn't prove it one way or the other. "I'm sorry. I know you don't want…"

His heart constricted. Had she been about to quote him? When he'd said he didn't want her? *Oh, Lord. Please, help me make it up to her somehow.*

"No." He shook his head, slowly, adamantly. "I do want you, Jazz Lamont."

Her eyebrows rose nearly to her hairline.

He breathed out a sigh. "I know what I said. I was wrong. So very, very wrong. I was afraid and didn't realize I'd become such a selfish person, only caring about what I wanted to do. I was afraid I'd lose my freedom if I cared for you."

"I would never want to make you feel trapped or like you weren't free."

"I know that. But the truth is, I haven't been living in freedom at all. I've been trapped by my own selfishness, serving those desires instead of the Lord. And I avoided relationships because I wanted to put myself first above all else."

He hooked his thumbs in his wet pockets to keep from touching her again, which everything in him yearned to do. "God showed me that tonight. I'm so sorry how stupid I was and for all the hurtful things I said to you. I don't mean them, and I wish I could take them back." He met Jazz's searching gaze. "I hope you'll forgive me, if you can."

Jazz watched him closely, as if trying to read something in his face or eyes. "I do."

Relief spread through Hawthorne. "Thank you." He managed to push the words from his tightening throat.

Not sure what I should do now, Lord. Hawthorne knew he loved Jazz, but she wasn't a Christian. He still couldn't go anywhere with his feelings. How would he explain that without hurting her all over again?

"God showed me some things tonight, too."

The gaze Hawthorne had dropped jumped back to Jazz. He'd never heard her talk about God like that before. Hope began to stir in his belly. "He did?"

She nodded. "All this time that I'd been looking to belong with someone, I already belonged to Him."

A smile cracked Hawthorne's face as the hope rushed through the rest of his body. He took a step toward her, his arms longing to hold her again. "Are you saying what I think you're saying?"

"I'm a Christian now."

A squeal pierced the air, making Jazz and Hawthorne jump and twist toward the sound.

Nevaeh dashed to Jazz, dropping her dog's leash and throwing herself at the taller woman. "Praise the Lord, you're saved!"

Jazz smiled as her excited friend pulled back from the

quick hug and hopped up and down, prompting Flash to jog to her with an excited tail wag.

"We're sisters for real and forever now!" Nevaeh's shout echoed in the night air. "Hallelujah!"

A laugh—that beautiful, musical laugh—tumbled from Jazz's lips as her friend came back and gripped her arms.

Jazz pulled Nevaeh into another hug. "Forever."

When the hug ended, Nevaeh shot a glance at Hawthorne. "Didn't mean to interrupt. Go for it." She gave him a grin with a wink, then darted away and jogged toward the fairgrounds with her K-9.

Jazz turned to him with a smile that almost looked shy.

Hawthorne's chest pinched. This beautiful, confident, smart woman with insane skills he didn't know the half of was uncertain with him. Because he had hurt her? Or did it mean something else—that she loved him?

"You don't have to say anything. Nev just likes to joke around." Those emerald eyes locked on him, clouding with doubt. But maybe hope, too.

He couldn't stand it anymore. He closed the gap between them and cradled her cheek in his hand. "I want to say something. Very badly."

Her eyes widened, tempting him to do more than just say things. But that would have to wait until he'd communicated what she needed to hear.

"I'm not sure when it happened, but somewhere along the way, I fell in love with my heroine."

Her lips parted in adorable surprise, distracting him even more.

He focused his mind on finishing what he had to say. "And now that we both belong to the same Lord, I guess we're free to do something about it. That is, if you could see your way to caring for the author who's putting you in his book."

Her eyes narrowed.

Hawthorne lowered his hand. Had he said something wrong?

"I expected to be in three books at least." A teasing glint lit her eyes.

He breathed again and wrapped both arms around her as he grinned. "I can promise you more than three, if you stick with me."

"All right. I guess I will, on those terms." A gorgeous smile curved her lips, ruining her attempt at a serious expression. She laid her palms against his chest. "But I have to make a confession."

"Oh?"

"This heroine has fallen in love with the author, too."

The thrill and joy that filled him was like nothing he'd ever felt. Wow, had he ever underestimated romance. Somehow, he managed to speak past his huge smile and the pounding of his heart. "Oh, really? What should we do about it?"

"Well, usually, if this were a romance novel, which I realize you don't actually write..." Her gaze lowered slightly.

To his lips?

Heat zinged through his chest. "The heroine would be kissed by the hero."

"Uh-huh." She gave a barely perceptible nod. "Think you could pretend to be the hero instead of the author?"

He grinned. "Oh, yeah. Research is very important."

A beaming smile lit her face.

Shifting to cradle her head with his hand, he leaned in for a kiss so full of love and passion that it could rival any romance novel.

Why had he been afraid of this? Of giving himself to Jazz?

He barely remembered. Because loving her like this, he'd never felt freer.

Anticipation and excitement crackled in the evening air as visitors gathered by the grandstand for the spectacular fireworks display that would end the Tri-City Fair.

A child laughed as he ran past, and Flash tugged slightly on the leash, wanting to follow. "Sorry, bud." Jazz gave him a scratch behind his ear.

"Aw, it's all right, boy." Hawthorne's voice filled Jazz with warmth, and she turned to see him approach with the large bucket of popcorn he'd gone to purchase for them. "I got you covered." He winked at Jazz, then bent over and dropped a handful of popcorn on the blacktop for Flash.

"Hey." Jazz feigned dismay, propping a hand on her hip. "You're not supposed to feed the security K-9s."

"Not sorry." Hawthorne popped a kernel into his mouth as he grinned at her. "Are we, Flash?" He glanced down at the dog who was busy scarfing down the popcorn feast.

"You're trying to buy his affections, so he'll like you better than me."

"Yep. It's a male bonding thing. I don't want to be outnumbered in my life now that Rebekah is moving in." Despite his protest, the joy in his eyes said he was pleased Rebekah wanted to stay with him at his new apartment.

"Is she still moving next week?"

"That's the plan. It times well with her lease expiring. But I don't plan to stay at the apartment very long."

"You don't?" In all the lengthy conversations she and Hawthorne had enjoyed over the past week, she hadn't heard him mention that. But she didn't feel even an ounce of worry. He wasn't leaving her. He'd made that clear. And she was learning with every day that passed, Hawthorne was a trustworthy man. Someone she could count on.

"I'm thinking of buying a house."

Jazz smiled. She loved the sound of permanence in that plan. The sound of settling down. "You are?"

He nodded, his lips closed in a smile that looked like he was struggling to hold back some secret he'd love to let out. He stepped closer to her, lowering the popcorn bucket as he slid his free arm around her back. "But I want you to help me pick it out. The house you want to live in."

A shiver tracked up her spine even as heat from his touch spiraled through her torso.

"For that future we've been talking about."

The future. Jazz's heart swelled with the happiness that had flooded her so many times in the past week that she thought she might burst. She finally had someone who wanted to have a future with her.

She'd been shocked when Hawthorne had brought up marriage a couple days ago. For a man who'd run from marriage and even committed relationships for most of his life, he was a surprisingly fast mover now that he'd changed his mind. Maybe because the change had come from God transforming his heart, as Hawthorne had explained.

Now she got the feeling Hawthorne might propose at any moment, but he probably wanted to wait for the right timing for her. Until the painful emotions from the upheaval in her family were a more distant memory.

In her whole life, she'd never cried as much as she had in the last week. Often on Hawthorne's shoulder, strengthened by his support and compassion.

She'd had to give statements to the police about all that

had happened with Pierce. Including the crimes he'd confessed to her and the attempt to kill her and Rebekah. The next challenge would be testifying at his trial. That wouldn't take place for a couple of months yet, but she already struggled with anxiety at the idea of testifying against her only living relative. Unless she counted his daughters, her cousins. But they had rebuffed her attempts to connect via phone or email.

They seemed to want to distance themselves from the whole affair, probably to keep their reputations unscathed from the scandal of having their father, prominent candidate for governor, exposed as the murderer of their own mother.

It was ironic he'd murdered two people and attempted two more killings all to cover up the original death that had started it all.

Nev and Hawthorne had helped Jazz search through her father's things, and they'd eventually found the evidence Pierce must have feared. Old photos of a dead soldier and a recording her dad had apparently captured secretly of a conversation between him and Pierce. Both offered proof that Pierce had killed the soldier.

The death had been accidental, according to the recorded conversation, but resulted from an altercation between the soldier and Pierce. The other soldier started the fight, and Pierce responded by trying to subdue him with a choke. Trouble was, Pierce unintentionally held the choke longer than the soldier could handle, and the young man died.

The only people present, Pierce and Jazz's dad, covered up the killing by using explosives to destroy the body in such a way that it would look like the soldier had encountered a land mine.

When Cora had searched the names of soldiers Jazz's dad had served with, she'd discovered that Pierce had been in the same unit. Phoenix had directed Cora to look deeper the moment she'd learned Pierce and Jazz's dad were in combat together overseas. The boss had suspected something during that time could give Pierce a reason to want Jazz dead.

Jazz knew they had served together, but what she hadn't known was Cora's further discovery—that they had been the only two people who'd witnessed a soldier's death.

And years after his successful cover-up, Pierce was still so worried about the truth coming out that he'd killed again. On purpose this time. More than once. Even murdering his own wife.

Jazz shook her head. She still couldn't wrap her head around Pierce murdering Aunt Joan.

"Hey." A light touch on Jazz's chin drew her gaze up to Hawthorne's. "You okay?"

"Yeah." She sighed. "I will be."

He gave her a squeeze, letting her cradle her head on his shoulder.

"Hey, lovebirds." Nev came up beside Jazz, people moving past her in droves to reach the grassy field where they could best see the fireworks.

Aunt Joan would have been so pleased with the huge turnout and the way attendance numbers had shot up for the last week of the fair. After the public had learned the danger was over and the culprits were no longer at large, her Tri-City Fair had been a success, once again.

"We're set up over there with blankets." Nev pointed toward a spot on the field where Sof, Michael, and their daughter, Grace, were spreading out a blanket next to one occupied by Bristol, Toby, and Remington. On the other side of Sof's family, Branson sat on another blanket.

"Blankets." Jazz stared at Nev. "I forgot one."

Nev waved the concern away with a hand. "I got you covered, girl. Ours is big enough to share."

"Even with your giant bodyguard fiancé?" Jazz grinned at her BFF.

Nev wrinkled her nose. "Hey, I plan to sit on his lap." She winked.

Jazz laughed.

Nev started forward with Alvarez on leash. "Oh, Becks said she's going to join us, too."

Jazz grinned at the nickname Nev had promptly created for Rebekah as soon as she'd learned the girl was going to be a big part of Jazz's life. "Where'd she get off to, anyway?" Jazz glanced at Hawthorne as they followed Nev toward the grass.

He winced. "I'm afraid she found a boy who wanted to take her on the Slingshot."

"Poor Hawthorne." Nev laughed and smiled over her shoulder at him.

Jazz linked her arm with Hawthorne's. "I'm proud of you."

He gave her a sidelong look as he pulled her closer with their intertwined arms. "For what? Not forbidding the kid to be alone with my baby sister?"

"Exactly." She beamed a smile at him, pride and appreciation swelling in her for how much he cared about his sister. "You're giving her space and still protecting her, letting her know she's loved. It's a tough balance."

He blew out a long breath as he looked forward. "That's an understatement." He turned his head toward Jazz again as they neared the blankets the PK-9 team had spread close together on the grass. "But I'm thankful to see her happier now that she has closure about Sam."

Jazz nodded. "That makes a big difference." Thanks to Pierce's claims that Butch was guilty of the sabotage and the discovery of Butch's motive to frame Desmond Patch, the police were open to hearing Hawthorne's suspicions that Butch had also killed Sam. Further investigation led to Randall from Best Life sharing that Butch had followed him outside the cult once and offered to pay him to give a note to Butch's ex-wife. Randall testified that Butch had become furious when he'd refused.

Given the possibility that Sam and Butch may have gotten into an altercation about the same issue at the fair, the police examined areas Hawthorne led them to at and around the designated smoking space where Sam was last seen. They found a tiny trace of dried blood on the bottom of a pipe behind the restroom facilities. Sam's blood.

The detectives and Hawthorne speculated that Butch had lured Sam to the more hidden location by offering to pay him to deliver a message. Given Sam's drunken state, he may have joked or insulted short-tempered Butch.

Butch's ex-wife shared that he had been physically abusive during their marriage, but she had never reported the incidents. So the theory that he'd become violent toward Sam was not only plausible, but almost certain.

Now Rebekah and Sam's parents could grieve knowing what had really happened and knowing his killer hadn't gotten away with it. Butch had fallen prey to his own schemes and revenge.

According to Rebekah, Sam's parents were back together. His mom had left the cult to join her husband, Gary, so they could grieve their son's death together, knowing the truth and finally being able to move on.

If only Hawthorne's parents would make a similar decision and flee the cult. But neither he nor Rebekah had heard anything from their parents so far. Hawthorne and Jazz were praying that God would change his parents' hearts, just as God had changed them.

Hawthorne stopped at the edge of the blanket where Nev kicked off her flip-flops and plopped down, basically in Branson's lap as she'd promised.

Hawthorne released Jazz's arm and made a sweeping gesture toward the blanket. "Milady."

"Ooh. How gentlemanly. Are you going to start writing medieval romances now?"

"I never know what you'll inspire me to do next." The heat in his eyes sent a tingle to her toes.

"Hey, Cora...Kent." Nev's greeting drew Jazz's attention to the lovely blond and her tall husband as they neared the group, Kent carrying a rolled-up blanket under one arm and a cooler in the other hand.

Cora held a pitcher and a large tote bag. "Hello." She

beamed a smile at the group. "I've brought snacks and lemonade for everyone."

Sweet Cora. Always thinking of their needs and doing her best to meet them.

"No Jana?"

Cora met Jazz's gaze as Kent rolled out their blanket. "No, the fireworks would be too much for her."

"I thought about leaving Flash home, too. But I think he'll be good with the cotton in his ears." Flash, like all the PK-9 dogs except for Jana, had been trained to be comfortable around loud noises, including gunshots. But Nev had left Alvarez home since those loud sounds were not his favorite thing, and Jazz had added insulation to Flash's ears to keep the fireworks from damaging his hearing.

Hawthorne slid his arm behind Jazz's back again. "Want to sit down?"

She gave him a warm smile. "In a second." Her gaze slid over the PK-9 team members as she stayed standing.

One person was missing. Phoenix. "Anyone know where Phoenix is?"

The other ladies looked at Cora, who was now sitting beside Kent and removing plated food from the cooler. She paused. "She's had to go away again on a trip."

"Too bad. She should be here." This time, Jazz didn't mean the words as a criticism. Because as much as she still didn't understand Phoenix, Jazz did know she'd been judging the boss unfairly. She'd allowed her own insecurities to skew the way she viewed the mysterious woman, just like Neveah had said.

In the days since Pierce had tried to kill her, Jazz had felt the full-on blessing of the Phoenix K-9 team. They'd supported her, checked on her, made sure she was safe and healing. Even ribbed her in all the ways they had before. They treated her like family.

And they always had. She'd missed seeing that because she'd been too busy trying to push them away before they could reject her.

But now that she was trying to embrace them, too, she was tasting the wonder of what it was like to have a family of choice. Like Marion Moore's family that Phoenix had shown her—a family formed through adoption, where love was a choice, not a biological duty.

Was that the real reason Phoenix had taken her to the Forever Home shelter? So she would see that family didn't have to be by birth, but by the choice to love?

Jazz wouldn't be surprised. She was starting to come around to Nev's way of thinking that Phoenix was trying to help all of her agents heal. And one of the ways she did that was by building this family of PK-9.

She also took care of her agents behind the scenes in ways Jazz hadn't known. Jazz had been flabbergasted to learn from Nev that Phoenix had patrolled with Dag outside Nev's house every night after the two thugs had broken in. Jazz still needed to eat humble pie and thank Phoenix for that.

Though maybe she didn't have to. The boss didn't seem to want credit or thanks for any of the good she did.

"I'd hoped she would be here, too." Bris stood up, and Remington rose beside her, wrapping his arm around her waist as they faced the others. "But I still want to make this announcement now, while we're at this sort of celebration, and before things get farther along."

Jazz glanced at Nev who looked at her with a shrug.

Huge smiles beamed from the couple as Bris lifted her hands in the air. "We're expecting a baby!"

Squeals, applause, and laughter sprang up from the group as they all got to their feet and went to congratulate the happy couple.

As Hawthorne and Jazz stepped away from the prospective parents to allow Nev and Branson access to them, Hawthorne ducked his head toward Jazz.

"What do you think?" His low murmur tickled her ear. "Should we have one of those?"

She turned into his arms with a soft giggle. "Maybe even more than one."

He braced his hands behind her back as she leaned against them, resting her palms on his chest.

"But don't you have a book baby coming out in a few months?" She grinned, using the term she'd learned from him as he'd spoken of his upcoming release.

"Oh, yeah. It's a new series about an amazing woman with intelligence, beauty, and brains—along with some crazy fight skills you wouldn't believe."

"Wow. She sounds too good to be true."

He pulled her in closer, tightening his arms as he brought his face close to hers. "She almost is. But I hope very soon, I'll get to call her mine."

The electricity in his teal eyes and the loving desire in his words sent thrills through every part of her being.

"Hawthorne?"

He leaned down farther, pressing his forehead to hers. "Yes?"

"There's something I've been wanting to ask you ever since we met."

His slowing breath tickled her cheeks. "What is it?"

"Would you sign my Carson Steele novels?"

He straightened, pulling his head away but rewarding her with a hearty laugh.

She joined in the laughter with him as contentment and joy filled her heart to the brim.

A pop of fireworks pulled their attention to the brilliant, colorful display of light that painted the sky.

Jazz turned toward the show, and Hawthorne closed his arms around her from behind, cradling her back against his chest.

Standing at the edge of Nev's blanket, she had a perfect view of the fireworks, but also of her Phoenix K-9 family. Love for them swelled in her heart as she looked at each woman one-by-one. How could she have almost missed out on being part of such a precious family?

Tears sprang to her eyes, and she sniffed, trying to hold them in.

Hawthorne ducked his head down by hers, his lips brushing her ear. "You aren't sad, are you?"

She rested her hands on his strong arms and leaned her head back against him, reveling in his embrace. "No. I'm happier than I ever dreamed."

Hawthorne responded with a gentle squeeze.

God hadn't given Jazz the dream she'd tried to force into reality. No, He'd given her far greater gifts than she'd dreamed of—a trustworthy man and a family of women who chose to accept her and love her.

Belonging to Jesus would have been enough. She'd learned that as she'd grown closer to Him every day, reading the Bible and learning all about who God really was.

He was the Father who had chosen her—Jazz Lamont— before He'd even created the universe.

And that wasn't a dream. It was so real and true and wondrous that Jazz wondered every day why she'd taken so long to come to Him.

Thank the Lord, He'd chased her down and brought her to Himself despite her resistance. No matter what happened from now on, she was safe in the arms of the God who had chosen to call her His, forever.

EXCERPT OF TERMINAL DANGER

Glock ready, Callum slowly opened the door and slipped through.

A noise—like an abbreviated yell—echoed through the damp garage.

Callum veered closer to the bumpers of parked cars and crouched as he continued toward the direction of the sound.

Movement. On the ground at the rear of a black car ahead.

What—

Callum raised his weapon as he approached, trying to make sense of the moving, shifting shape on the concrete floor.

The changing form became clearer as he neared. Two forms. Two people.

An obese man who fit the photographs of Willis Peterson, and...

A woman?

Was Willis attacking another victim?

Callum's muscles clenched, and his heart rate spiked as he quickly closed the distance between him and the figures, aiming his Glock.

But he froze six feet away.

Willis wasn't attacking the woman.

She lay on the ground beneath his heavy body, but she had her denim-clad legs wrapped around his neck.

She was choking him.

Willis reached for the woman's face with his one free arm, flailing wildly.

She blocked his attempted strikes with one arm as the rest of her body appeared not to move.

The man's arm soon dropped to the ground, and his body stiffened.

Callum lowered his weapon. "Ms. Gray." The baseball cap on the concrete a few feet away, the blond braid that disappeared behind her back, and the lovely profile he'd seen in the FBI office revealed her identity. Even if Callum still couldn't believe the scene he was witnessing.

Apparently, Phoenix Gray had also predicted the kidnapper's escape plan and decided to wait for him in the garage. Had Willis attacked her, and she was defending herself?

She didn't move, not even a twitch to suggest she was surprised Callum was there.

"Ms. Gray, the FBI frowns on chokeholds unless they are absolutely necessary, justified use of force."

She didn't loosen the triangle choke or show any sign she'd heard Callum.

He stepped closer.

A growl snapped Callum's attention to his right.

A dog emerged from the shadow between two cars, its teeth bared. The tan dog stared at Callum with startling blue eyes as it rumbled again.

Callum didn't dare move with her K-9 threatening him. But he could still speak. "I'm going to have to insist you let Peterson go. The FBI can't handle a suspect this way." Callum risked gradually angling his gaze away from the dog to check on Willis.

Phoenix unwrapped her legs from around his neck and quickly got to her feet.

Willis lay on the ground, unmoving.

"Dagian, stand down." She delivered the words in her

firm, deep voice as she walked toward Callum, stopping a few feet in front of him.

She watched him with eyes he hadn't been able to see very clearly before, thanks to the cap she'd worn at the meeting and her distance from him then. They appeared to be dark blue. And completely devoid of emotion. Shockingly so.

He'd looked into the eyes of many criminals—serial killers, rapists, pedophiles. But even the psychopaths and narcissists, who lacked empathy for others, showed emotion in their eyes. Hers were entirely apathetic, at least from what he could see. Maybe it was the dim lighting in the garage.

"Dag." She didn't look away from Callum as her dog passed him and stopped at her side. She held Callum in her unflinching stare while he searched it for any hint of emotion, dark or light, good or evil.

"Good thing I'm not FBI." She continued eye contact for one more moment, no defiance or triumph changing her expressionless features or infusing her monotone delivery.

She turned abruptly and moved away, her dog sticking close to her leg. She stalked past Willis and snatched up her gray baseball cap without breaking stride. Placing the cap on her head, she walked toward the closed door at the end of the garage.

Movement pulled Callum's gaze toward Willis. The man moaned as he touched his head and started to push himself up.

Callum hurried to him, pulling handcuffs from his pocket to secure the suspect. Phoenix knew what she was doing. She'd only held her choke long enough to keep Willis out for a matter of seconds.

Callum glanced up from cuffing the man's wrists just as the sound of the overhead garage door opening reached his ears.

Phoenix and her K-9 stepped out of the lit garage into the black night beyond.

But he could still see her in his mind's eye—the way she'd

stared at him with the eerie impassiveness he'd only seen on one other face. The face in a photo that had haunted him forever.

A girl wrecked by evil beyond belief.

The girl he was too late to set free.

This woman and her K-9 are being hunted. Exactly as she planned.

When a busload of schoolchildren disappears, Phoenix Gray knows the kidnapper is the unidentified serial killer she's spent her life trying to catch. This time, she'll find the killer and bring him to justice no matter what it takes. She and her Phoenix K-9 Security and Detection Agency join the search for the hostages, but they aren't the only ones who want the criminal captured.

Callum Ross, an FBI agent who specializes in catching serial criminals, is about to resign. But not until he finds one last culprit, the killer behind a famous twenty-year-old crime Callum vowed to solve.

Despite the FBI agent's uncanny understanding of her psyche, Phoenix refuses to be distracted from her goal. When the serial killer turns into the cat instead of the mouse, Phoenix thinks she's ready. But will she need the God she rejected to achieve the justice she's given her life to obtain?

Shop *Terminal Danger*
at TerminalDanger.com

She never invites visitors. But visitors sometimes invite themselves.

When a winter storm brings more than snow, May Denver is forced to flee from her home and fight for her life. Can she trust an unwanted neighbor and risk her greatest fear in order to survive?

GRAB THIS ROMANTIC SUSPENSE STORY FOR FREE
WHEN YOU SIGN UP FOR JERUSHA'S NEWSLETTER
www.FearWarriorSuspense.com

GUARDIANS UNLEASHED

"Fast-paced suspense
at its best."
– DiAnn Mills,
bestselling author of *Concrete Evidence*

GuardiansUnleashed.com

The Sisters Redeemed Series

JerushaStore.com

ABOUT JERUSHA

Jerusha Agen imagines danger around every corner but knows God is there, too. So naturally, she writes romantic suspense infused with the hope of salvation in Jesus Christ.

Jerusha loves to hang out with her big furry dogs and little furry cats, often while reading or watching movies.

Find more of Jerusha's thrilling, fear-fighting stories at www.JerushaAgen.com.

facebook.com/JerushaAgenAuthor
instagram.com/jerushaagen